A Long Petal of the Sea

A Long Petal of the Sea

A   N O V E L

ISABEL ALLENDE

Translated from the Spanish by

NICK CAISTOR *and* AMANDA HOPKINSON

BALLANTINE BOOKS

NEW YORK

Copyright © 2020 by Isabel Allende

English language translation © 2020 by Isabel Allende

All rights reserved.

Published in the United States by Ballantine Books, an imprint of Random House, a division of Penguin Random House LLC, New York.

BALLANTINE and the HOUSE colophon are registered trademarks of Penguin Random House LLC.

Originally published in Spain in 2019 as *Largo pétalo de mar*

LIBRARY OF CONGRESS CATALOGING-IN-PUBLICATION DATA

NAMES: Allende, Isabel, author. | Caistor, Nick, translator. | Hopkinson, Amanda, translator.

Title: A long petal of the sea: a novel / Isabel Allende; translated from the Spanish by Nick Caistor and Amanda Hopkinson.

OTHER TITLES: Largo pétalo de mar. English

DESCRIPTION: New York: Ballantine Books, [2020] | "Originally published in Spain in 2019 as Largo pétalo de mar"—Title page verso.

IDENTIFIERS: LCCN 2019037428 (print) | LCCN 2019037429 (ebook) | ISBN 9781984820150 (hardcover) | ISBN 9781984820167 (ebook)

SUBJECTS: LCSH: Spain—History—Civil War, 1936-1939—Fiction. | GSAFD: Historical fiction.

CLASSIFICATION: LCC PQ8098.1.L54 L3613 2020 (print) | LCC PQ8098.1.L54 (ebook) | DDC 863/.64—dc23

LC record available at https://lccn.loc.gov/2019037428

LC ebook record available at https://lccn.loc.gov/2019037429

International edition 9780593158425

Printed in the United States of America on acid-free paper

randomhousebooks.com

987654321

FIRST EDITION

Book design by Barbara M. Bachman

To my brother Juan Allende

To Victor Pey Casado and other navigators of hope

Foreigners, here it is,

This is my homeland,

Here I was born and here live my dreams.

—PABLO NERUDA
"Return"
SAILINGS AND RETURNS

PART ONE

War and Exodus

CHAPTER I

1938

Get ready, lads,
To kill again, to die once more
And to cover the blood with flowers.

— PABLO NERUDA
"Bloody was all the earth of man"
THE SEA AND THE BELLS

THE YOUNG SOLDIER WAS PART OF THE "BABY BOT-
tle Conscription," the boys called up when there were
no more men, young or old, to fight the war. Victor
Dalmau received him with the other wounded taken
from the supply truck and laid out like logs on mats
placed over the cement and stone floor of the Estacion
del Norte, where they had to wait for other vehicles to
take them to the hospital centers. The boy lay motionless, with the calm look of someone who has seen the
angels and now fears nothing. There was no telling
how many days he had spent being shifted from one
stretcher to another, one field hospital to another, one
ambulance to another, before reaching Catalonia on
this particular train.

At the station, doctors, paramedics, and nurses
evaluated the soldiers, immediately dispatching the

most serious cases to the hospital, and classifying the others according to the part of the body where they had been wounded: Group A: arms, Group B: legs, Group C: head, and so on. They were then transferred to the corresponding center with labels around their necks. The wounded arrived by the hundreds, and each diagnosis and decision had to be made in no more than a few minutes. But the chaos and confusion were misleading, for no one was left unattended, no one was left behind. Those in need of surgery were sent to the old Sant Andreu building in Manresa; those requiring treatment were dispatched to other centers; the remainder were left where they were, since nothing could be done to save them. Volunteer women would moisten their lips, whisper to them, and comfort them as if they were their own children, in the knowledge that somewhere else, another woman might be cradling their own son or brother. Later, the stretcher-bearers would take them to the morgue.

The little soldier had a wound in his chest, and the doctor, after a swift examination during which he could detect no pulse, decided the boy was beyond all help, and had no need of either morphine or consolation. On the battlefield they had strapped a bandage around his chest to protect the wound with an inverted tin plate, but nobody knew how many hours or days, how many trains ago that had been.

Dalmau was there to assist the doctors. Although it was his duty to leave the boy and attend to the next case, he thought that if the youngster had survived the shock, the hemorrhaging, and the journey to reach this station platform, he must really want to live; and so it would be a shame to surrender him to death now. Carefully removing the bandages, he saw to his amazement that the wound was still open and was as clean as if it had been painted onto his chest. He couldn't understand how the bullet had shattered the ribs and part of the sternum, and yet had left the heart intact. Having worked for nearly three years on the side of the Republicans in the Spanish Civil War, at first on the fronts at Madrid and Teruel, and then at the evacuation hospital at Manresa, Victor Dalmau thought he had seen everything, become immunized to the suffering of others, but he had never seen an actual beating heart.

Fascinated, he watched the final, increasingly slow and sporadic pulsation until it ceased completely, and the little soldier finally passed away without a sigh. For a brief moment, Dalmau simply stood there, contemplating the red hole where the heartbeats had ceased. This was to be his most stubborn, persistent memory of the war: that fifteen- or sixteen-year-old boy, still smooth-cheeked, filthy with the dirt of battle and dried blood, laid out on a stretcher with his heart exposed to the air. Victor was never able to explain to himself why he inserted three fingers of his right hand into the gaping wound, gently grasped the organ, and squeezed it rhythmically several times, quite calmly and naturally, for how long, he couldn't remember: perhaps thirty seconds, or perhaps an eternity. Suddenly he felt the heart coming back to life between his fingers, first with an almost imperceptible tremor, soon with a strong, regular beat.

"If I hadn't seen it with my own eyes, I never would have believed it," said one of the doctors who had approached without Dalmau noticing. He called over two stretcher-bearers, ordering them to rush the wounded youth to the hospital—this was a special case.

"Where did you learn that?" he asked Dalmau as soon as the men had lifted the little soldier onto the stretcher. The boy's face was still ashen, but he had a pulse.

Victor Dalmau, a man of few words, told the doctor that he had managed to complete three years of medical studies in Barcelona before leaving for the front as an auxiliary.

"But where did you learn that technique?" insisted the doctor.

"Nowhere, but I thought there was nothing to lose . . ."

"I see you have a limp."

"My left femur. I was injured at Teruel. It's getting better."

"Good. From now on you'll work with me. What's your name?"

"Victor Dalmau, comrade."

"I am not your comrade. Call me 'Doctor.' Understood?"

"Understood, Doctor. The same goes for me: you can call me Señor Dalmau. But the other comrades aren't going to like it one bit."

The doctor smiled to himself. The very next day, Dalmau began to learn a profession that would determine his destiny. Together with everyone else at Sant Andreu and other hospitals, he heard the story circulating that the team of surgeons had spent sixteen hours resurrecting the young soldier. Many called it a miracle. The advances of science, and the boy's constitution of an ox, claimed those who had renounced God and his saints. Victor promised himself he would visit the boy wherever he was transferred, but in the chaos of those days he found it impossible to keep track of those present and those missing, of the living and the dead. For a long while it seemed as though he had forgotten the heart he had held in his hand.

Yet years later, on the far side of the world, he still saw the soldier in nightmares, and from then on the boy visited him occasionally, a pale, sad ghost with his heart on a platter. Dalmau could not recall, or possibly never knew, his real name, but for obvious reasons he called him Lazaro.

The young soldier, though, never forgot the name of his savior. As soon as he could sit up and drink water on his own, he was told about the feat performed at the Estacion del Norte by an auxiliary who had brought him back from the land of death. He was assailed with questions: everyone wanted to know whether heaven and hell really existed, or had been invented by the bishops to instill fear in people. The boy recovered before the end of the war, and two years later in Marseilles had the name of Victor Dalmau tattooed beneath the scar.

———

LIKE ALMOST ALL YOUTHS his age, Victor had joined the Republican Army in 1936 and gone off with his regiment to defend Madrid, which had been partially occupied by Franco and his Nationalist forces, as the troops who rose against the government called themselves. Victor had worked recovering the wounded, because his medical studies meant he was more useful at that than shouldering a rifle in the trenches. Later on he was dispatched to other fronts.

In December 1937, during the icy cold of the battle for Teruel, Victor Dalmau was assigned to a heroic ambulance giving first aid to the wounded, while the driver, Aitor Ibarra, an immortal Basque who was constantly singing to himself and laughing out loud to mock death, somehow managed to maneuver the vehicle along shattered roads. Dalmau trusted that the Basque's good luck, which had allowed him to emerge unscathed from a thousand close scrapes, would be sufficient for both of them. To avoid being bombed, they often traveled at night. If there was no moon, somebody walked in front of the ambulance with a flashlight to illuminate the road, while Victor attended to the injured inside the vehicle with what limited supplies he had, by the light of another flashlight. They constantly defied the obstacle-strewn terrain and temperatures many degrees below freezing, crawling forward slowly like worms through the ice, sinking into the snow, pushing the ambulance up slopes or out of ditches and bomb craters, dodging lengths of twisted iron and frozen bodies of mules, amid strafing by Nationalist machine guns and bombs from the German Condor Legion planes swooping low above their heads. Nothing could distract Victor Dalmau from his determination to keep the men in his care alive, even if they were bleeding to death in front of his eyes. He was infected by the crazy stoicism of Aitor Ibarra, who always drove on untroubled, and had a joke for every occasion.

From the ambulance, Dalmau was sent to the field hospital that had been set up in some caves in Teruel to protect it from the bombs. There the staff worked by candlelight, rags soaked in engine oil, and kerosene lamps. They fended off the cold with braziers pushed under the operating tables, although that didn't stop the frozen instruments from sticking to their hands. The surgeons operated quickly on those they could patch up and send to the hospital centers, knowing full well that many would die on the way. The others, who were beyond all help, were left to await death with morphine—when there was any, since it was always in short supply; ether was rationed as well. If there was nothing else to relieve the dreadfully wounded men who cried out in pain, Victor would give them aspirin, telling them it was a powerful American drug. The bandages were washed with melted ice and snow and then reused. The most thankless task was disposing of the piles of amputated legs and arms; Victor could never get used to the smell of burning flesh.

It was at Teruel that he ran into Elisabeth Eidenbenz for the second time. They had met during the battle for Madrid, where she had arrived as a volunteer for the Association to Aid Children in War. She was a twenty-four-year-old Swiss nurse with the face of a Renaissance virgin and the courage of a battle-hardened veteran. Victor had been half in love with her in Madrid, and would have been so entirely if only she had given him the slightest encouragement. However, nothing could divert this young woman from her mission: to lessen the suffering of children in these awful times. Over the months since he had first met her, she had lost the innocence she had arrived with. Her character had been toughened by her struggles against military bureaucracy and men's stupidity; she kept her compassion and kindness for the women and children in her care. In a lull between two enemy attacks, Victor bumped into her next to one of the food supply trucks. "Hello there, do you remember me?" Elisabeth greeted him in a Spanish enriched by guttural German sounds. Of course he remembered her, but seeing her left him dumbstruck. She looked more mature and more beautiful than ever. They sat on a piece of concrete rubble; he began to smoke, and she drank tea from a canteen.

"What's become of your friend Aitor?" she asked him.

"He's still around in the thick of it, without a scratch."

"He's not afraid of anything. Say hello to him from me."

"What plans do you have for when this war is over?" Victor asked.

"To find another one. There's always war somewhere in the world. What about you?"

"If you like, we could get married," he suggested, overcome with shyness.

She laughed, and for a moment became a Renaissance maiden once more.

"Not on your life, man. I'm not going to get married to you or anyone else. I don't have time for love."

"Maybe you will change your mind. Do you think we'll meet again?"

"Without a doubt, if we survive. You can count on me, Victor, if there's any way I can help you . . ."

"The same goes for me. May I kiss you?"

"No."

IT WAS IN THE TERUEL CAVES that Victor acquired nerves of steel and the medical knowledge that no university could have offered him. He learned that you can get used to almost anything—to blood (so much blood!), surgery without anesthetics, the stench of gangrene, filth, the endless flood of wounded soldiers, sometimes women and children as well—while at the same time an age-old weariness sapped your will, and worst of all, you had to confront the insidious suspicion that all this sacrifice might be in vain. And it was there, as he was pulling the dead and wounded from the ruins of a bombardment, that the delayed collapse of a wall smashed his left leg.

He was seen by an English doctor from the International Brigades. Anyone else would have opted for a rapid amputation, but the Englishman had just begun his shift and had been able to rest for a few hours. He stammered an order to the nurse and made ready to reset the broken bones. "You're lucky, my lad. Supplies from the Red Cross arrived yesterday, so we can put you to sleep," said the nurse, covering his face with the ether mask.

Victor attributed the accident to the fact that Aitor Ibarra and his lucky star had not been with him to protect him. Aitor was the one who had taken him to the train that brought him to Valencia together with dozens of other wounded men. Victor's leg was immobilized by lengths of wood kept in place by bandages—his flesh wounds meant it couldn't be encased in plaster. He was wrapped in a blanket, shivering from cold and fever, and tormented by every jolt of the train, but grateful that he was in a better state than most of those lying with him on the floor of the wagon. Aitor had given him his last cigarettes, as well as a dose of morphine that he made Victor promise to use only in a dire emergency, because he wouldn't get any more. In the hospital at Valencia, they congratulated him on the good work the English doctor had done. If there were no complications, his leg would be like new, although a little shorter than the other one, they told him.

Once the wounds began to heal and he could stand using a crutch, they set his leg in plaster and sent him to Barcelona. He stayed at his parents' home playing endless games of chess with his father until he could move about unaided, and then went back to work at a local hospital, where he attended civilians. To him, this was like being on vacation; compared to what he had experienced on the battlefront, it was a paradise of cleanliness and efficiency.

He stayed there until the following spring, when he was sent to

Sant Andreu in Manresa. He said goodbye to his parents, and to Roser Bruguera, the music student the Dalmau family had taken in. During the weeks of his convalescence, Victor had come to think of her as one of the family. This modest, likeable girl who spent endless hours in piano practice had provided the company that Marcel Lluis and Carme were in need of ever since their own children had left home.

IT WAS NOT LONG AFTER that he returned to the front. A young militiawoman, her cap tilted to counter the ugliness of her uniform, was waiting for Victor Dalmau at the door to the operating room. The moment he came out, with three days' growth of beard and his white coat spattered with blood, she gave him a folded piece of paper with a message from the telephone operators. Dalmau had been on his feet for hours; his leg was aching, and he had just realized from the deep rumble in his stomach that he hadn't eaten since dawn. The work was relentless, but he was grateful for the opportunity to learn in the magnificent aura of Spain's leading surgeons. In other circumstances, a student like him would never even have gotten near them, but by this stage of the war, studies and diplomas were less valuable than experience; and he had more than his fill of that, as the hospital director assured him when allowing him to assist during surgery. By this time, Dalmau could work for forty hours at a stretch without sleeping, able to keep going thanks to tobacco and chicory coffee, and not even noticing the hindrance of his leg.

Unfolding the piece of paper the militiawoman had handed him, Victor Dalmau read the message from his mother, Carme. Even though the hospital was only sixty-five kilometers from Barcelona, he had not seen her in seven weeks, because he had not had a single free day when he could take the bus home. Once a week, always at the same time on a Sunday, she called him on the telephone, and on the same day also sent him some sort of gift, chocolate from the International Brigades, a sausage, a bar of soap bought on the black market, occasionally even cigarettes. To Carme the latter were the real treasure, because she couldn't live without nicotine. He wondered how she managed to get hold of them. Tobacco was so prized that the enemy planes used to drop it from the sky along with loaves of bread, mocking the shortages on the Republican side and showing off the abundance the Nationalists enjoyed.

A message from his mother on a Thursday could only mean there was an emergency. "I'll be at the telephone exchange. Call me." Her son calculated she must have been waiting almost two hours by now, the time he had been busy in the operating theater before he got her message. He went down to the offices in the basement and asked one of the operators to connect him to the Barcelona exchange.

Carme Dalmau came on the line and, in between bouts of coughing, told her son he had to come home because his father had only a short while to live.

"What happened to him? He was good and healthy when I last saw him!" Victor exclaimed.

"His heart has given out. Tell your brother so that he can come to say goodbye as well, because he could be gone before we know it."

It took Victor thirty hours to locate Guillem on the Madrid front. When they were finally able to communicate by radio, through a cacophony of static and sidereal crackles, his brother explained it was impossible for him to get leave to go to Barcelona. His voice sounded so distant and weary that Victor barely recognized it.

"Anybody who can fire a rifle is absolutely needed here, Victor, you know that. The Fascists have more troops and weapons than us, but they'll not pass," said Guillem. He was repeating the Republican slogan made popular by a woman named Dolores Ibarruri, appropriately known as La Pasionaria because of her ability to rouse fanatical enthusiasm among the Republicans. Franco had by now occupied most of Spain, but had been unable to take Madrid. Its defense, street by street, house by house, had become the symbol of the war. The Fascists could count on the colonial troops from Morocco, the feared Moors, as well as the formidable aid of Mussolini and Hitler, but the Republicans' resistance had held them up in the capital. At the outbreak of war, Guillem Dalmau had fought with the Durruti column in Madrid. Back then, the two armies faced each other at the Ciudad Universitaria; they were so close that in some places there was only a street between them; the adversaries could see one another's faces and hurl insults without even having to shout. According to Guillem, holed up in one of the buildings, the enemy shells had pierced the walls of the Faculty of Philosophy and Liberal Arts, the Faculty of Medicine, and Casa de Velazquez. There was no defense against the shells, he said, but they had calculated that three volumes of philosophy could stop bullets. He was nearby at the death of the legendary anarchist Buenaventura Durruti, who had come to fight in Madrid with part of his column after spreading and consolidating the revolution in the Aragon region. He died from a bullet fired point-blank into his chest in dubious circumstances. His column was decimated: more than a thousand militiamen and -women were killed, and among the survivors, Guillem was one of the few left unscathed. Two years later, after fighting on other fronts, he had been sent back to Madrid.

"Father will understand if you can't come, Guillem. We'll be waiting for you at home. Come whenever you can. Even if you don't see him alive, your presence will be a great comfort to Mother."

"I suppose Roser is with them."

"Yes."

"Say hello to her from me. Tell her that her letters go everywhere with me, and that I'm sorry I don't reply very often."

"We'll be waiting for you, Guillem. Take care of yourself."

They said a brief farewell, and Victor was left with a knot in his stomach as he wished for his father to live a little longer, for his brother to return unharmed, for the war to finally end, for the Republic to be saved.

THEIR FATHER, PROFESSOR MARCEL Lluis Dalmau, had spent fifty years teaching music. In addition to singlehandedly creating and passionately conducting the Barcelona Youth Orchestra, he had composed a dozen piano concertos, none of which had been played since the start of the war, as well as many songs, some of which were favorites with the militias. He had met his wife, Carme, when she was fifteen years old and dressed in a somber school uniform, and he was a young music teacher twelve years older than she was. Carme was the daughter of a stevedore, a charity pupil of the nuns, who had been preparing her to enter the order since childhood; and they never forgave her for leaving the convent to go off with an atheist good-for-nothing, an anarchist and perhaps even a freemason, who scorned the holy ties of matrimony. After living in sin for several years, until shortly before the birth of Victor, Marcel Lluis and Carme got married to avoid having their child stigmatized as a bastard, which in those days would be a serious obstacle in his life. "If we had had our children now, we wouldn't have married, because nobody is a bastard in the Republic," Marcel Lluis Dalmau declared in an inspired moment at the outbreak of hostilities. "If we had had our children now, I would have been pregnant as an old woman, and your children would still be in diapers," replied Carme.

Victor and his younger brother, Guillem, were educated at a nonreligious school and grew up in a small house in the Raval district of Barcelona, in a struggling middle-class Catalan home, where their father's music and their mother's books took the place of religion. The Dalmaus were not militants in any political party, but their shared mistrust of authority and any sort of government meant they were close to the anarchists. Marcel Lluis instilled in his sons, as well as all kinds of music, a curiosity for science and a passion for social justice. The former led Victor to study medicine, and the latter became an unshakable ideal for Guillem, who from his early days was angry at the world, and preached against big landowners, businessmen, industrialists, aristocrats, and priests—above all, against priests, with more messianic fervor than reasoned arguments. He was cheerful, boisterous, an impulsive giant. This made him a favorite with the girls, who tried in vain to seduce him, because he devoted himself body and soul to sports, bars, and male friends. Defying his parents, he enlisted in the first workers' militias organized to defend the Republican government against the Fascist rebels. He had the vocation of a soldier, born to wield a weapon and command others who were less resolute than he was.

His brother, Victor, on the other hand, looked like a poet, with his lanky limbs, unruly hair, and constantly preoccupied expression. He said little, and always had a book in his hands. At school, Victor had to put up with relentless attacks from other boys—why don't you become a priest, you faggot—and Guillem would step in, three years younger but much stronger, and always ready for a fistfight in a just cause. Guillem embraced the revolution like a lover, having discovered a cause worth laying down his life for.

The conservatives and the Catholic Church, who had invested money, propaganda, and apocalyptic sermons from the pulpit in the opposition cause, were defeated at the 1936 general elections by the Popular Front, a coalition of left-wing parties. Spain was split in two as if struck by an axe. Claiming they wanted to restore order to a situation they said was chaotic (even though this was far from the truth), the right wing immediately began plotting with the armed forces to overthrow the legitimate government made up of liberals, socialists, communists, and trade unionists, backed by the enthusiastic support of workers, peasants, and the majority of students and intellectuals.

Guillem had struggled to finish high school, and according to his father, a great lover of metaphors, he had an athlete's physique, the courage of a bullfighter, and the brain of an eight-year-old. The political atmosphere was ideal for Guillem: he took advantage of every opportunity to come to blows with his adversaries, even if he had trouble explaining his ideological position. He continued to find this difficult until he joined the militias, where political indoctrination was as important as training in the use of weapons. Barcelona was divided, the extremes coming together only to attack each other. There were bars, dances, sporting events, and parties for the Left, and others for the Right.

Even before he enlisted, Guillem was fighting. After clashes with insolent rich kids, he would return home battered and bruised, but contented. His parents had no idea that he went out to burn crops and steal animals from landowners' farms, to brawl, start fires, and destroy property, until one day he came home with a silver candelabra. His mother snatched it from him and hit him with it; if she had been taller, she would have split her son's head open, but the candelabra struck him in the middle of his back. Carme forced him to confess to what others knew, but which she had refused to admit until that moment: among other outrages, her son had profaned churches and attacked priests and nuns—in other words, doing exactly what the Nationalists' propaganda claimed. "Is this what I brought you up for? You'll make me die of shame, Guillem. Go and give it back at once, do you hear me?" Head bowed, Guillem left with the candelabra wrapped in newspaper.

IN JULY 1936, the armed forces rose against the democratic government; the uprising was soon led by General Francisco Franco, whose unremarkable appearance disguised a cold, vengeful, and brutal temperament. His most ambitious dream was to return Spain to past imperial glories; his most pressing one was to put a stop to disorderly democracy and to govern with an iron fist with the help of the armed forces and the Catholic Church. Franco's rebels were hoping to take over the whole country within a week, but came up against unexpected resistance from the working class, organized in militias and determined to defend the rights they had won. This saw the start of a period of unleashed hatred, vengeance, and terror that was to cost Spain a million lives. The strategy of the men under Franco's command was to spill as much blood as possible and to spread terror, the only way they could destroy any hint of resistance from the conquered people. By now, Guillem Dalmau was ready to participate fully in the Civil War. It was no longer a question of stealing a candelabra, but of picking up a weapon. Whereas before he had to find pretexts to cause mayhem, now that there was war he had no need to go looking for them. Although the principles inculcated in him at home prevented him from committing atrocities, they did not cause him to defend often-innocent victims from his comrades' reprisals. Thousands of murders were committed, above all of priests and nuns. This forced many people to seek refuge in France to escape the Red hordes, as the Nationalist press called them. The Republic's political parties soon gave the order to put a stop to this violence since it ran counter to revolutionary ideals, and yet the abuses continued. Among Franco's forces, however, the order was the exact opposite: they were to crush and punish people with fire and blood.

Meanwhile, absorbed in his studies, Victor turned twenty-three; he was still living with his parents, before he was recruited into the Republican Army. At home he would get up at dawn and before leaving for the university prepare breakfast for them, his only contribution to the household chores. He would return very late to eat what his mother had left him in the kitchen—bread, sardines, tomatoes, and coffee—and then continue studying. He stayed aloof from his parents' political passion and his brother's fanaticism. "We're making history. We're going to rescue Spain from centuries of feudalism. We're setting an example for Europe, the answer to Hitler and Mussolini," Marcel Lluis Dalmau would lecture his sons and friends at the Rocinante, a bar that looked gloomy but was lofty in atmosphere, where he met daily with friends to play dominoes and drink the lethal wine. "We're going to put an end to the privileges of the oligarchy, the Church, the big landowners, and all the other exploiters of the people. We have to defend democracy, but remember that not everything is politics. Without science, industry, and technology, no progress is possible, and without music and art, there's no soul," he would maintain.

Victor agreed with his father in principle, but tried to escape his lectures, which were almost always the same. Nor did Victor talk about politics with his mother; he restricted himself to helping her teach the militiamen literacy in the basement of a brewery. A high school teacher for many years, Carme thought education was as important as bread, and that anyone who could read and write had a duty to teach those abilities to others. For her, the classes they gave the militiamen were no more than her usual routine, but to Victor they were torture. "They're like donkeys!" he would protest, frustrated at spending two hours on the letter A. "They're no such thing! These boys have never seen an alphabet. I'd like to see how you'd manage behind a plow," his mother would respond.

It was thanks to Carme, afraid her son might end up as a hermit, that from an early age Victor learned to play popular tunes on his guitar. He had a caressing tenor voice that contrasted with his awkward physique and stern expression. Sheltering behind his guitar, he was able to conceal his shyness, avoid banal conversations that irritated him, and yet appear to be joining in with the others. Girls were unaware of his presence until they heard him sing, but when they did, they crowded around and invariably ended up singing along. Afterward they would whisper among themselves that the older Dalmau boy was quite good-looking, even though obviously he couldn't hold a candle to his brother, Guillem.

THE MOST OUTSTANDING PIANIST among Professor Dalmau's students was Roser Bruguera, a young girl from the village of Santa Fe de Segarra who, had it not been for the generous intervention of Santiago Guzman, would have shepherded goats all her life. Guzman, from an illustrious family that had fallen on hard times thanks to generations of lazy sons who squandered money and land, was spending his last years in an isolated mansion surrounded by mountains and rocks, but full of sentimental memories. He had been a professor of history at the Central University in the days of King Alfonso XII, and remained quite active despite his advanced years. He went out every day, in the fierce August sun and the icy January winds, walking for hours with his pilgrim's staff, battered leather hat, and hunting dog. His wife was lost in the labyrinths of dementia, and spent her days being cared for inside the house, creating monsters with paper and paint. In the village she was known as the Gentle Lunatic, and that's what she was: she didn't cause any problems, apart from her tendency to get lost as she set off toward the horizon, and to paint the walls with her own excrement.

Roser was about seven years old when, on one of his walks, Don Santiago saw her looking after a few skinny goats. Exchanging a few words with her was enough for him to realize that she possessed a lively and inquiring mind. The professor and the little goatherd established a strange friendship based on the lessons in culture he gave her, and her desire to learn. One winter's day, when he came upon her crouched, shivering in a ditch with her three goats, soaked from the rain and flushed with fever, Don Santiago tied up the goats and slung her over his shoulder like a sack, thankful she was so small and weighed so little. Even so, the effort almost killed him, and after a few steps he gave up. Leaving her where she was, he hurried on and called to one of his laborers, who carried her to the house. Don Santiago told his cook to give her something to eat, then instructed his housemaids to prepare a bath and bed for her, and the stable boy to go first to Santa Fe and find the doctor, and then to look for the goats before someone stole them.

The doctor said the girl had influenza and was malnourished. She also had scabies and lice. Since nobody came to the Guzman house asking after her either on that day or any of the following ones, they assumed she was an orphan, until in the end they asked her directly and she explained that her family lived on the other side of the mountain. In spite of being as frail as a partridge, the young girl recovered rapidly, because she turned out to be stronger than she looked. She allowed them to shave her head to get rid of the lice, and didn't resist the sulfur treatment they used for the scabies. She ate voraciously and showed signs of having a placid temperament that was at odds with her sad situation.

In the weeks she spent in the mansion, everyone, from the delirious mistress to all the servants, became deeply attached to her. They had never had a little girl in that stone house, which was haunted by semi-feral cats and ghosts from past ages. The most infatuated was the professor, who was vividly reminded of the privilege of teaching an avid mind, but even he realized that her stay with them could not go on forever. He waited for her to recover completely and to put some flesh on her bones, then decided to visit the far side of the mountain and tell her negligent parents a few hard truths. Ignoring his wife's pleas, he installed her, well wrapped up, in his carriage and took off.

They came to a low muddy shack at the edge of the village, one of many wretched places in the area. The peasants lived on starvation wages, working on the land as serfs for big landowners or the Church.

The professor called out, and several frightened children came to the door, followed by a witch dressed in black. She was not, as Don Santiago first thought, the girl's great-grandmother, but was in fact Roser's mother. These villagers had never received the visit of a carriage with gleaming horses before, and were dumbstruck when they saw Roser climbing out of it with such a distinguished-looking gentleman. "I've come to talk to you about this child," Don Santiago began in the authoritarian tone that had once struck fear into his university students. Before he could continue, the woman grabbed Roser by the hair and started shouting and slapping her, accusing her of the loss of their goats. The professor immediately understood there was no point reproaching this exhausted woman for anything, and on the spot came up with a plan that would drastically alter the girl's destiny.

Roser spent the rest of her childhood in the Guzman mansion, officially adopted and taken in as the mistress's personal servant, but also as the professor's pupil. In exchange for helping the maids and bringing the Gentle Lunatic solace, she was given board and an education. The historian shared a good part of his library with her, taught her more than she would have learned in any school, and let her practice on the grand piano once played by his wife, who now could no longer recall what on earth this huge black monster was for. Roser, who during the first seven years of her life had heard no music at all apart from the drunkards' accordions on Saint John's Eve, turned out to have an extraordinarily good ear. There was an old cylinder phonograph in the house, but as soon as Don Santiago realized his protégée could play tunes on the piano after listening to them only once, he ordered a modern gramophone from Madrid, together with a collection of records. Within a short time Roser Bruguera, whose feet still didn't reach the pedals, could play the music from the records with her eyes closed. Delighted, he found her a music teacher in Santa Fe, sent her there three times a week, and personally supervised her practice sessions. Roser, who was able to play anything from memory, didn't see much point in learning to read music or practicing the same scales for hours, but did so out of respect for her mentor.

By the time she was fourteen, Roser was far more accomplished than her teacher, and at fifteen Don Santiago installed her in a guest house for young Catholic ladies in Barcelona so that she could continue her music studies. He would have liked to keep her by his side, but his duty as an educator won out over his paternal instinct. He decided that the girl had received a special talent from God, and his role in this world was to help her develop it. It was around this time that the Gentle Lunatic began to fade away, and in the end died without any fuss. Alone in his mansion, Santiago Guzman began increasingly to feel the weight of his years. He had to give up his walks with his pilgrim's staff and spent his time reading by the hearth. His hunting dog also died, and he was loath to replace it because he didn't want to die first and leave the animal without a master.

The arrival of Spain's Second Republic in 1931 embittered the old man. As soon as the election results favoring the Left became known, King Alfonso XIII left for exile in France, and Don Santiago, monarchist, staunch conservative, and Catholic that he was, saw his world collapsing around him. He could never tolerate the Reds, much less adapt to their vulgar ways: those ruthless people were lackeys of the Soviets who went around burning churches and executing priests. The idea that everyone was equal was fine as a theoretical slogan, he said, but in practice it was an aberration. We are not equal in the eyes of God, because He was the one who created social classes and other distinctions among mankind. The agrarian reform stripped Don Santiago of his land, which was not worth a great deal but had belonged to his family forever. From one day to the next, the peasants began to speak to him without doffing their caps or lowering their eyes. His inferiors' insolence was more painful than the loss of his land because it was a direct affront to his dignity and the position he had always held in this world. He dismissed all the servants who had lived under his roof for decades, had his library, paintings, other collections, and memorabilia packed up, and closed his house under lock and key. All this filled three moving vans, but he couldn't take the biggest pieces of furniture or the grand piano, because they wouldn't fit into his Madrid apartment. A few months later, the Republican mayor of Santa Fe confiscated the house and turned it into an orphanage.

Among the many grave disappointments and reasons for anger Don Santiago suffered in those years was the transformation of his protégée. Under the bad influence of the troublemakers at the university, and in particular that of a certain Professor Marcel Lluis Dalmau, a communist, socialist, or anarchist—in the end, it was all the same thing—his Roser had turned into a Red. She had left the guest house for young ladies of good repute and was living with some hoydens who dressed as soldiers and practiced free love, which is what promiscuity and indecency had come to be called. He had to admit that Roser never showed him any lack of respect, but since she took it upon herself to ignore his warnings, he naturally had to withdraw his support for her. She wrote him a letter thanking him with all her soul for everything he had done for her, promising she would always follow the right path according to her own principles, and explaining she was working at night in a bakery and continuing to study music by day.

Don Santiago Guzman, installed in his luxurious Madrid apartment, where he could barely make his way through the clutter of furniture and other objects, and protected from the noise and vulgar uproar in the streets by heavy drapes the color of bull's blood, socially isolated by his deafness and boundless pride, was blissfully unaware of how the most terrible rancor was surfacing in his country, a rancor that had been feeding on the wretchedness of some and the arrogance of others. He died alone and irate in his apartment in the Salamanca district four months before the uprising spearheaded by Franco's troops. He was lucid to the end, and so accepting of death that he prepared his own obituary, to avoid some ignorant person publishing untruths about him.

He said farewell to no one, possibly because there was nobody close to him still alive, but he did remember Roser Bruguera, and in a noble gesture of reconciliation left her the grand piano, which was still being stored in the new orphanage at Santa Fe.

PROFESSOR MARCEL LLUIS DALMAU rapidly distinguished Roser from the rest of his students. In his desire to teach his pupils what he knew of music and life, he slipped in political and philosophical ideas that doubtless had more influence on them than he ever suspected. In this at least Santiago Guzman had been right. Experience had taught Dalmau to beware of those students who had too much facility with music, because as he often said, he had not yet come across any Mozarts. He had seen cases like that of Roser, youngsters with a good ear who could play any instrument, who soon became lazy, convinced this was enough for them to be able to master their art, and therefore could do without study or discipline. More than one ended up earning a living in popular bands, playing at parties, hotels, and restaurants, as what he called "cheap wedding entertainers." He set out to save Roser Bruguera from this fate, and took her under his wing. When he heard she had been left on her own in Barcelona, he opened the doors of his home to her, and later on when he learned she had inherited a piano and had nowhere to put it, he removed the furniture from his living room and never once objected to her endless practicing of scales during her daily visits to them after her classes. Since Guillem was away at the war, Carme lent her the bed he normally slept in; this meant she could snatch a few hours' sleep before she went to the bakery at three in the morning to bake loaves for the new day. From lying so often with her head on the pillow of the younger of the Dalmau boys, breathing in traces of Guillem's manly smell, the girl fell in love with him, and would not allow distance, time, or war to dissuade her.

Roser came to be part of the family as easily as if she were a blood relation; she became the daughter the Dalmaus had always wished for. They lived in a modest house, rather gloomy and run down because it had not been looked after for many years, but spacious. When his two sons had gone off to war, Marcel Lluis suggested Roser come to live with them: that way she could reduce her costs, work fewer hours, practice the piano whenever she liked, and at the same time help his wife with the household tasks. Although some years younger than her husband, Carme looked older, because she went around panting for breath and coughing, whereas he was full of energy. "I hardly have the strength to teach the militiamen to read and write, and when that's no longer absolutely necessary, there'll be nothing for me to do but die," she would sigh. In his first year of medical studies, her son Victor diagnosed her lungs as being like cauliflowers. "Damn it, Carme, if you're going to die, it'll be because you smoke so much," complained her husband when he heard her coughing, without taking into account the tobacco he himself smoked or ever imagining that death would come for him first.

So it happened that Roser Bruguera, who was so close to the Dalmau family, was with the professor when he had a heart attack. She stopped going to her classes, but went on working at the bakery and took turns with Carme to attend him. In the empty hours she would entertain him by playing the piano, filling the house with music that soothed the dying man. She was present when the professor gave his last words of advice to his eldest son.

"When I'm gone, Victor, you'll be responsible for your mother and Roser, because Guillem is going to die fighting. We've lost the war, my son," he told him, pausing all the time to draw breath.

"Don't say that, Father."

"I realized it back in March, when they bombed Barcelona. Those were Italian and German planes. Reason is on our side, but that won't help stave off defeat. We're on our own, Victor."

"Everything could change if France, England, and the United States intervene."

"You can forget the United States: they're not going to help us in any way. I've heard Eleanor Roosevelt has tried to convince her husband to intervene, but the president has public opinion against him."

"They can't all be against it, Father: you can see how many American young men in the Lincoln Brigade have come to Spain and are willing to die alongside us."

"They're idealists, Victor, and there are very few of those in the world. A lot of the bombs that fell on us in March were American."

"But Hitler and Mussolini's Fascism will spread throughout Europe if we don't stop them here. We cannot lose this war: that would mean the end of all that the people have achieved and a return to the past, to the feudal misery we've lived under for centuries."

"Listen to me, son: nobody will come to our aid. Even the Soviet Union has abandoned us. Stalin is no longer interested in Spain. And when the Republic falls, the repression will be dreadful. Franco has imposed what he calls cleansing, that is, outright terror, utter hatred, the bloodiest revenge; he won't negotiate or pardon. His troops are committing unspeakable atrocities . . ."

"So are we," retorted Victor, who had seen a lot.

"How dare you compare the two! There'll be a bloodbath in Catalonia. I won't live to suffer it, my son, but I want to die in peace. You must promise me you'll take your mother and Roser abroad. The Fascists will take it out on Carme because she teaches soldiers to read and write: they shoot people for a lot less than that. They'll take revenge on you because you work in an army hospital, and on Roser because she's a young woman. You know what they do to them, don't you? They hand them over to the Moors . . . I've got it all planned. You're to go to France until the situation calms down. In my desk you'll find a map and some money I've saved. Promise me you'll do as I ask."

"I promise, Father," replied Victor, without any real intention of doing so.

"You must understand, Victor—this isn't cowardice, it's a question of survival."

Marcel Lluis Dalmau wasn't the only one who had doubts about the future of the Republic, but nobody dared express them openly, because the worst betrayal would be to sow despair or panic among an exhausted population that had already suffered too much.

The next day Professor Marcel Lluis Dalmau was buried. His family wanted this to be a discreet affair because it was not a time for private grief, but the news got out and the Montjuic cemetery was filled with his friends from the Rocinante tavern, university colleagues, and middle-aged former students—all the younger ones were fighting on the battlefronts or were already beneath the earth. Leaning on Victor and Roser, and dressed in deep mourning that included a veil and black stockings despite the June heat, Carme walked behind the coffin containing the love of her life. There were no prayers, eulogies, or tears. Dalmau was given a send-off by some of his former students, who played the second movement of Schubert's string quintet, its melancholy ideally suited to the occasion, and then sang one of the militia songs he had composed.

CHAPTER 2

1938

Nothing, not even victory,
Can wipe away the terrible hole of blood.

—PABLO NERUDA
"Hymn to the Glory of the People at War"
OFFENDED LANDS

ROSER BRUGUERA FELL IN LOVE FOR THE FIRST
time at Professor Dalmau's house, where he had invited her with the excuse of helping her with her studies, even though both of them knew it was more an act
of charity. The professor suspected that his favorite
student ate very little and needed a family, especially
somebody like Carme, whose maternal instincts found
little response in Victor, and none at all in Guillem.
Earlier that year, disgusted with the military regime of
the boardinghouse for respectable young ladies, Roser
had left it to live in the port area of Barceloneta with
three girls from the popular militias in the only room
she could afford. She was nineteen years old, and while
the other girls were only four or five years her senior,
they were twenty years older in terms of experience
and mentality. The militiawomen, who lived in a very

different world from Roser, nicknamed her "the novice" and completely ignored her most of the time. They slept in a bedroom containing four bunk beds (Roser took one of the top bunks), a couple of chairs, a washbowl, jug, chamber pot, a kerosene burner, with nails in the wall to hang their clothes on, and a bathroom shared with the thirty or more lodgers in the house. These cheerful, feisty women enjoyed the freedom of those turbulent times to the fullest. They wore militia uniforms, boots, and berets, but also put on lipstick and curled their hair with tongs heated in a brazier. They trained with sticks or borrowed rifles, desperate to go to the front and defy the enemy face-to-face rather than carry out the transport, supply, cooking, and nursing roles assigned to them with the argument that there were barely enough Soviet and Mexican weapons for the men, and they would be wasted in female hands.

A few months later, when the Nationalist troops had occupied two-thirds of Spain and were continuing their advance, the young women's desire to be in the vanguard was fulfilled. Two of them would be raped and have their throats cut in an attack by Moroccan troops. The third survived the three years of civil war and the following six of the Second World War, wandering in the shadows from one end of Europe to the other, until she was able to emigrate to the United States in 1950. She ended up in New York married to a Jewish intellectual who had fought in the Lincoln Brigade—but that's another story.

Guillem Dalmau was a year older than Roser Bruguera. Whereas she lived up to her "novice" nickname with old-fashioned dresses and a serious demeanor, he was cocky and defiant, completely sure of himself. Yet Roser only had to be with him once or twice to realize that hidden beneath his brash exterior lay a childish, confused, romantic heart. Each time Guillem returned to Barcelona he seemed more resolute: there was nothing left of the foolish youth who stole a candelabra. Now he was a mature man, with furrowed brow and a huge charge of contained violence that could explode at the slightest provocation. He would sleep in the barracks but spend a couple of nights at his parents' house, above all because of the chance of seeing Roser. He congratulated himself that he had avoided the sentimental ties that caused so much anguish to the soldiers separated from their girlfriends or families. He was completely immersed in the war, but his father's pupil was no danger to his bachelor independence: she was nothing more than an innocent bit of fun. Depending on the angle and the light, Roser could be attractive, but she did nothing to enhance her looks, and her simplicity struck a mysterious chord in Guillem's soul. He was accustomed to the effect he had on women in general, and was aware he did the same to Roser, even if she was incapable of any coquettishness. *The girl is in love with me, and how could it be otherwise: all the poor thing has in her life is the piano and the bakery; she'll get over it,* he thought. "Be careful, Guillem, that girl is sacred, and if I catch you showing her any disrespect . . ." his father had warned him. "What are you saying, Father! Roser is like a sister to me." But fortunately, she wasn't his sister. To judge by the way his parents took care of her, Roser must be a virgin, one of the few remaining in Republican Spain. He wouldn't dream of going too far with her, but no one could blame him for showing a little tenderness, a brush of knees under the table, an invitation to the movies to touch her in the darkness when she was crying at the film and trembling with shyness and desire. For more daring caresses he could rely on some of his female comrades, experienced and willing militiawomen.

After his brief furloughs in Barcelona, Guillem would return to the front intending to concentrate only on surviving and defeating the enemy, and yet he found it hard to forget Roser Bruguera's anxious face and clear gaze. Not even in the most silent recesses of his heart would he admit how much he needed her letters, packets of candies, and the socks and scarves she knitted for him. The only photograph he carried in his billfold was of her. Roser was standing beside a piano, possibly during a recital, wearing a modest dark dress with a longer than usual skirt, short sleeves, and a lace collar, an absurd schoolgirl's dress that hid all her curves. In this black-and-white card, Roser looked distant and blurred, a woman lacking any spark, ageless and expressionless. One had to guess at the contrast between her amber-colored eyes and black hair, her straight Grecian nose, expressive eyebrows, protruding ears, long fingers, the way she smelled of soap: all details that were painful to Guillem when they suddenly engulfed him or invaded him in his sleep. Details that could distract him and cost him his life.

ON SUNDAY AFTERNOON NINE DAYS after his father's burial, Guillem Dalmau turned up unannounced in a battered military vehicle. Roser went out to see who it was, wiping her hands on a dishcloth. For a moment she didn't recognize the thin, haggard man being helped in by two militiawomen. She hadn't seen him for four months: four months nourishing her hope on the rare phrases he sent her from time to time, describing the fighting in Madrid but without a single affectionate word; messages like reports, on sheets torn out of a notebook, penned in a schoolboy's handwriting. *Everything the same here, you'll have heard how we're defending the city, the walls are full of holes like colanders from the mortars, ruins everywhere, the Fascists have Italian and German weapons, they're so close sometimes we can smell the tobacco they're smoking, the bastards. We can hear them talking, they shout to provoke us but they're drunk with fear—apart, that is, from the Moors, who are like hyenas and aren't afraid of anything. They prefer their butchers' knives to rifles, hand-to-hand fighting, the taste of blood; the Nationalists receive reinforcements every day, but they don't advance a single meter; on our side we have no water or electricity and food is in short supply, but we manage; and I'm fine. Half the buildings have collapsed; we are barely able to recover the bodies; they lie where they fall until the next day, when the mortuary attendants come. Not all the children have been evacuated—you should see how stubborn some of the mothers are, they refuse to leave or be separated from their offspring, it makes no sense. How is your piano going? How are my parents? Tell Mother not to worry about me.*

"Dear Jesus! What's happened to you, for God's sake!" exclaimed Roser on the front doorstep, her Catholic upbringing resurfacing. Guillem didn't respond: his head was drooping on his chest, his legs unable to support him. Then Carme also appeared from the kitchen, and her terrified cry rose from her feet to her throat, producing an outburst of coughing.

"Stay calm, comrades. He's not wounded; he's sick," one of the militiawomen said firmly.

"This way," Roser directed, leading them to the room that had once been Guillem's and which she now occupied. The two women laid him down on the bed and withdrew, only to return a minute later with his rucksack, blanket, and rifle. Then they left, after bidding the family a brief goodbye and good luck. Carme was still coughing desperately, so Roser took off Guillem's tattered boots and filthy socks, struggling to control the nausea she felt at his stinking body. There was no way they could take him to a hospital, where he would only get infected, or try to find a doctor—doctors were all far too busy with the war wounded.

"We have to wash him, Carme, he's filthy. I'll run to the telephone exchange to call Victor," said the girl, who didn't want to see Guillem naked, covered in excrement and urine. On the telephone Roser explained the symptoms to Victor: a very high fever, difficulty breathing, diarrhea.

"He groans whenever we touch him. He must be in a lot of pain, in the stomach I think, but the rest of the body as well. You know your brother never complains."

"It's typhus, Roser. There's an epidemic of it among the soldiers.

It's transmitted by lice, fleas, contaminated water, and dirt. I'll try to come and see him tomorrow, but it's very hard for me to leave my post. The hospital is full to overflowing—every day we receive dozens of newly wounded people. For now you need to give him boiled water with a little sugar and salt to drink to keep him hydrated, and wrap him in cold damp towels to lower the fever."

For the next two weeks, Guillem Dalmau was looked after by his mother and Roser, supervised from Manresa by his brother, whom Roser called every day to report on Guillem and receive instructions on how to avoid contagion. They had to get rid of the lice in his clothes—the best way was to burn them—to wash everything with bleach, use different cooking pots for Guillem, and to wash their own hands thoroughly each time they attended him. The first three days were critical. Guillem's temperature rose to 104 degrees; he was delirious, beside himself with headaches and nausea, his body racked with a dry cough; his feces were a green liquid like pea soup. On the fourth day, his fever abated, but they couldn't wake him. Victor told them to shake him and force him to drink water, but to let him sleep the rest of the time. He needed to rest and recover.

The main responsibility for looking after him fell on Roser, because Carme, due to her age and the state of her lungs, was more vulnerable to catching the disease. While Roser spent the day at home, reading or knitting beside Guillem's bed, Carme continued to go out to teach and stand in line for food. Roser went on with her night job, because she was paid with bread. Rations of lentils had been reduced to half a cup per person per day; there were no cats or pigeons left for stews. Roser's bread was a dark, heavy block that smelled of sawdust; oil had become a luxury item, and was mixed with engine oil to make it go further. Many people grew vegetables in their bathtubs or on their balconies. Family heirlooms and jewels were traded for potatoes and rice.

Although Roser didn't see her family, she had stayed in touch with a few peasants in the countryside, and so could get vegetables, a piece of goat cheese, a sausage on the rare occasions a pig was killed. Carme's budget didn't allow her to buy on the black market, where there were very few foodstuffs, but which was a last resort for cigarettes and soap. Guillem was as skinny as a skeleton, and they had to help him regain his strength, so Carme dipped into the little savings her husband had left and sent Roser back to Santa Fe to buy anything they could put in a soup. She knew Marcel Lluis had intended the money to be used to send the family out of Spain, but the fact was that none of them could seriously consider emigrating. What would they do in France or anywhere else? They couldn't leave their home, their neighborhood, their language, their relatives and friends. The possibility that they would win the war was increasingly remote, and they had silently resigned themselves to a negotiated peace and Nationalist repression, but even that was preferable to exile. However ruthless Franco was, he couldn't execute the entire Catalan population.

Roser spent the money on two live chickens. She traveled with them hidden in a sack tied around her waist under her dress so that they wouldn't be stolen by some desperate person or confiscated by soldiers. Thinking she must be pregnant, the other passengers gave up their seat for her on the bus. She sat there covering the bulge as best she could, praying the birds didn't start moving around. Carme covered the floor of one of the rooms with sheets of newspaper and they installed the chickens there. They fed them with scraps and leftovers from the Rocinante bar, as well as a little barley and buckwheat Roser smuggled out of the bakery. The birds recovered from the trauma of being in the sack, and soon Guillem could count on one or two eggs for breakfast.

After a few days' convalescence, their patient wanted to return to life, but had barely enough energy to sit up in bed and listen to Roser play the piano in the living room or read detective novels out loud to him. He had never been much of a reader: as a boy he got through school thanks to his mother, who supervised his homework, and to Victor, who often did it for him. At the front in Madrid, where he found himself growing bored in endless waits while nothing happened, it would have been wonderful to have Roser read to him. There were more than enough books, but to him the words seemed to dance all over the page. During pauses in her reading, he told Roser about his life as a soldier, about the volunteers from more than fifty countries who had come to Spain to fight and die in a war that wasn't theirs, about the Americans in the Lincoln Brigade who were always in the vanguard, and always the first to fall. "They say that more than thirty-five thousand men and several hundred women from other countries came to fight against Fascism. That's how important our war is, Roser." He told her about how the corridors of the buildings were full of rubble, garbage, dust, and broken glass. "In the quiet moments we teach and we learn. Mother would be in her element teaching the boys who can't read or write; lots of them have never been to school."

What he didn't mention to Roser were the rats and lice, the feces, urine, and blood, the wounded comrades waiting hours losing blood until the stretcher-bearers could reach them, the hunger and mess tins with hard beans and cold coffee, how some comrades were irrationally brave and faced the bullets nonchalantly, whereas others were terrified, especially the youngest, the newest arrivals, the boys in the Baby Bottle Conscription. Fortunately, he had not had to fight alongside any of them because he would have died of pity. Much less did he confess to Roser the mass executions carried out by his own comrades: how they tied enemy prisoners together in pairs, took them off in a truck to some waste ground, shot them on the spot, and then buried them in mass graves. More than two thousand in Madrid alone.

———

IT WAS THE START of summer. Night fell later, and the days grew longer in hot, languid hours. Guillem and Roser spent so much time together they came to know each other very well. However much they shared reading or conversing, there were lengthy silences steeped in a sweet feeling of intimacy. After supper, Roser would lie down on the bed she now shared with Carme and sleep until three in the morning. Then she would set off for the bakery to prepare the bread that was handed out as rations at first light.

The news on the radio, in the papers, and from the loudspeakers in the streets was always optimistic. The air was filled with the militias' songs and the incendiary speeches of La Pasionaria: better to die on one's feet than to live on one's knees. There was never any talk of an enemy advance: it was always called a tactical withdrawal. Nor was there any mention of the rationing and shortages of almost everything, from food to medicine. Victor Dalmau gave his family a more realistic account than the one from the loudspeakers. He could judge how the war was going by the trainloads of wounded and the numbers of dead that mounted up tragically in the hospital. "I have to get back to the front," Guillem would say, but couldn't even get his boots on before collapsing back on the bed, exhausted.

The daily rituals of caring for Guillem through the miseries of typhus, washing him with a sponge, emptying the chamber pot, feeding him with spoonfuls of a child's pap, watching over his sleep and then washing him again, emptying the pot, and feeding him in an endless routine of concern and affection, only strengthened Roser's conviction that he was the only man she could love. She was sure there could be nobody else.

On the ninth day of his convalescence, seeing how much better he looked, Roser understood she had no more excuses for keeping him in bed, where she could have him all to herself. Guillem would very soon have to return to the front. There had been such huge losses in the past year that the Republican Army was recruiting adolescents, old men, and evil-looking prisoners who were given the choice of either going to the front or rotting in jail. Roser announced to Guillem that it was time for him to get up, and the first step would be a good bath. She heated water in the biggest pan in the kitchen, helped Guillem into the washtub, soaped him from his hair down to his feet, and afterward rinsed him and dried him until he was pink and shiny. She knew him so well by now that she didn't even notice his nakedness. For his part, Guillem was no longer embarrassed in front of her; in Roser's hands he was returning to childhood.

I'm going to marry her when the war is over, he told himself in a moment of profound gratitude. Until then, nothing had been further from his mind than putting down roots and getting married. The war had saved him from planning any possible future. *I'm not made for peace,* he had told himself, far better to be a soldier than a factory worker—and what else could he do with no education and such an impetuous character? But Roser, with her freshness and innocence, her unflagging kindness, had gotten under his skin. The image of her accompanied him in the trenches, and the more he remembered her, the more he needed her and the prettier she seemed. In the worst days of typhus, when he was drowning in a tide of pain and fear, he clung desperately to Roser to stay afloat. In his confused state, his only compass was her concerned face leaning over him; his only anchor her wild eyes that suddenly became smiling and gentle.

This first bath in the washtub brought Guillem back to the land of the living, after many days sweating at death's door. He returned to life thanks to being rubbed with the soapy cloth, the foam in his hair, the buckets of warm water, and Roser's hands on his body, the hands of a pianist: strong, gentle, precise. He surrendered completely, thankfully. She dried him, helped him into a pair of his father's pajamas, shaved him, and cut his hair and his fingernails, which had grown into claws. Guillem still had sunken cheeks and red eyes, but he was no longer the scarecrow who had arrived at the house dragged along by two militiawomen. Then Roser heated what was left of the coffee from breakfast and poured in a splash of brandy, to give herself courage.

"I'm ready for us to go out and dance," said Guillem when he saw himself in the mirror.

"You're ready to go back to bed," announced Roser, handing him a cup. "With me," she added.

"What did you say?"

"You heard."

"You can't be thinking of . . ."

"Of exactly the same as you ought to be thinking," she replied, pulling her dress up over her head.

"What are you doing? Mother could be back at any minute."

"It's Sunday. Carme is dancing *sardanas* in the square, and then she'll go and line up at the telephone exchange to call Victor."

"I might infect you . . ."

"If you didn't infect me at the start, it's not likely to happen now. That's enough excuses. Get a move on, Guillem," Roser ordered him, slipping off her bra and panties, and pushing him aside to get into bed.

Never before had she appeared naked in front of a man, but she had lost her shyness in these days of being forced to live with rationing, in a permanent state of alert, mistrusting neighbors and friends, with the angel of death always hovering nearby. Her virginity, so prized at the nuns' school, now weighed on her at twenty like a blemish. Nothing was certain; the future did not exist; all they had was this moment to savor before the war snatched it from them.

DEFEAT BECAME CLEAR WITH the battle of the River Ebro. It began in July 1938, lasted four months, and left more than thirty thousand dead. Among them would be Guillem Dalmau.

The Republicans' situation was desperate: their only hope was that France and Great Britain would intervene on their behalf, but the days went by without any sign of this happening. In order to gain time, the Republicans concentrated all their efforts and the bulk of their troops in a crossing of the River Ebro. The idea was to thrust into enemy territory and occupy it, seize their supplies and ammunition, demonstrate to the world that the war was not lost and that with the necessary aid, Spain could defeat Fascism. Eighty thousand men were transported stealthily by night to the eastern bank of the river. Their task was to cross it and confront the enemy forces, who were far superior in numbers and weaponry. Guillem was part of the mixed brigades of the 45th International Division, fighting alongside English, American, and Canadian volunteers. They were the advance guard, the shock troops, what they themselves called the cannon fodder. They were fighting in rugged terrain and with harsh summer weather, the enemy in front of them, the river at their backs, and German and Italian planes in the skies above them.

This surprise attack gave the Republicans an initial advantage. Arriving at the front, the soldiers crossed the river on improvised craft, pulling along terrified, loaded-down mules. The engineers built pontoon bridges that were bombed by day and replaced by night. In the vanguard, Guillem spent days with no food or water when the supply chain failed. He went weeks without bathing, sleeping on the rocks, sick from sunstroke and diarrhea, constantly exposed to enemy fire, mosquitoes, and rats that ate anything they could find and attacked anybody who fell. The hunger, thirst, churning guts, and exhaustion were made worse by the fierce summer heat. Guillem was so dehydrated he no longer produced any sweat. His skin was burned, cracked, and blackened, as leathery as a lizard's. He sometimes spent hours crouching, rifle in hand, jaws clenched, every fiber of his body taut as he waited for death, until his legs gave out under him. He thought he must have been weakened by the bout of typhus, and was no longer as strong as he once had been. His comrades were falling at a terrifying rate, and he wondered when it would be his turn. The wounded were evacuated at night in vehicles without lights to avoid being strafed by enemy planes; some of the most badly wounded begged to be given the coup de grâce, because the possibility of falling into enemy hands was worse than a thousand deaths. The bodies that couldn't be removed before they began to stink under the merciless sun were covered with stones or burned, as were the horses and mules: it was impossible to dig graves in this rocky ground, where the earth was as hard as cement. Guillem risked exposure to bullets and grenades to reach the bodies and rescue some kind of personal item to send back to their families.

None of the combatants could understand why they had been sent to die on the banks of the River Ebro. It made no sense to push into territory Franco controlled, and the cost in lives of maintaining their position was absurd. But to voice any objection out loud was an act of cowardice or treason, paid for dearly. Guillem fought under a lion-hearted American officer who had been a university student in California before joining the Lincoln Brigade. Despite having no military training, the American showed he was made for warfare, a born soldier who knew how to give orders: his men worshipped him.

Guillem had been one of the first volunteers for the militias in Barcelona, at a time when the socialist ideal of equality reigned. The revolution had extended this to every sector of society, including the army, where no one was considered superior to anyone else, or entitled to have more. The officers lived alongside the rest of the troops

without privileges; they ate the same food and wore the sar
forms. There was no hierarchy, no protocol, no standing at attention,
no special tents, weapons, or vehicles for officers, no shiny boots,
fawning adjutants, or cooks, as in conventional armies and definitely
in Franco's. All this changed over the first year of war, when the revolutionary enthusiasm died down to a great extent. A disgusted Guillem saw how in Barcelona there was a subtle return to bourgeois ways
of living: social classes, the arrogance of some and the servility of
others, bribes, prostitution, the privileges of the rich, who had plenty
of everything—food, tobacco, fashionable attire—while the rest of
the population suffered shortages and rationing. He also saw changes
in the military. Made up of conscripts, the Popular Army absorbed the
voluntary militias and reimposed traditional hierarchies and discipline.

Despite this, the American officer still believed in the triumph of
socialism. To him, equality was not only possible, but inevitable, and
he practiced it like a religion. The men under his command called him
comrade, but never questioned his orders. He had learned enough
Spanish to be able to explain the Ebro campaign to his men. The aim
was to protect Valencia and to restore contact with Catalonia, separated from the rest of Republican territory by a broad swath the Nationalists had conquered. Guillem respected the officer and would
have followed him anywhere, with or without explanations.

In mid-September, the American was machine-gunned from behind. He fell alongside Guillem without a single moan, continuing to
encourage his men from the ground until he lost consciousness. Guillem and another soldier lifted him up and laid him behind a pile of
rubble until nightfall, when the stretcher-bearers could come and take
him to a first aid post. A few days later, Guillem heard that if the officer didn't die, he would be an invalid for the rest of his life. He
wished him a speedy death with all his heart.

The American died a week before the Republican government announced the withdrawal of foreign fighters from Spain, in the hope that Franco, who relied on German and Italian troops, would follow suit. That didn't happen. Buried in an unmarked grave, the Lincoln Brigade officer did not live to march with his comrades through the streets of Barcelona, cheered by a grateful population in a massive ceremony that every one of them would remember forever. The most memorable farewell speech was given by La Pasionaria, whose incandescent enthusiasm had kept Republican morale high throughout the war. She called them freedom crusaders, heroes and idealists who were both brave and disciplined, and who had left their homes and countries to give everything, only asking in return the honor of dying for Spain. Nine thousand of those crusaders stayed forever, buried on Spanish soil. La Pasionaria ended by telling the departing foreigners that after the victory they would return to Spain, where they would find a homeland and friends.

Franco's propaganda called on the Republican troops to surrender through loudspeakers and pamphlets dropped from planes, offering bread, justice, and freedom, but all the combatants knew that deserting meant they would end up in a prison or a mass grave that they themselves would be forced to dig. They had heard that in the towns and villages conquered by Franco, the widows and families of those executed were obliged to pay for the bullets used by the firing squads. And the number of the executed was in the tens of thousands. So much blood ran that the following year the peasants swore that when they pulled up their onions they were red, and that they found human teeth in their potatoes. Even so, the temptation to go over to the enemy for a loaf of bread led to many fighters deserting—usually the youngest recruits. On one occasion, Guillem had to grapple with a youngster from Valencia who was so terrified he lost his nerve; Guillem pushed his pistol against the boy's temple and swore he would kill him if he left his post. It took two hours to calm the boy down, but Guillem succeeded in doing so without anybody else noticing. Thirty hours later, the youngster was dead.

And in the midst of that hell, where they couldn't rely on even the most essential supplies, every so often an ambulance appeared with a sack of mail. The driver was Aitor Ibarra, who had set himself this task to raise the combatants' spirits. Personal correspondence was one of the lowest priorities on the Ebro front, and in fact most of the men did not receive letters: those in the International Brigades because they were so far from their loved ones, and many of the Spaniards, especially those from the south, because they came from families where no one could read or write. But Guillem Dalmau did have someone to write to him. Aitor would joke he was risking his life to bring letters to a single recipient. Sometimes he handed Guillem a thick packet of several letters tied up with a string. There were always one or two from Guillem's mother and brother, but most came from Roser. She would write one or two paragraphs every day until she had filled a couple of pages, then put them in an envelope and take it to the military mail office, singing to herself the most popular militia song: *If you want to write / you know where I'll be / Third Mixed Brigade / in the first line of fire.* She had no idea that Ibarra greeted Guillem with the same or a similar song when he handed him the letters. The Basque sang even when he was asleep to ward off fear and beguile his good luck fairy.

AFTER CONQUERING MOST OF the country, Franco's troops continued their inexorable advance; it was obvious that Catalonia would fall as well. Panic gripped Barcelona; many made preparations to leave, lots more had already done so. In mid-January 1939, Aitor Ibarra arrived at Manresa hospital in a battered truck with nineteen gravely wounded men. There had been twenty-one when they started out, but two had died on the journey, and their bodies had been left by the wayside. Some doctors had already fled the city, while those who remained were trying to avoid panic among their patients. The members of the Republican government had also chosen to go into exile, hoping to continue to govern from Paris. This finally undermined the spirit of the civilian population. By now, the Nationalists were less than twenty-five kilometers from Barcelona.

Ibarra had gone fifty hours without sleeping. After delivering his pitiful cargo, he collapsed, exhausted, into Victor Dalmau's arms when the doctor came out to receive the wounded. Victor installed Aitor in what he called his regal chamber—a camp bed, kerosene lamp, and chamber pot constituted his entire lodging ever since he had begun living in the hospital in order to save time. Some hours later, when there was a lull in the frenetic activity in the operating theater, Victor took his friend a bowl of lentil soup, the dried sausage his mother had sent him that week, and a pot of chicory coffee. He had difficulty waking up Aitor, but still dizzy with fatigue, the Basque ate voraciously and told him in detail about the battle of the Ebro, which Victor already knew about in outline from the accounts of all the injured he had treated in the previous months. The Republican Army had been decimated and, according to Ibarra, it only remained for them to prepare for the final defeat. "In the hundred and fifteen days of combat, more than ten thousand of our men died. I don't know how many thousands more were taken prisoner, or how many civilian victims there were in the bombed towns and villages, and that's not counting the losses among the enemy," added the Basque. As Professor Marcel Lluis Dalmau had predicted before he died, the war was lost. There would be no negotiated peace, as the Republican high command was claiming; Franco would accept nothing less than unconditional surrender. "Don't believe the Francoist propaganda: there'll be no mercy or justice. There'll be a bloodbath, just like there has been in the rest of the country. We're done for."

To Victor, who had shared moments of tragedy with Ibarra without him ever losing his defiant smile, his songs and jokes, the gloomy expression on his friend's face was even more eloquent than his words. Aitor took a small bottle of liquor out of his rucksack, poured it into the watery coffee, and offered it to Victor. "Here, you're going to need it," he told him. For a long while he had been searching for the best way to give Victor the sad news about his brother, but in the end could only blurt out that Guillem had died on the eighth of November.

"How?" was all that Victor managed to ask.

"A bomb in the trench. I'm sorry, Victor, I prefer to spare you the details."

"Tell me what happened," Victor insisted.

"The bomb blew several men to pieces. There was no time to reconstitute the bodies, so we buried the pieces."

"So then you weren't able to identify them."

"We couldn't identify them individually, Victor, but we knew who was in the trench. Guillem was one of them."

"But you can't be sure, can you?"

"I'm afraid I can," said Aitor, taking a charred billfold from his rucksack.

Victor carefully opened the billfold, which seemed to be about to fall to pieces. He took out Guillem's army identity card, and a miraculously intact photograph. It was the image of a young girl standing next to a grand piano. Victor Dalmau remained seated for several minutes at the foot of the camp bed, unable to speak. Aitor didn't have the heart to embrace him as he would have liked, but sat beside him without moving, also silent.

"It's his girlfriend, Roser Bruguera. They were going to get married after the war," said Victor finally.

"I'm so sorry, Victor, but you'll have to tell her."

"She's pregnant: six or seven months, I think. I can't tell her without being sure that Guillem has died."

"What more certainty do you need, Victor? Nobody came out of that hellhole alive."

"But he might not have been there."

"If that were the case, he would still have his billfold in his pocket, he would be alive somewhere, and we would have news of him. Two months have gone by. Don't you think the billfold is proof enough?"

That weekend, Victor Dalmau went home to his mother's house in Barcelona. She received him with *arròs negre* made with a cup of rice she had bought on the black market, a few cloves of garlic, and an octopus that she bartered for her husband's watch down at the port. The fishing catch was reserved for the soldiers, and what little was distributed among the civilian population was meant to go to hospitals and children's centers, although everyone knew there was no shortage on the tables of the politicians or in the hotels and restaurants frequented by the bourgeoisie.

When he saw his mother so thin and shriveled, looking so aged with worry and concern, and a radiant Roser with a bulging stomach and the inner glow that pregnant women have, Victor couldn't bear to tell them about Guillem's death; they were still in mourning for Marcel Lluis. He tried to do so several times, but the words froze in his chest, and so he decided to wait until Roser gave birth, or the war came to an end. With a baby in their arms, Carme's grief at losing her son, and Roser's at losing her great love, would be more bearable. Or so he thought.

CHAPTER 3

1939

The days of a century passed by
And the hours followed your exile.

—PABLO NERUDA
"Artigas"
CANTO GENERAL

THE DAY NEAR THE END OF JANUARY IN BARCELONA when the exodus that became known as the Retreat began, it dawned so cold that water froze in the pipes, vehicles and animals got stuck on the ice, and the sky, shrouded in dark clouds, seemed to be in deep mourning. It was one of the coldest winters in living memory. Franco's Nationalist troops were advancing down from Tibidabo, and panic gripped the civilian population. Hundreds of Nationalist prisoners were dragged from their cells and shot. Soldiers, many of them wounded, began the trek toward the French border, following thousands upon thousands of civilians: entire families, grandparents, mothers, children, breast-feeding infants, everyone carrying whatever they could take with them. Some traveled in buses or trucks, others on bicycles, horse-drawn carts, horses, or mules, but the majority went on foot, hauling their belongings in sacks, a pitiful procession of the desperate. Behind them they left shuttered homes and treasured objects. Pets followed their owners for some of the way, but soon became lost in the chaos and were left behind.

Victor Dalmau had spent the night evacuating those among the wounded who could be transferred in the few available ambulances, trucks, and trains. Around eight o'clock in the morning, he realized he ought to follow his father's orders and save his mother and Roser, but he couldn't abandon his patients. He managed to locate Aitor Ibarra and convince him he should leave with the two women. The Basque driver had an old German motorcycle with a sidecar. In peacetime it had been his pride and joy, but for the past three years he had kept it safe in a friend's garage, unable to use it due to the shortage of fuel. Given the circumstances, Aitor thought extreme measures were justified, and he stole two jerry cans of gasoline from the hospital. The bike lived up to the reputation of Teutonic technological excellence and kicked into life at the third try, as if it had never spent a day buried in a garage. At half past ten, Aitor turned up outside the Dalmau house, engine roaring and in a cloud of exhaust fumes, having zigzagged with difficulty through the crowds thronging the streets. Carme and Roser were expecting him, because Victor had found a way to alert them. His instructions had been clear: they were to stay close to Ibarra, cross the frontier, and once over it, get in touch with the Red Cross to try to find a friend of his called Elisabeth Eidenbenz, a nurse who could be trusted. She would be their contact point when they were all in France.

The two women had packed warm clothing, a few provisions, and some family photos. Roser was loath to go without Guillem, but reassured herself that she would be able to reunite with him in France. Until the last moment, Carme was also doubtful about whether or not she should leave. She felt incapable of starting a new life elsewhere: she said that nothing lasted forever, however bad, and perhaps they could wait to see how things turned out. Aitor provided her with vivid details of what would happen when the Fascists came. First, there would be flags everywhere, and a solemn Mass in the main square that everybody would be forced to attend. The conquerors would be received with cheers by a crowd of enemies of the Republic who had lain low in the city for three years, and by many more who, impelled by fear, would try to ingratiate themselves and pretend they had never participated in the revolution. *We believe in God, we believe in Spain. We believe in Franco. We love God, we love Spain, we love the Generalisimo Francisco Franco.* Then the purge would begin. First the Fascists would arrest any combatants they could lay their hands on, wounded or not, along with those denounced by others as collaborators or suspected of any activity considered anti-Spanish or anti-Catholic. This included members of trade unions, left-wing parties, followers of other religions, agnostics, freemasons, teachers at all levels, scientists, philosophers, students of Esperanto, foreigners, Jews, gypsies—and so on in an endless list.

"The reprisals are ferocious, Doña Carme. Did you know they take children from their mothers and put them in orphanages run by nuns in order to indoctrinate them in the one true faith and the values of the fatherland?"

"My children are too old for that to happen."

"That's just an example. What I'm trying to say is that your only course is to come with me, because otherwise you'll be shot for teaching revolutionaries to read and write, and for not going to Mass."

"Listen, young man. I'm fifty-four years old and have a consumptive's cough. I'm not going to live much longer. What kind of a life would I have in exile? I prefer to die in my own home, my own city, with or without Franco."

Aitor spent another fifteen minutes trying in vain to persuade her, until finally Roser intervened.

"Come with us, Doña Carme, your grandchild and I need you.

After a while, when we've settled and can see how things are in Spain, you can return if you wish."

"You're stronger and more capable than I am, Roser. You'll get along fine on your own. Don't cry, now . . ."

"How can I not cry? What will I do without you?"

"All right, so long as it's understood I'm doing this for you and the baby. If it were up to me, I'd stay and put a brave face on it."

"That's enough, ladies, we need to leave right now," insisted Aitor.

"What about the hens?"

"Set them loose, somebody will find them. Come on, it's time to go."

Roser wanted to sit astride the motorbike behind Aitor, but he and Carme convinced her to use the sidecar, where there was less danger of damaging the child or causing a miscarriage. Carme, wrapped in several cardigans and a black woolen Castilian blanket that was rainproof and as heavy as a rug, clambered onto the pillion seat. She weighed so little that if it hadn't been for the blanket she could have blown away. They made very slow progress, dodging around people, other vehicles, and draft animals, skidding on the icy surface and fighting off desperate individuals trying to force their way onto the bike.

The exodus from Barcelona was a Dantesque spectacle of thousands of people shivering with cold in a stampede that soon slowed to a straggling procession traveling at the speed of the amputees, the wounded, the old folks, and the children. Those hospital patients able to walk joined the exodus; others were taken by train as far as possible; the rest were left to face the Moors' knives and bayonets.

They left the city behind and found themselves in open country. Peasants deserted their villages, some with their animals or wagons loaded down with baggage, and mingled with the slowly moving

mass. Anyone with valuables bartered them for a place in the few vehicles on the road: money was worthless now. Mules and horses
struggled under the weight of carts, and many of them fell gasping for
breath. When they did so, men attached themselves to the harnesses
and pulled, while the women pushed from behind. The route became
strewn with objects that could no longer be carried, from crockery to
pieces of furniture; the dead and wounded also lay where they fell;
nobody stopped to attend to them. Any capacity for compassion had
gone: everyone looked after only themselves and their loved ones.
Warplanes swooped low overhead, spreading death and leaving in
their wake a spattering of blood that mingled with the mud and ice.
Many of the victims were children. Food was in short supply: the
most farsighted had brought enough provisions to last a day or two;
the rest went hungry, unless some farmer was willing to make an exchange for food. Aitor cursed himself for having left the hens behind.

Hundreds of thousands of terrified refugees were escaping to
France, where a campaign of fear and hatred awaited them. Nobody
wanted these foreigners—Reds, filthy fugitives, deserters, delinquents, as the French press labeled them. Repugnant beings who were
going to spread epidemics, commit robberies and rape, and stir up a
communist revolution. For three years there had been a trickle of
Spaniards escaping the war: there was little sympathy for them, but
they were dispersed throughout France and were almost invisible.
After the Republican defeat, the authorities knew that the flow would
increase; they were expecting an unknown number of refugees, possibly ten or fifteen thousand, a figure that already alarmed the French
Right. No one imagined that within a few days there would be almost
half a million Spaniards, in the last stages of confusion, terror, and
misery, clamoring at the border. France's first reaction was to close
the ports of entry while the authorities reached an agreement as to
how to deal with the problem.

———

NIGHT CAME EARLY, BRINGING with it enough rain to soak their clothes and turn the ground into a quagmire. Then the temperature fell several degrees below freezing and a biting wind rose, chilling them to the bone. The lines of refugees came to a halt: there was no way they could continue in the darkness. They huddled together on the ground wherever they could, covered in wet blankets, the women hugging their children, the men trying to protect their families, the old people praying. Aitor Ibarra settled the two women in the sidecar, telling them to wait for him. Pulling a cable from the motorbike engine so that nobody could steal it, he stepped off the road a little way to relieve himself: he had been suffering from diarrhea for months, like almost all those who had been at the front. In a crack in the rocks his flashlight picked out a motionless mule, perhaps with broken legs or simply overcome with exhaustion. It was still alive. Aitor took out his pistol and shot it in the head. This single gunshot, different from the enemy strafing, attracted several onlookers. Aitor was trained to receive orders, not to give them, but at that moment an unexpected gift of command surfaced in him: he organized the men to butcher the animal, and the women to roast the meat in small fires that would not attract the attention of the warplanes. His idea quickly spread through the crowd, and soon single shots could be heard in different spots. Aitor took two pieces of this tough meat back to Carme and Roser, together with mugs of water heated on one of the campfires. "Imagine it's a *carajillo*, all that's missing is the coffee," he told them, pouring a slug of brandy into each mug. He kept some of the meat, confident it would not go bad in the cold, and half a loaf of bread that he had bartered for with a pair of goggles that once belonged to a crashed Italian pilot. He thought those goggles must have passed from hand to hand twenty times before reaching him, and would continue going round the world until they fell apart.

Carme refused to eat the meat; she said she would break her teeth chewing on a leather sole like that, and gave her portion to Roser. She was already beginning to think she could take advantage of the darkness to slip away and vanish. The cold was making it hard for her to breathe; each time she drew breath she started coughing, her chest hurt and she felt she was suffocating.

"I wish I could catch pneumonia and that would be an end to it," she muttered.

"Don't say that, Doña Carme, think of your children," answered Roser, who had overheard her.

If she didn't die of pneumonia, to die frozen was a good option, Carme told herself; she had read that this was how old people at the North Pole committed suicide. She would have liked to get to know the grandson or granddaughter that was soon to be born, but this wish faded in her mind like a dream. All that mattered was for Roser to reach France safe and sound, for her to give birth there and be reunited with Guillem and Victor. Carme didn't want to be a burden on the young people; at her age, she was an obstacle; without her they would go farther and more rapidly. Roser must have guessed her intentions, because she watched over Carme until she herself was overcome by tiredness and fell asleep curled up. She didn't notice when Carme slipped away from her as stealthily as a cat.

Aitor was the first to discover her absence. It was still dark, and without waking Roser he set off to look for Carme in the midst of this mass of suffering humanity. He shone the flashlight on the ground to make sure he wasn't treading on anyone; he calculated that Carme would have found it difficult to go far. Daylight found him wandering among the confusion of people and bundles, calling out to her along with others also shouting their relatives' names. A girl who must have been about four years old, hoarse from so much crying, soaking wet and blue with cold, clung to one of his legs. Regretting he didn't have anything to cover her with, he wiped her nose and lifted her onto his shoulders to see if anybody could identify her, but no one was interested in anybody else's fate. "What's your name, pretty one?"

"Nuria," the little girl murmured, and he entertained her by singing the militiamen's popular verses everyone knew by heart and that he had on the tip of his tongue for months. "Sing with me, Nuria, because singing helps you forget your sorrows," he said, but she went on crying.

He walked with her on his shoulders for a good while, pushing his way through the crowd and calling out Carme's name as he went. Finally he came across a truck pulled up by the roadside, where a couple of nurses were distributing milk and bread to a gaggle of children. He explained that Nuria was looking for her family, and they told him to leave her with them; the children in the truck were lost as well. An hour later, still not having found Carme, Aitor went back to where he had left Roser. When he arrived, he noticed that Carme had left without taking the Castilian blanket.

With the new day, the desperate mass began to spread out slowly like a huge stain. The rumor that the border had been closed and that more and more people were crowding at the crossings went from mouth to mouth, only increasing the panic. No one had eaten for hours, and the children, old folks, and wounded were growing weaker and weaker. Hundreds of vehicles, from carts to trucks, had been abandoned by the roadside, either because the draft animals couldn't go on or for lack of fuel. Aitor decided to get off the main road, where the endless lines made it impossible to advance, and to risk heading into the mountains in search of a less well-guarded pass.

At first, Roser refused to leave without Carme, but he convinced her that Carme would be bound to reach the frontier with the rest of the column, and they could meet up again in France. They spent some time arguing, until Aitor lost patience and threatened to continue on his own and leave Roser stranded. Roser, who didn't know him, thought he meant it.

As a boy, Aitor used to hike in the Pyrenees with his father; what he wouldn't give to have the old man with him now, he thought. He wasn't the only one with the idea: other groups were heading cross-country into the mountains. If the journey was going to be hard on Roser, with her heavy belly, swollen legs, and sciatica, it would be far worse for the families with children and grandparents, or soldiers with amputated limbs and bloody bandages. The motorcycle would only be useful as long as there was a track, and he doubted whether in her state Roser would be able to continue on foot.

AS AITOR HAD CALCULATED, the motorcycle took them as far as the mountains, where it began coughing and pouring out smoke until it eventually stalled. From there they would have to travel on foot. Aitor gave a farewell kiss to the machine, which he considered more faithful than a devoted wife, before hiding it in some bushes, promising it he would return. Roser helped him organize and distribute their things, which they strapped on their backs. They had to leave most of their possessions behind and carry only the essentials: warm clothing, a spare pair of shoes, the small amount of food they had, and the French money that Victor, always thinking ahead, had given Aitor. Roser donned the Castilian blanket and two pairs of gloves, because she had to look after her hands if she was ever to play the piano again.

They began the climb. Roser was walking slowly but determinedly, and didn't stop. Aitor pushed or pulled her up the steep parts, joking and singing all the way to encourage her, as if they were going on a picnic. The few other refugees who had chosen this route and had reached the same heights overtook them with a brief greeting.

Soon they were all alone. The narrow, icy goats' track they had been following petered out. Their feet sank into the snow, and they had to avoid rocks and fallen tree trunks on the edge of the precipice. One false step and they would crash to the ground a hundred yards below. Aitor's boots, which like the goggles had once belonged to an enemy officer fallen in battle, were worn out, but they protected his feet better than Roser's thin city shoes. After a while, neither of them could feel their feet anymore. The enormous, snow-topped mountain loomed high above them, silhouetted against a purple sky. Aitor was afraid he had gotten lost, and realized that at best it would take them several days to reach France; if they couldn't join a group, they would never succeed. He silently cursed his decision to leave the main road, but reassured Roser, promising her he knew the terrain like the back of his hand.

As night was falling they saw a dim glow in the distance, and with one last, desperate effort drew near to a tiny camp. From a distance they could make out human figures, and Aitor decided to run the risk of them being Nationalists, because the alternative was to spend the night buried in the snow. Leaving Roser behind, he crept closer, until by the light of a small campfire he could see four thin, bearded men dressed in rags. One of them had a bandaged head. They had no horses, uniforms, boots, or tents: they were a disheveled group that didn't look like enemy soldiers, but could well be bandits. As a precaution, Aitor cocked the pistol he carried hidden beneath his overcoat, a German Luger he had acquired some months earlier in one of his miraculous exchanges. He approached them, arms raised in a conciliatory gesture. One of the men advanced, pointing his rifle, with another two close behind covering his back with shotguns. All three were as wary and suspicious as he was.

They came to a halt, sizing one another up. On a hunch, Aitor called out in Catalan and Basque: *bona nit! kaixo! gabon!* After a pause that to him seemed an eternity, the one who appeared to be their leader welcomed him with a brief *ongi etorri burkide!* Aitor realized they were fellow comrades, no doubt deserters. His knees buckled with relief. The men surrounded him, but seeing he was no threat, were soon patting him on the back in a friendly manner. "I'm Eki and these are Izan and his brother Julen," the man with the rifle said. Aitor introduced himself in his turn and explained he had a pregnant woman with him, and so they all set off to get her. Two of the men almost carried her to the miserable camp that seemed the height of luxury to the new arrivals, because there was a canvas shelter, warmth, and food.

From then on they passed the time exchanging bad news and sharing cans of beans heated in the fire, as well as the small amount of liquor left in Aitor's canteen. He also offered them the remaining meat from the mule and the hunk of bread he was carrying in his rucksack. "Keep your provisions, you'll need them more than we do," Eki declared. He added that the next day they were expecting a local guide who was bringing them food. Aitor insisted on repaying their generous hospitality by giving them his tobacco. For the past two years only the rich and political leaders had smoked cigarettes bought on the black market; everyone else had to make do with a mixture of dried grass and licorice that was consumed in a single puff. Aitor's bag of English tobacco was received with religious solemnity. The men rolled cigarettes and smoked in silent ecstasy. They served Roser a portion of beans, then installed her in the improvised tent, settling her down with a hot water bottle for her frozen feet. While she was resting, Aitor told their hosts about the fall of Barcelona, the Republic's imminent final defeat, and the chaos of the Retreat.

The four men received the news without reacting—they had been expecting it. Nearly two years earlier, they had escaped alive from Guernica when it was bombed by the much-feared Condor Legion planes that razed the historic Basque town and sowed death and destruction in their wake. Afterward, they had survived the fires started by incendiary bombs dropped in the nearby forests, where they had sought refuge, and went on to fight in the Euzkadi Army Corps until the final day of the battle for Bilbao. Before the city fell into enemy hands, the Basque high command organized the evacuation of the civilian population to France, while the soldiers continued fighting, dispersed among different battalions. A year after the defeat at Bilbao, Izan and Julen learned that their father and younger brother, prisoners in Nationalist jails, had been shot by firing squad. The two of them were the only ones left of a large family. It was then they decided to desert as soon as they got the chance: democracy, the Republic, and the war no longer meant anything; they no longer knew what they were fighting for. After that they wandered through forests and over steep mountainsides, staying in the same place for no more than a few days at a time, and tacitly following Eki, who knew the region well. In the previous few weeks, as the inevitable end of the war was approaching, they had come upon the other wounded man on the run. They weren't safe anywhere. In France they wouldn't be treated with the respect due to a vanquished army or retreating combatants, not even as refugees. They would be regarded as deserters, arrested, and deported back to Spain, into Franco's clutches.

With nowhere to go, Republican deserters wandered about in small bands. Some hid in caves or the most inaccessible areas, hoping to lie low until the situation returned to normal; others were suicidal, determined to carry on fighting guerrilla warfare against the might of the conquering army. However, such was not the case of the brothers on the mountain. They were disillusioned with everything, as was Eki, who was only interested in surviving in order to one day return to his wife and children. The man with the bandaged head, who looked very young and took no part in the conversation, turned out to be from Asturias. His wound had left him deaf and confused. Jokingly, the others explained to Aitor that they couldn't get rid of him as they would have wished, because he was such a good shot: he could hit a hare with his eyes closed, didn't waste a single bullet, and it was thanks to him that they could occasionally eat meat. In fact, they had with them some rabbits they were planning to exchange for other provisions with the mountain guide when he arrived the next day. Aitor couldn't help but notice the clumsy tenderness they showed the Asturian youth, as if he were a backward child. The men thought Aitor and Roser were married, and so obliged him to sleep in the tent with his wife; that meant two of the men would have to stay out in the cold. "We'll take turns," they said, and refused to allow Aitor to take one as well: what kind of hospitality would that be, they protested.

Aitor settled down next to Roser, who was curled up protecting her belly. He lay behind her, hugging her to him for warmth. His bones were aching, he was numb with cold, and he was concerned not just for the safety but for the life of the mother-to-be. He had promised Victor he would be responsible for her. During the arduous climb up the mountainside, Roser had assured him she had strength to spare, and that he shouldn't worry about her. "I grew up in the mountains looking after goats in winter and summer, Aitor. I'm used to the cold and rain, so don't think I tire easily."

As they lay together, she must have sensed his fear, because she took hold of his hand and placed it on her stomach so that he could feel the baby moving. "Don't worry, Aitor, the child is safe and happy as can be," she said, between two yawns. At this, the cheerful, valiant Basque who had witnessed so much death and suffering, so much violence and cruelty, secretly wept, head buried in the neck of the young woman, whose smell he would never forget. He shed tears for her, because she didn't yet know she was a widow; for Guillem, who would never get to meet his child or ever again embrace his beloved; for Carme, who had vanished without saying goodbye; and for himself, because for the first time in his life he doubted his lucky star.

THE NEXT DAY THE MOUNTAIN GUIDE they were expecting arrived early on an old horse, riding at walking pace. He introduced himself as "Angel, at your service," and boasted that the name suited him, because he was an angel to fugitives and deserters. He brought much-needed provisions, cartridges for their shotguns, and a bottle of spirits that would help relieve their boredom and treat the Asturian's injury. When they changed the youth's bandage, Aitor saw he had a deep wound and a hollow in his skull. He thought the intense cold must have prevented it from becoming infected; the youngster must have had an iron constitution to still be alive.

The mountain guide confirmed the news that France had closed the border two days earlier, and that thousands of refugees were blocked there, half-dead from cold and hunger. Armed guards were preventing them from crossing. Angel claimed he was a shepherd, but Aitor wasn't fooled: just like his own father, Angel had the look of a smuggler, a much more lucrative profession than tending goats. Once this was clarified, it turned out the guide knew the elder Ibarra: in this region everyone in the profession knew one another, he said. There were only a few passes through the mountains, there were many difficulties, and the weather was as fierce as the authorities on both sides of the frontier. In such circumstances, solidarity was unavoidable. "We're not criminals. We provide an essential service, as I'm sure your father explained to you. It's the law of supply and demand," he added.

He insisted it was impossible to reach France without a guide, because the French had reinforced the passes, so they would have to take a secret route that was dangerous at any time, but even more so in winter. He knew it well, because at the onset of war he had taken it to lead International brigadiers into Spain. "Those foreigners were good lads, but lots of them were city boys, and some of them didn't make it. Anyone who fell behind or fell down a ravine was left where they fell." He offered to take the two of them across himself, and accepted payment in French money. "Your wife can ride my horse, and we'll walk," he told Aitor.

Midmorning, after sharing a drink that purported to be coffee,

Aitor and Roser said goodbye to the four men and continued on their way. Their guide warned them they would have to keep going while there was daylight, and if they managed to walk without stopping, they could spend the night in a shepherds' hut. Aitor was keeping a close eye on him. In this lonely spot, in a region he didn't know, the man could easily cut their throats, not so much for their money but for his Luger, his penknife, his boots, and the Castilian blanket. They walked for hours on end, frozen stiff, exhausted, their feet sinking into the snow. For long periods Roser walked as well, to spare the horse, which its owner looked after like an elderly relative. They stopped only briefly to rest, drink melted snow, and eat the remains of the mule meat and bread. When it began to grow dark and the temperature dropped so much they could barely see for the frost on their eyelashes, Angel pointed to a promontory in the distance.

It was the promised shelter. It turned out to be a round domed hut with slates used as bricks and a narrow doorless opening that they had to force the horse through to prevent it from freezing to death outside. Inside, the single round low-roofed room was much bigger and warmer than it seemed from outside. There was a pile of firewood, bales of straw, a big bucket full of water, a couple of axes, and some cooking pots. Aitor made a fire to cook one of Angel's rabbits, and from his saddlebags the guide brought out some sausage, hard cheese, and a dark, dry bread that was better than the one Roser had baked with wartime rations back in Barcelona.

After eating and feeding the horse, they lay down on the straw, wrapped in their blankets, warmed by the fire. "Before we go tomorrow we have to leave this just as we found it. We'll have to chop wood and fill the bucket with snow. And another thing, *gudari*, you don't need your weapon, you can sleep peacefully. I'm a smuggler, not a murderer. Besides, your father, old man Ibarra, was my friend," said Angel.

—

THE CROSSING TO FRANCE took them three long days and nights, but thanks to Angel they didn't once get lost or have to sleep out in the open. Each day's march ended somewhere where they could spend the night. They passed the second one in the hut of two charcoal burners who had a dog resembling a wolf. The men, who made a living collecting hawthorn wood to make charcoal, were rough and unwelcoming, but agreed to put them up if they paid. "Keep your eye on these fellows, *gudari*, they're Italian," Angel warned Aitor in a whisper. This gave the Basque the idea to make things more friendly by singing the half dozen Italian songs he knew. Once the first mutual suspicion had been dispelled, they all ate and drank, then settled down to play cards with a very greasy pack. Roser was unbeatable: she had learned to play *tute* and cheat at the nuns' school. Their hosts found this hilarious, and willingly accepted the loss of the piece of dried salami they had bet.

Roser fell asleep on some sacks on the floor, her nose buried in the dog's rough coat as it snuggled up to her for warmth. When they said farewell the next morning, she followed the charcoal-burners' custom by kissing them three times on the cheeks, and told them she couldn't have been more comfortable in a feather bed. The dog followed them for a good while, trotting along at Roser's heels.

On the afternoon of the third day, Angel announced that from then on they were on their own. They were safe now; they only needed to descend into France. "Follow the mountain edge and you'll come to a ruined farmhouse. You can shelter there." He gave them bread and cheese, took his money, and said goodbye with a brief embrace. "Your woman is worth her weight in gold, *gudari*, look after her. I've been the guide for hundreds of men, from battle-hardened soldiers to criminals, but I've never known anyone who put up with everything without a single complaint the way she has. And with that belly of hers, on top of everything."

An hour later, as they were approaching the farmhouse, a man armed with a rifle strode out toward them. They came to a halt, holding their breath. Aitor had the pistol ready behind his back. For what seemed like an eternity, they stood staring at one another from fifty meters, then Roser took a step forward and shouted that they were refugees. When the man realized she was a woman and that the new arrivals appeared more frightened than he was, he lowered his weapon and called out to them in Catalan: *Veniu, veniu, no else faré res.* He told them they weren't the first refugees to pass through there, and they wouldn't be the last. He added that his own son had fled to France that morning, scared that Franco's troops would pick him up. He led them to a hovel with a beaten earth floor and half the roof missing, gave them some leftovers from his stove, and let them lie down in a simple but clean bed where his son used to sleep. A few hours later, three more Spaniards arrived and were also given lodging by this good man. At dawn the next day he offered them a salty broth with bits of potato and herbs in it, which he said would help them bear the cold. Before showing them the path they had to take, he gave Roser his last five sugar lumps, to sweeten the baby's journey.

Led by Roser and Aitor, the group set off for the frontier. It took them the whole day, but just as the Catalan had said, at nightfall they came to a rise and suddenly saw houses with lights. They knew this must mean they were in France, because in Spain nobody switched on lights for fear of bombardment. They continued the descent toward the houses until they came to a main road. Soon afterward, a van full of *gardes mobiles,* the French rural police, pulled up alongside them. They gave themselves up cheerfully: they were in the France of solidarity, of liberty, equality, and fraternity, the France with a left-wing government presided over by a socialist. The gendarmes searched them roughly and took Aitor's pistol, penknife, and what little money he had left. The other Spaniards were unarmed.

The gendarmes led them to a large stone building, the granary for a mill that had been adapted to receive the refugees arriving by the hundreds. It was packed with people: terrified men, women, and children crammed together, all of them hungry and desperately trying to breathe because of the lack of ventilation and the clouds of dust from the grain floating in the air. All they had for their thirst were some drums filled with dubiously clean water. There were no latrines, only a few holes outside the building, where they had to crouch under guard. Humiliated, the women wept while the guards laughed.

Aitor insisted on staying with Roser, and when they saw her bulging belly, the guards made no objection. Curled up in a corner, the two shared the last piece of bread and the Italians' dried salami, while Aitor tried to protect her from the crush and sudden ripples of despair that ran through the detained refugees. Word went around that this was a transit point and that they would soon be taken to a *centre de rétention administrative*. No one knew what that meant.

The next day, the women and children were taken away in army trucks. This was agony for the families; the gendarmes had to use their batons to force them apart. Roser hugged Aitor, thanked him for all he had done for her, assured him she would be fine, and walked off calmly to the waiting truck. "I'll come and look for you, Roser, I promise!" he managed to shout, before he fell to his knees, cursing furiously.

WHILE MUCH OF THE CIVILIAN population was escaping to the French border by any means possible, followed by what was left of the defeated army, Victor Dalmau, together with the doctors still at their posts and a few volunteers, transported the wounded from the hospital in trains, ambulances, and trucks. The situation was so dire that the director, who was still in charge, had to make the harrowing decision to leave the most seriously wounded behind, since they were bound to die on the journey anyway, and fill the vehicles with those who had a chance of surviving. Crammed into cattle trucks or battered vehicles, lying on the floor, freezing cold, constantly jolted, with no food, combatants who had just been operated on, or were wounded, blind, had amputated limbs, or were delirious from fever, typhus, dysentery, or gangrene, made their way out of Barcelona. The medical staff had nothing with which to relieve their suffering, and could offer only water, words of comfort, and sometimes, if a dying man asked for it, a final prayer.

For more than two years, Victor had been working alongside the most expert doctors. He had learned a great deal at the battlefront and later at the hospital, where nobody asked what qualifications he had: there, only dedication counted. He himself often forgot that he needed several more years' study to graduate, and pretended to his patients he was a qualified doctor, in order to reassure them. He had seen dreadful wounds, assisted at amputations without anesthetics, helped more than one unfortunate youngster die, and thought he had developed the hide of a crocodile; and yet that tragic journey in the wagons he was in charge of destroyed his spirit. The trains reached as far as Gerona, then stopped to wait for other means of transport.

After thirty-eight hours without eating or sleeping, trying to give water to an adolescent dying in his arms, something gave way in Victor's chest. *My heart is broken*, he told himself. It was at that moment he understood the profound meaning of that common phrase: he thought he heard the sound of glass breaking and felt that the essence of his being was pouring out until he was empty, with no memory of the past, no awareness of the present, no hope for the future. He concluded this must be what it was like to bleed to death, like so many men he had been unable to help. There was too much pain, too much that was despicable in this war between brothers; defeat had to be better than to continue killing and dying.

France was watching in horror as the border became jammed with a crush of people that the authorities managed to keep barely in check by employing armed soldiers and the fearsome colonial troops from Senegal and Algeria, with their turbans, rifles, and whips. The whole country was overwhelmed by this massive influx of undesirables, as they were officially called. In the face of international protests, on the third day the French government allowed in women, children, and the elderly. Then came the turn of the remaining civilians and finally the defeated combatants, who marched across the border exhausted from hunger and fatigue, but singing and with their fists raised. They left mountainous piles of weapons on both sides of the border, before they were marched to hastily improvised concentration camps. *Allez! Allez-y!* the mounted guards goaded them on with threats and insults, lashing them with their whips.

After they had more or less been forgotten, the wounded who had survived were also brought into France. With them were Victor and the few remaining doctors and nurses accompanying them. They were allowed in more easily than the first waves of refugees, but didn't receive any warmer a welcome. The wounded were tended in a rough and ready way in schools, railway stations, and even in the street, because the local hospitals couldn't cope and nobody wanted them, even though they were the most needy among the hordes of "undesirables." There were not enough resources or medical staff for so many patients. Victor was allowed to stay with the men in his care, and so could enjoy relative freedom.

AFTER SHE WAS SEPARATED from Aitor Ibarra, Roser was taken with other women and children to the camp at Argeles-sur-Mer, thirty-five kilometers from the border, where tens of thousands of Spanish refugees were already interned. The camp was fenced off on the beach, guarded by gendarmes and Senegalese soldiers. Sand, sea, and barbed wire. Roser soon realized that as prisoners they had to fend for themselves, and swore she would survive, come what may; if she had been strong enough to cross the Pyrenees, she could deal with whatever was thrown at her, for the sake of the child she was bearing, for herself, and for the possibility of meeting Guillem again.

The refugees were left out in the open day and night, exposed to the cold and rain. Hygiene was nonexistent: they had no latrines or drinkable water. The water that came from the wells they dug was salty, cloudy, and polluted with excrement, urine, and the corpses that were not carried away quickly enough. The women gathered in tight groups to defend themselves against the sexual aggression of the guards and some of the male detainees, who, having lost everything, no longer had even a sense of decency. Roser dug a pit with her hands to sleep in, protected from the *tramontana*, the icy wind that whipped up the sand. The stinging grains of sand cracked skin, blinded eyes, filtered in everywhere, producing wounds that grew infected. Once a day there was a distribution of watery lentils, and occasionally cold coffee or loaves of bread thrown from passing trucks. The men fought savagely to pick them up; the women and children got the crumbs if and when someone took pity and shared their ration. Between thirty and forty people died every day, first the children from dysentery, then the elderly from pneumonia, and later on the others, one by one.

At night somebody would stay awake to prod others every ten or fifteen minutes so that they could move and avoid freezing to death. One woman, who had dug her own nest next to Roser, woke up one morning embracing her dead five-month-old daughter, after the temperature had fallen below freezing in the night. Other refugees took the little girl's body away and buried it farther down the beach. Roser spent the day with the mother, who said nothing and didn't weep, but simply stared at the horizon. That night she went to the water's edge and waded out into the sea until she disappeared. She was not the only one. Many years later, the exact statistics became known to Roser:

almost fifteen thousand people died in those French camps, from hunger, starvation, mistreatment, and illnesses. Nine out of every ten children perished.

Eventually the authorities installed the women and children on another part of the beach, separated from the men by a double row of barbed wire. Material began to arrive to build huts. The refugees constructed them with their bare hands, and some of the men were sent to complete the roofs for the women. Roser asked to speak to the officer in charge of the camp and convinced him to organize the distribution of what little food there was so that the women would not have to fight for a few crusts of bread for their children.

Soon afterward, two Red Cross nurses arrived to give vaccinations and dole out powdered milk. They advised the mothers to filter water through cloths and boil it for several minutes before using it in their feeding bottles. They also brought blankets and warm clothing for the children, as well as the names of French families willing to employ some of the Spanish women as maids or in home industries. They usually specified: no children.

Through the Red Cross nurses, Roser sent a message to Elisabeth Eidenbenz, as Victor had instructed her to do. "Tell her I'm Victor Dalmau's sister-in-law and that I'm pregnant."

ELISABETH HAD BEEN WORKING first with the combatants on the Spanish battlefront and then, when defeat was imminent, with the flood of fugitives on their journey into exile. She had crossed the border into France wearing her white apron and blue cape without anyone being able to stop her. Roser's message was among hundreds of pleas for aid she received, and perhaps she would not have given it priority had it not been for the name of Victor Dalmau. She remembered him fondly as the shy man who played the guitar and wanted to marry her.

The day after she got the message, she traveled to Argeles-sur-Mer to look for Roser Bruguera. Even though she knew how dreadful conditions in the camp were, she was shocked when she saw this disheveled, filthy young woman, ashen-faced and with purple lines under eyes inflamed by sand. She was so thin that her belly seemed to stick out directly from her skeleton. Despite her appearance, Roser met her standing erect, with a firm voice and the dignity she had always shown. Nothing in what she said revealed anguish or resignation, as if she were in complete control of her situation.

"Victor gave us your name, señorita. He said you could serve as a contact point for us to meet up again."

"Who is with you now?"

"For the moment it's just me, but Victor and his brother, Guillem, will be arriving: Guillem is the father of my child. Also a friend by the name of Aitor Ibarra, and possibly Victor and Guillem's mother, Carme Dalmau. When they do get to France, please tell them where I am. I hope they find me before the birth."

"You can't stay here, Roser. I'm trying to help the pregnant women and those with breastfeeding children. No newborn child can survive in these camps."

Elisabeth told her she had opened a house to shelter mothers-to-be, but as the demand was so great and space so limited, she had her eye on an abandoned mansion in Elne. Her dream was to set up a proper maternity home, an oasis for the women and children in the midst of so much suffering. But it would have to be built up out of the ruins, and that would take months.

"But you can't wait, Roser, you must get out of here right away."

"How?"

"The camp commander knows you'll be coming with me. The truth is, the only thing they want is to get rid of the refugees. They're trying to force them back into Spain, but anybody who can find a sponsor or a job can go free. So come with me."

"There are lots of women and children here. Pregnant women too."

"I'll do what I can. I'll come back with more help."

OUTSIDE THE CAMP, A car with the Red Cross insignia was waiting for them. Elisabeth decided that what Roser needed most was hot food, and so stopped at the first restaurant they came to. The few customers there at that time of day couldn't conceal their disgust at this smelly beggar accompanying the neat and tidy nurse. Roser ate all the bread put on the table even before the chicken stew arrived. After the meal, the young Swiss nurse drove the car as if it were a bicycle, zigzagging between other vehicles on the road, climbing onto sidewalks and proudly ignoring all the crossroads and traffic lights, which she considered optional. They arrived at Perpignan in no time at all. She took Roser to the house being used as a maternity unit, where there were eight young women, some in the last month of pregnancy, others with newborn babies in their arms.

Roser was received with the unsentimental warmth typical of Spanish women: she was handed a towel, soap, and shampoo and sent off for a shower. An hour later, Roser reappeared in front of Elisabeth, clean, her hair soaking, and wearing a black skirt, a short woolen tunic that covered her belly, and high-heeled shoes. That same evening, Elisabeth took her to the home of an English Quaker couple she had worked with when they were on the Madrid front, offering food, clothing, and protection to child victims of the conflict.

"You can stay with them as long as necessary, Roser, at least until you give birth. After that, we'll see. They're really good people. Quakers are always to be found where they're most needed. They're saints; the only saints I respect."

CHAPTER 4

1939

I celebrate the virtues and vices
Of the suburban middle classes.

— PABLO NERUDA
"Suburbs"
THE YELLOW HEART

THE *REINA DEL PACIFICO* LEFT THE CHILEAN PORT of Valparaiso at the start of May, to dock in Liverpool twenty-seven days later. In Europe, spring was giving way to an uneasy summer, threatened by the drumbeats of an unavoidable war. The previous fall, the European powers had signed the Munich peace treaty, which Hitler had no intention of respecting. Paralyzed, the Western world looked on as the Nazis continued their expansion.

And yet on board the *Reina del Pacifico*, the echoes of the approaching conflict were muffled by distance as well as the sound of the diesel engines that propelled this 17,702-ton floating city across two oceans. The 162 passengers in second class and the 446 in third found the crossing rather long, but in first class the inconveniences of sea travel vanished in a refined atmosphere where the days flew by and the rolling waves couldn't spoil the pleasure of the journey. The noise from the ship's engines barely reached the upper deck, where it was replaced by the soothing sounds of background music, conversation in several languages among the 280 passengers, the comings and goings of seamen and officers dressed in white from head to foot and waiters in uniforms with gold buttons, an orchestra and a female string quartet, the endless clink of crystal glasses, porcelain crockery, and silver cutlery. The kitchen only closed during the darkest hour before dawn.

In her suite with two bedrooms, two bathrooms, a salon, and a balcony, Laura del Solar groaned as she struggled into a girdle, her ball gown still waiting for her on the bed. She had kept it especially for tonight, the second to last of the journey, when the first-class passengers showed off all that was most elegant in their trunks and their most impressive jewelry. Her dressmaker in Santiago had already let six centimeters out on the seams of the pleated blue satin gown she had ordered from Buenos Aires, but after several weeks at sea, Laura could hardly fit into it. Her husband, Isidro del Solar, smiled contentedly as he adjusted the white tie of his tuxedo in the mirror's beveled glass. Less sweet-toothed and more disciplined than his wife, he hadn't put on weight, and at fifty-nine was still good-looking. He had changed little over their years of marriage, unlike his wife. Laura sank into the Gobelin upholstered armchair, head down and shoulders drooping. She was in despair.

"What's wrong, Laurita?"

"Do you mind if I don't accompany you tonight, Isidro? I've got a headache."

Her husband stood in front of her with the annoyed expression that always overcame her resistance.

"Take a couple of aspirins, Laurita. It's the captain's dinner tonight. We're at an important table, I had to work wonders bribing the maitre d' to get seats. There are only eight of us; your absence would be noted."

"The thing is, I don't feel well, Isidro . . ."

"Make an effort. For me, this is a business dinner. We're going to be sharing the table with Senator Trueba and two English business-men who're interested in buying my wool. I told you about them, re-member? I already have an offer from a military uniform factory in Hamburg, but it's hard to do deals with Germans."

"I don't think Señora Trueba will be there."

"That woman is very eccentric. They say she talks with the dead," said Isidro.

"Everyone talks to the dead now and then, Isidro."

"What nonsense you come out with, Laurita!"

"I can't fit into the dress."

"What do a few extra kilos matter? Wear another one. You always look pretty," he said, in the tone of someone who has repeated the same thing a hundred times.

"How do you expect me not to get fat, Isidro? All we've done on board is eat and eat."

"Well, you could have taken some exercise—swum in the pool, for example."

"Surely you don't imagine I was going to show myself in a swim-suit?"

"I can't force you, Laura, but let me say again that your presence at this dinner is important. Don't leave me stranded. I'll help you do up your dress. Wear the sapphire necklace, it'll look perfect."

"It's very showy."

"Not a bit, it's modest compared to the jewels we've seen on other women here on the boat," Isidro ruled, opening the safe with the key he carried in his vest pocket.

Laura missed their house in Santiago, with its terrace of camellias, a refuge where little Leonardo played and where she could knit and pray in peace, protected from her husband's noisy whirlwind of frenetic activity. Isidro del Solar was her destiny, but marriage weighed on her like a burden. She often envied her younger sister, sweet Teresa, a cloistered nun who spent her days in meditation, pious reading, and embroidering the trousseaus for brides-to-be in Chilean high society. An existence devoted to God, without all the distractions Laura suffered from: without having to worry about the melodramas of children and relatives, or do battle with domestic staff, waste time on social visits, and fulfill her role as a dutiful wife. Isidro was omnipresent: the universe revolved around him, his wishes and demands. That was how his grandfather and father had been, that was how all men were.

"Cheer up, Laurita," said Isidro, struggling with the tiny clasp on the necklace he had already hung around her neck. "I want you to have a good time, for this trip to be memorable."

What had been memorable was the journey they had made several years earlier on board the newly launched liner *Normandie*, with its dining room for seven hundred guests, Lalique lamps and chandeliers, art deco design, and a winter garden with exotic caged birds. In just five days between France and New York, the del Solars had experienced a luxury unknown in Chile, where sobriety was a virtue and the more money one had, the more care was taken to hide it. Only Arab immigrants grown rich in commerce flaunted their wealth, but Laura did not know anyone of that ilk—they were outside her circle and always would be.

She and her husband had traveled on the *Normandie* on a second honeymoon, after leaving the five children with their grandparents, the English governess, and the maids. The surprise result was another pregnancy, when Laura was least expecting it. She was convinced it was during that short trip that they produced Leonardo, the poor innocent, her Baby. The child was born several years after Ofelia, who until then had been the youngest in the family. Ofelia had come with them on this voyage, and was staying in the other bedroom in the suite.

Although the *Reina del Pacifico* could not compete in terms of luxury with the *Normandie,* it was more than adequate. Laura took breakfast in bed, then dressed around ten for Mass in the chapel, after which she went to get some fresh air on the top deck in the chaise longue reserved for her, where a waiter brought her oxtail broth and bread rolls. From there she went in for lunch, which consisted of at least four courses, and soon it was time for high tea, with sandwiches and cakes. She barely had time to take a nap and play a few rounds of canasta before she had to dress for cocktails and dinner, where she had to force herself to smile and listen to other people's opinions. Afterward she was obliged to dance. Isidro was fleet of foot and had a good ear, but she moved as heavily as a seal on sand. While the orchestra took a break, the passengers were served a midnight snack of foie gras, caviar, champagne, and desserts. She abstained from the first three, but couldn't resist the sweets. The previous night the chef, a gargantuan Frenchman, had served up an orgy of chocolate in different shapes, crowned with an ingenious fountain that spouted melted chocolate from the mouth of a crystal fish.

To Laura, this journey was simply another of her husband's impositions. Where vacations were concerned, she preferred to go to their estate in the south of Chile or their beach house at Viña del Mar, where the days were spent in languorous leisure. Long strolls, tea in the shade of the trees, the family rosary with children and domestic staff. For her husband, this journey to Europe was an opportunity to strengthen social ties and plant the seeds of new business opportunities. He had a full agenda for each of the capitals they were to visit. Laura felt defrauded: this was not really a vacation.

Laura's family regarded the ability to make money in commercial enterprises as suspicious, typical of the new rich, of the parvenus.

They put up with this defect in Isidro because no one could doubt his solid Castilian-Basque lineage, with not a drop of Arab or Jewish blood in his veins. He came from a branch of the del Solars of irreproachable honor, the one exception being his father, who in his mature years fell in love with a modest schoolteacher and had two children with her before the affair was discovered. His numerous family and others in the same social class closed ranks around his wife and legitimate offspring, but he refused to leave his mistress. The scandal was the end of him.

Isidro had been fifteen at the time. That was the last he saw of his father, who continued to live in the same city but descended a couple of steps in the strict hierarchy of the Chilean class system and disappeared from his former entourage. The drama was never mentioned, but everyone knew about it. The abandoned wife's brothers helped her with a minimal pension and took on Isidro, the eldest child, who was forced to leave school and start work. He turned out to be more intelligent and hardworking than all his relatives put together, and within a few years had attained an economic position appropriate to his family name. He was proud of the fact that he did not owe anyone anything.

At the age of twenty-nine he had asked for the hand of Laura Vizcarra, on the basis of his good reputation and some business ventures that were acceptable in his social milieu: a sheep farm in Patagonia, the import of antiques from Ecuador and Peru, a country estate that produced little profit but considerable prestige. The bride-to-be's family—descended from Don Pedro de Vizcarra, an interim governor of the colony in the sixteenth century—was a Catholic, ultraconservative, uneducated, and inward-looking clan. Its members lived, married, and died among themselves, refusing to mix with anyone else and with no intention of getting to learn the century's new ideas. They were immune to science, art, and literature. Isidro was accepted because he won their sympathy, and because he could prove he was linked to the Vizcarras on his mother's side.

ISIDRO DEL SOLAR SPENT the twenty-something days at sea cultivating his contacts and doing sports: he played ping-pong and took fencing lessons. He began the day running several laps round the track on deck, and ended it past midnight with friends and acquaintances in the bar and the smokers' saloon, where ladies weren't welcome. The gentlemen talked business casually, with feigned indifference: it was in bad taste to show too great an interest; political debate, however, did arouse passions. They received news thanks to the ship's newsletter: two printed sheets taken from the telegraph that were handed out to passengers each morning. By the afternoon, the news was already out of date; everything was changing so quickly—the world they knew had been turned upside down.

Compared to Europe, Chile was a happily backward and distant paradise. It was true that at this moment it had a center-left government: the president was from the Radical Party and a freemason. He was detested by the Right, and his name was never mentioned by the "best families," but he wasn't going to last long. The Left, with its coarse realism and vulgarity, had no future; the owners of Chile would make sure of that.

Isidro met up with his wife to eat and for the evening entertainment. The ship offered movies, theater, music, circuses, ventriloquists, and turns by hypnotists and clairvoyants, who fascinated the ladies and were laughed at by the men. Outgoing and jovial, Isidro enjoyed everything with a cigar in one hand and a glass in the other, not permitting himself to be discouraged by the attitude of his wife, who was scandalized by this forced revelry that had more than a whiff of sin and dissipation about it.

Laura looked at herself in the mirror, fighting back the tears. The gown would look wonderful on another woman, she thought; she didn't deserve it, just as she didn't deserve most of what she had. She was well aware of her privileged position, of her good fortune at being born into the Vizcarra family, of marrying Isidro del Solar, and of so many other benefits obtained mysteriously, without any effort or planning on her part. She had always been protected and waited on. She had given birth to six children without ever having changed a diaper or prepared a bottle—the person who saw to all this was Juana, who supervised the wet nurses and servants. Juana had raised the children, including Felipe, who would soon be celebrating his twenty-ninth birthday. It had never occurred to Laura to ask Juana how old she was, nor how many years she had been working in the del Solars' house; nor could Laura remember how she first arrived.

God had bestowed too much on her. Why her? What was He asking in return? She had no idea, and this debt to the Almighty tormented her. On board the *Normandie,* curiosity had led her to get a glimpse of life on the third-class deck, disobeying the instructions about not mixing with passengers from other classes for sanitary reasons, as the sign on the door to her suite made clear. If by any mischance there was an outbreak of tuberculosis or any other infectious disease, everyone could end up in quarantine, as the official explained when he intercepted her. Laura saw something she had observed when she accompanied the Catholic Ladies to distribute charity in the Santiago slums: poor people were a different color, with a strange smell; their skin was darker, their hair didn't shine, their clothes were faded. Who were these people in third class? They didn't look like beggars or delinquents, but they had the same ashen aspect. Why them and not me? Laura had wondered with a mixture of relief and shame. The question continued to echo in her mind. On board the *Reina del Pacífico* the class division was akin to that of the *Normandie,* but the contrast was less dramatic, because times had changed and this was a less luxurious boat. The passengers on the lower decks, in what was now called the tourist class, had embarked in Chile, Peru, and other ports on the Pacific coast and were civil servants, employees, students, small traders, immigrants returning to visit their families in Europe. Laura noted that they were having a much better time than the passengers in first class: the atmosphere was relaxed and festive, with singing, dancing, beer, competitions, and games. No one put on tweed jackets for lunch, silk dresses for tea, formal wear for dinner.

In front of the mirror on this penultimate night of the sea journey, sheathed in her ball gown, perfumed and wearing the necklace she had inherited from her mother, all Laura wished for was a small glass of sherry with a few drops of valerian, then to settle down in her bed and sleep and sleep for months until the end of the journey, until she woke up back in her own home with its cool rooms, back in her world, with Leonardo. She missed him terribly; it was torture to spend so long far away from her son: perhaps when she returned he might not even recognize her—his memory was so fragile, like everything else about him. What if he fell ill? Better not to think of that. God had given her five children, and in addition had sent her this innocent, this pure soul.

Frustration flared up in her stomach; she could feel heartburn in her chest. *I'm always the one who has to give in, what Isidro wants he gets: it's him first, second, and third—that's what he tells me, as if it were some kind of joke, and I accept it! What wouldn't I give to be a widow!* thought Laura. She had to combat this recurrent temptation with prayers and penitential acts. To wish for another person's death was a mortal sin; Isidro might be short-tempered, but he was an excellent husband and father. He didn't deserve this perverse wish of his wife, the woman who, when they married, had sworn at the altar to be loyal and obedient. "I'm crazy as well as fat," she sighed, and all of a sudden that conclusion seemed amusing. She couldn't suppress a contented smile, which her husband took to be one of acquiescence.

"That's what I like to see, darling," he said, singing under his breath as he headed for the bathroom.

OFELIA ENTERED HER PARENTS' suite without knocking. At nineteen, she was still an impetuous girl. *When is she going to grow up?* her father would sigh halfheartedly, because she was his pampered child, the only one who was as daring and stubborn as he was, someone impossible to subdue. She had been out of her depth at school, and after failing her final exam was only allowed to graduate because the nuns wanted to get rid of her. She had learned very little during her twelve years' education, but managed to hide her ignorance by being so beguiling, by knowing when to keep quiet, and thanks to her ability to observe. Her memory had not been good enough for her to pass her history exam or to learn the times tables, but she knew the words to all the songs played on the radio. She was absentminded, flirtatious, and too pretty: her father was afraid she would be easy prey for unscrupulous men. He was sure that all the officers on board, and half the male passengers, including the elderly ones, had her in their sights. More than one had commented how talented his daughter was, referring to the watercolors Ofelia painted on deck, but they did not crowd around her to admire her banal little compositions. Isidro was hoping to see her married soon, when she would become the responsibility of Matias Eyzaguirre and no longer his, so that he could breathe more easily. Although it would be better for her to wait awhile, because if she married very young, like her sisters, within a few years she would turn into an embittered matron.

Coming from Chile, in the far south of America, the journey to Europe was a long, expensive odyssey that few families could afford. The del Solar family were not among the truly rich, as they might have been had Isidro's father left what he himself had received rather than throwing it away entirely before he abandoned his family, but they were comfortably well-off nevertheless. However that might be, social position depended less on money than on lineage. Unlike many rich families who still had their provincial mentalities, Isidro thought it was important to see the world. Chile was an island, bounded to the north by the most inhospitable desert, to the east by the impenetrable cordillera of the Andes, to the west by the Pacific Ocean, and to the south by the frozen continent of Antarctica. This explained why Chileans spent their time navel-gazing, while beyond their borders the twentieth century went galloping along. To Isidro, travel was a necessary investment. He had sent two of his sons to the United States and Europe as soon as they were old enough, and would have liked to do the same for his daughters, but they married before he found the right moment to do so. He was determined not to make that mistake with Ofelia; he had to get her out of the narrow, sanctimonious atmosphere in Santiago and give her at least a veneer of culture.

Secretly, he had in mind something that not even his wife knew at present: to leave Ofelia in a girls' finishing school in London at the end of their trip. One or two years of a British education would be good for her; she could improve her English, which she had studied since childhood with a governess and private tutors, as all his children had (except, of course, Leonardo). English could well be the language of the future, unless Germany took over Europe. A school in London was what his daughter needed before she married Matias Eyzaguirre, her eternal fiancé, who was carving out a career for himself in the diplomatic corps.

Ofelia occupied the second bedroom in the suite, separated by a door from her parents. For weeks, chaos had reigned in her cabin: trunks and hatboxes lay open, while clothes, shoes, and cosmetics were strewn everywhere, along with tennis rackets and fashion magazines. Brought up by servants, she went everywhere sowing confusion, never asking herself who picked up or sorted out the typhoon she left in her wake. At the sound of a bell, someone appeared as if by magic to attend her. That night she had rescued a flimsy, tight-fitting gown from the maelstrom. When he saw it, her father exploded with disgust.

"Where did you get that sluttish dress?"

"It's fashionable, Papa. Do you want to see me in a nun's habit, like Aunt Teresa?"

"Don't be impertinent. What would Matias think if he saw you like that?"

"He'd stand there with his mouth wide open, like he always does. Don't get your hopes up, I'm never going to marry him."

"Well then, you shouldn't keep him hanging on."

"He's so devout, Papa."

"Would you prefer him to be an atheist?"

"Not in a month of Sundays, Papa. Mama, I came to ask if I could borrow Grandma's necklace, but I see you're already wearing it. It looks wonderful on you."

"You take it, Ofelia, you'll show it off much better than I will," her mother said quickly, raising her hands to the clasp.

"Don't be silly, Laura! Didn't you hear that I want you to wear it tonight?" her husband cut in.

"What does it matter, Isidro? It will look better on her . . ."

"It matters to me! That's enough. Ofelia, wear a shawl or cardigan, that neckline is too low," he ordered. He couldn't forget how embarrassed he had been during the masked ball held when they crossed the equator, when Ofelia appeared as a harem girl, wearing a veil and a revealing pair of pajamas.

"Just pretend you don't know me, Papa. Luckily I don't have to sit at your table with those boring old crocks. I hope I'm with some good-looking young fellows . . ."

"Don't be so vulgar!" her father managed to exclaim before she swept out of the room, twirling like a flamenco dancer.

To Laura and Ofelia del Solar the captain's dinner seemed endless. After the dessert—a volcano of ice cream and meringue with a lit candle in the center—the mother retired to her suite with a migraine, while her daughter made up for it dancing in the ballroom to soaring trumpets. She overdid the champagne and ended up in a corner of the deck kissing a Scottish officer with carrot-colored hair and wandering hands. Her father swooped down to rescue her at the last minute. "For God's sake, the trouble you cause me! Don't you know that rumor has wings? You'll see, Matias is going to hear about this before we even dock in Liverpool!"

IN THE DEL SOLAR HOUSE on Calle Mar del Plata back in Santiago, a sense of perpetual vacation floated in the air. The master and mistress had been away for four weeks, and not even the dog was missing them. Their absence didn't change the routines or lighten the servants' tasks, but none of the servants was in any great hurry. The radios poured out soap operas, boleros, and soccer. There was time for siestas. Even Leonardo, who normally clung to his mother, seemed happy and had stopped asking for her. This was the first time they had been apart, and far from regretting it, Baby took advantage to explore all the forbidden nooks and crannies of this three-story house: the basement, garage, cellar, and attic.

Felipe, the eldest son, who had been left in charge of the house and his younger brother, took his responsibilities lightly, because he was not cut out to be the head of the family, and his mind was on more interesting affairs. The burning issue of political life in Chile at the time was the question of the Spanish refugees, and so he couldn't care less if they served watery soup or crab at table or if Baby slept with the dog on his bed. He didn't check the household expenses, and if he was asked for instructions, told the staff they should do as they always did.

Juana Nancucheo, of mixed criollo and Mapuche heritage from the deep south, was a woman of indeterminate age. Short of stature and as solid as the ancient tree trunks of her native forests, with a long black plait and olive skin, she was rough in manner and steadfastly loyal, and had been in charge of the household since time immemorial. She strictly supervised the three maids, cook, laundress, gardener, and the man who polished the floors, fetched the firewood and coal, looked after the hens, and did all the heavy work (nobody could remember his name: he was simply "the little fellow who did all the chores"). The only one to escape Juana's control was the driver, who lived above the garage and received orders directly from the masters, although in her view this led to many abuses. She had her eye on him: she was sure he couldn't be trusted, that he smuggled women up to his room. "There are too many domestic staff in this house," Isidro would often say. "So who are you thinking of getting rid of, *patron*?" Juana would retort. "No one, I'm just saying it," he would immediately bluster. He was right in a way, Juana admitted to herself: the children were grown up and several of the bedrooms had been closed off. The two elder daughters were married and had children of their own; the second son was away studying climate whims in the Caribbean, even though in Juana's opinion there was nothing to be studied about that, you simply had to put up with it. Felipe lived in his own house. The only ones left were the youngest daughter, Ofelia, who was going to marry the agreeable young Matias—such a gentleman, so much in love—and Baby, her little angel, who was going to stay with her forever, because he would never grow up.

Her master and mistress had traveled abroad before, when the children were younger, and before Leonardo was born, and she had been left in charge of the house. On that occasion she had carried out her duties without anyone complaining, but this time they had decided to leave Felipe in charge, as if she were a useless idiot. All those years serving the family, she thought, and they repaid her in such a shabby fashion. Tempted as she was to gather her things and leave, she had nowhere to go. She must have been six or seven when she was given to Laura's father, Vicente Vizcarra, in payment for a favor. In those days, Señor Vizcarra traded in hardwoods—although by now there was nothing left of the fragrant forests of the Mapuche region, chopped down with axe and saw and replaced by nondescript trees planted in rows like soldiers, destined for paper mills. Juana was a barefoot youngster who understood no more than a few words of Spanish: her mother tongue was Mapudungun. Although she looked to him like a young savage, Vizcarra accepted her, because to refuse would have been a tremendous insult to his debtor. He took her back to Santiago with him, and handed her over to his wife, who in turn passed her on to the maids for them to train the girl in basic housework. Juana learned everything else for herself, her only schooling being her ability to listen and her willingness to obey. When Laura, one of the Vizcarra family daughters, married Isidro del Solar, Juana was dispatched to be their servant. She calculated that this must have been when she was about eighteen, although her birth had never been registered and so legally she didn't exist.

From the outset Isidro and Laura del Solar made her the housekeeper, for they trusted her blindly. One day she plucked up the courage to stammer out a request that her employers could perhaps pay her something, not a lot, and forgive her for asking, but she had a few expenses, a few needs . . .

"Goodness me, you're part of the family, why would we pay you?" was their answer.

"I'm sorry, but I'm not part of the family, I'm only part of the household."

And so for the first time Juana Nancucheo began to receive money, which she spent on candies for the children and a new pair of shoes every year; the rest, she saved. Nobody knew the members of the family better than she did; she was the guardian of all their secrets. When Leonardo was born, and it was obvious from his sweet moon face that he was different, Juana swore she would live long enough to take care of him until his dying day. Baby had heart problems and, according to the doctors, wasn't going to live long, but Juana's instinct and affection for him made her reject that diagnosis. With great patience she taught him to eat by himself and to use the toilet. Other families hid any children they had resembling him, ashamed as if it was a punishment from God, but thanks to Juana, it wasn't the same for Leonardo. When he was clean and not shouting or screaming, his parents presented him as simply another one of their offspring.

FELIPE, THE DEL SOLARS' eldest son, was the apple of Juana's eye, and continued to be her favorite even after the birth of Leonardo, because there were different kinds of love. She thought of Felipe as her mentor, the stick she could lean on in her old age. He had always been a good boy, and to her he still was, even though now he was grown up. He was a lawyer, but reluctantly so, because his passions were art, conversation, and ideas. Nothing very useful in this world of ours, as his father often commented.

During his studies at the religious school where the children of the leading, most conservative families in Chile were educated, Felipe had taught Juana to read, write, and do sums. This created a close bond between them. Juana covered up any mischief he got into, and he kept her informed about the world outside. "What are you reading at the moment, *niño* Felipe?" "Wait until I finish the book and I'll tell you—it's about pirates" or alternatively: "Nothing that would interest you, Juana. It's about the Phoenicians, who lived many centuries ago and who nobody cares a bit about—I don't know why the priests teach us such stupid things." Felipe had grown in size and years, but still went on telling her what he was reading and explaining what was going on in the world. Later on, he helped her invest her savings in shares on the stock exchange: the same ones his father, Isidro, bought. He showed some delicate touches: he would steal into her room to leave money or candy under her pillow. She was always concerned about his health, because her *niño* Felipe was frail, catching cold from the slightest draft and suffering from indigestion whenever he was upset or ate heavy meals. Unfortunately, her Felipe was another innocent like Leonardo, unable to see other people's falsity and treachery. An idealist, as they say. In addition, he was so absentminded he kept losing things, and had such a gentle character that people took advantage of him. He was always lending money that nobody ever repaid, and contributing to noble causes that Juana considered pointless because the world never changes. Inevitably, he had never married: what woman would put up with his crazy ideas, they might be all right for saints, but not for any right-minded gentleman, as Juana would say.

Isidro del Solar was another one who didn't appreciate his son's generosity, which went beyond his charitable impulses and affected the clarity of his ideas. "One of these days he's going to surprise us with the news that he's become a communist," he would sigh. The arguments between father and son were a sight to behold. They ended with slammed doors over matters that had nothing to do with the family, such as the state of the country and of the world—which according to Juana was none of their business. After one of these clashes, Felipe chose to go and live in a house he rented six blocks away. Juana was up in arms because a proper son only leaves the family home when he is married, and not before, but the rest of the family accepted it without a fuss. This didn't mean, though, that Felipe disappeared completely: he came for lunch every day, expected his meals prepared and his clothes washed and ironed how he liked them. Juana would go to his house and supervise the work done by his two servants—a couple of lazy, dirty Indians in her view. More work for her when all was said and done: it would have been better for him to stay in his bachelor's bed, she muttered. The feud between Felipe and his father seemed likely to go on forever, until Doña Laura suffered a serious bout of hepatitis that forced them to make up.

Juana could well recall the reason for the split between the two men: it was impossible to forget, because it shook the entire country, and was still talked about on the radio. It had happened in spring the previous year, when there had been a presidential election. There were three candidates: Isidro del Solar's favorite, a conservative millionaire with the reputation of being a speculator; a man from the Radical Party, an educator, lawyer, and senator, whom Felipe was going to vote for; and a general who in the past had occupied the presidency as a dictator, and was running this time with the support of, among others, the Nazi Party. Nobody in the family liked him. As a boy, Felipe had a collection of lead soldiers from the Prussian Army, but he lost all sympathy for the Germans when Hitler came to power. "Have you seen the Nazis marching through the center of Santiago saluting with an arm raised in the air, Juana? How ridiculous!" Yes, she had seen them, and also knew of somebody called Hitler, because Felipe had told her about him.

"Your father was sure his candidate was going to win."

"Yes, because here the right wing always wins. The general's supporters wanted to stop him winning, and tried to carry out a coup. They didn't succeed."

"They said on the radio that some youngsters were shot down like dogs."

"It was a handful of hotheaded Nazis, Juana. They stormed the University of Chile building and another one opposite the presidential palace. The military police and army quickly cornered them.

They surrendered with their hands up, and they were unarmed, but they were shot down all the same. The authorities had given orders that none of them was to be left alive."

"Your father says they deserved it for being such idiots."

"No one deserves that, Juana. My father ought to be more careful in his opinions. It was a massacre unworthy of Chile. The whole country is furious, and that's what cost the right wing the election. So Pedro Aguirre Cerda won, as you know, Juana, and now we've got a Radical president."

"What does that mean?"

"He's a man with progressive ideas. According to my father, he's a man of the Left. Anybody who doesn't think like my father is of the Left."

For Juana, left and right meant directions in the street, not people, and the president's name meant nothing to her. He wasn't from any well-known family.

"Pedro Aguirre Cerda represents the Popular Front, made up of center and left-wing parties, similar to what they had in Spain and France. Do you remember I explained the Spanish Civil War to you?"

"In other words, the same thing could happen here."

"I hope not, Juana. If you could vote, you would have voted for Aguirre Cerda. Someday, I promise you, women will be able to vote in elections."

"And who did you vote for, *niño* Felipe?"

"For Aguirre Cerda. He was the best candidate."

"Your father doesn't like him."

"But I do, and so do you."

"I don't know anything about it."

"It's bad you don't know, Juana. The Popular Front represents the workers, peasants, the miners in the north, people like you."

"I'm none of those, and neither are you. I'm a domestic servant."

"You belong to the working class, Juana."

"As I see it, you're my master, so I don't see why you voted for the working class."

"What you need is education. The president says that to govern is to educate. Free, compulsory education for all Chilean children. Public health for everyone. Better wages. Making the trade unions stronger. What do you think of all that?"

"It's all the same to me."

"Juana! How can it all be the same to you? You really should have gone to school."

"And you may have a lot of education, *niño* Felipe, but you can't even blow your own nose. And while we're at it, let me tell you you're not to bring guests into the house without warning. The cook gets angry, and I don't want any trouble, or having visitors leave here saying we don't know how to treat them properly. Those pals of yours may have a lot of education as well, but they drink your father's liquor without asking permission. Just wait till he gets back, and we'll see what he says when he discovers all that's missing from the wine cellar."

IT WAS THE SECOND to last Saturday of the month, the day of the informal meeting of the Club of the Enraged, as Juana Nancucheo called the group of Felipe's pals. Usually they met at Felipe's place, but since his parents had been away, he received them in the family's house on Calle Mar del Plata, where the food was excellent. Despite the trouble these people caused her, Juana did her best to get fresh oysters and to serve them the finest stews prepared by the cook, a formidable woman whose temper was as foul as her cooking was superb. Like all young men of their class, Felipe's friends were members of the Club de la Union, where they discussed personal matters as much as the country's financial and political affairs; but those big,

gloomy rooms with dark wood paneling, chandeliers, and plush armchairs were not exactly suitable for the animated philosophical discussions the Enraged held. Besides, the Club de la Union was for men
only, and what would their gatherings be like without the refreshing
presence of a few unmarried women: free spirits, artists, writers, and
stylish adventuresses, including one amazon with a Croatian surname
who traveled alone to places that didn't figure on any map. The most
frequently recurring topic over the past three years had been the situation in Spain, and in recent months the fate of the Republican refugees who, since that January, had been left to rot and die in French
concentration camps.

The massive exodus of people from Catalonia toward the border
with France had coincided with the worst earthquake ever to hit
Chile. Even though Felipe boasted that he was an incurable rationalist, he saw in this coincidence a call for compassion and solidarity.
The earthquake left a total of twenty thousand or more dead and
whole towns flattened, but the Spanish Civil War, with hundreds of
thousands dead, wounded, or refugees, was by comparison a far
greater tragedy.

That evening the Salon had a special guest: Pablo Neruda, who at
the age of thirty-four was considered the best poet of his generation,
which was some feat as in Chile poets flourished like weeds. Some of
his *Twenty Love Poems* had already become part of Chilean folklore,
and even those who couldn't read or write recited them. Neruda was a
man from the south, from rain and timber, the son of a railway worker,
who recited his verses in a booming voice and described himself as
having a hard nose and minimal eyes. A polemical figure because
of his fame and left-wing sympathies, especially for the Communist
Party, in which he would later become a militant, he had been a consul in Argentina, Burma, Ceylon, Spain, and most recently France,
because, according to his political and literary enemies, the successive
governments in Chile preferred to keep him as far away as possible. In

Madrid, where he had been consul shortly before the war broke out, he had made friends with numerous intellectuals and poets, among them Federico Garcia Lorca—murdered by the Francoists—and Antonio Machado, who died in a town close to the French border during the Retreat. Neruda had published a hymn to the glory of the Republican fighters called "Spain in the Heart," five hundred numbered copies of which were printed while war was raging by the militiamen of the Eastern Army in Montserrat Abbey. Copies were done on paper made from anything they could lay their hands on, from bloody shirts to an enemy flag. The poem was also published in Chile in an ordinary edition, but Felipe had one of the original copies. *And along the streets the blood of the children flowed simply, like the blood of children . . . Come and see the blood in the streets, come and see the blood in the streets.*

Neruda had a passionate love of Spain; he loathed Fascism and was so concerned about the fate of the defeated Republicans that he had managed to convince the new Chilean president to allow a certain number of them to come to Chile, in defiance of the intransigent opposition of right-wing parties and the Catholic Church. This was what he had been invited to come to the meeting of the Enraged to talk about, as he was briefly in Santiago, having spent weeks in Argentina and Uruguay organizing economic aid for the refugees. In Chile, the right-wing newspapers claimed that other countries offered money, but none wanted to welcome Reds, those rapists of nuns, murderers, bandits, unscrupulous atheists, and Jews, who were bound to put the country's security in jeopardy.

Neruda told Felipe and his friends that he would be leaving in a few days for Paris, where he'd been appointed a special consul for Spanish emigration. "They don't like me in the Chilean Legation in Paris, they're all right-wing stooges determined to obstruct my mission," the poet told them. "Our government is sending me there with no money, and I have to find a ship. I'll have to see what I can do."

He explained that his orders were to select qualified workers who could teach their trades to their Chilean counterparts. They had to be peace-loving and honorable, not politicians, journalists, or potentially dangerous intellectuals. According to Neruda, Chilean immigration policy had always been racist: consuls were given confidential instructions to refuse visas to several categories, races, and nationalities, from gypsies, negroes, and Jews to the so-called Orientals, a vague term that could mean almost anything. Now a political dimension had been added to this xenophobia: there were to be no communists, socialists, or anarchists—but since this had not yet been officially sanctioned, there was still some room for maneuver. Neruda had a herculean task ahead of him: he had to finance and equip a boat, select the immigrants, and provide them with the amount of money demanded by the government for their upkeep if they didn't have any family or friends to receive them in Chile. This was three million Chilean pesos, which had to be deposited in the Central Bank before they embarked.

"How many refugees are we talking about?" Felipe asked him.

"Let's say fifteen hundred men, but there'll be more than that, because how can we leave their wives and children behind?"

"When will they arrive?"

"At the end of August or the start of September."

"That means we've got more or less three months to raise funds and find them housing and work. We also need a campaign to counteract the right-wing propaganda and mobilize public opinion in favor of those Spaniards," said Felipe.

"That'll be easy. Popular sympathy is on the side of the Republicans. Most of the Spanish colony here in Chile, the Basques and Catalans, are ready to help."

The Enraged said their farewells at one in the morning, and Felipe drove the poet in his Ford to the house where he was staying. On his return, he found Juana waiting for him in the dining room with a jug of hot coffee.

"What's wrong, Juana? You ought to be asleep."

"I was listening to what those pals of yours were saying."

"Spying on us?"

"Your pals eat like jailbirds, not to mention how they drink. And those women with painted faces drink even more than the men. And they're so rude: they don't ever say hello or thank you."

"I can't believe you waited up just to tell me that."

"I waited up so that you could explain to me why that poet is famous. He started reciting and would never shut up: more and more nonsense about fish in vests and crepuscular eyes—who knows what kind of illness that is."

"They're metaphors, Juana. That's what poetry is."

"Go teach your grandmother, may she rest in peace, to suck eggs. I know what poetry is: Mapudungun is pure poetry. I bet you didn't know that! And I'm sure that Neruda of yours didn't either. I haven't heard my language in many years, but I still remember. Poetry is what stays in your head and isn't forgotten."

"Of course, and music is what you can whistle, isn't it?"

"You said it, *niño* Felipe."

ISIDRO DEL SOLAR RECEIVED the telegram from his son Felipe on the last day of their stay at the Savoy Hotel, after spending a whole month in Great Britain with his wife and daughter. In London they visited the usual tourist sights, went shopping, attended the theater and horse races. The Chilean ambassador, yet another of Laura Vizcarra's many cousins, put an official car at their disposal so that they could tour the countryside and visit the Oxford and Cambridge colleges. He also had them invited for lunch at the castle of a duke or marquess—they weren't sure of the exact rank, as titles of nobility had long since been abolished in Chile, and no one remembered them.

The ambassador warned them about the proper codes of behavior and dress: they were to pretend that the servants did not exist, but it was best to make a fuss over the dogs; they were not to comment on the food, but to go into raptures about the roses; to wear simple and, if possible, old clothes—no flounces or silk neckties, because nobles dressed like the poor in the country. They traveled to Scotland, where Isidro had secured a deal for his Patagonian wool, and to Wales, where he was hoping to do the same, but which fell through.

Behind the back of his wife and daughter, Isidro visited a ladies' finishing school that dated from the seventeenth century, based in a magnificent mansion opposite Kensington Palace and Gardens. There Ofelia would learn etiquette, the art of social relations, how to deal correctly with invitations and selecting a menu, good manners, comportment, grooming, and household management, among other virtues of which she was greatly in need. What a shame his wife had not learned any of that, thought Isidro; it would be a good business opportunity to found a similar establishment in Chile, to refine all the uncouth young women down there. He would look into the possibility. For the moment, though, he hid his plans from Ofelia: she would only kick up a fuss and ruin the rest of their trip. He would tell her at the very end, when there was no time for tantrums.

They were in the hotel salon with its glass-domed ceiling (a symphony in white, gold, and ivory) enjoying the customary five o'clock tea served on floral porcelain, when the bellboy in his admiral's uniform came up bearing Felipe's telegram. "Poet exiles need rooms STOP Juana refuses keys STOP Send instructions STOP." Isidro read it three times, and passed it to Laura and Ofelia.

"What is this crap about?"

"Please, Isidro, don't talk like that in front of the child."

"I hope Felipe hasn't started drinking," he growled.

"What are you going to answer?" asked Laura.

"Tell him to go to hell."

"Don't get angry, Isidro. Better not to answer anything; these things always sort themselves out."

"But what does my brother mean?" Ofelia wanted to know.

"I've no idea. Nothing that concerns us," her father retorted.

ANOTHER IDENTICAL TELEGRAM REACHED them at their Paris hotel. Isidro could only with great difficulty scan *Le Figaro* because he had learned some French at school, but since he understood even less English, he had not caught up with the news in England. He now read that the French Communist Party and the Spanish Refugee Evacuation Service had chartered a cargo boat, the *Winnipeg,* and were fitting it out to send almost two thousand exiles to Chile. He nearly had a fit. This was all that was needed in this time of disasters, he grunted, first a Radical Party president, then the apocalyptic earthquake, and now they were going to pack Chile with communists. The sinister meaning of the telegram became clear: his son intended to install this rabble in his own house, no less. Thank God for Juana, who refused to hand over the keys.

"Explain to me what exiles are, Papa," Ofelia insisted.

"Listen, sweetheart, in Spain there was a revolution of bad people. It was a catastrophe. The military rose against it and fought for the values of the fatherland and morality. Naturally, they won."

"What did they win?"

"The Civil War. They saved Spain. The exiles Felipe talks of are the cowards who escaped and are in France."

"Why did they escape?"

"Because they lost and had to face the consequences."

"I think there are lots of women and children among the refugees, Isidro. The newspaper says there are hundreds of thousands of them . . ." Laura commented timidly.

"That may be. But what does Chile have to do with all of it? Neruda's the one to blame! That communist! Felipe has no common sense, it's as if he weren't my son. I'm going to have to set him straight when we get back."

Laura seized on this to suggest it might be better to return to Santiago before Felipe did anything crazy, but the newspaper said the *Winnipeg* would be leaving in August. They had more than enough time to go to the spa at Evian, visit Lourdes, as well as the shrine of San Antonio of Padua in Italy to fulfill Laura's many vows, as well as the Vatican to receive a private blessing from the new Pope Pius XII, which had cost Isidro a lot of pulling of strings and money, before they came back to England. There they would leave Ofelia at the finishing school, by force if need be, and then he would embark with his wife for the journey back to Chile on board the *Reina del Pacifico*. In other words, a perfect trip.

PART TWO

Exile, Loves, and
Misunderstandings

CHAPTER 5

1939

Let's keep anger, pain, and tears,
Let's fill the desolate void
And may the nightly bonfire recall
The light of the deceased stars.

— PABLO NERUDA
"*José Miguel Carrera, 1810*"
CANTO GENERAL

VICTOR DALMAU SPENT SEVERAL MONTHS IN THE concentration camp at Argeles-sur-Mer, never once suspecting that Roser had been there as well. He had not heard any news of Aitor, but supposed he had kept his promise to get his mother and Roser out of Spain. At this point the inhabitants of the camp were almost exclusively male, tens of thousands of Republican soldiers, who suffered hunger and deprivation, as well as blows and constant humiliation from their jailers. Although the conditions were still inhuman, at least the harshest days of winter were behind them.

In order to survive without going mad, the prisoners organized themselves. The different political parties held revolutionary meetings separately, just as they had during the war. They sang, read whatever they could lay their hands on, taught those who needed it to read and write, published a newspaper of sorts—a handwritten sheet of paper that was passed from reader to reader—and sought to preserve their dignity cutting one another's hair and checking each other for lice and washing their clothes in the freezing seawater. They divided the camp into streets with poetic names, outlined absurd squares and *ramblas* like those in Barcelona in the sand and mud, created the illusion of an orchestra without instruments to perform classical and popular music, and restaurants with invisible food that the cooks described in great detail while the others savored the tastes with their eyes closed. With what little building supplies they had, they managed to construct sheds, barracks, and huts. They were constantly alert for news from the outside world, which was on the brink of another war, and for the possibility of being set free. The more skilled among them were often employed in the countryside or in industry, but the majority had been farm laborers, woodcutters, shepherds, or fishermen, and so had no skills usable in France. They came under constant pressure from the authorities to be repatriated to Spain, and were sometimes fooled into being taken to the Spanish border.

Victor stayed in the camp with a small team of doctors and nurses, because on that infernal beach they had a mission: to serve the sick, the wounded, and the crazy. The legend that he had restarted the heart of a dead young soldier at the Estacion del Norte had preceded him, and this gave his patients a blind trust in him, although he always insisted that if they were seriously ill they should see one of the doctors. There were never enough hours in the day for his work. The boredom and depression that were the scourge of most of the prisoners didn't affect him: on the contrary, he found in his work a stimulus that was close to happiness. He was as skinny and weak as the rest of the men in the camp, but didn't feel hungry, and more than once gave his ration of dried cod to someone else. His comrades said he must have been eating sand. He began work at first light, but after sunset still had several hours to fill, so he would pick up his guitar and sing.

He had done so only rarely during the years of the Civil War, but he remembered the romantic ballads his mother had taught him to combat his shyness, and of course revolutionary songs, during which others joined in for the chorus. The guitar had belonged to a youngster from Andalusia who kept it with him throughout the war, went into exile without letting go of it, and played it at Argeles-sur-Mer until the end of February, when he was carried off by pneumonia. Victor cared for him in his final days, and so the boy left him the instrument by way of inheritance. It was one of the few real instruments in the camp; most were fantasy ones whose sounds were imitated by men who were good mimics.

As the months went by, overcrowding in the camp gradually diminished. The old and infirm died off and were buried in a cemetery adjacent to the camp. The luckiest among the prisoners obtained sponsors and visas to emigrate to Mexico and South America. Many of the soldiers joined the French Foreign Legion, despite its brutal discipline and its reputation for harboring criminals, since anything was better than remaining in the camp. Those with suitable qualifications were recruited for the Foreign Workers Companies created to replace the French workforce called up in preparation for the coming war. Later on, others were to go to the Soviet Union to fight with the Red Army or join the French Resistance, and thousands of them died in Nazi death camps or Stalin's gulags.

One day in April 1939, when the unbearable winter cold had given way to spring and the first warmth of summer was on the horizon, Victor was called to the camp commander's office. He had a visitor. It was Aitor Ibarra, wearing a straw boater and white shoes. It was almost a minute before Aitor recognized Victor in the ragged scarecrow standing in front of him. When he did, they embraced with great emotion, both with moist eyes.

"You can't imagine the trouble I've had finding you, brother, you're not on any list; I thought you were dead," Aitor said.

"Almost. And you: how come you're all dressed up as a pimp?"

"As a businessman, you mean. I'll tell you later."

"Tell me first what happened to my mother and Roser."

Aitor told him how Carme had disappeared. He had made inquiries but had not heard anything concrete, except that she had not returned to Barcelona. The Dalmau house had been commandeered, and another family was living there now. He had good news about Roser, though. He briefly told Victor about how they had escaped from Barcelona, then crossed the peaks of the Pyrenees on foot, and how they were separated after reaching France. For a while, he'd had no news of her.

"I escaped as soon as I could, Victor. I don't know why you haven't tried: it's easy."

"They need me here."

"Thinking like that means you'll always be in trouble."

"That's true, but what can I do? Tell me about Roser."

"I had no difficulty finding her once I remembered the name of your friend the nurse. Roser was here, in this same camp, but she got out thanks to Elisabeth Eidenbenz. She's living in Perpignan with a family who took her in, working as a seamstress and giving piano lessons. She had a healthy baby boy, who's a month old already and is a fine-looking fellow."

Aitor had got by as ever, buying and selling. During the war he got hold of the most saleable items, from cigarettes and sugar to shoes and morphine, and bartered them for other things in an exchange that was laborious but always left him with a profit. He also picked up real treasures, similar to the German pistol and the American penknife that had impressed Roser so much. He would never have relinquished them, and was still angry when he remembered how they were taken from him. Eventually he had managed to get in touch with some distant cousins who had emigrated to Venezuela several years earlier, and they were going to sponsor him and find him work in that country. Thanks to his innate talent he had already saved enough money for the passage and visa.

"I'm leaving in a week, Victor. We have to get out of Europe as quickly as possible: another war is on the horizon, and it will be far worse than the last one. As soon as I get to Venezuela I'll sort out the paperwork so that you can emigrate, and I'll send you the boat ticket."

"I can't leave Roser and her child."

"For them as well, of course."

Aitor's visit left Victor speechless for several days. He was convinced he was trapped yet again, stuck in limbo, unable to control his fate. After hours walking on the beach, weighing up his responsibility to the sick in the camp, he decided that the moment had come to give priority to his responsibility toward Roser, her child, and his own destiny. On April 1, Franco, as Caudillo of Spain (a title he had bestowed on himself in December 1936), had declared an end to the war that had lasted nine hundred and eighty-four days. France and Great Britain had recognized his government. Victor's homeland was lost; there was no hope of returning.

He bathed in the sea, rubbing himself clean with sand because he had no soap, had his hair cut by a comrade, shaved carefully, and asked for a pass to go and fetch the medical supplies provided by a local hospital, something he did every week. At first a guard had always accompanied him, but after several months of coming and going he was allowed to go alone. He left the camp without a problem, and simply didn't return. Aitor had given him some money, which he spent on his first decent meal since January, a gray suit, two shirts, and a hat, all of them secondhand but in good condition, as well as a pair of new shoes. As his mother used to say: good shoes, warm welcome. A truck driver gave him a lift, and so he reached Perpignan and the Red Cross office, where he asked for his friend the nurse.

———

ELISABETH EIDENBENZ RECEIVED VICTOR in her makeshift maternity home with a baby on each arm. She was so busy she didn't even remember the romance that had never happened between them. Victor had not forgotten it, though. Seeing her calm, clear-eyed, and in her spotless uniform, he concluded she was perfect and that he must have been an idiot ever to think she would notice him: Elisabeth had the soul of a missionary, not a lover. When she finally recognized him, she handed the children to another woman and embraced him with genuine affection.

"How changed you are, Victor! You must have suffered a lot, my friend."

"Less than others. I've been lucky, all things considered. You, on the other hand, look as well as you always did."

"You think so?"

"How do you manage to stay looking so impeccable, so tranquil, and keeping a smile on your face? You were like that when I met you in the midst of battle, and you're still the same, as if the evil times we're living through didn't affect you at all."

"These evil times force me to be strong and to work hard, Victor. You came to see me about Roser, didn't you?"

"I don't know how to thank you for all you've done for her, Elisabeth."

"There's nothing to thank me for. We're going to have to wait until eight o'clock, though; that's when she finishes her last piano class. She doesn't live here. She's with some Quaker friends."

While they were waiting, Elisabeth introduced him to the mothers living in the house, and then they sat to have tea and biscuits while they talked about everything that had happened to them since they last saw each other at Teruel. At eight, Elisabeth drove him in her car, paying more attention to their conversation than to the road. Victor thought how ironic it would be to have survived the war and the concentration camp only to die squashed like a cockroach in his improbable girlfriend's vehicle.

The Quakers' house was twenty minutes away; Roser herself opened the door to them. When she saw Victor she gave a loud cry and buried her face in her hands, as though having a hallucination; he folded her in his arms. He remembered her as being skinny, with narrow hips and a flat chest, thick eyebrows and strong features: the kind of woman who has no false pride about her looks, and who, with age, would become lean or masculine. The last time he had seen her was in December, with a bulging belly and a face covered in acne. Becoming a mother had softened her, giving her curves where before she had only angles. She was breastfeeding her baby, and had large breasts, clear skin, and lustrous hair.

Their meeting was so charged with emotion that even Elisabeth, who was more than accustomed to heartrending scenes, was moved. Victor's nephew was plump and bald: all babies that age looked like Winston Churchill to him. A closer look, though, showed he had some familiar traits, including the deep black eyes of the Dalmaus.

"What's his name?" he asked Roser.

"For now we call him 'little one.' I'm waiting for Guillem to appear so we can name him at the Registry Office."

This was the moment to give her the bad news, but yet again Victor's courage failed him.

"Why not call him Guillem?"

"Because Guillem warned me that none of his children were to be called that. He didn't like his name. We agreed that if it was a boy he'd be Marcel, and if it was a girl, Carme, in honor of your mother and father."

"Well, there you are then."

"I'm going to wait for Guillem."

The Quaker family, consisting of the father, mother, and two children, invited Victor and Elisabeth for dinner. Despite being English, they served an edible meal. They spoke Spanish well since they had spent the war years in Spain helping children's organizations and, since the Retreat, had been working with refugees. That is what they would always do, they said: as Elisabeth had insisted, there's always a war somewhere.

"We're truly grateful to you," Victor told them. "It's thanks to you the child is alive. He would never have survived in the Argeles-sur-Mer camp. And I don't think Roser would have either. We hope not to have to abuse your hospitality for very long."

"There's nothing to thank us for. Roser and the boy are already part of the family. What's the rush to leave?"

Victor explained about his friend Aitor Ibarra and the plan to emigrate to Venezuela once he had succeeded in helping them. It seemed to be the only viable solution.

"If you want to emigrate, maybe you could consider going to Chile," suggested Elisabeth. "I saw an item in the newspaper about a boat taking Spaniards to Chile."

"Chile? Where's that?" Roser wanted to know.

"At the far end of the earth, I think," said Victor.

The next day, Elisabeth found the article and sent it to Victor. On the Chilean government's instructions, the poet Pablo Neruda was fitting out a boat called the *Winnipeg* to transport Spanish exiles to his country. Elisabeth gave Victor money to take the train to Paris and try his luck with the poet, whose work he didn't know.

THANKS TO A CITY MAP, Victor Dalmau found his way to the elegant Chilean Legation at No. 2 Avenue de la Motte-Picquet, near Les Invalides. There was a line at the door, controlled by a bad-tempered porter. The employees inside the building were equally hostile, and didn't even respond to a greeting. To Victor this seemed like a bad omen, just like the heavy, tense atmosphere of this Paris spring. Hitler was gobbling up European territories, and the storm clouds of war were already darkening the sky. The people in the line spoke Spanish, and nearly all of them were holding the press announcement. When Victor's turn came, he was pointed toward a staircase, which began with marble and bronze on the bottom floors and ended as narrow, bare steps into a sort of attic. There was no elevator, and Victor had to help another Spaniard who was much lamer than he was—he had a leg missing and could barely climb the stairs holding tight to the banister.

"Is it true they only take communists?" asked Victor.

"So they say. What are you?"

"Simply a Republican."

"Don't complicate matters. Better tell the poet you're a communist and be done with it."

In a tiny room furnished with three chairs and a desk, he was received by Pablo Neruda. The poet was still a young man, with piercing eyes and drooping Arab eyelids, hefty shoulders and a slight stoop. He looked more weighty and portly than he really was, as Victor realized when he stood up to say goodbye. The interview lasted only ten minutes and left him feeling that he had failed. Neruda asked him several routine questions: age, marital status, education, and work experience.

"I heard you're only taking communists . . ." said Victor, surprised that the poet had not asked his political affiliation.

"You heard wrong. We're working with quotas for communists, socialists, anarchists, and liberals. The decision depends on the Spanish Refugee Evacuation Service and me. What's most important is the person's character and how useful they can be in Chile. I'm studying hundreds of requests, and as soon as I've made a decision, don't worry, I'll let you know."

"If your decision is favorable, Señor Neruda, please take into account the fact that I won't be traveling alone. A friend with a baby only a few months old would come as well."

"A friend, you say?"

"Roser Bruguera, my brother's girlfriend."

"In that case, your brother will need to come to see me and fill out a request."

"We think my brother died at the battle of the Ebro."

"I'm very sorry. You do understand I have to give priority to immediate family members, don't you?"

"I understand. If you allow me, I'll come back and see you again in three days' time."

"In three days I won't have an answer, my friend."

"But I will. Thank you."

Victor took the train back to Perpignan that same afternoon. He arrived tired after dark, and slept in a flea-infested hotel where he couldn't even have a shower. The next morning he presented himself at Roser's workshop. They went out into the street to talk. Victor took her by the arm and led her to an isolated bench in a nearby square. He told Roser about his experience at the Chilean Legation, but didn't mention the harsh attitude of the Chilean staff or Neruda's lack of a firm offer.

"If that poet does accept you, Victor, you must go anyway. Don't worry about me."

"Roser, there's something I should have told you months ago, but every time I try, I can feel an iron hand throttling me, and I can't say a word. I wish it didn't have to be me who . . ."

"Guillem? Is it something about Guillem?" Roser asked in alarm.

Victor nodded, not daring to look at her. He pulled her to his chest and let her weep out loud like a desperate, trembling child, her face buried in his secondhand jacket. Eventually she ran out of tears. It seemed to Victor that Roser was releasing feelings she had suppressed for a long while, that the terrible news wasn't really a surprise. She must have suspected it for a long time, because that was the only explanation for Guillem's silence. Of course, in war people get lost, couples are forced apart, families are split up, and yet her instinct must have told Roser that he had died. She didn't ask for proof, but he showed her the charred billfold and the photograph Guillem had always carried with him.

"Do you see why I can't leave you behind, Roser? If they'll take us, you must come with me to Chile. There's going to be war in France as well. We have to protect the child."

"What about your mother?"

"Nobody has seen her since we left Barcelona. She was lost in the chaos; if she were alive she would have been in touch with me or you by now. If she does reappear in the future, we'll work out how best to help her. For the moment, you and your son are the most important thing, do you see that?"

"Yes, I see it. What do I have to do?"

"I'm sorry, Roser . . . you'll have to marry me."

She gave him such a terrified look that Victor couldn't help but smile, even though it didn't exactly fit the solemnity of the moment. He repeated what Neruda had said about giving priority to families.

"You're not even my sister-in-law, Roser."

"I was married to Guillem without any certificate or blessing by a priest."

"I'm afraid that doesn't count in this case. To be frank, Roser, you're a widow without really being one. We're going to get married today, if possible, and register the child as our son. I'll be his father; I promise I'll care for him and protect him, and love him as if he were my own. And the same goes for you."

"But we're not in love . . ."

"You're asking a lot, Roser. Isn't affection and respect enough for you? At times like these, that's more than sufficient. I'm never going to force you into a relationship you don't want."

"What does that mean? That you're not going to sleep with me?"

"Exactly that, Roser. I'm not a scoundrel."

And so, in a few minutes on that bench in the square, they made the decision that was to determine the rest of their lives, as well as that of the child. In the rush to flee, many of those forced out of Spain arrived in France without any identity papers; others lost them en route or in the concentration camps; but Victor and Roser still had theirs. Their Quaker friends acted as witnesses to the wedding in a brief ceremony held in the town hall. Victor had polished his new shoes and was wearing a borrowed tie; Roser, who was calm by now although her eyes were puffy from so much crying, wore her best dress and a spring hat. After the ceremony, they registered the child as Marcel Dalmau Bruguera, which would have been his name had his father lived. They celebrated with a special dinner at Elisabeth Eidenbenz's maternity home that ended with a crème Chantilly cake. The married couple cut the cake and distributed slices to everyone there.

As Victor had promised Pablo Neruda, after exactly three days he returned to the office of the Chilean Legation in Paris and placed the marriage certificate and his son's birth certificate on the poet's desk. Neruda gazed at him from behind his sleepy-looking eyelids and studied him for several seconds, intrigued.

"I see you have a poet's imagination, young man. Welcome to Chile," he said at length, stamping the form. "Did you say your wife's a pianist?"

"Yes, sir. And also a seamstress."

"We have seamstresses in Chile, but we need pianists. Go with your wife and child to the Trompeloup port at Bordeaux, next Friday, as early as possible. You'll leave on the *Winnipeg* at nightfall."

"We can't pay for the passages . . ."

"Nobody can. We'll see. And don't worry about paying for Chilean visas, as some consuls insist. I think it's shameful to charge refugees for a visa. We'll take care of that in Bordeaux as well."

———

THAT SUMMER DAY, AUGUST 4, 1939, remained forever engraved on the minds of Victor Dalmau, Roser Bruguera, and the other two thousand or more Spaniards sailing toward that long, narrow South American country that clung to the mountains so as not to topple into the sea. None of them knew anything about Chile. Years later, Neruda was to define it as a *long petal of sea and wine and snow . . .* with a *belt of black and white foam,* but that would not have left the migrants any the wiser. On the map, it looked slender and remote.

The square in Bordeaux was teeming with people, a huge crowd that grew minute by minute, suffocating in the heat under a bright blue sky. Trains, trucks, and other vehicles crammed with new arrivals kept pulling up. Most of them had come straight from the concentration camps and were hungry, weak, and unwashed. Since the men had spent several months separated from their women and children, the re-encounter between couples and families produced dramatic, emotional scenes. They hung out of train windows, shouting when they recognized loved ones and falling sobbing into each other's arms. A father who thought his son had died at the battle of the Ebro, two brothers who had heard nothing about each other since the Madrid front, a battle-hardened soldier who discovered a wife and children he had never expected to see again. And all this without any trouble, with a natural instinct for discipline that made the job of the French guards much easier.

Pablo Neruda, dressed from head to toe in white, together with his wife, Delia del Carril, also decked out in white and wearing a big, broad-brimmed hat, was overseeing the process of identification, health checks, and selection like a demigod. He was aided by consuls, secretaries, and friends seated at long trestle tables. Permission to board was granted with his signature in green ink and a rubber stamp from the Spanish Refugee Evacuation Service. Neruda solved the visa problem by issuing collective ones. The Spaniards were put into groups and had their photograph taken. Each one was quickly developed, and then someone cut out the faces and stuck them on the permits. Charity volunteers handed out snacks and toiletries for everyone. Each of the three hundred and fifty children received a complete set of clothes: Elisabeth Eidenbenz took charge of distributing them.

This was the day of departure, and the poet still needed a lot of money to pay for this immense transfer of migrants. The Chilean government refused to contribute, arguing that it would be impossible to justify the expense to a hostile, divided public at home. To everyone's surprise, a small group of very formally dressed people suddenly appeared on the quay, volunteering to pay half of every passage. When Roser saw the group in the distance, she handed Victor the baby and ran to greet them. Among them were the Quakers who had taken her in. They had come in the name of their community to fulfill the duty they had set for themselves ever since their origins in the seventeenth century: to serve mankind and promote peace. Roser repeated to them what she had heard from Elisabeth, "You always appear where you're most needed."

Victor, Roser, and the baby were among the first to embark. The ship was an old nine-thousand-ton cargo boat that brought goods from Africa and had been used as a troop ship in the Great War. Built to accommodate twenty seamen for short voyages, it had been converted to take more than two thousand people for a month. Triple bunks had been built in the hold, and a kitchen, dining room, and sick bay with three doctors had been installed. As soon as the Dalmau family arrived on board they were assigned to their sleeping quarters: Victor with the men in the prow, Roser with the women and children in the stern. Over the next few hours, the lucky passengers finished coming on board, while several hundred other refugees had to remain at dockside as there was no more room.

At nightfall the *Winnipeg* weighed anchor with the high tide. On deck, some were weeping silently; others had their hands on their hearts as they sang the Catalan song of the emigrant: *Dolça Cataluña / pàtria del meu cor / quan de tu s'allunya / d'enyorança es mor.* Perhaps they knew in their hearts they would never return to their homeland. Pablo Neruda stood on the quay waving a handkerchief until they disappeared from view. That day was engraved on his memory too, and years later he would write: *Critics can erase all my poetry if they wish. But this poem, that I recall today, cannot be erased by anyone.*

The bunks were like niches in a cemetery: the refugees had to crawl into them and lie without moving on straw mattresses. Even so, this seemed to them the height of luxury compared to the holes they had made in the wet sand of the concentration camps. There was a latrine for every fifty people and three sittings for the dining room, which were strictly respected. Coming, as most of the passengers did, from wretched conditions and near starvation, they thought this was paradise: they had not had a hot meal in months. On the boat the food was very simple but tasty, and they could have second helpings of as many vegetables as they liked. They had been tormented by lice and bedbugs, and could now wash in basins with clean water and soap. They had been prisoners of despair, and now were sailing toward freedom. There was even tobacco! And beer and spirits in a small bar for those who could afford them. Almost all the passengers volunteered to help with the work on board, from the engine room to peeling potatoes or scrubbing the deck. On their first morning at sea, Victor introduced himself to the doctors in the sick bay. They greeted him warmly, lent him a white coat, and told him that several of the refugees showed symptoms of dysentery and bronchitis; there were also a couple of cases of typhus that had escaped the health authorities' attention.

The women organized themselves to look after the children. They put up some barriers on deck to create room for a kindergarten and school. From the first day there was a nursery, games, art, exercise, and classes—an hour and a half in the morning, and an hour and a half in the afternoon. Like almost everybody else, Roser was seasick, but as soon as she could get up she began teaching the little ones to make music with a xylophone and drums made out of buckets. Once she had begun her lessons, the first mate, a Frenchman from the Communist Party, approached with the good news that Neruda had arranged for a piano and two accordions to be brought on board for her and anyone else who could play them. Some other passengers had a couple of guitars and a clarinet. From then on there was music for the children, concerts and dances for the adults, and a stirring Basque choir.

Fifty years later, when Victor Dalmau was interviewed on television about the odyssey of his exile, he said that the *Winnipeg* had been the ship of hope.

FOR VICTOR, THE SEA JOURNEY was a pleasant holiday, but Roser, who had spent several months comfortably installed in her Quaker friends' house, suffered at first from the crowded conditions and the smells. She never dreamed of mentioning it (that would have been the height of discourtesy) and she quickly became so used to them she didn't even notice. She put Marcel in a makeshift sling and went everywhere with him on her back, even while she was playing the piano. Victor took turns with the baby whenever he wasn't working in the sick bay. Roser was the only one who could breastfeed—the other malnourished mothers could count on a reliable supply of bottles for the forty babies on board. Several women offered to wash clothes and diapers for Roser so that she wouldn't spoil her hands. One peasant woman, toughened by years of hard toil, examined Roser's hands in amazement, mystified as to how she could play the piano without looking at the keys. Her husband had worked collecting cork before the war, and when Neruda had told him there were no cork oaks in Chile, he replied drily: well, there will be. The poet thought this was a splendid riposte, and so accepted him on board, together with fishermen, farm and factory workers, manual laborers, and intellectuals as well, despite instructions from his government to avoid anyone with ideas. Neruda simply ignored that instruction: it made no sense to leave behind men and women who had defended their ideals so heroically. In his heart of hearts he was hoping they would rouse his country from its insular somnolence.

The migrants stayed out on deck until very late each evening, because down below the ventilation was awful and there was little room to move around. They created a newspaper with news from the outside world; this grew steadily worse as Hitler continued to occupy more territory. After nineteen days at sea, when they learned of the nonaggression pact between the Soviet Union and Nazi Germany, many of the communists who had fought against Fascism in Spain felt badly betrayed. The political divisions that had split the Republican government persisted on board. Occasionally fights broke out due to blame and past resentments; these were rapidly stifled by other passengers before the ship's captain could intervene. Captain Pupin was a man of right-wing beliefs who had no sympathy for the passengers he was transporting, but did have an unshakable sense of duty. The Spaniards, blind to this aspect of his character, suspected he might betray them, change course, and take them back to Europe. They kept their eye on him as well as on the route the ship was taking. The first mate and most of the seamen were communists, so they also had Pupin in their sights.

Evenings were filled with recitals by Roser and the choir, dances, and games of cards and dominoes. Victor organized a chess club for those who knew how to play and those who wished to learn. Chess had rescued him from despair in the empty moments during the war and in the concentration camp, when he was at his wit's end and was tempted to lie down like a dog and let himself die. At moments like that, if he didn't have an opponent, he played from memory against himself with an invisible board and pieces. On board the *Winnipeg* there were also lectures on science and many other topics, aside from politics, because their commitment to the Chilean government was to avoid spreading any doctrines that might lead to a revolution. In other words, gentlemen, don't come and set the cat among the pigeons, as one of the few Chileans on board put it. These Chileans gave talks to the others to prepare them for what they were likely to find in Chile. Neruda had handed them all a short leaflet and a reasonably realistic letter about the country: *Spaniards: possibly of all our vast America, Chile was for you the most remote region. It was that for your ancestors as well. The Spanish conquistadors faced many dangers and much hardship. For three hundred years they lived continually at war with the indomitable Araucanians. That harsh existence has bequeathed a race that is accustomed to the difficulties of life. Chile is far from being a paradise. Our land only rewards those who work hard in it.*

This warning, and others issued by the Chileans, didn't frighten any of the refugees. The Chileans explained that the doors to their country had been opened thanks to the Popular Front government led by President Pedro Aguirre Cerda, who had defied the opposition parties and the terror campaign by the Right and the Catholic Church. "In other words, we're going to find the same enemies we had in Spain," sighed Victor. This news inspired several artists on board to paint a huge banner in homage to the Chilean president.

The migrants also learned that Chile was a poor country, with an economy based on minerals—above all copper—but that there was a lot of fertile land, thousands of kilometers of coastline for fishing, endless forests, and sparsely populated areas where they could settle and prosper. Nature there was spectacular, from the lunar desert in the north to the southern glaciers. Chileans were used to shortages and to natural disasters such as earthquakes, which often sent everything crashing to the ground, but the exiles regarded this as a lesser evil compared to what they had lived through, and what Spain would be like under Franco's rod of iron. They heard they should be prepared to repay what they were offered, because that would be a lot. Collective hardships didn't make Chileans mean, but hospitable and generous: they were always ready to open their arms and their homes. *Now it's my turn, tomorrow it'll be yours,* was their slogan. The unmarried men were also warned to beware of Chilean women: if one of them set their sights on you, you'd have no means of escape. They were seductive, strong, and bossy: a lethal combination. All of this sounded like a fantasy world to the Spaniards.

Two days into the voyage, Victor was present at the birth of a little girl in the sick bay. He had seen the most terrible wounds and death in all its guises, but he had never seen the very beginnings of life, and when the newborn was placed on her mother's breast, he could barely hide his tears. The captain made out the birth certificate in the name of Agnes America Winnipeg.

Then one morning the man who slept in one of the top bunks in Victor's dormitory didn't show up for breakfast. Thinking he must still be asleep, nobody disturbed him until Victor went to wake him for lunch and discovered he was dead. This time, the captain had to sign a death certificate. That evening, after a brief ceremony, they launched his body into the sea wrapped in a tarpaulin. His comrades formed up on deck to bid him farewell, singing one of their battle songs in unison with the Basque chorus. "You see, Victor, how life and death always go hand-in-hand," said an emotional Roser.

The couples made up for the lack of privacy by using the lifeboats. They had to take orderly turns to make love, just as they did for everything else, and while the loving couple was enjoying themselves in the boats, a friend would stand guard to ward off other passengers and distract the attention of any crew member who drew near. When they learned that Victor and Roser were newly married, more than one couple offered them their turn. They began by refusing these offers with a great show of thanks, but suspicions would have been aroused if the whole month went by without them showing the least desire to make love, and so once or twice they made their way to the assignation separately, as all the couples did, following a tacit protocol. Roser was scarlet with embarrassment, and Victor felt like an idiot, while a volunteer walked up and down the deck with Marcel in his arms.

Inside the lifeboat it was airless, uncomfortable, and stank of rotten cod, but the opportunity for Victor and Roser to be alone brought them closer together than if they had made love. Lying side by side with her head on his shoulder, they talked about those who were missing: Guillem and Carme, whom neither of them wanted to believe were dead, and speculated about the unknown land awaiting them at the end of the earth, while they planned their future. The most pressing question was to settle and find whatever work they could: after that, they could divorce and both of them be free.

Roser asked Victor to promise they would always remain friends, as he was the only family she and her son had left. She didn't feel she belonged to her family back in Santa Fe—she had only very rarely visited them since Santiago Guzman took her to live with him, and no longer had anything in common with them. Victor repeated his promise of being a good father to Marcel. "As long as I can work, you two will lack for nothing," he added. This wasn't what Roser had meant, because she felt more than capable of both looking after herself and bringing up the child, but she preferred to say nothing. They both avoided talking about their deepest feelings.

THEIR FIRST PORT OF CALL was the island of Guadeloupe, a French colony where they docked to take on food and water. Then they sailed on to Panama, where they were held up for many hours at the entrance to the canal, unable to discover what was going on until they heard through the ship's loudspeakers that they had run into an administrative hitch. This almost caused a revolt among the passengers, convinced that Captain Pupin had found a good excuse to head back to France. Victor and two other men who had a reputation for being coolheaded were delegated to find out what was going on and to negotiate a solution. An irate Pupin explained that the people who had organized the voyage were to blame because they hadn't paid the fees for using the canal, and now he was wasting time and money in this hellhole. Had they any idea how much it cost just to keep the *Winnipeg* afloat? Sorting out the problem took five days of anxious waiting, crammed aboard the ship in an oven-like heat, until finally they were given permission to enter the first lock.

Victor, Roser, and the other passengers and crew looked on in amazement at the system of sluices taking them from the Atlantic to the Pacific. The maneuvers were a miracle of precision in a space so narrow they could talk from the deck to the men working on land on both sides of the ship. Two of these men turned out to be Basque, and were entertained by the chorus of their fellow countrymen singing in Euskera. It was here in Panama that the migrants felt definitively cut off from Europe; the canal separated them from their homeland and their past.

"When will we be able to return to Spain?" Roser asked Victor.

"Soon, I hope. The Caudillo can't live forever. But everything depends on the war."

"Why is that?"

"War in Europe is imminent, Roser. It will be a war of ideologies and principles, a war between two ways of understanding the world and life, a war between democracy and Nazis and Fascists, between freedom and authoritarianism."

"Franco will align Spain with Hitler. Which side will the Soviet Union be on?"

"It's a democracy of the proletariat, but I don't trust Stalin. He could ally himself with Hitler and become an even worse tyrant than Franco."

"The Germans are invincible, Victor."

"So they say. That remains to be seen."

Those sailing for the first time in the Pacific Ocean were surprised at its name, because it wasn't in the least peaceful. Like many others who thought they had gotten over their initial seasickness, Roser found herself laid low again by the fury of the waves, but Victor was scarcely affected. While the sea was so rough he was busy in the sick bay helping with the birth of another child.

After leaving behind Colombia and Ecuador, they entered Peruvian territorial waters. The temperature dropped because they were in the southern winter, and now that the tremendous heat had passed, the passengers' spirits rose considerably. They were far from the Germans, and there was less possibility that Captain Pupin would change course.

Approaching their destination with a mixture of hope and fear, they realized from the news on the ship's telegraph that in Chile opinions were divided, that their situation was the cause of heated discussions in Congress and the press, but they also learned there were plans to help house them and find them work from not only the government but left-wing parties, trade unions, and associations of Spanish immigrants who had arrived much earlier. They would not be left stranded.

CHAPTER 6

1939–1940

Slender is our homeland
and on its naked blade
burns our delicate banner.

—PABLO NERUDA
"Yes, comrade, it's time for the garden"
THE SEA AND THE BELLS

At the end of August, the *Winnipeg* arrived at Arica, the most northerly port in Chile. It was very different from the idea the refugees had of a South American country: there were no exuberant jungles or luminous, palm tree–lined beaches—it looked more like the Sahara Desert. They were told it had a temperate climate and was the driest inhabited region on earth. From the sea they could make out the coastline and a chain of purple mountains in the distance resembling brushstrokes of watercolor against a clear lavender sky. The ship anchored out to sea and shortly afterward a boat appeared, bringing officials from Immigration and the Consular Department of the Foreign Ministry. The captain gave up his cabin so that they could interview the passengers, provide them with identity papers and visas, and tell them which region of the country they were to reside in, according to their skills. In the narrow compartment, Victor and Roser, with Marcel in their arms, presented themselves to a young consular official named Matias Eyzaguirre, who was busy stamping all the visas and adding his signature.

"It states here that your place of residence will be in the province of Talca," Matias explained. "But the idea that you're told where you should settle is some nonsense dreamed up by the Immigration people. In Chile there's absolute freedom of movement. Don't pay any attention to it, go wherever you like."

"Are you Basque, señor? From your name, I mean . . ." Victor asked him.

"My great-grandparents were Basque. Here we are all Chilean. Welcome to Chile."

Matias Eyzaguirre had traveled by train to Arica to receive the ship, which arrived several days late due to the problem in Panama. He was one of the youngest members of the Consular Department, and had to accompany his boss. Neither of them was exactly pleased, because they were completely opposed to the policy of accepting the refugees into Chile. They considered them to be a mob of Reds, atheists, and possibly criminals, who were coming to take jobs from Chileans just at a moment when there was terrible unemployment and the country hadn't yet recovered from the Great Depression or the recent earthquake—but they were determined to do their duty. When they reached the port, they'd boarded a rickety boat that struggled through the waves out to the *Winnipeg*, where they had to climb a rope ladder swaying in the wind, pulled up by some very rough French sailors. Once on board, Captain Pupin received them with a bottle of cognac and Cuban cigars.

The officials had heard that Pupin had undertaken this journey against his will and that he detested his human cargo, but he surprised them. It turned out that after sharing his vessel with the Spaniards for a month, Pupin had gradually altered his opinion of them, even though his political convictions were still intact. "These people have suffered a great deal, gentlemen. They are upright, disciplined, and respectful, and are coming to your country ready and willing to work and rebuild their lives," he told them.

Matias Eyzaguirre came from a family that considered itself aristocratic, and had been brought up in a Catholic, conservative background. He was against immigration, but like Captain Pupin, when he came face-to-face with the individual refugees—men, women, and children—his views changed. He had been educated at a religious school, and lived his life protected by the privileges his clan enjoyed. His grandfather and father were Supreme Court judges, and two of his brothers were lawyers, so he studied law as his family expected, even though he was not cut out for the profession. He doggedly attended university for a couple of years, and then entered the Foreign Ministry thanks to his family connections. He started from the bottom and by the age of twenty-four, when he found himself stamping visas on the *Winnipeg*, he had already shown he had the makings of a good public servant and diplomat. In a couple of months he was being sent to Paraguay on his first foreign mission, and he was hoping to do so married, or at least engaged, to his cousin Ofelia del Solar.

The documentation complete, a dozen passengers were taken off the ship, as there was work for them in the north, and then the *Winnipeg* sailed on toward the south of Neruda's "long petal." The Spanish exiles were agog with silent expectation. On September 2, they glimpsed the outline of Valparaiso, their final destination, and at nightfall the ship dropped anchor outside the harbor. The passengers' anxiety came close to collective hysteria: more than two thousand eager faces crowded onto the upper deck, waiting for the moment to set foot on this unknown land. However, the port authorities decided that the disembarkation should take place the next day, with early morning light and a calmer atmosphere.

Thousands of twinkling lights in the port and dwellings on the hills of Valparaiso competed with the stars: it was impossible to tell where the promised land ended and the sky began. Valparaiso was an idiosyncratic city of stairways, elevators, and narrow streets wide enough only for donkeys. Houses hung dizzily from steep hillsides; like almost all ports, it was full of stray dogs, was poor and dirty, a place of traders, sailors, and vices, and yet it was marvelous. From the ship it shone like a mythical, diamond-studded city. Nobody went to sleep that night: they all stayed out on deck admiring the magical spectacle and counting the hours. In the years to come, Victor would always remember that night as one of the most beautiful in his life. The next morning, the *Winnipeg* finally docked in Chile, with the enormous banner of President Pedro Aguirre Cerda and a Chilean flag draped from its side.

Nobody on board was expecting the welcome they received. They had been warned so often about the Right's negative campaign, the Catholic Church's uncompromising opposition, as well as the proverbial Chilean reserve, that at first they didn't understand what was going on in the port. The crowds crammed behind barriers with placards and flags of Spain, the Republic, Euskadi, and Catalonia, cheering them in a deafening roar of welcome. A band played the national anthems of Chile and the Spanish Republic, and hundreds of voices joined in. The Chilean one summed up in a few rather sentimental verses the hospitable spirit and vocation for freedom of the country receiving them: *Sweet fatherland, accept the vows given by Chile on your altars, that you will either be the tomb of the free, or the refuge against oppression.*

On deck, battle-hardened combatants who had undergone so many brutal challenges wept openly. At nine, the disembarkation began in single file down a gangway. On shore, each refugee first had to go to a Health Department tent to be vaccinated, and then fell into the arms of Chile, as Victor Dalmau expressed it many years later, when he was able to thank Pablo Neruda personally.

September 3, 1939, the day of the Spanish exiles' splendid arrival in Chile, the Second World War broke out in Europe.

FELIPE DEL SOLAR HAD made the journey to the port of Valparaiso the day before the arrival of the *Winnipeg* because he wanted to be present at what he called a "historic event." According to his pals in the Club of the Enraged, he was taking things too far. They said his enthusiasm for the refugees was less because he had a kind heart and more because he wanted to annoy his father and his clan.

Felipe spent most of the day greeting the newcomers, mingling with all those who had gone to receive them, and talking to acquaintances he met. Among the excited crowd on the quayside were members of the government; representatives of the workers and the Catalan and Basque communities with whom he had been in contact in recent months to prepare for the arrival of the *Winnipeg*; artists, intellectuals, journalists, and politicians. Also present was a doctor from Valparaiso, Salvador Allende, a Socialist Party leader who a few days later would be named health minister. Despite being so young, he was prominent in political circles, admired by some, rejected by others, but respected by all. He had taken part more than once in the gatherings of the Enraged, and when he recognized Felipe del Solar in the crowd, he waved to him from afar. Felipe had managed to secure an invitation to board the special train transporting the newcomers from Valparaiso to Santiago. That gave him several hours to hear firsthand what had happened in Spain; until then he knew only what was reported in the press and what he had gleaned from the testimonies of a few individuals, such as Neruda. Seen from Chile, the Spanish Civil War had been something so remote it was as if it had occurred in another time.

The train traveled without stopping, but slowed down whenever it came to a railway station, because at each one there was a crowd ready to greet the refugees with flags and songs, as well as meat pies or cakes that they ran with along the tracks to pass in through the carriage windows. In Santiago, such a dense, frantic multitude was waiting for them at the main station it was impossible to move; many of them had climbed the columns and were hanging from the roof beams, shouting greetings, singing, and throwing flowers in the air. The police had to force a way through so that the Spaniards could leave the station and attend the dinner in their honor (with a resoundingly Chilean menu) prepared by the Refugee Committee.

On the train, Felipe del Solar had heard many different stories, linked by a common thread of misfortune. He ended up between two carriages, smoking a cigarette with Victor Dalmau, who gave him his view of the war from the perspective of the blood and death he had witnessed in the first-aid stations and evacuation hospitals.

"What we suffered in Spain is a taste of what people are going to suffer all over Europe," Victor concluded. "The Germans tested out their weaponry on us; they left entire towns reduced to rubble. It will be worse still in the rest of Europe."

"For the moment, only England and France are standing up to Hitler, but they're bound to find allies they can count on. The Americans will have to make up their minds."

"And what will Chile's position be?" asked Roser, who had come out to join them, her child on her back in the same sling she had been using for months.

"This is Roser, my wife," said Victor, presenting her.

"Pleased to meet you, señora. Felipe del Solar, at your service. Your husband has told me about you. Madam is a pianist, isn't she?"

"Yes, but please don't be so formal," said Roser, repeating her question.

Felipe told her about the large German colony established in the country for several decades, and mentioned the Chilean Nazis, but added there was nothing to fear, and that Chile would undoubtedly stay neutral in the war. He showed them the list of industrialists and businessmen willing to offer employment to Spaniards depending on their skills, but none of these suited Victor. He would be unable to dedicate himself to the only thing he knew—medicine—without a diploma. Felipe advised him to enroll at the University of Chile, which was free and very prestigious, where he could study. They might possibly recognize the courses he had taken in Barcelona and the knowledge acquired during the war, but even so it would take him years to obtain his title.

"First of all, I need to earn my living," replied Victor. "I'll try to find a night job so that I can study by day."

"I need work as well," observed Roser.

"It'll be easy for you. We always need pianists down here."

"That's what Pablo Neruda said," Victor added.

"For now, you're to come and live with me," Felipe insisted. He had two empty rooms and, in preparation for the arrival of the *Winnipeg*, had taken on more domestic staff. He now had a cook and two maids, so as to avoid any further conflict with Juana. Her refusal to hand over the keys to the empty rooms in the family home had given rise to the only argument they had had in more than twenty years, but they loved each other too much to allow that to force them apart. When the telegram arrived from his father in Paris making it clear that no Red was to set foot in his house, Felipe had already decided to organize things to receive Spaniards under his own roof. The Dalmau family seemed ideal.

"I'm really grateful, but I understand the Refugee Committee has found us lodging in a boardinghouse and is going to pay the first six months," said Victor.

"I have a piano, and spend all my days at work. You'll be able to practice without anyone disturbing you, Roser."

That clinched it. The house was in a neighborhood that, to the new guests, seemed as grand as the best parts of Barcelona. From the outside it was elegant, and was almost empty on the inside, because Felipe had bought only the most indispensable pieces of furniture: he detested his parents' fussy style. There were no drapes on the beveled glass windows, no rugs on the parquet floors; there were no flower pots or plants to be seen, and the walls were bare. But despite this lack of decoration, the house had an air of undeniable refinement. The Dalmaus were offered two bedrooms, a bathroom, and the exclusive use of one of the maids, to whom Felipe assigned the role of nanny. Marcel would have someone to look after him while his parents were at work.

Two days later, Felipe took Roser to a radio station run by a friend of his, and that same evening they invited her to play the piano to accompany a program. This advertised her talent as a soloist and music teacher, and meant she would never be short of work. He also found Victor a job at the bar of the Equestrian Club thanks to the same networking system, where merit was much less important than connections. Victor's shift was from seven at night to two in the morning, which would allow him to study as soon as he could put his name down for the School of Medicine. Felipe said that would be no problem, because the president of the school was a relative of the Vizcarras, his mother's family. Victor began hauling crates of beer and washing glasses, until he learned to distinguish between different wines and to prepare cocktails, when he was put behind the bar. He had to wear a dark suit, white shirt, and bow tie, and only had one change of underclothes and the suit he had bought with Aitor Ibarra's money when he escaped from Argeles-sur-Mer, but Felipe put his entire wardrobe at Victor's disposal.

Juana Nancucheo held out for a week without asking about Felipe's lodgers, but in the end her curiosity got the better of her pride and so, armed with a tray of freshly baked bread rolls, she went to see what was going on. The door was opened by the new nanny, with the baby in her arms. "The master and mistress aren't at home," she said. Juana pushed her aside and strode in. She inspected everything from top to bottom, and was able to verify that the Reds, as Don Isidro called them, were quite clean and tidy. She looked into the pans in the kitchen and gave orders to the nanny, who she thought looked too young and dumb. "Where's the mother of the brat traipsing about? A fine thing to have children and abandon them. But I must say, little Marcel is sweet. Big eyes, nice and plump, and not shy at all: he threw his arms around my neck and tugged on my braid," she later told Felipe.

IN PARIS ON SEPTEMBER 4, 1939, Isidro del Solar was getting his wife used to the idea of the young ladies' college in London where he had already enrolled Ofelia, when they were caught unaware by the news that war had been declared. The conflict had been looming for months, but Isidro had managed to put the collective apprehension out of his mind, lest it interfere with his vacation. The press was exaggerating. The world was always on the verge of some military confrontation or other: what need was there to get into a state about this one?

But he only had to open the door of their suite to realize the seriousness of what was going on. Outside there was frenzied activity: hotel staff running to and fro with suitcases and trunks, guests thronging the exit, ladies with their lap dogs, men fighting over taxis, confused children wailing. The streets were in turmoil as well: half the city seemed to want to escape to the countryside until the situation became clearer. The traffic was at a standstill because there were so many vehicles loaded to the roof trying to force their way through rushing pedestrians; loudspeakers were blaring out urgent instructions, while police on horseback tried to keep order. Isidro del Solar was forced to accept that his plans to return calmly to London to drop off his daughter, pick up the latest model automobile he was shipping to Chile, and then embark on the *Reina del Pacifico* had gone up in smoke. He had to get out of Europe as quickly as possible.

He called the Chilean ambassador in France, then had to wait anxiously for three days until the legation found passages for them on the last departing Chilean ship, a cargo boat full to bursting with three hundred passengers instead of the regulation fifty. In order to make room for the del Solar family, the authorities were about to disembark a Jewish family who had paid for their tickets and bribed a Chilean consul with their grandmother's jewels to obtain visas. Already, some ships had refused to accept Jews, and liners had returned with them to their point of departure because no country would accept them. This family, like several others among the passengers, had fled Germany after suffering dreadful harassment and had been forbidden to take anything of value. For them, leaving Europe was a question of life or death.

Ofelia heard them pleading with the captain and volunteered (without consulting her parents) to let them have her cabin, even though this meant sharing a narrow bunk with her mother. One has to adapt in times of crisis, Isidro said, but he was unhappy about being thrown together with people of different social standing, the sixty Jews, the awful food that was simply rice and more rice, the lack of enough water for a bath, and the fear of sailing without lights to be invisible to enemy planes. "I don't know how we're going to survive a month crammed like sardines in this rust bucket," he would complain, while his wife prayed and his daughter kept busy entertaining the children and drawing portraits and scenes of shipboard life. Soon Ofelia, prompted by her brother Felipe's generosity, gave some of her clothes to the Jews who had boarded with nothing more than what they were standing in. "All that money spent in shops only for that child to give away what we bought. Thank heavens her trousseau is safely in the trunks in the hold," muttered Isidro, taken aback by this gesture from his daughter, who had always seemed to him so frivolous. It was only months later that Ofelia learned that the Second World War had saved her from the ladies' college.

In normal times, the voyage to Chile took twenty-seven days, but their ship took twenty-two, traveling at full speed, dodging floating mines and avoiding warships from both navies. In theory they were safe because they flew the neutral flag of Chile, but in practice there could be a tragic misunderstanding and they could be sunk by the Germans or the Allies.

In the Panama Canal they met with extraordinary protective measures against any sabotage: nets and divers searching for any possible bombs in the locks. For Laura and Isidro del Solar the heat and mosquitoes were pure torture, the discomfort unbearable, and the tension produced by the war had their stomachs in knots. For Ofelia, on the other hand, the experience was more rewarding than the journey on the *Reina del Pacifico*, with its air-conditioning and orgies of chocolate.

Felipe was waiting for them in Valparaiso with his car and a rented van to carry all their baggage, driven by the family chauffeur. He was surprised at seeing his sister again, as she had always seemed to him shallow-minded, prissy, and trivial. She seemed older and more serious; she had grown up, and her features were better defined—she was no longer the doll-faced girl who had left Chile, but an interesting young woman. If she hadn't been his sister, he would have said she was very pretty. Matias Eyzaguirre was at the port as well, with his car and a bouquet of roses for his reluctant fiancée. Like Felipe, he was impressed when he saw Ofelia. She had always been attractive, but now she seemed to him so beautiful he was struck by the terrible thought that some other more intelligent or richer man might snatch her from him. He decided to bring his plans forward. He would tell her at once of his first diplomatic mission, and as soon as they were on their own he would offer her his great-grandmother's diamond ring. He was sweating so nervously his shirt was soaked: who could tell how this impetuous young woman would react at the prospect of getting married and going to live in Paraguay?

They passed a group of about twenty young people bearing swastika armbands protesting against the Jews disembarking the boat and hurling insults at all those who had come to welcome them.

"Poor people, they've escaped from Germany and look what they find when they get here," said Ofelia.

"Don't pay these protesters any attention. The police will disperse them," Matias reassured her.

During the four-hour journey up a winding dirt road to Santiago, Felipe, who was with his parents in one of the cars, had time to tell them how the Spaniards were adapting wonderfully: in less than a month the majority had found somewhere to live and jobs. Many Chilean families had taken them in: it was embarrassing that with half a dozen empty bedrooms they weren't doing the same. "I know that you've got some atheist communists in your house," said Isidro. "You're going to regret it."

Felipe pointed out that they were definitely not communists, possibly anarchists, and as for being atheists, that remained to be seen. He told them about the Dalmau family and how decent and well educated they were, and about the boy, who was in love with Juana. Isidro and Laura already knew that the faithful Juana Nancucheo had betrayed them, that she went every day to see Marcel in order to supervise his meals and take him to the park to get some sun with Leonardo, because as she put it, his mother was always out on the streets and never at home, using the piano as an excuse, and her husband spent all his time in a bar. Felipe was amazed that his parents had obtained so much information in mid-ocean.

THAT DECEMBER MATIAS EYZAGUIRRE left for Paraguay to serve an ambassador who was despotic toward his subordinates and servile toward those of a higher social rank. Matias entered into this second category. He left alone, as Ofelia had rejected his ring on the pretext that she had promised her father to stay single until she was twenty-one. Matias was well aware that if she had wanted to get married, nobody would have been able to stop her, but he resigned himself to wait, with all the risks that implied. Ofelia had her choice of admirers, but his future in-laws assured him they would keep an eye on her. "Give the girl time, she's very immature. I'm going to pray for you both, for you to be married and very happy," Doña Laura promised him. Matias thought he could win Ofelia over once and for all with a constant stream of correspondence, a flood of love letters: that was what the mail was for, and he could be much more eloquent when he wrote than when he spoke. Patience. He had loved Ofelia since they were children; he hadn't the slightest doubt that they were made for each other.

As he did every year, a few days before Christmas, Isidro del Solar had a suckling pig brought from their country property, and hired a butcher to slaughter it in the most distant yard behind the house, out of sight of Laura, Ofelia, and Baby. Juana supervised the transformation of the hapless beast into meat for the barbecue, sausages, chops, ham, and bacon. She was also in charge of the Christmas Eve dinner for the whole family, as well as of making a crib in the hearth with plaster figures brought from Italy.

Early on Christmas Eve, when she went to take Don Isidro his coffee in the library, she paused in front of him.

"Is something wrong, Juana?"

"In my opinion, we ought to invite *niño* Felipe's communists."

Isidro del Solar raised his eyes from the newspaper and stared at her in amazement.

"I mean for little Marcel's sake."

"Who?"

"You know who I'm talking about, *patron*. The little brat, the communists' child."

"Communists don't give a damn about Christmas, Juana. They don't believe in God, and couldn't care less about the baby Jesus."

Juana stifled a cry. Felipe had explained to her a lot of communist nonsense about equality and the class struggle, but she had never heard of anyone who didn't believe in God and couldn't care less about the baby Jesus. It took her a minute to recover her voice.

"That may be so, *patron,* but that's not the brat's fault. As I see it, they should dine here on Christmas Eve. I've already told *niño* Felipe and he agrees. So do Señora Laura and little Ofelia."

SO IT WAS THAT the Dalmaus spent their first Christmas in Chile with the extended del Solar family. Roser wore the same dress she had worn for her wedding in Perpignan, navy blue with white flowers around the neckline. She gathered her hair up in a net with black beads and a jet clasp Carme had given her when she learned Roser was expecting a child by her son Guillem. "You're my daughter-in-law now, there's no need for any paperwork," she had told Roser. Victor had on one of Felipe's three-piece suits that was a little baggy and short in the leg.

When they arrived at the house on Calle Mar del Plata, Juana took charge of Marcel and swept him off to play with Leonardo, while Felipe propelled the Dalmaus into the big drawing room for the obligatory presentations. He had told them that in Chile the social classes were like a mille-feuille cake, easy to reach the bottom but almost impossible to reach the top of, because money could not buy pedigree. The only exceptions were talent, as in the case of Pablo Neruda, and the beauty of certain women. That had been the case with Ofelia's grandmother, the daughter of a modest English shopkeeper, a beauty with the bearing of a queen who came to improve the race, as her descendants, the Vizcarras, claimed. If the Dalmaus had been Chilean, they would never have been invited to the del Solars' table, but for the moment, as exotic foreigners, they were floating in limbo. If things went well for them, they would end up in one of the numerous subdivisions of the Chilean middle class. Felipe warned them that in his parents' house they would be observed like wild animals in a circus by people who were conservative, religious, and intolerant, but once that initial curiosity had been satisfied they would be welcomed with the obligatory Chilean hospitality.

And so it proved. Nobody asked them about the Civil War or the reasons for their exile—partly out of ignorance (according to Felipe they only ever read the society pages of *El Mercurio*) but also out of kindness: they didn't want to upset the guests. Victor suddenly relapsed into the adolescent shyness he thought he had left behind long ago, and remained standing in a corner of the French-style room between two Louis XV armchairs upholstered in moss-green silk, speaking as little as possible. Roser, on the other hand, was in her element, and didn't need to be asked twice to play cheerful tunes on the piano, accompanied by several of the guests who had drunk one glass too many.

It was Ofelia who was most impressed by the Dalmaus. What little she knew about them was based on Juana's comments, and she had imagined a pair of gloomy Soviet officials, even though Matias had spoken of his pleasant experience with Spaniards, in general, when he had to stamp their visas on the *Winnipeg*. Roser Dalmau was a young woman who radiated confidence but without the least hint of vanity or social climbing. She explained to a gaggle of ladies, all dressed in black with pearl necklaces (the uniform of distinguished Chilean matrons), that she had been a goatherd, a baker, and a seamstress before she made a living from the piano. She said this so naturally it was celebrated as if she had done all of it on a whim. Then she sat at the piano and completely won them over.

Ofelia felt a mixture of envy and shame when she compared her existence as an unenlightened, idle young woman to that of Roser, who Felipe had told her was only a couple of years her senior, but had lived three lives already. She had been born into poverty, had survived a war on the losing side, and suffered the desolation of exile; she was a mother and wife, had crossed the seas and reached the ends of the earth without a penny to her name, and yet she was afraid of nothing. Ofelia wished she could be worthy, strong, and brave—she wished she could be Roser.

As if reading her thoughts, Roser came over, and the two women spent some time on their own, smoking out on the balcony to escape the heat. Roser thought that to celebrate Christmas in the middle of summer made no sense. Ofelia surprised herself by confessing to this stranger her dream of going to Paris or Buenos Aires and dedicating herself to painting, and how crazy that was because she had the misfortune of being a woman, a prisoner of her family and social convention. She added with a mocking smile that disguised her impulse to cry that the worst obstacle was being financially dependent: she would never be able to earn a living with her art. "If it's your vocation to paint, sooner or later that's what you'll do, so the sooner the better. Why does it have to be Paris or Buenos Aires? Discipline is all you need. It's like the piano, isn't it? It only rarely brings in enough to live on, but you have to try," argued Roser.

That evening, more than once Ofelia felt Victor Dalmau's ardent gaze following her around the room, but since he remained in his corner and made no attempt to approach her, she whispered to Felipe for him to make the introductions.

"This is my friend Victor, from Barcelona. He was a militiaman in the Civil War."

"In fact, I was a medical auxiliary; I never had to fire a gun," said Victor.

"A militiaman?" queried Ofelia, who had never heard that term before.

"That was what the Republican fighters were called before they joined the regular army," Victor explained.

Felipe left them on their own, and Ofelia spent some time trying to get Victor to talk, but she was unable to discover anything they had in common, and received little encouragement from him. She asked about the bar, because Juana had mentioned it, and managed to drag out of him the fact that he wanted to complete the medical studies he had begun in Spain. In the end, irritated by the lengthy pauses, she left him.

Soon afterward, she caught him staring at her once more, and his boldness annoyed her, although she too was secretly observing him, fascinated by his ascetic face, aquiline nose, and prominent cheekbones, his veined hands with long fingers; his wiry, hard body. She would like to paint him, she thought, to do his portrait in black and white brushstrokes on a gray background, a full-length picture with him holding a rifle, and naked. The thought made her blush; she had never painted anyone naked, and had learned what little she knew of male anatomy in European museums, where most of the statues were mutilated or had parts covered by a fig leaf. Even the most daring were disappointing, like Michelangelo's *David*, with his enormous hands and baby peepee. She had never seen Matias naked, but they had fondled each other enough for her to guess what was concealed beneath his trousers. She would have to see to judge. Why did the Spaniard have a limp? It could be a heroic war wound.

Victor was just as curious as Ofelia. He concluded they came from different planets, and that this young woman was of another species, unlike any woman he had met before. War distorts everything, including memory. Possibly in the past there had been girls like Ofelia: fresh, kept from the ugliness of the world, with spotless lives like blank pages where their destinies could be written in elegant handwriting without a single crossing-out, but he couldn't remember anyone of the sort. Her beauty intimidated him: he was used to women prematurely marked by poverty or war. She seemed tall, because everything about her was vertical, from her long neck to her slender feet, but when she came over he realized she only reached his chin. Her thick hair was various shades of wood color, tied up with a black velvet ribbon; her mouth was constantly half-open, as if she had too many teeth, and was painted ruby red. Her most striking feature was her blue eyes, set far apart and with the distant expression of somebody staring out to sea from beneath arched brows. He decided it must be because she was slightly cross-eyed.

After dinner, the whole family, together with the children and servants, went in procession to Midnight Mass in the local church. The del Solars were surprised that the supposedly atheist Dalmaus accompanied them, and that Roser followed the rite in Latin, as the nuns had taught her. On the way, Felipe caught Ofelia by the arm and kept her back so that he could speak freely. "If I catch you flirting with Dalmau, I'll tell Father, understood? We'll see how he reacts to you setting your cap at a married man, an immigrant without a penny to his name." She feigned surprise at his warning, as if the idea had never occurred to her. Felipe did not take Victor to task in the same way because he didn't want to humiliate him, but decided to prevent him seeing his sister again at all costs. The attraction between the two of them was so overpowering that others must have noticed it as well.

He was right. Later on that night, when Victor went to say good night to Roser, who slept in the other bedroom with Marcel, she advised him not to fall into that temptation.

"That girl is out of your reach. Put her out of your mind, Victor. You'll never be part of her social circle, let alone her family."

"That's the least of it. There are far greater obstacles than social class."

"Yes, that's true. Apart from being poor and morally suspect in the eyes of that inward-looking clan, you're not exactly personable."

"You're forgetting the main thing: I have a wife and child."

"We can get divorced."

"In this country there is no divorce, and according to Felipe, there never will be."

"You mean we're trapped forever!" Roser exclaimed in horror.

"You could have put it more delicately. As long as we're living here, we'll be legally married, but when we return to Spain we'll get divorced and that's that."

"That could be a long time away. Meanwhile, we've got to settle here. I want Marcel to grow up as a Chilean."

"As a Chilean, if you wish, but our home will always be Catalan, and proud of it."

"Franco has forbidden speaking Catalan," she reminded him.

"For exactly that reason, Roser."

CHAPTER 7

1940–1941

I have slept with you
the whole night long
while the dark earth turns
with the living and the dead.

——PABLO NERUDA
"Night on the Island"
THE CAPTAIN'S VERSES

VICTOR DALMAU ENROLLED AT THE UNIVERSITY
to complete his medical studies thanks to the fact that
its president was a Vizcarra, and to the infallible system
of social connections so common in Chile. Felipe del
Solar introduced him to Salvador Allende, a co-
founder of the Socialist Party, the president's right-
hand man, and the minister of health. Allende had
followed with passionate interest the triumph of the
Republic in Spain, the defeat of democracy, and Franco's dictatorship, as though sensing an echo of his future. Allende listened to the brief account Victor
Dalmau gave him about war and exile, and guessed the
rest. It took him a single telephone call to get the
School of Medicine to validate the courses Victor had
taken in Spain and allow him to complete his studies in
three years to obtain his professional diploma.

The courses were intensive. Victor knew as much as his professors about practice, but very little about theory: it was one thing to mend broken bones, and quite another to be able to identify them by name. He went to the minister's office to thank him, with no idea how he could repay him. Allende asked if he knew how to play chess, and challenged Victor to a game on the board he kept in his office. The minister ended up losing good-humoredly. "If you want to repay me, come and play whenever I call you," Allende told him by way of goodbye. Chess became the basis of the friendship between the two men.

Roser, Victor, and the boy lived with Felipe for several months, until they could afford to rent somewhere else. They refused any aid from the committee, because others needed it more. Felipe wanted them to stay on at his house, but they felt they had already been given more than enough, and it was time for them to stand on their own feet. The person worst affected by this change was Juana Nancucheo, because now she had to catch a tram to see Marcel.

The friendship between Victor and Felipe continued, although it was hard to maintain as they belonged to different circles and were both extremely busy. Realizing how much he had to offer, Felipe tried to get Victor to join the Club of the Enraged, whose meetings were gradually losing their intellectual tone and becoming increasingly frivolous, but it was plain Victor had nothing in common with those friends of Felipe's. On the only occasion Victor attended the group, he gave monosyllabic answers to the bombardment of questions about his hazardous life and the war in Spain. The members of the club quickly grew tired of getting only crumbs of information out of him, and proceeded to ignore him. In order to avoid him encountering Ofelia again, Felipe also didn't take him to his parents' house.

Victor's night job in the bar barely paid him enough to live on, but it helped him learn that curious trade and to study the customers. This was how he came to know Jordi Moline, a Catalan widower who had emigrated to Chile twenty years earlier and owned a shoe factory. He would often come and sit at the bar to drink and chat in his mother tongue. During one of the long nights when he sat cradling his glass of spirits, he told Victor that manufacturing shoes was boring, however profitable, and now that he was on his own and growing old, the moment had come to do as he wanted. He suggested they open a Catalan-style tavern: he would put up the money initially, and Victor would contribute his experience. Victor replied that medicine was his vocation, not running a tavern, but later that night when he told Roser about the Catalan's bizarre proposal, she thought it was a splendid idea: better to have one's own business than to work for other people—and if it wasn't successful, they wouldn't have lost much, because the shoemaker was risking the capital.

The tavern was inspired by the Rocinante, the Barcelona inn where Victor's father played dominoes until his final days. They set up in a hole-in-the-wall with barrels for tables, hams and strings of garlic hanging from the ceiling, and a smell of sour wine, but it was in a good spot in the center of Santiago. Roser became the bookkeeper, since she had a better head for figures and knowledge of mathematics than either of the two partners. She would arrive dragging Marcel along and install him with a toy or two in a corner behind the counter, while she did the accounts. Not so much as a single glass of beer escaped her meticulous eye. They found a cook capable of preparing Catalan sausages with diced eggplant, anchovies and squid with garlic, tuna with tomato, and other delicacies from the old country, and soon had a faithful clientele of Spanish immigrants. They named the tavern the Winnipeg.

In the eighteen months that they had been married, Victor and Roser developed a perfect relationship as brother and sister and comrades. They shared everything apart from a bed: Roser because of the memory of Guillem, and Victor to avoid trouble. Roser had decided that love only strikes once, and that she had had her share. For his part, Victor depended on her to fight his phantoms: she was his best friend and he came to love her more and more as he grew to know her. From time to time he wished he could cross the invisible frontier between them, take her by the waist in a carefree moment, and kiss her, but that would betray his brother and could have disastrous consequences. One day they would need to have the discussion about how long mourning lasts, how long the dead are allowed to haunt us. Roser would decide when that moment arrived, as she decided almost everything: until then his thoughts strayed to Ofelia del Solar, like someone wasting their time imagining they're going to win the lottery. He had fallen in love with her at first sight with adolescent intensity, but as he didn't see her again, love rapidly became a myth to him. In his daydreams he would conjure up the details of her face, the way she moved, her dress, her voice. Ofelia was a flickering mirage that vanished at the slightest hesitation. He loved her theoretically, like the troubadours of olden days.

From the outset, Victor and Roser adopted a system of trust and mutual aid. They agreed that Marcel would be the most important thing for them until he reached eighteen. Victor scarcely remembered that Marcel was not his son but his nephew, but Roser always bore it in mind, and that was why she loved Victor as much as he loved the boy. The money they earned was stored in a cigar box for their shared expenses. Roser took charge of their finances. Each month she divided the funds into four envelopes, one for each week, and they kept strictly to that amount, even if they had to eat beans and nothing but beans. Lentils were out of the question: Victor had grown tired of them in the French concentration camp. If there was anything left over, they took the child out for an ice cream.

They were completely different, which was why they got on so well. Roser never gave in to the sentimental attitude of many exiles, refusing to look back or idealize a Spain that no longer existed. There was a reason why they had left. Her resolute sense of reality saved her from frustrated desires, pointless reproaches, deep regrets, and the vice of constantly complaining. She was oblivious to fatigue and despair: she had a tank-like determination to crush any obstacles in her way. Her plans were crystal clear. There was no way she was going to continue playing the piano for radio soap operas, where it was always the same repertoire: music that was sad, romantic, bellicose, or sinister, depending on the plot. She was thoroughly fed up with the march from *Aida* and *Blue Danube*. Her main object in life was serious music; to hell with the rest. But she had to wait. As soon as the tavern provided them with a livelihood and Victor graduated, she would enroll at the Faculty of Music. She was going to follow the path of her mentor and become a teacher and composer like Marcel Lluis Dalmau.

Her husband, on the other hand, was often overwhelmed by sad memories and the pangs of nostalgia. Only Roser was aware of these dark moments, because Victor continued to attend medical school and work in the tavern in the evening as usual. Yet he went around closed in on himself with the absent air of a somnambulist, not so much from the tiredness of someone who only sleeps in short bursts standing on his feet as horses do, but because he felt worn down, caught in a web of responsibilities. Whereas Roser imagined a bright future, he saw shadows all around them. "At twenty-seven I'm already an old man," he would say, but whenever Roser heard that, she would berate him fiercely. "Why don't you have more guts? We've all been through hard times. If you keep complaining you won't be able to appreciate what we have: there's a ghastly war on the other side of the ocean, and yet here we are living in peace with full stomachs. And I'm telling you we're going to be here for a long time, because the Caudillo, curse him, is in very good health and evil people lead long lives."

And yet at night, if she heard him crying out in his sleep, Roser softened. She would go and wake him up, slip into his bed, and hug him like a mother, letting him unburden himself of his nightmares of amputated limbs and smashed chests, shrapnel, dripping bayonets, pools of blood, and graves littered with bones.

IT WAS A YEAR and two months before Ofelia and Victor met again. During that time, Matias Eyzaguirre rented a mansion on one of Asuncion's main streets, which was hardly appropriate to his position as second-in-command or his salary as a public servant. The ambassador regarded this as impertinent and never missed an opportunity to make a sarcastic comment. Matias filled the house with a shipment of furniture and decorations sent from Chile, and his mother made a special trip there to train the domestic staff, which proved difficult as they spoke only Guarani. His recalcitrant fiancée had finally agreed to marry him, thanks to his constant stream of letters and the efficacy of the Masses and novenas said by his future mother-in-law, Doña Laura.

Early in December, when Ofelia turned twenty-one, Matias traveled to Santiago for the official engagement, which took place in a ceremony in the garden of the del Solars' house with the two families' closest relatives, about two hundred people altogether. The wedding rings were blessed by Father Vicente Urbina, Doña Laura's nephew. He was a charismatic, scheming, and energetic priest, better suited to a colonel's uniform than a cassock. Although not yet forty, Urbina exerted a fearsome influence on his ecclesiastical superiors as well as on his congregation in the fashionable heights of Santiago. It was a privilege having him in the family. The date for the wedding was set for September the following year, the month for elegant nuptials. Matias placed the antique diamond ring on the fourth finger of her right hand, as a sign to any possible rival that the young woman was taken; he would transfer it to the other hand on the day of their marriage, to demonstrate that she was his once and for all. He wanted to tell her in great detail about the preparations he had made to receive her like a queen in Paraguay, but she interrupted him in a rather offhand way: "What's the hurry, Matias? Lots of things could happen between now and September." Alarmed, he asked what things she was referring to, and she said that the Second World War might reach Chile, there could be another earthquake, or a catastrophe in Paraguay. "In other words, nothing that concerns us," Matias concluded.

Ofelia enjoyed this period of waiting and anticipation by laying out her trousseau in trunks, wrapped with tissue paper and sprigs of lavender, sending tablecloths, sheets, and towels to her aunt Teresa's convent to be embroidered with her initials and those of Matias intertwined, being invited by her female friends to tea at the Hotel Crillon, repeatedly trying on her wedding dress and going-away outfit, and learning the rudiments of household management from her sisters. She showed a surprising aptitude for this, given her reputation as a lazy, disorganized young woman. There were nine months to go before the wedding, but she was already thinking up ways of lengthening this period of truce. She was afraid of taking the irrevocable step of marrying for the rest of her life, living with Matias in another country where she didn't know a soul, far from her family and surrounded by Guarani Indians, and of having children and ending up repressed and frustrated like her mother and sisters. And yet the alternative was worse. To stay a spinster meant depending on the generosity of her father and Felipe, and becoming a social pariah. The possibility of working to earn a living was a dream as absurd as that of going to Paris to paint in a Montmartre attic.

She was planning a whole rosary of excuses for postponing the wedding, without ever imagining that heaven would send her the only true one: Victor Dalmau. When she bumped into him two months after becoming engaged and seven before the date fixed for the wedding, she discovered the love she had read about in novels, the kind of love she had never felt for Matias despite all his stubborn faithfulness. At the end of Santiago's hot, dry summer, when all those who could migrated en masse to the beach or countryside, Victor and Ofelia met in the street. The encounter paralyzed them both, as if they had been caught out; an eternal minute went by before she took the lead and greeted him with a smothered, barely audible "hello" that he took as a sign of encouragement. A whole year believing he was in love with her without the slightest hope, and it turned out she had been thinking of him as well, as was plain from the way she reacted like a nervous foal.

She was prettier than he recalled, with light-colored eyes and tanned skin, a low-cut dress and curls escaping from her schoolgirl's straw hat. He recovered sufficiently to begin an innocuous conversation, learning that the del Solar family had been spending the three summer months between their country property and their beach house in Viña del Mar; Ofelia had come to Santiago to get her hair cut and visit the dentist. He in turn told her in four sentences about Roser, the boy, the university, and the tavern. They soon ran out of things to say and stood there in silence, sweating in the scorching sun, only too aware that when they separated they would be passing up a wonderful opportunity. As she turned to go, Victor took her by the arm, dragged her into the nearest patch of shade under a pharmacy awning, and begged her breathlessly to spend the evening with him.

"I have to get back to Viña. The chauffeur is waiting for me," she said, without conviction.

"Tell him to wait. We need to talk."

"I'm going to get married, Victor."

"When?"

"What does that matter? You're married."

"That's exactly what we have to talk about. It's not what you think. Let me explain."

He took her to a cheap hotel even though he couldn't afford it, and she returned to Viña del Mar close to midnight, just as her parents were about to inform the police she was missing. Thanks to a generous bribe, the chauffeur told them a tire had burst on the way back.

EVER SINCE HER FIFTEENTH BIRTHDAY, when she had reached her full height and developed feminine curves, Ofelia had attracted men with completely unintentional powers of seduction. She wasn't even aware of the broken hearts she sowed in her wake, except for the few occasions when the lovelorn youth became a threat and her father had to intervene. She was pampered and protected in her tranquil existence: this was a double-edged sword, because even though on the one hand the risks were reduced, on the other, so much protection prevented her from acquiring any astuteness or intuitive sense. Concealed beneath her flirtatious attitude was an astonishing naïveté.

Over the following years as she came into womanhood, she discovered that her looks opened doors and made almost everything easy for her. This was the first, and sometimes the only, thing that others saw; she didn't need to make any effort, as her ideas and opinions went unnoticed. In the four hundred years since the days of the rough colonial conquistador who had founded their dynasty, the Vizcarra family refined their genetic heritage with pure European blood (although Felipe del Solar maintained that everyone in Chile, however white they appeared, had some indigenous blood in them, apart from newly arrived immigrants). Ofelia was part of a clan of pretty women, but she was the only one to inherit her English grandmother's spectacular blue eyes. Laura del Solar was convinced the devil bestows beauty with the sole aim of leading souls to perdition, both the person so endowed and those whom it attracts. As a result, physical attributes were never mentioned in her house: that was in bad taste, pure vanity. Her husband appreciated beauty in other women, but considered it a problem in his own daughters, because he was the guardian of their virtue, especially Ofelia's.

For her part, Ofelia came to accept the family theory that good looks were contrary to intelligence: one could possess one or the other, but not both together. This would explain the difficulties she had at school, her laziness in pursuing her talent for painting, and her inability to keep to the path of righteousness preached by Father Urbina. Her sensuality, which she was unable to identify, was a torment to her. Urbina's insistent query as to what she wanted to do with her life went round and round in her head without finding any answer. Her destiny of marriage and having children seemed to her as stifling as entering a convent, and yet she accepted it as inevitable: all she could do was postpone it awhile. And, as everyone constantly told her, she ought to be thankful Matias Eyzaguirre existed: such a good, noble, and handsome young man. She was to be envied.

Matias had been in love with her from childhood. She discovered and explored desire with him as far as her strict Catholic upbringing and his natural chivalry allowed, even though she often tried to push beyond those limits: after all, what was the difference between petting and fondling until they almost fainted while keeping their clothes on, and committing a sin naked? The divine punishment would be the same. In view of her weakness, Matias assumed the responsibility for their abstinence. He respected her in the same way that he demanded others respect his sisters, and was convinced he would never betray the trust deposited in him by the del Solar family. He believed the desires of the flesh could only be satisfied in a union sanctified by the Church in order to have children. He would not have admitted even in the deepest reaches of his heart that the main reason for abstinence was not to avoid a sin, but the fear of pregnancy. Ofelia never talked of this with her mother or sisters, but was convinced this kind of transgression, however slight, could only be erased through matrimony. The sacrament of confession absolves the sin, but society does not pardon or forget; the reputation of a decent young woman is made of white silk, and any stain ruins it, as the nuns insisted. Who knew how many stains she had accumulated with Matias.

That hot evening Ofelia went to the hotel with Victor Dalmau, she was well aware this would be very different from the exhausting skirmishes with Matias that left her puzzled and angry. She was amazed at the decisive way she agreed in an instant and the lack of inhibition with which she took the initiative once alone in the room with Victor. She found she possessed knowledge she had had no possibility of acquiring, and a lack of shame that normally comes from long experience. With the nuns she had learned how to undress gradually: first she put on a long-sleeved nightdress that covered her from head to toe, then fumbled to remove her clothes beneath it—but that evening with Dalmau her modesty simply evaporated. She let her dress, petticoat, and all her undergarments fall to the floor and stepped out of them naked and Olympian, with a mixture of curiosity about what was going to happen and continuing irritation at Matias for being so sanctimonious. *Serves him right that I'm unfaithful,* she decided enthusiastically.

Victor didn't suspect that Ofelia was a virgin, because nothing about her astonishing confidence suggested it, and because he couldn't imagine such a thing. Virginity had been relegated to his uncertain, almost forgotten adolescence. He came from a different reality, a revolution that had abolished social differences, old-fashioned habits, and religious authority. In Republican Spain, virginity was obsolete; the militiawomen and nurses he had briefly had affairs with enjoyed the same sexual freedom as he did. Nor did it occur to him that Ofelia had agreed to accompany him on a spoiled young woman's caprice rather than out of love. He himself was in love, and automatically thought she must be as well. It was only later when they were resting after making love that he came to ponder the magnitude of what had happened, their bodies entwined in a bed with sheets yellow from use and stained with virginal blood. He told her how and why he had married Roser, and confessed he had been dreaming of Ofelia for more than a year.

"Why didn't you tell me it was the first time for you?" he asked.

"Because you would have backed out," she replied, stretching like a cat.

"I should have been more considerate, Ofelia. I'm sorry."

"There's nothing to be sorry about. I'm happy. My body is tingling. But I have to go, it's very late."

"Tell me when we'll meet again."

"I'll send word when I can escape. We're returning to Santiago in three weeks; it'll be easier then. We'll have to be very, very careful, because if this gets out, we're going to pay dearly for it. I can't bear to think what my father would do."

"I'll have to talk to him at some point . . ."

"Are you out of your mind? What are you thinking? If he finds out I'm going with an immigrant who's married and has a child, he'll kill both of us. Felipe has already warned me."

USING THE DENTIST AS an excuse, Ofelia managed to return to Santiago a second time. In the weeks apart from Victor, she discovered somewhat fearfully that her initial curiosity had given way to an obsession to recall every last detail about that evening in the hotel, an unbearable need to see him and make love, to talk and talk, to tell him her secrets and find out about his past. She wanted to ask him why he limped, to count all his scars, to learn about his family and the feelings he had for Roser. He was a man with so many mysteries that unraveling them was going to be a lengthy task: what did words like "exile" and "military uprising" mean, or "mass grave," "concentration camp," what were "shattered mules" or the "bread of war"? Victor Dalmau was more or less the same age as Matias Eyzaguirre, but he seemed far older, as tough as cement on the outside and impenetrable inside, sculpted with a chisel, marked by scars and bad memories. Unlike Matias, who enjoyed her explosive temperament and her whirlwind moods, Victor grew impatient at her childishness, wanting her to be clearheaded and intelligent. He wasn't interested in anything superficial. If he asked her a question, he would listen to her reply as closely as a schoolmaster, and not permit her to evade it with a joke or change of topic. Ofelia was confronted for the first time with the challenge of being taken seriously.

The second time she awoke from dozing a few minutes after their lovemaking, Ofelia decided she had found the man of her life. None of the pretentious, pampered young men in her circle, their futures secure thanks to their families' wealth and power, could compete with him. Victor was moved by this confession on her part, because he too felt she was the one for him, and yet he didn't lose his head: he took into account the bottle of wine they had shared and the novelty of this situation for her. The circumstances encouraged an exaggerated response; but they would have to talk when their bodies had cooled down.

Ofelia would have willingly broken off her engagement with Matias Eyzaguirre, but Victor made her see that he wasn't free and had nothing to offer her apart from these hasty, forbidden encounters. She suggested they elope to Brazil or Cuba, where they could live beneath the palm trees and nobody would know them. They might be condemned to secrecy in Chile, but the world was a big place.

"I have a duty to Roser and Marcel; besides, you have no idea what poverty and exile mean. You wouldn't be able to stand a week with me under those palm trees," Victor replied good-humoredly.

Ofelia began not answering Matias's letters, in the hope that he would grow tired of her indifference, but that didn't happen, as her stubborn suitor attributed her silence to nervousness typical of a sensitive fiancée. Meanwhile, surprised at her own duplicity, she continued to display to her family a delight she was far from feeling over the wedding arrangements.

She let several months go by without making up her mind, still meeting Victor in stolen moments, but as September drew closer, she realized she had to find the courage to break off her engagement, whether or not Victor agreed; the invitations had been sent out, and the wedding announced in *El Mercurio*. Finally, without a word to anyone, she went to the Foreign Ministry to ask a friend to send a package to Paraguay in the diplomatic bag. The package contained the ring and a letter explaining to Matias that she was in love with somebody else.

No sooner had he received Ofelia's package than Matias Eyzaguirre flew to Chile, sitting on the floor of a military plane, because in the midst of a world war fuel was too scarce for unplanned private flights. He burst into the Calle Mar del Plata house while she was having tea, crashing into fragile tables and chairs with curved legs. Ofelia found herself confronted by a total stranger. Her obliging, conciliatory fiancé had been taken over by a madman who laid into her, scarlet with rage and bathed in sweat and tears. His reproachful shouting drew the attention of the family, and this was how Isidro del Solar learned what had been going on under his nose for months.

Isidro succeeded in removing the irate suitor from the house with the promise that he would deal with the situation in his own way, but his overbearing authority came up against his daughter's resolute stubbornness. Ofelia refused to give any explanation or reveal the name of her lover, much less to repent her decision. She simply kept her mouth shut, and there was no way to get a word out of her. She remained impervious to her father's threats, her mother's tears, and the apocalyptic arguments of Father Vicente Urbina, who was called for urgently as her spiritual guide and administrator of God's thunderbolts. Seeing it was impossible to reason with her, her father forbade her to leave the house, and gave Juana the task of keeping her in quarantine. Juana Nancucheo took this to heart, because on the one hand she had a great deal of affection for Matias Eyzaguirre—that young man was a real gentleman, one of those who greet the domestic staff by name—on the other, he adored Ofelia, so what more could she ask for? She genuinely wanted to carry out her master's instructions, but her efforts as a jailer failed completely thanks to the lovers' guile.

Victor and Ofelia managed to see each other at the most unexpected times and places: in the Winnipeg bar when it was closed; in sordid hotels, parks, and movie houses, almost always with the complicity of the family chauffeur. Once she had evaded Juana's vigilance, Ofelia had plenty of free time, but Victor, who lived from minute to minute, running from one place to the next to keep up with his studies and the tavern, found it hard to steal an hour here and there to spend with her. He neglected his family completely. Noting the change in his habits, Roser confronted him in her usual frank way. "You're in love, aren't you? I don't want to know who she is, but you have to be discreet. We're guests in this country, and if you get into trouble we'll be deported. Is that clear?" Victor was offended by her harshness, even though it corresponded perfectly to their strange matrimonial agreement.

That November, President Pedro Aguirre Cerda died of tuberculosis, after only three years in office. The poor people in Chile, who had benefited from his reforms, shed tears for him as for a beloved father in the most spectacular funeral ever seen. Even his right-wing enemies were forced to concede he was honest and grudgingly accepted his vision—he had promoted national industry, health, and education—but there was no way they were going to allow Chile to shift to the Left. Socialism was fine for the Soviets, who lived far away and were barbarians, but it was not for their own homeland. The deceased president's secular, democratic spirit was a dangerous precedent that was not to be repeated.

Felipe del Solar met the Dalmaus at the funeral. They had not seen one another in months, and after the procession he invited them to lunch to catch up with their news. He learned they were getting ahead and that Marcel, who was still not three years old, spoke in Catalan as well as in Spanish. Felipe told them about his family: Baby had a heart problem, and his mother wanted to take him on a pilgrimage to the shrine of Santa Rosa of Lima because in Chile there was a sore lack of national saints; his sister Ofelia's wedding had been postponed.

Nothing about Victor betrayed the shock he felt inside on hearing about Ofelia, but Roser could sense the reaction on her own skin and so knew beyond doubt who her husband's lover was. She would have preferred the identity to remain a mystery, because uncovering Ofelia's name made her into an incontrovertible reality. The situation was far worse than Roser had imagined.

"I told you to forget her, Victor!" she reproached him that night when they were alone.

"I can't, Roser. Do you remember how you loved Guillem? How you still love him? It's the same with me and Ofelia."

"What about her?"

"She loves me too. She knows we can never be together openly and accepts it."

"How long do you think that girl is going to put up with being your mistress? She has a privileged future ahead of her. She would be crazy to sacrifice it for you. And let me tell you again, Victor: if this gets out, they'll throw us out of this country. Those people are very powerful."

"Nobody will find out."

"Everything gets out sooner or later."

OFELIA'S WEDDING WAS CANCELED with the excuse that she was unwell. Matias Eyzaguirre returned to the post in Paraguay that he had abandoned precipitously. He received a warning for his escapade that had little impact, as he had shown an unusual ability for diplomacy and had succeeded at gaining acceptance in the political and social circles where the ambassador, a rancorous and rather dim man, was struggling. Ofelia was punished with enforced leisure. At twenty-one, she was made to sit at home doing nothing, with Juana Nancucheo keeping a close eye on her. She was bored to death, but it was no use arguing that she had come of age: she had nowhere to go and was incapable of fending for herself, as she was clearly told. "Be very careful, Ofelia, because if you leave by the front door, you'll never enter this house again," her father threatened her. She tried to win sympathy from Felipe or her sisters, but the clan closed ranks to defend the family honor, and so in the end she could rely only on help from the chauffeur, a man of negotiable honesty. Her social life was over, for how could she go out and enjoy herself if she was meant to be ill? Her only outings were visits to the Santiago slums with the Catholic Ladies, to family Mass, and to her art classes, where it was unlikely she would meet anyone from her own circle. Thanks to throwing an epic tantrum, she had managed to get her father to yield over these classes. The chauffeur was told to wait at the door for the three or four hours the sessions lasted. Several months went by without Ofelia making any artistic progress, which only went to show she had no talent, as the family already knew. In fact, she would enter the art school carrying her canvases, easel, and paints, walk through the building, and leave by the back door, where Victor was waiting for her. They met only infrequently, as he found it hard to make his rare free time coincide with her class schedule.

Victor was tired, with dark shadows under his eyes from lack of sleep. He was so exhausted that sometimes he nodded off even before his lover managed to remove her clothes in their hotel room. Roser, on the other hand, displayed an irrepressible energy. She was adapting to the city and learning to understand Chileans, who deep down were as generous, muddle-headed, and dramatic as Spaniards. She had set herself to win friends and carve out a reputation as a pianist, and now played on the radio, in the Hotel Crillon, at the cathedral, in clubs, and in private houses. Word got around that she was well turned-out and well-mannered, and that she could play by ear anything she was asked for. All people had to do was whistle a couple of bars and within a few seconds she could play the tune on the piano, which made her ideal for both parties and solemn occasions. She earned a lot more than Victor with his Winnipeg, but had been obliged to neglect her role as a mother. Until he was four, Marcel didn't call her "mother" but "señora." The first words he said were "white wine" in Catalan, spoken in his playpen behind the tavern counter. Roser and Victor took turns carrying him in the sling until he became too heavy. It was so snug and warm that, clinging to his mother's or father's body, he felt secure. He was a calm, quiet little boy who made his own amusement and rarely asked for anything. His mother would take him to the radio station, and his father to the tavern, but he spent most of his time at the house of a widow who had three cats and looked after him for a modest amount.

Contrary to expectation, the relationship between Victor and Roser was strengthened during this chaotic time when their lives barely coincided and his heart had gone out to another woman. Their longstanding friendship turned into a deeper complicity in which there was no room for secrets, suspicion, or offense; they started from the principle that they would never hurt each other and that if this happened, it would be unintentional. They protected each other, which made their present hardships and the ghosts of the past bearable.

In the months Roser had spent in Perpignan living with the Quakers, she had learned to sew. In Chile, she used her first savings to buy a Singer sewing machine: it was a shiny black treadle model, with gilt lettering and flowers, a wonder of efficiency. Its rhythmic sound was similar to her piano exercises, and whenever she finished a dress or a romper for her son, she was as pleased as she was with an audience's applause. She copied styles from fashion magazines and was always well-dressed. For her performances she made herself a long, steel-colored gown to which she added and subtracted different-colored bows, short or long sleeves, collars, flowers, and brooches so that she looked different on every occasion. She wore her hair in the old-fashioned way, in a chignon held by combs or clasps, and painted her nails and lips bright red, as she would into her old age when her hair was streaked with gray and her lips dry.

"Your wife is very pretty," Ofelia told Victor. She had run into Roser at the funeral of one of her uncles, when Roser was playing solemn music on the organ as the deceased man's relatives walked past offering their condolences to the widow and children. When she saw Ofelia, Roser stopped playing, kissed her on the cheek, and whispered in her ear that she could count on her for anything she might need. This confirmed for Ofelia the truth of Victor's assertion that they were like brother and sister.

Ofelia's comment about Roser's looks surprised Victor: whenever he thought of Roser, the image that sprang to mind was that of the skinny, unassuming girl he had known in Spain, the defenseless goat-herd his parents had adopted, or simply Guillem's girlfriend. Whether Roser was that or the woman Ofelia admired did not change the essential fact that he loved her. Not even the irresistible temptation of eloping with Ofelia to a palm tree–fronded paradise could make him leave Roser or her child.

CHAPTER 8

1941–1942

Take note:
If little by little you stop loving me,
I'll stop loving you little by little.

If suddenly you forget me
Don't come looking for me,
I'll already have forgotten you.

—PABLO NERUDA
"*If you forget me*"
THE CAPTAIN'S VERSES

WHEN OFELIA WAS CONFINED TO THE HOUSE ON
Calle Mar del Plata, her amorous encounters with Victor in the hotel became increasingly sporadic and brief. In this new life where he could not see Ofelia so often, Victor Dalmau found he occasionally had time to accept Salvador Allende's invitation to play chess. The young woman was imprinted on his soul, but he no longer suffered from the permanent anxiety to escape to her clandestine embrace, and didn't need to spend all hours of the night studying to make up for the hours with her. At medical school, he skipped the classes in theory where no one took attendance, because he could

study that material on his own from books and notes. He concentrated on the lab work, autopsies, and hospital practice, where he had to conceal his knowledge so as not to humiliate his professors. He never missed his hours at the tavern, using the slack periods to study, and meanwhile keeping an eye on Marcel in his pen.

Jordi Moline, the Catalan shoemaker, turned out to be the ideal business partner, always happy with the Winnipeg's modest earnings and pleased to have somewhere of his own to go that was more welcoming than his widower's home. He talked with his friends, drank a mixture of Nescafé and brandy, enjoyed dishes from his home country, and played tunes on the accordion. Victor had offered to teach him chess, but Moline could never see the point of moving pieces here and there on a board without any money being at stake. On those nights when he saw how tired Victor was, Jordi sent him off to sleep and was delighted to replace him, although he only served customers wine, beer, and brandy. He knew nothing about cocktails, regarding them as a fashion brought in by queers. His respect for Roser was matched by his affection for Marcel. He could spend hours crouched behind the counter playing with him; the little boy had become the grandson he never had.

When one day Roser asked him if he still had any family in Catalonia, he told her he had left his village to seek fame and fortune more than thirty years earlier. He had been a seaman in Southeast Asia, a lumberjack in Oregon, a train driver and builder in Argentina; in short, he had many trades before coming to Chile and becoming well off thanks to his shoe factory.

"Let's just say that, in principle, I still have family over there, but God knows what has happened to them. In the war they were divided: some of them were Republican, others supported Franco; there were communist militiamen on one side, and priests and nuns on the other."

"Are you in contact with any of them?"

"Yes, with a couple of relatives. In fact, I have a cousin who was in hiding until the end of the war and is now the town mayor. He's a Fascist, but he's a good man."

"One of these days I'm going to ask you a favor . . ."

"Ask away, Roser."

"The thing is, during the Retreat my mother-in-law, Victor's mother, went missing, and we don't know what happened to her. We looked for her in the French concentration camps, we've made inquiries on both sides of the border, but have heard nothing."

"That happened to lots of people. So many dead, so many exiled or displaced, so many living clandestinely! The prisons are full to overflowing: every night they choose prisoners at random and take them out and shoot them on the spot, without a trial or anything. That's Franco's justice for you. I don't want to be pessimistic, Roser, but your mother-in-law could have died . . ."

"I know. Carme preferred death to exile. She was separated from us during the Retreat to France. She disappeared one night without saying goodbye or leaving any trace. If you have any contacts in Catalonia, maybe they could ask around after her."

"Give me her details and I'll make sure to do it. But I don't hold out much hope, Roser. War is a hurricane that destroys a lot in its path."

"Tell me about it, Don Jordi."

Carme Dalmau wasn't the only person Roser was looking for. One of her occasional but regular recitals was at the Venezuelan embassy, a mansion buried among the trees of a leafy garden, where a single peacock strutted. The ambassador, Valentin Sanchez, was a sybarite who loved good food, fine liquor, and above all, music. He came from a line of musicians, poets, and dreamers. He had made several journeys to Europe to rescue forgotten musical scores, and in his music room had an extraordinary collection of instruments, from a harpsichord said to have belonged to Mozart to his most precious treasure: a prehistoric flute that, according to its owner, was carved from a mammoth's tooth. Roser said nothing about her doubts concerning the authenticity of the harpsichord or the flute, but was grateful for the books Valentin Sanchez lent her on art history and music, as well as the honor of being the only person he allowed to play some of the instruments in his collection.

On one of those nights she stayed behind with her host after all the guests had left, sharing a drink and talking of the extravagant project that had occurred to her, inspired by the ambassador's collection: to create an orchestra of ancient instruments in Chile. It was an idea that both of them were passionate about: she wanted to conduct the orchestra, and he wanted to be its patron. Before saying good night, Roser plucked up her courage and asked if he could help her find somebody she had lost in exile. "His name is Aitor Ibarra, and he went to Venezuela because he had relatives there in the construction industry," she told him.

Two months later, a secretary called her from the embassy with details of Iñaki Ibarra and Sons, a building supplies firm in Maracaibo. Roser wrote several letters, convinced she was throwing a bottle into the sea. She never received any reply.

THE PRETEXT OF OFELIA's ill health that her family used for several months to explain the postponement of her marriage to Matias Eyzaguirre worked perfectly at the start of the following year, when Juana Nancucheo realized the girl was pregnant. First came the morning sickness, which Juana treated unsuccessfully with infusions of fennel, ginger, and cumin; soon afterward, she calculated that nine weeks had gone by without her seeing any sanitary towels in the laundry. One day when she saw Ofelia throwing up in the bathroom, she confronted her, arms akimbo. "Either you're going to tell me who you've been with, or else you will have to tell your father," she challenged her. Ofelia was almost completely ignorant about her own body; until the moment Juana asked her who she had been with, she hadn't linked Victor Dalmau to the cause of her sickness. She had thought it was a stomach virus. She now understood what was happening to her, and the sense of panic left her speechless.

"Who is the fellow?" Juana insisted.

"I'd rather die than tell you," Ofelia replied, once she could speak again. That was to be her only answer for the next fifty years.

Juana took matters into her own hands, believing that prayers and homemade remedies could solve the problem without arousing the family's suspicions. She offered a bunch of aromatic candles to Saint Jude, the patron saint of lost causes, gave Ofelia rue tea, and pushed parsley stalks into her vagina. She gave her the rue knowing it was poisonous, but thought a perforated stomach was less serious than a *huacho,* a bastard. After a week this only brought an increase in the vomiting and an insurmountable tiredness; then Juana decided to turn to Felipe, the person she had always trusted. First she made him promise he wouldn't tell a soul, but when she explained to him what was happening, Felipe convinced her it was too great a secret for the two of them to bear on their own.

Felipe found Ofelia prostrate on her bed, doubled up with stomach pains from the rue and feverish with anxiety.

"How did this happen?" he asked, trying to stay calm.

"How it always does," she replied.

"This has never occurred before in our family."

"That's what you think, Felipe. It occurs all the time, but men aren't even aware of it. They're women's secrets."

"Who did you . . ." he mumbled, not knowing how to say it without offending her.

"I'd rather die than tell you," Ofelia insisted.

"You'll have to tell me, sister, because the only way out is for you to marry whoever did this to you."

"That's impossible. He doesn't live here."

"What do you mean, he doesn't live here? Wherever he may be, we'll find him, Ofelia. And if he doesn't marry you . . ."

"What do you mean? That you'll kill him?"

"My God! The things you say. I'll talk firmly to him, but if that doesn't work, Father will get involved . . ."

"No! Not Father!"

"We have to do something, Ofelia. It's impossible to hide this: soon everybody will realize what's going on, and there'll be a terrible scandal. I'll help you all I can, I promise."

In the end they agreed to tell their mother, so that she could get her husband used to the idea; after that, they would see. Laura del Solar greeted the news persuaded that God was finally settling her debts with Him for all she owed. Ofelia's drama was part of the price she had to pay to heaven, and the other, more costly one, being that her son Leonardo's heart was always either beating wildly or remaining silent. As the doctors had forecast when he was born, his organs were weak and his life would be short. Slowly but surely, Baby was fading, but his mother, clinging to prayer and her dealings with the saints, refused to accept the obvious signs. Laura felt as if she were sinking in thick mud, dragging her family with her. Her headaches began at once, a pounding in the back of her neck that clouded her vision, leaving her blind.

How was she going to tell Isidro? She had no way of softening the blow or his reaction. All they could do was wait awhile to see if divine goodness resolved Ofelia's problem naturally—many pregnancies were frustrated early in the belly—but Felipe convinced her that the longer they waited, the worse the situation would become. He himself took on the task of braving his father in the library, while Laura and Ofelia, cowering at the back of the house, prayed with all the fervor of martyrs.

More than an hour went by before Juana came to find them, with the message that they were to go at once to the library. Isidro del Solar met them on the threshold and immediately gave Ofelia two resounding slaps before Laura could shield her or Felipe grab his arm.

"Who's the swine that ruined my daughter? Tell me who he is!" he roared.

"I'd rather die," said Ofelia, wiping the blood from her nose on her sleeve.

"You're going to tell me even if I have to whip you!"

"Go on and do it then. I'm never going to tell you!"

"Father, please," Felipe interrupted them.

"Shut up! Didn't I give orders that this damned brat be locked up? Where were you, Laura, to allow this to happen? I suppose you were at Mass, while the devil was strolling around our house. Do you realize the shame, the scandal of this? How will we be able to face people?" He continued shouting at the top of his voice until Felipe managed to interrupt him a second time.

"Calm down, Father, and let's try to find a solution. I'll make some inquiries . . ."

"Inquiries? What do you mean?" asked Isidro, suddenly relieved because he hadn't been the one to suggest the obvious.

"He means that I have an abortion," said Ofelia, without losing her calm.

"Can you think of any other solution?" Isidro barked.

At this point Laura del Solar spoke up for the first time. In a trembling but very clear voice she said an abortion didn't even bear thinking about, because that was a mortal sin.

"Sin or not, this mess won't be sorted out in heaven, but down here on earth. We'll do whatever is necessary, and God will understand."

"We're not going to do anything until we've spoken to Father Urbina," said Laura.

———

VICENTE URBINA ANSWERED THE family's call that same night. He calmed them down just by being there, radiating intelligence and the strength of purpose of someone who knew how to deal with troubled souls and has a direct line to God. Accepting the glass of port he was offered, he declared he would speak to each of them separately, beginning with Ofelia, who by this time had a swollen face and a closed eye. He spoke with her for almost two hours, but he wasn't able either to get her to confess the name of her lover, or reduce her to tears. "It's not Matias, don't blame him for this," Ofelia repeated twenty times like a refrain. The priest was accustomed to hypnotizing his flock with fear, so this girl's icy calm almost drove him out of his mind. It was past midnight by the time he had finished talking to the sinner's parents and brother. He also questioned Juana, who was unable to clarify anything, because she had no idea who the mysterious lover might be. "It must be the Holy Spirit, Reverend," she concluded slyly.

Any idea of an abortion was dismissed out of hand by a scandalized Urbina. Not only was it a crime according to the law, but it was an abominable sin in the eyes of God, the one arbiter in matters of life and death. There were alternatives, which they could consider in the following days. What was most important was to keep the matter within the four walls of the house: no one was to find out, not even Ofelia's sisters or her other brother, who fortunately was away measuring typhoons in the Caribbean. Rumors have wings, as Isidro rightly said; the main thing was to safeguard Ofelia's reputation and the family's honor. Urbina encouraged each of them with his advice: Isidro was to avoid violence, as that can have unfortunate consequences, and at that moment what was needed was extreme caution; Laura was to continue to pray and contribute to the church's charitable works; Ofelia should repent and confess, because the flesh is weak, but God's mercy is infinite. He took Felipe aside and told him he had to take the lead in this crisis, and that he should come to see him in his office; he had a plan.

Father Urbina's plan turned out to be extremely simple. Ofelia would spend the next few months far from Santiago, and then, when the size of her belly could no longer be hidden, she was to go to a convent, where she would be well looked after until she gave birth and would receive the spiritual aid she so desperately needed.

"And then?" asked Felipe.

"The boy or girl will be given in adoption to a good family. I personally will see to that. You must reassure your parents and sister and take care of the details. Of course, there will be some expenses . . ."

Felipe promised he would see to everything and reward the nuns. He asked that, when the delivery date was close, permission be given to Aunt Teresa, a nun in a different order, to be with her niece.

The months that followed in the family's country property were a marathon of prayers, vows to the saints, penances, and acts of charity from Doña Laura, while Juana Nancucheo took charge of the domestic routine. She looked after Baby, who had regressed to the days of diapers and had to be fed a pap of mashed vegetables with a spoon, and kept her eye on the fallen girl, as she called Ofelia. Installed in their Santiago house, Isidro del Solar pretended to have forgotten the drama taking place far away among the womenfolk, certain that Felipe had taken the necessary steps to silence any gossip. He was more worried about the political situation, which could affect his businesses. The Right had been defeated in the elections, and the new Radical Party president apparently intended to continue with his predecessor's reforms. Chile's position in the Second World War was vitally important to Isidro, as his wool exports to Scotland and Germany, which continued via Sweden, depended on it. The Right defended neutrality—why commit yourself if you might get it wrong?—but the government and general public supported the Allies. If that support became policy, his sales to Germany would go to the devil, he kept telling himself.

Ofelia managed to send Victor Dalmau a letter via the family chauffeur, before he was spectacularly sacked and she was sent off as a prisoner to the countryside. Juana, who detested the chauffeur, accused him without proof that she had seen him whispering with Ofelia. "I did tell you, *patron,* but you won't listen. That oaf is the reason. It's his fault *niña* Ofelia is pregnant." The blood rushed to Isidro del Solar's head so swiftly he thought his brain would explode. It was only natural that the boys in the family took advantage of the maids occasionally, but he couldn't imagine his daughter doing the same with his pockmarked servant. He had a fleeting vision of his naked daughter in the arms of the chauffeur, that lowborn son of a bitch, in the room above the garage, and he almost passed out. He was enormously relieved when Juana explained that he was merely the go-between. Isidro summoned him to the library and shouted questions to get him to reveal the name of the man to blame; he threatened to have him arrested so that the police could beat and kick the truth out of him; when that had no effect, he tried to buy him off, but the man couldn't tell him anything, because he had never seen Victor. All he could tell him were the times he'd left and picked up Ofelia from the art school. Isidro realized that his daughter had never been to her classes; she had always gone from the school on foot or in a taxi to her lover's arms. The blasted girl was less stupid than he had imagined, or lust had made her cunning.

Ofelia's letter contained the explanation she should have given Victor personally, but in the rare moments when she was able to call him, he didn't answer at either his house or the Winnipeg. At their country estate she would be cut off from the outside world: the closest telephone was fifteen kilometers away. She wrote him the truth: that her passion had been like a drunken spree that had clouded her reason; that she now understood what he had always maintained—the obstacles keeping them apart were insurmountable. She admitted in a business-like fashion that in reality what she had felt was a loss of control of her feelings, rather than love; she had been swept away by the novelty of it, but couldn't sacrifice her reputation and her life for him. She told him she would be going away on a trip with her mother for some time, and after that, when her mind had cleared, she would consider the possibility of going back to Matias. She ended the letter with a categorical farewell, and warned him not to try to communicate with her ever again.

Victor received Ofelia's letter with the resignation of someone expecting it, and prepared for it. He had never believed their love would prosper, because as Roser indicated from the start, it was a plant without roots that was bound to wither. Nothing can grow in the shade of secrets, she would say, love needs light and space to flourish. Victor read the letter twice and handed it to Roser. "You were right, as ever," he told her.

Roser had only to glance at it rapidly to read between the lines and grasp that Ofelia's deathly cold tone only barely concealed an immense anger. She thought she understood the reason, which was not merely the lack of a future with Victor or a capricious young woman's reaction. She guessed Ofelia had been kidnapped by her family to hide the shame of a pregnancy, but decided not to share her suspicion with Victor, because it seemed too cruel. What need was there to torment him with yet more doubts? She saw Ofelia as very vulnerable and naïve, and felt a mixture of sympathy and pity for her; she was a Juliet swept up in the whirlwind of an adolescent passion, but instead of a youthful Romeo, she had become involved with a battle-hardened man.

She left the letter on the kitchen table, took Victor by the hand, and led him to the couch, the one piece of comfortable furniture in their modest house. "Lie down, I'll scratch your head." As Victor lay on the couch with his head in Roser's lap and surrendered to the gentle touch of her pianist's fingers in his hair, he felt certain that as long as she existed, he wouldn't be alone in this world of misfortune. If with Roser the worst memories were bearable, so too would be the hole Ofelia had left in the center of his chest. He would have liked to unburden himself of the pain choking him, but he didn't have the words to describe what he had experienced with her, or how at a certain point she had wanted them to run away together, how she had sworn they would always be lovers. He couldn't tell her, but Roser knew him only too well and, doubtless, was already aware of it. They were interrupted when Marcel woke from his siesta and screamed for them.

Roser's intuition had not failed her regarding Ofelia's emotions. As the days went by after her condition became known to her family, her passion was gradually transformed into a smoldering anger raging inside her. She spent hours analyzing her behavior and examining her conscience as Father Urbina demanded, but instead of repenting for her alleged sin, it was her obvious stupidity she repented of. It had never occurred to her to ask Victor what they should do to avoid a pregnancy, because she assumed he had it under control and that, anyway, they met so infrequently it wouldn't happen. Magical thinking. Since he was older and more experienced, Victor was to blame for this unforgivable accident; and yet as the victim, she had to pay for both of them. That was a monumental injustice.

She could scarcely recall why she had clung so tightly to that hopeless love for a man with whom she had so little in common. After being in bed with him, always in some sordid room, rushed and uncomfortable, she was as frustrated as with Matias's clumsy fumbling. She supposed it would have been different if they had been more trusting and had more time to get to know each other, but she didn't have that with Victor. She had fallen in love with the idea of love, romance, and the heroic past of her warrior, as she would often call him. She had lived an opera whose outcome had to be tragic. She knew Victor was in love with her—at least, as much in love as a heart full of scars can be, but on her side it was nothing more than an impulse, a fantasy, another of her whims. She felt so nervous, trapped, and ill that the details of her adventure with Victor, even the happiest ones, were distorted by her terror that she had ruined her life. For him it had been pleasure with no risk; for her there was risk with little pleasure. And now finally she was suffering the consequences, while he could carry on with his life as if nothing had happened.

She hated him. She hid from him the fact that she was pregnant, fearing that if he knew it, Victor would claim his position as father and refuse to leave her in peace. She was the one who had to make all the decisions concerning her pregnancy; no one else had any right to give their opinion, least of all that man who had already caused her enough harm. None of this was in the letter, but Roser sensed it.

At the end of three months, Ofelia was no longer sick, and was filled with an upsurge of energy she had never before experienced. By sending her letter to Victor she had closed that chapter, and within a few weeks no longer tormented herself with memories or speculation over what might have been. She felt liberated from her lover, strong, healthy, with the appetite of an adolescent. She strode out for long walks in the countryside followed by her dogs; went into the kitchen to bake an endless supply of biscuits and buns to be handed out to the children on the estate; and enjoyed herself painting daubs with Leonardo, huge colored splotches that seemed to her more interesting than the landscapes and still lifes she had painted in the past; to the laundry maid's consternation, she took to doing the ironing, and spent hours surrounded by heavy flat irons, perspiring and happy. "Let her be, she'll soon get over it," Juana predicted. Doña Laura was shocked by Ofelia's sunny disposition: she was expecting to see her bathed in tears as she knitted baby clothes, but Juana reminded her that she herself had experienced several months of euphoria during her pregnancies before the weight of her belly became unbearable.

Felipe visited the estate once a week to deal with the accounts, the expenses, and instructions for Juana, who ran the house as usual while her mistress was preoccupied with complex negotiations with the saints. He brought news from the capital, which nobody was interested in, pots of paint and magazines for Ofelia, teddy bears and rattles for Baby, who no longer spoke and had gone back to crawling everywhere. Vicente Urbina appeared once or twice with his odor of sanctity, as Juana Nancucheo called it, but which in reality was nothing more than the stench of his sweaty cassock and shaving lotion. He came to take stock of the situation and guide Ofelia along her spiritual path, and to encourage her to make a full confession. She listened to his wise words with an absent air like a deaf person, showing not the slightest emotion at the prospect of becoming a mother, as if it was a tumor she had in her stomach. Father Urbina thought this would make adoption far easier.

THEIR STAY IN THE COUNTRY would last throughout the summer and into the winter, and had the virtue of gradually easing Doña Laura's frantic pleas to the heavens. She didn't dare ask for the miracle of a miscarriage, which would have solved the family's problem, because that was as serious as wishing her husband dead, but she subtly hinted at it in her prayers. The peacefulness of nature, with its unchanging, tranquil rhythm, the long days and quiet nights, the warm, frothy milk from the barn, the huge bowls of fruit and the delicious-smelling bread fresh from the clay oven, all suited her timid temperament much more than the hustle and bustle of Santiago. If it had been up to her, she would have lived there permanently. Ofelia also relaxed, and her hatred for Victor gave way to a feeling of vague resentment; he was not the only one to blame, she too was partly responsible. She began to think of Matias Eyzaguirre with a certain nostalgia.

The house was colonial and ancient: thick adobe walls, red roof tiles, wooden beams, and tiled floors. Unlike other houses in the region, it had resisted the 1939 earthquake well: only some of the walls were cracked and only half the tiles fell off. In the disorder following the earthquake, attacks on properties in the area increased; there were good-for-nothings scavenging, and a high level of unemployment, the result of the worldwide economic depression of the 1930s as well as the crisis in the saltpeter industry, when natural saltpeter was replaced by a synthetic one, causing thousands of workers in Chile to lose their jobs. The effects of these events were still being felt nearly a decade later. In the countryside robbers poisoned guard dogs and got in at night to steal fruit, hens, sometimes a pig or a donkey to sell.

But Ofelia was unaware of any of this. During the summer days, which seemed to stretch out endlessly, she avoided the heat by resting in the cool corridors or drawing bucolic scenes, now that Baby was no longer able to join her in daubing big canvases with a brush. On small pieces of card stock, she sketched the hay cart pulled by oxen, sleepy-eyed cows in the dairy, the hen yard, washerwomen, the grape harvest. Isidro made no money from his wine, but to him it was essential to be seen as a wine producer, part of that exclusive club of well-known families.

THE SIXTH MONTH OF OFELIA'S pregnancy coincided with the start of autumn: the sun set early, and the dark, cold nights seemed endless. They kept warm with blankets and coal braziers, and used candles for lighting, as it would be years before electricity was installed in these remote regions. Ofelia was not greatly affected by the cold, as the euphoria of the previous months had given way to a sea lion–like heaviness that was not merely bodily (she had put on thirty-five pounds and her legs were swollen like hams) but of the soul as well. She no longer sketched on her cards, took walks through the fields, read, knitted, or embroidered, because she would fall asleep within five minutes. She allowed herself to continue putting on weight, and was so negligent that Juana Nancucheo had to force her to bathe and wash her hair. Her mother warned her that she herself had borne six children, and that if she had taken care of herself she might have kept some of her youthful good looks. "What does it matter, Mama? Everyone says I'm ruined, so who cares how I look? I'm going to be a fat old spinster."

She placed herself meekly in the hands of Father Urbina and her family, and played no part in the decisions about the imminent baby. In the same way that she agreed to stay hidden in the countryside and live in secret, taking upon herself the shame the priest and circumstances finally inculcated in her, so she became convinced that adoption was inevitable. There was no other way out for her. Around the seventh month she could no longer imagine she had a tumor in her stomach, and could clearly feel the presence of the being she was carrying. Previously, the signs of life had been no more than the flutter of a frightened bird's wing, but now when she felt her belly she could follow the tiny body's outline, identify a foot or the head. She took up her pencil once more to draw boys and girls who looked like her, with not a single one of Victor Dalmau's features.

Every two weeks a midwife came to see Ofelia, sent by Father Urbina. Her name was Orinda Naranjo and, according to the priest, she knew more than any doctor about women's illnesses, as he called anything related to reproduction. She inspired confidence at first glance, with the silver cross around her neck, her nurse's uniform, and her medicine bag containing all the tools of her trade. She measured Ofelia's stomach, took her blood pressure, and talked to her in the mawkish tone of someone addressing a dying person. Ofelia was profoundly suspicious of her, but made an effort to be friendly, knowing the woman would be crucial at the moment of birth. Since she had never kept track of her menstruation or of the meetings with her lover, she had no idea when she had become pregnant; Orinda Naranjo calculated the approximate due date by the size of her stomach. She predicted that as this was Ofelia's first child and she had grown fatter than normal, it would be a difficult birth, but there was no need to worry, because she had brought more children into the world than she could remember. She recommended they transfer Ofelia to the convent in Santiago, which had an infirmary containing all that was necessary and was close to a private clinic. They followed her advice. When Felipe came in the family car to transport his sister, she was unrecognizable: fat, blotchy-faced, dragging her enormous feet along in a pair of slippers, and wearing a poncho that smelled of lamb. "Being a woman is a misfortune," she told him by way of explanation. Her baggage consisted of two maternity dresses as voluminous as tents, a man's thick cardigan, her paint box, and a suitcase filled with the fine clothes her mother and Juana had prepared for the baby. What little she herself had knitted turned out misshapen.

ONE NIGHT A WEEK after her arrival at the convent, Ofelia suddenly awoke from a troubling dream covered in sweat and with the sensation that she had slept for months in a lengthy twilight. She had been given a cell containing an iron camp bed, a horsehair mattress, two rough raw woolen blankets, a chair, a drawer to keep her clothes in, and an unpolished wooden table. She didn't need anything more, and was thankful for this Spartan simplicity, which suited her state of mind. The cell window gave on to the nuns' garden, with a Moorish fountain at its center, surrounded by old trees, exotic plants, and wooden boxes filled with medicinal herbs. The garden was crossed by narrow stone paths with wrought iron arches that would be covered with climbing roses in the springtime.

After her abrupt awakening amid the wintry light of late morning and the cooing of a dove outside her window, it took her a minute or two to realize where she was and what had happened to her and why she was imprisoned in this mountain of flesh that was so heavy she could hardly breathe. Lying there still for several minutes allowed her to recall details of the dream, in which she was the light, agile young woman she had once been, dancing barefoot on a black sand beach, with the sun on her face and her hair ruffled by the salty breeze. All at once the sea became rougher, and a wave threw a little girl covered in scales like a mermaid's offspring up onto the shore. Ofelia remained in bed when she heard the bell for Mass, and was still there an hour later when a novice came by banging a triangle for breakfast. For the first time in months, she had no appetite, and preferred to doze for the rest of the morning.

At the rosary hour that same evening, Father Urbina came to visit her and was received by a flurry of black habits and white wimples, a noisy throng of fawning women kissing his hand and asking his blessing. He was still a haughty young man, who seemed to wear his cassock as a disguise. "How is my protégée?" he inquired good-naturedly once he was installed with a cup of thick hot chocolate. The nuns sent for Ofelia, who waddled in like a frigate, swaying on her massive legs. Urbina held out his consecrated hand for the customary kiss, but she shook it in a firm greeting.

"How do you feel, my child?"

"How do you expect me to feel with a watermelon in my belly?" she retorted.

"I understand, my child, but you must accept your discomfort. It's normal in your condition: offer it up to God Almighty. As the holy scriptures say: man has to work by the sweat of his brow, and woman has to give birth in pain."

"As far as I can tell, Father, you don't sweat when you work."

"Well, well, I can see you're agitated."

"When is my aunt Teresa coming? You said you would arrange permission for her to be with me."

"We'll see, my child. Orinda Naranjo tells me we can expect the birth in a few weeks. Call on Our Lady of Hope to come to your aid, and make sure you are free of sin. Remember that many women render up their souls to God in the act of giving birth."

"I have confessed and taken communion every day since I've been here."

"Has it been a complete confession?"

"You want to know if I told my confessor the name of the father of this child . . . It didn't seem to me necessary, because what matters is the sin, not with whom one sins."

"What do you know about categories of sin, Ofelia?"

"Nothing."

"An incomplete confession is the same as not having confessed at all."

"You're dying of curiosity, aren't you, Father?" said Ofelia with a smile.

"Don't be so insolent! My priestly duty is to lead you along the right path. I suppose you know that."

"Yes, Father, and I'm truly grateful. I don't know what I would have done in my situation without your help," she said in such a humble tone it sounded like irony.

"Well, my child, you have been lucky all the same. I've brought good news. I've carried out rigorous searches for the best possible couple to adopt your baby, and I can tell you now that I believe I've found them. They're very good, hardworking people, in a comfortable economic position, and Catholic, of course. I cannot tell you anything more, but don't worry, I'll watch over you and your child."

"It's a girl."

"How do you know?" asked the startled priest.

"Because I dreamed it."

"Dreams are just that: dreams."

"There are prophetic ones. But whether it's a boy or a girl, I'm its mother and I intend to bring it up. You can forget about adoption, Father Urbina."

"What are you saying, for the love of God!"

Ofelia's decision proved unshakable. The priest's argument and threats couldn't make her change her mind. Later on, when her mother and her brother Felipe arrived to try to convince her, backed up by the mother superior, she listened to them slightly amused, as if they were speaking the language of pharisees. However, the avalanche of excessive reproaches and dire warnings eventually had their effect, or perhaps it was one of those winter viruses that killed dozens of old people and children every year. Ofelia came down with a high fever, talking deliriously about mermaids, prostrate from back pain and exhausted by a cough that kept her from eating or sleeping. The doctor Felipe brought prescribed tincture of opium diluted in red wine and several medicines in blue bottles labeled only with numbers. The nuns treated her with herbal infusions from the garden and hot linseed poultices for her congested lungs.

Six days later, her chest had been somewhat burned by the poultices, but she felt better. Assisted by two novices who had been at her side day and night, she got up and managed to shuffle to the small leisure room in the convent, where the nuns met during their free moments. It was a cheerful place bathed in natural light, with a shiny wooden floor and potted plants, presided over by a statue of the Virgin of Carmen, Chile's patron saint, holding the infant Jesus in her arms, both wearing imperial crowns of gilded tin. Ofelia spent the morning covered with a blanket in an armchair, staring blankly at the cloudy sky through the window and raised to paradise by the miraculous combination of opium and alcohol. Three hours later, when the novices helped her stand up, they saw the stain on the chair and the blood trickling down her legs.

Following Father Urbina's instructions, they didn't call a doctor, but Orinda Naranjo. She arrived looking quite professional and announced in her plaintive whine that the birth could come at any time now, even though according to her calculations it wasn't due for another two weeks. She advised the nuns to keep the patient lying flat with her legs up, and to put cold compresses on her stomach. "Pray, because the heartbeats are faint; the baby is very weak," she added. On their own initiative, the nuns stemmed the hemorrhage with cinnamon tea and warm milk with mustard seeds.

When he heard the midwife's report, Father Urbina ordered Laura del Solar to move into the convent to be with her daughter. It would be good for both of them, he said, and help them to be reconciled. She insisted they weren't angry with each other, but he explained that Ofelia was furious with everyone, even God. Laura was given a cell identical to her daughter's, and for the first time in her life was able to experience the peace of religious life she had so much desired. She adapted at once to the icy blasts inside the building and the rigid litany of religious offices. She would get out of bed before dawn to wait for first light in the chapel praising the Lord, attend Mass at seven, and have a lunch of soup, bread, and cheese with the congregation in silence while someone read aloud the scripture selection of the day. In the afternoon she had a few hours for private meditation and prayer, and then at dusk she would join the nuns for vespers. Supper was also eaten silently, and was as frugal as lunch, although a little fish was added. Laura was happy in this female haven, and even the rumbles of hunger and lack of sweet things pleased her with the thought of how much weight she was losing. She loved the enchanted garden, the high, wide corridors where footsteps resounded like castanets, the perfume of candles and incense in the chapel, the creak of the heavy doors, the sound of the bells and chants, the murmur of prayer. The mother superior exempted her from work in the garden, the embroidery workshop, the kitchen or laundry, so that she could fully attend to the physical and spiritual needs of Ofelia, who, at Father Urbina's urging, she had to convince to accept adoption, which would legitimize this poor creature born of lust, and offer Ofelia the chance to rebuild her life. Ofelia would drink the magic potion in another glass of wine and doze like a lifeless doll on her horsehair mattress, watched over by the novices and lulled by her mother's purring voice, although she didn't take in a word of what her mother was saying. Father Urbina did them the favor of visiting them, and after witnessing yet again this misguided young woman's stubbornness, he took Laura del Solar out into the garden under an umbrella while a rain as fine as dew fell on them. Neither of them ever repeated the subject of their conversation.

Ofelia had no recollection of the birth, which she was told was long and difficult, or of the days that followed. It was as if she hadn't lived through them, thanks to the ether, morphine, and Orinda Naranjo's mysterious potions that left her unconscious for the rest of that week. She came around gradually, so lost that she couldn't even remember her name. As her mother was constantly at prayer bathed in tears, it fell to Father Urbina to give Ofelia the bad news. He appeared at the foot of her bed as soon as the drugs had been reduced and she had recovered sufficiently to ask what had happened and where her daughter was. "You gave birth to a little boy," the priest informed her in the most compassionate tone he could muster, "but God in his wisdom took him a few minutes after he was born." He explained that the baby had been strangled by the umbilical cord around his neck, but fortunately they succeeded in having him baptized, so that he did not go to limbo but to heaven with the angels. God spared the innocent child suffering and humiliation on this earth, and in his infinite mercy was offering her redemption. "Pray a lot, my child. You must overcome your pride and accept divine will. Ask God to forgive you, and to help you bear this secret alone, with dignity and in silence, for the rest of your life."

Urbina tried to console her with quotations from the holy scriptures, but Ofelia began to howl like a she-wolf and to thrash around in the strong hands of the novices who were trying to restrain her, until she was forced to swallow another glass of wine laced with opium. And so, from glass to glass, she survived almost two weeks half-asleep, until even the nuns thought this was enough of praying and potions, and that she should be brought back to the land of the living. When she was able to get to her feet, they saw she had deflated considerably and was again shaped like a woman rather than a zeppelin.

Felipe went to fetch his sister and mother from the convent. Ofelia insisted on seeing her son's grave and so they visited the cemetery in the nearby village, where she laid flowers on the spot marked with a white wooden cross inscribed with the date of death but no name, where the child who had not lived lay. "How can we leave him all alone here? It's so far to come and visit him," sobbed Ofelia.

On their return to Calle Mar del Plata, Laura didn't tell her husband all that had gone on in the previous few months, because she thought Felipe had kept him informed, and because Isidro preferred to know as little as possible, remaining faithful to his habit of staying away from the emotional extravagances of the female members of the family. He greeted his daughter with a kiss on the forehead as he did on every normal morning; he was to die thirty-three years later without ever asking after his grandson. Laura sought solace in the church and sweet things. Baby had reached the last stage of his short life, and took all the attention of his mother, Juana, and the rest of the family, which meant Ofelia was left in peace with her sadness.

THE DEL SOLAR FAMILY could never be entirely sure they had avoided the scandal of Ofelia's pregnancy, as traditionally those sorts of rumors darted like birds in the periphery of the family. Ofelia could not fit into any of her old dresses, and her keenness to buy and have new ones helped distract her somewhat from her sorrow. It was at night that the tears flowed, since in the dark the memory of her child was so intense she could clearly feel him kicking playfully in her belly, and drops of milk dripped from her nipples. She went back to her painting classes, seriously this time, and took her place once more in society, unperturbed by the curious looks and whispers behind her back.

Rumors reached Matias Eyzaguirre in Paraguay, but he dismissed them as yet another example of the prudishness and spite typical of his homeland. When he heard that Ofelia was ill and had been taken to the countryside, he wrote to her once or twice. When she didn't reply, he sent a telegram to Felipe inquiring after his sister's health. "It's following the usual course," Felipe answered. This would have seemed suspicious to anyone but Matias, who wasn't stupid, as Ofelia thought, but one of those rare good men. At the year's end, the obstinate suitor was given permission to leave his post for a month to take a vacation in Chile, far from the humid heat and windstorms of Asuncion.

He arrived in Santiago one Thursday in December, and by Friday was already standing at the door of the French-style house on Calle Mar del Plata. When she admitted him, Juana Nancucheo was as frightened as if it had been the police, because she imagined he had come to take Ofelia to task for what she had done, but Matias had a very different objective: he was carrying his great-grandmother's diamond ring in his pocket. Juana led him through the house, darkened both because in summer the shutters were left closed and in anticipation of little Leonardo's death. There were none of the usual fresh-cut flowers or the smell of peaches and melons from the country estate that usually filled the air, no music on the radio, not even the dogs' noisy welcome. All that remained was the looming presence of the heavy French furniture and the centuries-old portraits in their gilded frames.

He found Ofelia out among the camellias on the terrace, seated beneath a canopy as she sketched with a pen and China ink, shielded from the sun by a straw hat. He paused for a moment to observe her, as in love as ever, oblivious to the extra pounds she had put on. Rising to her feet, Ofelia was so bewildered she took a step backward: she had never expected to see him again. For the first time, she could appreciate him in full for what he was and not as the begging, indulgent cousin she had duped for more than a decade. She had thought of him a great deal in recent months, adding her loss of Matias to the price she was paying for her mistakes. The aspects of his character that had bored her in the past now seemed like rare virtues. To her he appeared different, more mature and solid, handsomer.

Juana brought them iced tea and dulce de leche pastries, then hovered behind the camellias trying to overhear them. As she often told Felipe when he scolded her for listening behind doors, her position in the family meant she had to stay well informed. "Why did Ofelita have to break young Matias's heart? He's such a good person; he doesn't deserve to suffer like that. Just imagine, *niño* Felipe, before he could even ask she told him everything that had happened. And in detail."

Matias had listened in silence, wiping the sweat from his face with a handkerchief, overwhelmed by Ofelia's confession, the heat, and the sweet scent of roses and jasmine in the garden. When she had finished, it took him a good while to calm his emotions and conclude that, in reality, nothing had changed. Ofelia was still the most beautiful woman in the world, the only one he had ever loved and would continue to love to the end of his days. He tried to tell her as much with the eloquence he had shown in his letters, but the flowery language was beyond him.

"Please, Ofelia, marry me."

"Didn't you hear what I've been telling you? Aren't you going to ask me who the father of the child was?"

"That doesn't matter. The only thing that does is if you still love him."

"It wasn't love, Matias. It was lust."

"Then it needn't concern us. I know you require time to recover, although I suppose no one truly recovers from the death of a child, but when you are ready, I'll be waiting for you."

He took the little velvet box from his pocket and placed it delicately on the tea tray.

"Would you say the same if I had an illegitimate child in my arms?" she challenged him.

"Of course I would."

"I imagine that nothing I've said comes as a surprise to you, Matias: you must have heard the rumors. My bad reputation will follow me wherever I go. It could ruin your diplomatic career, and your life as well."

"That's my problem."

BEHIND THE CAMELLIAS, Juana Nancucheo couldn't see Ofelia take the small velvet box and examine it closely in the palm of her hand as if it were an Egyptian scarab; all she noticed was the silence. She didn't dare poke her head through the bushes, but when she thought this had gone on long enough, she emerged from her hiding place and approached them to remove the tea tray. It was then she saw the ring on Ofelia's fourth finger.

They wanted to be married without any fuss, but for Isidro del Solar that was tantamount to admitting guilt, besides which his daughter's wedding was a wonderful opportunity to repay a thousand social obligations, and while they were at it give a slap in the face to the bastards spreading gossip about Ofelia. He himself hadn't heard any, but on more than one occasion in the Club de la Union he thought he heard people laughing behind his back. Preparations for the wedding were minimal, since the bride and groom had everything ready from the year before, including sheets and tablecloths embroidered with their initials. They published the announcement in the society pages of *El Mercurio,* and the dressmaker quickly made a wedding gown similar to the previous one, but a few sizes larger.

Father Vicente Urbina did them the honor of marrying them. His presence itself was a vindication of Ofelia's reputation. When readying the couple for the sacrament of marriage with the usual warnings and advice, he delicately avoided the question of the bride's past. Ofelia, however, took great pleasure in telling him that Matias knew what had happened and so she wouldn't have to carry the secret alone for the rest of her life. The two of them would bear it together.

Before leaving for Paraguay, Ofelia wanted to go to the country cemetery where her child was buried. Matias accompanied her. They straightened the white cross, laid a bunch of flowers on the grave, and said prayers. "One day, when we have our own plot in the Catholic cemetery, we'll transfer your little boy to be with us, as it should be," said Matias.

They had a week's honeymoon in Buenos Aires, then traveled overland to Asuncion. Those few days were enough for Ofelia to sense that in marrying Matias she had made the best decision of her life. *I'm going to love him as he deserves, I'll be faithful to him and make him happy,* she promised herself.

And so at last this man, as stubborn and determined as an ox, was able to cross the threshold of his lavish and meticulously prepared house, carrying his wife in his arms. She weighed more than he had bargained for, but he was strong.

PART THREE

Returns and Roots

CHAPTER 9

1948–1970

Every being
Will have the right
To land and life
And that will be the bread of tomorrow.

— PABLO NERUDA
"Ode to Bread"
ELEMENTAL ODES

THE SUMMER OF 1948 SAW THE BEGINNING OF A
Dalmau family tradition that was to last a decade.
Roser and Marcel spent the month of February in a
cabin they rented by the beach. Like most Chilean husbands of his standing, who boasted they never took
holidays because they were indispensable at work, Victor stayed in the city and joined them on weekends.
According to Roser, this was simply another expression of Chilean *machismo:* how could they give up the
freedom that being summer bachelors offered them? It
would have been frowned upon for Victor to take a
whole month off from the hospital, but the main reason
for him remaining was that the beach always brought
back bitter memories of the Argeles-sur-Mer intern-
ment camp. He had promised himself never again to
set foot on sand.

In February 1948 Victor finally had the chance to return the favor he owed Pablo Neruda for choosing him among those to emigrate to Chile. The poet was a senator, but had already fallen out with the president, who was at loggerheads with the Communist Party even though it had supported him in his rise to power. Neruda didn't spare his insults about someone he saw as *the product of political machinations.* He regarded him as a traitor, a *small, vile, and bloody vampire.* Accused of slander and calumny by the government, Neruda was stripped of his post as senator and hunted by the police.

Two leaders of the Communist Party, which was soon to be outlawed, appeared at the hospital to talk to Victor.

"As you know, there's an arrest warrant out for Comrade Neruda," they told him.

"I read about it in the newspaper today. I can hardly believe it."

"He has to be hidden while he's outlawed. We think the situation will soon be resolved, but if it isn't, he'll have to be somehow smuggled out of the country."

"How can I help?" asked Victor.

"You can put him up for a while. Not long. He has to change houses frequently, to avoid the police."

"Of course. It'll be an honor."

"It goes without saying that nobody is to hear about this."

"My wife and son are on vacation. I'm alone in my house. He'll be safe there."

"We must warn you that you could face a serious problem as an accessory."

"That doesn't matter," Victor replied, and gave them his address.

THIS WAS HOW PABLO NERUDA and his wife, the Argentine painter Delia del Carril, came to live clandestinely in the Dalmau family home for two weeks. Victor gave up his bed for them and took them food prepared by the cook at the Winnipeg, in small containers so as not to attract the neighbors' attention. The poet couldn't help but notice the coincidence of the restaurant's name. He also had to be supplied with newspapers, books, and whisky, the only thing that calmed him down. He was desperate for conversation, as visits were restricted. He was an extrovert who lived life to the full; he needed not only his friends but his ideological adversaries with whom to practice his polemical verbal fencing. During the endless evenings in that reduced space, he went over the list of refugees he had granted a place on board in Bordeaux that distant August 1939 day, as well as other exiled Spanish men and women who arrived in Chile in the years that followed. Victor pointed out that Neruda's refusing to stick to the government's order to select only skilled workers, and instead including artists and intellectuals, had enriched the country with a wide range of talent, knowledge, and culture. In under a decade they had provided outstanding scientists, musicians, painters, writers, journalists, and even a historian whose dream was the monumental task of rewriting the history of Chile from its origins.

Being shut in was driving Neruda mad. He paced tirelessly up and down like a caged animal within the house's four walls: he couldn't even look out the window. His wife, who had given up everything, including her art, to be with him, had to struggle to keep him indoors. The poet grew a beard and filled the time by furiously writing his *Canto General.* To repay Victor's hospitality, he read in his inimitably lugubrious voice earlier poems and some still unfinished. Listening to him infected Victor with an addiction to poetry that was to last throughout his life.

One night, without warning, two strangers arrived in dark coats and hats, even though the summer heat was still intense at that hour. They looked like detectives, but identified themselves as party comrades. Without explanation, they took the couple with them, barely giving them time to pack two suitcases with clothes and the unfinished poems. They refused to tell Victor where he could visit the poet, but warned him he might have to put Neruda up again, because it was hard to find refuges. There was a squad of more than five hundred policemen sniffing out the fugitive's tracks. Victor explained that in a week's time his family would be returning from the seaside, and his house would no longer be safe. In any event, it was a relief to recover peace and quiet. His guest had filled every nook and cranny with his huge presence.

Victor was to see Neruda again thirteen months later, when, together with two friends, he had to organize the poet's flight on horseback through Andean mountain passes and into Argentina. For months Neruda, unrecognizable with his heavy beard, had hidden in the houses of friends and party comrades, with the police hot on his heels. Just as with Neruda's poetry, this journey to the frontier left an indelible impression on Victor. They rode through the magnificent scenery of cold forests, age-old trees, mountains, and water: water everywhere, flowing down in hidden streams among ancient trunks, cascading from the sky, sweeping everything away in turbulent rivers the travelers had to cross, their hearts racing. Many years later, Neruda recalled that crossing in his memoirs: *Each one moved along, intoxicated by that boundless solitude, by that green and white silence. It was all the dazzling and secretive work of nature, and at the same time a growing threat of cold, snow, and pursuit.*

Victor said goodbye to him at the border, where gauchos were waiting for him with spare horses to continue the journey. "Governments come and go, but poets remain, Don Pablo. You'll return in glory and majesty. Remember my words," he said, hugging him.

Neruda managed to get out of Buenos Aires using the passport of Miguel Angel Asturias, the great Guatemalan novelist with whom he shared a certain physical resemblance: they were both *long-nosed, with plenty to spare in face and body*. In Paris he was greeted as a brother by Pablo Picasso and feted at the World Congress of Partisans for Peace.

The Chilean government meanwhile told the press that this man was an impostor, Neruda's double; the real one was in Chile, and the police knew where he was.

ON MARCEL DALMAU BRUGUERA's tenth birthday, a letter arrived from his grandmother Carme. It had traveled halfway around the world before finally reaching its recipient. His parents had told him about her, but he had never seen a photograph, and the stories about his legendary family in Spain were so distant from his reality that he put them in the same category as the make-believe horror and fantasy novels he collected. At that age, he refused to speak Catalan, only doing so with old Jordi Moline at the Winnipeg tavern. With the rest of humanity he spoke Spanish with an exaggerated Chilean accent and vulgar expressions that often earned him resounding slaps from his mother. Apart from this oddity, he was an ideal child, taking charge of his schooling, transport, clothes, also often his food, and even making his own appointments at the dentist and barber. He was like an adult in short trousers.

Returning from school that day, Marcel picked up the mail from the box, separated his weekly magazine of aliens and the wonders of nature, and left the rest on the hall table. He was accustomed to finding the house empty. As his parents worked unpredictable hours, they had given him the house key at the age of five, and he had traveled alone on trams and buses since he was six. He was bony and tall with well-defined features, his black eyes had an absorbed expression, and his stiff straight hair was kept in place with brilliantine. Apart from his

tango-singer hairstyle, he imitated Victor Dalmau's measured gestures and his tendency to say little and avoid giving details. He knew
Victor wasn't his father but his uncle, but this information was as ir-
relevant as the legend of that grandmother of his who had gotten off
a motorcycle in the middle of the night and became lost in the midst
of a despairing throng.

First Roser arrived with a birthday cake, and then Victor. He had
been on duty at the hospital for thirty hours, but hadn't forgotten to
bring Marcel the present he had been longing for over the last three
years. "It's a professional telescope, like the ones grown-ups use. It'll
last you until you get married," Victor joked, giving him a hug. He
was more demonstrably affectionate than the boy's mother, and a
much softer touch. It was impossible to get around her, but Marcel
knew a dozen tricks to get his own way with Victor.

After having supper and sharing the cake, Marcel brought the mail
into the kitchen. "Well! It's from Felipe del Solar. I haven't seen him
in months," exclaimed Victor when he saw the sender's name. It was
a large envelope with the stamp of the del Solar law firm. Inside was a
note saying it was time they met for lunch one of these days, and
apologizing for the delay in sending the attached letter, which had arrived at his former home after being sent one place and another until
it reached him, because he now lived in an apartment opposite the
golf club. A minute later, Roser and Marcel were startled to hear Victor give a loud shout: they had never heard him raise his voice before.
"It's Mother! She's alive!" he said, breaking into sobs.

Marcel wasn't really interested in the news. He would have preferred one of his aliens to materialize rather than his grandmother,
but he changed his mind when they told him about their trip. From
then on, everything was a matter of preparing to travel to meet
Carme: letters that came and went without waiting for any reply; tele-
grams crossing in midair; freeing up Roser's timetable of classes and
concerts and Victor's work at the hospital. Neither of them was con-

cerned about Marcel missing months at school if need be; his resurrected grandmother was more important.

They traveled on a Peruvian airline, making five stops before they reached New York. From there they took a boat to France, a train from Paris to Toulouse, and finally arrived in the Principality of Andorra on board a bus that climbed a road that slithered like a weasel among the mountains. None of them had flown before, and the experience served to reveal the only weakness they ever discovered in Roser: her terror of heights. In her everyday life, when she had to go out onto a balcony on a top floor, for example, she disguised her vertigo with the same stoicism that she used to put up with any aches or pains or the struggle to get by. "Clench your teeth and carry on without fuss" was her motto, but in the plane her nerves and equanimity deserted her. Her husband and son had to hold her hands, comfort her, distract her attention, support her head whenever she was sick during the countless hours in the air. At each stopover they almost had to carry her, because she could hardly walk. When they reached Lima from Antofagasta on the second stage of their odyssey, Victor thought she looked so ill he decided to send her back home overland and continue on his own with Marcel. Roser confronted him with her usual determination. "I'll fly to hell itself if necessary," she said, and reached New York quivering with fear and still vomiting in the paper airsickness bags. In fact, she was preparing herself, as she knew she was going to have to travel by air in the future if the project of the Ancient Music Orchestra that she was planning ever came to fruition.

Carme was waiting for them at Andorra la Vella bus station, sitting ramrod-stiff on a bench, smoking as ever. She was dressed in mourning for the dead, for those lost, and for Spain, wearing an absurd hat, and with a bag on her lap out of which poked the head of a little white dog.

The three adults had no difficulty recognizing one another, because none of them had changed a great deal over the ten years they had been apart. Roser was the same as before, although she had adopted a style suited to her position; Carme found herself slightly intimidated by this confident, well-dressed woman wearing makeup. She had last seen her on a terrible night, when she was pregnant, exhausted, and shivering with cold in a motorcycle sidecar. The only one reduced to tears of emotion was Victor; the two women greeted each other with a kiss on the cheek, as though they had seen each other the day before, and as if the war and exile had been insignificant episodes in their otherwise tranquil existences.

"You must be Marcel. I'm your *àvia*. Are you hungry?" was the grandmother's way of greeting her grandson. Without waiting for his reply, she handed him a sweet roll from her voluminous bag, where the dog sat beside the cakes. Fascinated, Marcel studied the complicated geography of *Àvia*'s wrinkles, her yellow, nicotine-stained teeth, her stiff, gray hair poking like straw from her hat, and her twisted, arthritic fingers. It seemed to him that if she had had antennae, she could have been one of his aliens.

They rode with her in a twenty-year-old taxi that wheezed its way through a city nestling between mountains. According to Carme, this was the capital of spying and smuggling, practically the only two profitable enterprises in those years. She herself dabbled in the latter, because to be a spy you had to have good connections with the European powers and the Americans. More than four years had passed since World War Two ended in 1945, and the devastated cities were recuperating from hunger and ruin, but there were still hordes of refugees and displaced people searching for their place in the world. She explained that during the war Andorra had been a nest of spies, and thanks to the Cold War, it still was. In the past it had been an escape route for those fleeing the Germans, especially Jews and escaped prisoners, who were sometimes betrayed by their guides and ended up murdered or handed over to their enemy to be robbed of the money and jewels they were carrying. "There are several shepherds who became rich all of a sudden, and every year when the thaw comes, bodies appear, their wrists tied with wire," said the taxi driver, who joined in their conversation. After the war, it was German officers and Nazi sympathizers who passed through Andorra, fleeing to possible destinations in South America. They were hoping to cross into Spain and receive help from Franco. "As for smuggling, it's almost nothing, just a service to society," Carme insisted. "Tobacco, alcohol, and little things like that, nothing dangerous."

Installed in the rustic house that Carme shared with the peasant couple who had saved her life, they sat down to eat a tasty rabbit and chickpea stew with two *porrones* of red wine and told one another of all their adventures during the previous decade. In the Retreat, when the grandmother decided she didn't have the strength to go on and the idea of exile was unbearable, she abandoned Roser and Aitor Ibarra to lie down and die of cold as far away from them as possible. To her great regret, she woke the next morning, stiff and ravenous but more alive than she would have wished. She remained where she was, motionless, while all around her the throng of fugitives dragged itself along, in ever decreasing numbers, until by evening she found herself alone, curled up like a snail on the frozen ground.

Carme told them she couldn't remember what she felt, but she realized it's hard to die, and to invite death is cowardice. Her husband was dead, and so too perhaps were her two sons, but Roser and Guillem's child was still alive. That made her determined to go on, but she couldn't raise herself from the ground. Then a stray puppy came by, following the trail of the refugees, and she let it snuggle up alongside her for some warmth. That animal was her salvation. An hour or two later, a peasant couple, who had sold their produce to the stragglers in the refugee column and were returning home, heard the dog whining and mistook it for a baby. When they saw Carme, they came to her aid.

She lived with them, working the land with great effort and poor results, until the family's eldest son took them to Andorra. They spent the Second World War there, smuggling anything that came their way between Spain and France, including people, if the opportunity arose.

"Is this the same dog?" asked Marcel, who had it on his lap.

"The very same. He must be eleven years old, and he's going to live many more. He's called Gosset."

"That's not a name. It means 'little dog' in Catalan."

"It's name enough. He doesn't need another one," his grandmother retorted between two drags on her cigarette.

DURING THE MEAL, Carme told them she had found them at long last thanks to Elisabeth Eidenbenz, who had returned to Vienna, still completely devoted to her mission of helping women and children. Vienna had been ferociously bombed, and when she arrived shortly after the end of the war, its starving inhabitants were digging in the garbage for food while hundreds of lost children were living like rats among the ruins of what had once been the most beautiful of imperial cities. In the south of France in 1940, Elisabeth had carried out her plan to create a model maternity home in an abandoned mansion in Elne, close to Perpignan, where she took in pregnant women so that they could give birth in safety. At first these had been Spanish women rescued from the concentration camps, then later Jews, gypsies, and other women escaping from the Nazis. Protected by the Red Cross, the Elne maternity home was meant to stay neutral and not aid political refugees, but Elisabeth paid little attention to this, despite being closely watched. As a result, the Gestapo closed the home in 1944. By then, she had managed to save more than six hundred babies.

As chance would have it, Carme later met one of the lucky mothers in Andorra, who told her how she had her child thanks to Elisabeth. Carme made the connection between that nurse and the name of the person who was to be her family's contact in France, if they succeeded in getting across. She wrote to the Red Cross, and from one of their offices to another, one country to another, through a persistent correspondence that overcame bureaucratic obstacles and crisscrossed Europe, she finally managed to locate Elisabeth in Vienna.

The nurse wrote to Carme that at least one of her sons, Victor, was still alive, had married Roser, who had a boy called Marcel, and the three of them were in Chile. She had no means of getting in touch with them, but Roser had written to the family that took her in when she left Argeles-sur-Mer. It was difficult to trace the Quakers, who by then were living in London. They had to search in their attic to find Roser's envelope with the only address they had for her, that of Felipe del Solar's house in Santiago. And so, after a delay of several years, Elisabeth Eidenbenz succeeded in reuniting the Dalmaus.

Roser, Victor, and Marcel had to return to Chile without her, as it would take a whole year before Carme Dalmau decided she was willing to emigrate and rejoin her family. As she knew nothing about Chile, that long worm at the far south of the map, she began searching in books and asking people if they knew any Chileans she could question, but none passed through Andorra in all that time. She was held back by her friendship with the peasants who had taken her in, and with whom she had lived for many years, as well as her dread at having to travel halfway round the world accompanied by an elderly dog. She was afraid she wouldn't like Chile. "My uncle Jordi says it's the same as Catalonia," Marcel reassured her in one of his letters. Once her mind was made up, she said goodbye to her friends, took a deep breath, and dismissed her worries, ready and willing to enjoy the adventure. She traveled unhurriedly by land and sea for seven weeks with the mutt in a bag, allowing herself time to be a tourist and appreciate other landscapes and languages, try exotic dishes, and compare customs different from her own. Day by day she grew more distant from the past she had known and entered another dimension.

During her years as a schoolteacher she had studied and taught the world, but now she was discovering it was nothing like the descriptions in books or photographs. It was much more complex and colorful, much less frightening. She shared her thoughts with her pet, and wrote them in a school notebook together with her recollections, as a precaution, in case at some point her memory began to fail her. She embellished the facts, because she was aware that life is how we tell it, so why would she jot down trivia?

The last stage of her pilgrimage was the same voyage down the Pacific that her family had taken in 1939. Her son had sent her enough money to travel first-class, arguing that she deserved it after all the hardships she had suffered, but she preferred to travel tourist-class, where she would be more at ease. The war and her years as a smuggler had made her very discreet, but she resolved to speak to strangers, since she had discovered that people like to talk, and it only took a couple of questions to make friends and find out lots of things. Everybody had a story and wanted to tell it.

Gosset, who had been suffering from the aches and pains of old age, was gradually rejuvenated. By the time they were approaching Chile, he was a different dog, more alert and smelling less like a skunk.

Victor, Roser, and Marcel were there to receive the grandmother and her dog in the port of Valparaiso. They were accompanied by a stout, talkative gentleman who introduced himself as "Jordi Moline, at your service, madame." He added in Catalan that he was ready to show her the best this beautiful country had to offer. "Do you realize you and I are almost the same age? I'm a widower too," he said rather coquettishly.

On the train to Santiago, Carme learned about how Jordi had adapted perfectly to the role of great-uncle. By now Victor was a cardiologist in the San Juan de Dios hospital, and so no longer worked nights in the Winnipeg. Roser was busy with her music, although she still kept an eye on the accounts. Marcel went almost every day to the bar to do his homework, and so as not to be at home alone.

IN THE MID-1960S, Roser traveled to Caracas, invited once more by her friend Valentin Sanchez, the former Venezuelan ambassador, who by this time was retired from diplomacy and devoted himself entirely to his passion for music. In the twenty-five years that had elapsed since the arrival of the *Winnipeg*, Roser had become more Chilean than anyone born in that country. The same was true of the majority of the Spanish refugees, who were not only citizens, but many of whom fulfilled Pablo Neruda's dream of rousing Chilean society from its slumbers. By now nobody remembered there had once been opposition to their arrival, and nobody could deny the magnificent contribution made by the people Neruda had invited to Chile. After years of planning, extensive correspondence, and many trips, Roser and Sanchez had succeeded in creating the Ancient Music Orchestra, the first of its kind on the continent, sponsored by oil, the inexhaustible treasure gushing out of the Venezuelan earth. While he traveled across Europe acquiring precious antique instruments and digging out unknown scores, she trained the musicians through a strict selection process from her position as vice-rector of the National Conservatory of Music. There were more than enough candidates who came from different countries in the hope of becoming part of this utopian orchestra. Chile didn't have the means to support such an enterprise— there were other priorities in the cultural field, and on the few occasions Roser managed to awaken interest in the project, there would be another earthquake, or a change of government, and her hopes would be dashed. But in Venezuela, with the right influence and connections, any dream was possible. Valentin had plenty of both, as he had been one of the few politicians capable of navigating safely through dictatorships, military coups, attempts at democracy, as well as the compromise government then in power, with a president who was one of his personal friends. His country was struggling against a guerrilla group inspired by the Cuban revolution, like many others on the continent, apart from Chile where a revolutionary movement that was more theoretical than real was just in its infancy. However, none of this affected Venezuela's prosperity or the love Venezuelans had for music, ancient or not. Valentin often visited Chile, where he kept an apartment in Santiago that he could use whenever he felt like it. Roser paid him visits in Caracas, and they had traveled to Europe together on orchestra business. She had learned to travel by plane thanks to tranquilizers and gin.

This friendship didn't trouble Victor Dalmau because he knew that his wife's friend was openly homosexual, but he suspected there could be a hypothetical lover. Each time Roser returned from Venezuela she was rejuvenated. She came back with new clothes, perfumed like an odalisque, or wearing a discreet jewel, a gold heart hanging round her neck from a slender chain, none of which she would buy for herself, as she was Spartan when it came to personal spending. What was most revealing for Victor was her renewed passion, as if when they met again she wanted to try out some acrobatics she had learned with another man, or else atone for her guilt. To be jealous would have been ridiculous in the relaxed kind of relationship they had, so relaxed that if Victor had to define it, he would have said they were comrades. He discovered the truth of his mother's saying that jealousy bites worse than fleas. Roser enjoyed the role of wife. In the days when they were poor and he was still in love with Ofelia del Solar, without telling him, she bought two wedding rings in monthly installments, and demanded they both wear them until such day as they could divorce. According to the agreement they had made at the start always to tell each other the truth, she ought to have told him about her lover, but she was of the belief that a kind omission is worth more than a pointless truth, so Victor deduced that if she applied this principle to small things, all the more reason she would do so when it came to being unfaithful.

Theirs was a marriage of convenience, but they had been together for twenty-six years, and loved each other with something more than the quiet acceptance of an arranged marriage in India. Marcel had reached eighteen long ago, the birthday that was supposed to mark the end of the commitment they had made to be together, but it merely served to underscore their mutual affection and their intention to stay married awhile longer, in the hope that they would never part.

Over the years they became increasingly close in their tastes and foibles, but not in character. They had few reasons to argue and none to fight; they agreed about all things fundamental and felt as much at ease together as if they were on their own. They knew each other so well that making love for them was an easy dance that left them both contented. They didn't repeat the same routine, because that would have bored Roser, as Victor well knew. The Roser naked in bed was very different from the elegant, sober woman up on a stage, or the strict professor at the Conservatory of Music. They had been through many ups and downs together before they reached the placid years of maturity when they had no great economic or emotional worries.

They lived on their own, as Carme had moved to Jordi Moline's house after the death of the very old, blind, and deaf Gosset, who remained lucid to the last. Marcel was living with two friends in an apartment. He had studied mining engineering, and was working for the government in the copper industry. He had not inherited the least trace of the musical talent of his mother or his grandfather Marcel Lluis Dalmau, the fighting spirit of his father, nor any inclination toward medicine like Victor or for teaching like his grandmother Carme, who at eighty-one was still a schoolteacher.

"How strange you are, Marcel! Why on earth are you so interested in stones?" Carme asked him when she learned of his chosen career.

"Because they don't have opinions or talk back," her grandson retorted.

HIS FAILED RELATIONSHIP WITH Ofelia del Solar left Victor Dalmau with a silent, suppressed anger that persisted for several years. He interpreted it as atonement for having behaved so cruelly, for having allowed that young virgin to fall in love with him when he knew he wasn't free, but had responsibility for a wife and child. That had been a long time ago. Since then, the burning nostalgia left by that love gradually merged into that gray area of memory where what we have lived fades away. He sensed he had learned a lesson, although the precise meaning of that lesson wasn't clear to him. For many years, that was his only amorous adventure, as he was constantly overwhelmed by the demands of his work. The occasional hasty encounter with a willing nurse didn't count; this happened only rarely, usually when he was on duty for two successive days at the hospital. Those furtive embraces never created a complication: they had no past or future, and were forgotten within hours. His unshakable affection for Roser was the anchor of his existence.

In 1942, shortly after Victor had received Ofelia's final letter, when he was still entertaining the fantasy of winning her again, although that would have been like rubbing salt on his wounded heart, Roser decided he needed a drastic cure to drag him out of his introspection. So one night she had slipped uninvited into his bed, just as she had years before with his brother, Guillem. That had been the best thing she had ever done, because the result was Marcel. On this occasion she thought she was going to surprise Victor, but found that he was waiting for her. He wasn't startled to see her half-naked in his doorway, her hair flowing: he simply moved over in bed to make room and took her in his arms as naturally as a real husband. They frolicked for most of the night, knowing each other in the biblical sense clumsily but good-naturedly. They both realized they had been longing for this moment from their first skirmishes in the *Winnipeg* lifeboat, when they whispered together chastely while, outside, other couples were waiting their turns to make love. That night they had no thought of Ofelia or Guillem, whose ever-present ghost had accompanied them on board the *Winnipeg*, but who in Chile had wandered off to explore new discoveries. Little by little Guillem had withdrawn to a discreet corner of their hearts, where he was no trouble at all. From that first night on, they always slept in the same bed.

Now Victor's sense of pride prevented him from spying on Roser or raising his suspicions with her. He didn't link his doubts to the persistent stomachache that troubled him, which he attributed to an ulcer, although he did nothing to confirm the diagnosis, simply taking milk of magnesia in alarming quantities. His feelings for Roser were so different from the foolish passion he had felt for Ofelia that it took a year of suffering before he could finally put a name to it. To alleviate his jealousy, he took refuge in the suffering of his hospital patients and in study. He needed to stay up to date with the latest advances in medicine, which were so fabulous there was even talk of being able to successfully transplant a human heart. Two years earlier, a chimpanzee's heart had been transferred to a dying man in Mississippi, and even though the patient lived only ninety minutes longer, the experiment raised the possibilities of medical science to the level of miracles. Like thousands of other doctors, Victor Dalmau dreamed of repeating the feat by using a human donor. Ever since he had held Lazaro's heart in his hands, he had been obsessed with that magnificent organ.

Apart from putting all his energy into work and studying, Victor had succumbed to one of his melancholy periods. "You're in a dream, son," Carme told him over one of their Sunday lunches at Jordi Moline's. They usually spoke Catalan there, but Carme changed to Spanish when Marcel was present, because at the age of twenty-seven her grandson refused to speak the family's mother tongue.

"*Àvia* is right, Papa. What's the matter?" asked Marcel.

"I miss your mother," Victor replied without thinking.

This came as a revelation to him. Roser was in Venezuela for another series of concerts, which to him seemed to occur increasingly often. Victor continued turning over in his mind what he had blurted out, because until the moment he had admitted his need for her, he hadn't fully realized how much he loved her. Although they discussed anything and everything openly, an inexplicable shyness prevented them both from expressing their love in words; what need was there to proclaim their feelings—it was enough to show them. If they were together it was because they loved each other, so why complicate such a simple truth?

One or two days later, as he was still mulling over the idea of surprising Roser with a formal declaration of love and the wedding ring he should have given her years before, she returned to Santiago unexpectedly, and Victor's plans were shelved indefinitely. As on her previous trips, she came back euphoric, with that air of utter satisfaction that roused so much suspicion in her husband, and wearing a flamboyant red-and-black-checked miniskirt no longer than a kitchen apron, that seemed to him completely at odds with her discreet nature.

"Don't you think it's too short for someone your age?" Victor asked, rather than giving the speech he had so carefully prepared.

"I'm forty-eight, but I feel as if I were twenty," she replied good-humoredly. This was the first time she had given in to the latest fashion: until then she had remained faithful to the styles she always wore.

Her challenging tone convinced Victor it was best to leave things as they were and avoid the risk of an explanation that might be very painful or definitive.

Years later, when it was no longer in any way important, Victor Dalmau learned that Roser's lover had been his old friend Aitor Ibarra. Their relationship had been happy, if sporadic, since they only met whenever she was in Venezuela and in between times were not in contact at all. It had lasted seven long years.

It began with the first concert given by the Ancient Music Orchestra, which was the cultural event of the season in Caracas. Aitor saw the name Roser Bruguera Dalmau in the newspaper. He thought it would be too much of a coincidence for this to be the same pregnant woman he had crossed the Pyrenees with during the Retreat at the end of the Civil War, but bought a ticket just in case. The orchestra gave its first performance in the Grand Hall at the Central University, with its Calder mobiles and the best acoustics in the world. On the huge stage, conducting the musicians with their precious instruments (some of which the audience had never seen before), Roser looked tiny. Through a pair of binoculars, Aitor examined her from the back. The only thing he recognized was her chignon, worn exactly the same way as in her younger days. He identified her for certain when she turned to acknowledge the applause, but she had more difficulty recognizing him when he appeared in her dressing room, because little remained of the lanky, jovial young man who was always in a hurry and to whom she owed her life. He had turned into a prosperous businessman with measured gestures, a few too many pounds, thinning hair, and a bushy moustache, although there was still a gleam in his eye. He was married to a splendid woman who had been a beauty queen, had four children and many grandchildren, and had made a fortune. Arriving in Venezuela with fifteen dollars in his pocket thanks to some relatives, he dedicated himself to doing what he knew best, repairing vehicles. He set up a garage, and in a short space of time had others in several cities; from there to the trade in vintage models for collectors was a short step. Venezuela was the perfect country for someone as enterprising and visionary as Aitor. "Opportunities drop from the trees like mangos here," he told Roser.

Those seven years of passion were intense in emotion and relaxed in expression. They would spend a whole day shut up in a hotel room making love like adolescents, laughing all the time, eating bread and cheese washed down with a bottle of Riesling. Both were amazed at their intellectual affinity and their shared unquenchable desire. It was unique in their lives, and never before or afterward would they feel anything similar. They managed to keep their love in a sealed, secret compartment of their lives so that it didn't spoil either of their happy marriages. Aitor loved and respected his beautiful wife, as Roser loved Victor. From the outset, when they came close to losing their heads over the surprise at their mutual love, they decided that the only possible future for this tremendous attraction was to keep it in the realm of the clandestine. They wouldn't allow it to turn their lives upside down or harm their families. They kept that promise throughout those seven blessed years, and would have stayed together many more if a stroke hadn't left Aitor hemiplegic, needing to be cared for by his wife. Victor knew none of this until Roser told him everything much later.

Victor Dalmau often saw Pablo Neruda, who had returned from exile in 1952, from a distance in public meetings, and occasionally at the house of Senator Salvador Allende, where he would go to play chess. Victor was also invited by the poet to gatherings in his house on Isla Negra, an organic dwelling resembling a beached ship, built in a crazy fashion on top of a promontory facing the sea. This was his place of inspiration and writing. *The sea of Chile, the tremendous sea, with its waiting barges, its towers of black and white foam, its coastal fishermen educated in patience, the natural, torrential, infinite sea.* He lived there with Matilde, his third wife, amid a ridiculous accumulation of the objects from his collections, from dusty bottles bought at flea markets to figureheads from shipwrecks. It was there that he received dignitaries from all over the world who came to honor him and bring invitations. Local politicians, intellectuals, and journalists, but above all personal friends, among them several of the refugees from the *Winnipeg*, also visited the poet there. Neruda was a celebrity, translated into every language, and by then not even his worst enemies could deny the power of his verses.

What the poet most wanted was to write without interruption, cook for his friends, and to be left in peace, but that was impossible even on the rocky outcrop of Isla Negra. All kinds of people came to knock on his door and remind him that he was the voice of long-suffering peoples, as he defined himself. So it was that one day his party comrades came to demand he represent them in the presidential campaign. Salvador Allende, the ideal candidate for the Left, had already run for president three times unsuccessfully, and it was thought that he had bad luck. The poet set aside his notebooks and fountain pen with green ink and set out to tour Chile in cars, buses, and trains, meeting the people and reciting his poetry to a chorus of workers, peasants, fishermen, railway workers, miners, students, and craftsmen, who were thrilled by the sound of his voice. This experience gave new impetus to his combative poetry and led him to understand he wasn't cut out to be a politician. As soon as he could, he withdrew and backed the candidacy of Salvador Allende. Against all odds, Allende became leader of Popular Unity, a coalition of left-wing parties. Neruda actively supported him in his campaign.

Now it was Allende's turn to travel north and south on trains, rousing the crowds who gathered at every station to listen to his passionate speeches, in tiny villages scorched by sand and salt, and in others darkened by eternal rain. Victor Dalmau went with him on several occasions, officially as his doctor, but really as his chess partner. That was the only way the candidate could relax, since on the train he had no Western films, his other means of relieving tension.

Allende was so energetic, determined, and insomniac that no one could keep up with him, and his entourage had to rotate their shifts. Victor took on the hours late at night, when the exhausted candidate needed to clear his mind of the noise of the crowds and the sound of his own voice via a game of chess that went on sometimes until dawn or was left pending until the following night. Allende slept very little, but took advantage of ten minutes here and there to doze off wherever he was sitting, and would wake up as refreshed as if he'd just had a shower. He walked erect, chest thrust out as if ready for the fray. He talked with an actor's voice and the eloquence of a missionary; his gestures were sparing, he was quick-witted and unshakable in his fundamental beliefs. Thanks to his lengthy political career he had come to know Chile like his own backyard, and never lost his belief that there could be a peaceful revolution, a Chilean path to socialism. Inspired by the Cuban revolution, some of his supporters maintained it was impossible to make a true revolution and escape U.S. imperialism without violence: it could only be achieved through armed struggle. For Allende, however, there was plenty of room for the revolution within the solid Chilean democracy, and he respected its constitution. Right to the end he believed it was above all a question of denouncing, explaining, proposing, and calling on others to act so that the workers could rise up and seize their destiny in their own hands. But he was also well aware of the power of his adversaries. In public he behaved with a dignity that had something pompous about it, which his enemies called arrogance, but in private he seemed simple and jovial. He always kept his word; he couldn't imagine betrayal, and that was what eventually cost him his life.

As a very young man, Victor Dalmau had found himself caught up in the Spanish Civil War on the Republican side. He fought, worked, and went into exile because of that, adopting his side's ideology unquestioningly. In Chile he kept the promise of refraining from political activism that had been demanded of all the *Winnipeg* refugees. He didn't join any party, but his friendship with Salvador Allende gradually came to define his ideas with the same clarity as the Civil War had defined his feelings. Victor admired him in the political sphere, and also, with a few reservations, in his personal life. Allende's image as a socialist leader was contradicted by his bourgeois habits, his expensive clothes, the refined way he surrounded himself with unique works of art he owned thanks to spontaneous gifts from other governments and every important Latin American artist: paintings, sculptures, original manuscripts, pre-Columbian artifacts. He was vulnerable to flattery and pretty women: he could spot them at a glance in a crowd, and attracted them thanks to his personality and the trappings of power. Victor was upset by these lapses, ones he only commented upon when he was alone with Roser. "How fussy you are, Victor! Allende isn't Gandhi," she would retort. They both voted for him, although neither really believed he would be elected. Allende himself doubted it, but in September 1970 he won more votes than any other candidate. As there was no absolute majority, Congress was meant to choose between the two candidates with the greatest number of votes. The eyes of the world were on Chile, that long narrow stain on the map that was defying convention.

Supporters of the utopian socialist revolution in democracy didn't wait for Congress's decision. They poured onto the streets to celebrate this long-awaited triumph. Dressed in their Sunday best, entire families, from grandparents to grandchildren, came out singing, euphoric, astonished but without the slightest hint of disorder, as if they had all agreed on some mysterious form of discipline. Victor, Roser, and Marcel mingled with the crowd waving flags and singing that the people united would never be defeated. Carme didn't go with them, because as she said, at the age of eighty-five she wasn't going to live long enough to get enthusiastic about anything as unpredictable as politics. In reality, by now she went out very little, devoting herself entirely to looking after Jordi Moline, who was suffering the pangs of old age and rarely wanted to leave home. He had remained young in spirit until he lost his tavern. The Winnipeg, which had become a landmark in the city, had disappeared when the whole block was razed to make way for some tall towers that Moline was convinced would be toppled by the next earthquake.

Carme, by contrast, was as healthy and energetic as ever. She had shrunk until she looked like a plucked bird, a heap of bones and skin, with little hair left and a cigarette permanently dangling from her lips. She was tireless, efficient, brusque in manner but secretly sentimental. She did all the housework and looked after Jordi as she would a backward child. The pair planned to watch the spectacle of the Left's electoral victory on the television with a bottle of red wine and Spanish serrano ham. They saw the columns of people with banners and torches, and witnessed their fervor and optimism. "We've already lived this in Spain, Jordi. You weren't there in '36, but I can tell you it's the same thing. I just hope it doesn't end badly like it did over there," was Carme's only commentary.

AFTER MIDNIGHT, WHEN THE CROWDS in the streets began to thin out, the Dalmaus bumped into Felipe del Solar, unmistakable in his camel-hair jacket and mustard-colored suede cap. They embraced like the good friends they were: Victor soaked in sweat and hoarse from shouting, and Felipe as impeccable as ever, smelling of lavender, with the elegant aloofness he had been cultivating for more than twenty years. He bought his clothes in London, where he went twice a year, and British sangfroid suited him well. He was at the demonstration with Juana Nancucheo, whom the Dalmaus recognized instantly because she looked exactly the same as in those far-off days when she took the tram to visit Marcel.

"Don't tell me you voted for Allende!" Roser exclaimed, embracing Felipe and Juana in turn.

"Of course not, Roser. I voted for the Christian Democrats, even though I don't believe in the virtues of either democracy or Christianity, but I couldn't give my father the pleasure of voting for his candidate. I'm a monarchist."

"A monarchist? Good God! Weren't you the only progressive among those troglodytes in your clan?" Victor exclaimed good-humoredly.

"A sin of youth. A king or queen is what we need in Chile, just as in England, where everything is more civilized than here." Felipe laughed, chewing on the unlit pipe he always carried with him as a fashion accessory.

"What are you doing in the street, then?"

"We're taking the pulse of the rabble. Juana voted for the first time. Women have had the vote for twenty years, but it's only now she's used it to vote for the Right. I can't get it into her head that she belongs to the working class."

"I vote the same as your father, *niño* Felipe. As Don Isidro says, we've seen this story of the mob emboldened before."

"When?" asked Roser.

"She means Pedro Aguirre Cerda's government," Felipe explained.

"It's thanks to that president that we're here, Juana. If you remember, he brought over the refugees on the *Winnipeg*," said Victor.

"I must be almost eighty, but there's nothing wrong with my memory, youngster."

Felipe told them his family was barricaded in Calle Mar del Plata waiting for the Marxist hordes to invade the upper class neighborhoods. They believed in the terror campaign they themselves had created. Isidro del Solar had been so convinced the conservatives would win that he had planned a celebration with friends and fellow right-wingers. The chefs and waiters were still at the house, waiting for divine intervention to change the course of events so that they could serve the champagne and oysters. Juana was the only one who had wanted to see what was going on in the street, out of not political sympathies but curiosity.

"My father announced he was going to take the family to Buenos Aires until this godforsaken country regains its senses, but my mother refuses to move. She doesn't want to leave Baby alone in the cemetery," Felipe added.

"What news is there of Ofelia?" asked Roser, realizing Victor didn't have the nerve to mention her.

"She missed the madness of the election. Matias was appointed chargé d'affaires in Ecuador. He's a career diplomat, so the new government can't dismiss him. Ofelia has taken the opportunity to study with the painter Guayasamin. Savage expressionism, sweeping brushstrokes. The family thinks they're hideous, but I have several of her paintings."

"And her children?"

"Studying in the United States. They're going to spend this political cataclysm far from Chile as well."

"But you're staying?"

"For the moment, yes. I want to see what comes of this socialist experiment."

"I hope with all my heart it's a success," said Roser.

"Do you think the right wing and the Americans are going to permit it? Remember what I say: this country is headed for ruin," Felipe retorted.

——

THE JOYOUS DEMONSTRATIONS ENDED without any trouble, and the following day, when scared people rushed to the banks to withdraw their money and buy airline tickets to escape before the Soviet hordes invaded the country, they found the streets were being cleaned as normal, and no thugs were going around brandishing garrotes and threatening decent folk. There was no great hurry after all. They calculated that it was one thing to win the most votes, and another to actually become president; there were two months left for Congress to decide, and to twist the situation in their favor.

The tension was palpable, and the plan to put a stop to Allende had already swung into action even before he took office. Over the following weeks, a plot supported by the North Americans ended with the assassination of the army commander in chief, a general who respected the constitution and therefore had to be gotten out of the way. This crime had the opposite effect to the one intended. It led to widespread indignation and strengthened the traditional respect for the laws that most Chileans had. They were repelled by these gangster tactics: that could happen in some banana republic or other, but never in Chile, where, as the newspapers insisted, disputes weren't resolved by the use of a gun. Congress ratified Salvador Allende, who became the first democratically elected Marxist head of state. The idea of a peaceful revolution no longer seemed so absurd.

In those troubled weeks between the election and the transfer of power, Victor had no opportunity to play chess with Allende. The future president was caught up in political bargaining, agreements and disagreements behind closed doors, a tug of war within his own coalition parties over how much power each was to have, and constant harassment by the opposition. Allende used every means possible to denounce the U.S. government's intervention. Nixon and

Kissinger had sworn to prevent the Chilean experiment from suc-
ceeding, as it might spread like wildfire through the rest of Latin
America and Europe. When they failed to achieve this through brib-
ery and threats, they began to woo the military.

Although Allende didn't underestimate his enemies at home and
abroad, he had an irrational belief that the people would defend his
government. It was said he had "the knack" for turning any situation
to his advantage, but over the next dramatic three years he was going
to need more good luck than any knack could offer. His games of
chess with Victor were renewed the following year, when the president managed to establish a certain routine in his complicated existence.

CHAPTER 10

1970–1973

In the middle of the night I ask myself:
what will happen to Chile,
what will become of my poor dark homeland?

— PABLO NERUDA
"Insomnia"
NOTES FROM ISLA NEGRA

WHILE THE COUNTRY WAS BEING SHAKEN BY A
whirlwind of change, Victor's and Roser's lives returned to normal, he at the hospital and she with her
classes, concerts, and trips abroad. Two years prior to
the election, a surgeon with golden hands had trans-
planted a human heart into a twenty-four-year-old
woman in a Valparaiso hospital. This feat had been
achieved once before in South Africa, but it remained a
challenge to the laws of nature. Victor Dalmau followed every detail of the operation and crossed off
every one of the 133 days the patient survived on his
calendar. He dreamed again of Lazaro, the young soldier he rescued from death on a platform at the Estacion del Norte shortly before the end of the Civil War.
The recurring nightmare of Lazaro with his lifeless
heart on a tray was replaced by a luminous dream in

which the youngster had a window open in his chest, where his heart beat healthily surrounded by golden rays, like the image of the sacred heart of Jesus.

One day, Felipe del Solar went to consult Victor at the hospital with stabbing pains in his chest. He had never before set foot in a public hospital, always preferring to use private clinics, but his friend's reputation led him to venture down from the wealthy hillsides above Santiago to the gray area where the other classes lived. "When are you going to set up your office somewhere more suitable? And don't give me the nonsense that health is everyone's right and not the privilege of a few; I've already heard it," was his greeting. He wasn't in the habit of taking a number and waiting his turn on a metal chair. After examining him, Victor announced with a smile that his heart was perfectly healthy, and that perhaps his chest pains were due to his uneasy conscience or to anxiety. As he was getting dressed, Felipe commented that due to the political situation, half of Chile was suffering from an uneasy conscience and anxiety, but he held that the much-vaunted socialist revolution would never take place. Instead, the government would become paralyzed, caught up in power struggles among different parties.

"If it fails, Felipe, it won't just be because of what you're saying, but because of all the machinations of its adversaries and Washington's intervention," said Victor.

"I'll wager there'll be no fundamental changes."

"You're mistaken. The changes are already visible. Allende has been dreaming of this political project for forty years, and is pursuing it full steam ahead."

"It's one thing to plan, another to govern. You'll see how there'll be political and social chaos in this country, and how the economy will be bankrupted. These people lack experience and training, they spend their time in endless discussions and are unable to agree on anything," Felipe said.

"The opposition, on the other hand, has a single objective, doesn't it? To overthrow the government at any cost. And it may succeed, because it has huge resources and very few scruples," Victor retorted angrily.

During his campaign, Allende had announced the measures he intended to take: nationalize the copper industry, transfer companies and banks to state ownership, expropriate land. The effect of all this shook the country. In the early months, the reforms brought good results, but then the uncontrolled printing of money led to such rampant inflation that no one knew how much bread would cost from one day to the next. Just as Felipe del Solar had prophesied, the political parties in government fought among one another, the companies taken over by the workers were badly run, production dropped sharply, and the opposition's cunning sabotage produced shortages. In the Dalmau family, Carme was the one who complained the most.

"Going out shopping is a disaster, Victor. I never know what I'll find. I'm not much of a cook; the person who does the cooking at home is Jordi, but as you know he's turned into a scared, tearful old man who won't go out anymore. I have to leave him for hours on end, and he gets frightened when I'm not there. Just think: to come to the end of the world and have to line up for cigarettes!"

"You smoke too much, Mother. Don't waste time on that."

"I don't waste time, I pay the professionals."

"What professionals?"

"You must buy on the black market only if you have not heard of the professionals, son. There are unemployed youths or old-age pensioners who keep your place in line for a reasonable price."

"Allende has explained the reasons for the shortages. I suppose you've seen him on television?"

"Yes, and I have heard him about a hundred times on the radio. Telling us that, for the first time, the people have the means to buy, but the businessmen won't let them because they'd rather see themselves ruined if it creates discontent. Blah, blah . . . do you remember Spain?"

"Yes, Mother, I remember it very well. I have contacts, I'll see if I can get some things for you."

"Such as what?"

"Toilet paper, for example. There's a patient who sometimes brings me rolls of toilet paper as a gift."

"Goodness! That's more precious than gold, Victor."

"So I've heard."

"Listen, do you have any contacts for condensed milk and oil? I can wipe my ass with newspaper. And get me my cigarettes."

IT WAS NOT ONLY FOOD that disappeared, but spare parts, tires, cement, diapers, baby formula, and other essential articles. On the other hand, there was a glut of soy sauce, capers, and nail polish. When they started rationing fuel, Chile was filled with novice cyclists zigzagging their way around pedestrians.

And yet the people were still euphoric. At last they felt represented by the government. Everybody was equal: it was comrade here, comrade there, comrade president. Scarcity, rationing, and the feeling of continual precariousness were nothing new for those who had always just gotten by or had been poor. Victor Jara's revolutionary songs could be heard everywhere. Marcel knew them by heart, even though in the Dalmau family he was the one least passionate about politics. Walls were covered with murals and posters, plays were performed in public squares, and books published for the price of an ice cream so that each home could have its own library. The military was silent in their barracks, and if some were plotting, nothing came to light. The Catholic Church officially remained above the political fray; some priests showed themselves worthy of the Inquisition, stirring up hatred and rancor from the pulpit, while other priests and nuns supported the government, not for ideological reasons, but because they served those most in need. The right-wing press published headlines like *Chileans, gather your hatred!* and the scared, enraged bourgeoisie goaded the military to revolt: *Chickens, faggots, take up your weapons!*

"What we saw in Spain can happen here," Carme kept repeating like a refrain.

"Allende says there'll never be fratricidal conflict here. The government and people will prevent it," said Victor, trying to reassure her.

"That comrade of yours is too naïve by half. Chile is divided into irreconcilable groups, son. Friends are fighting, families are split down the middle; it's impossible to talk to anyone who doesn't think as you do. I don't see many of my old friends anymore so that we won't fight."

"Don't exaggerate, Mother."

Yet Victor too could sense the violence in the air. One night Marcel was coming back from a Victor Jara concert and stopped to watch a group of young people perched on a couple of ladders painting a mural of doves and rifles. Suddenly out of nowhere, two cars appeared. Several men armed with iron bars and clubs jumped out, and within a couple of minutes they had left the artists sprawled on the ground. Before Marcel could react, they leaped back into their vehicles, which were waiting with engines running, and sped off. Alerted by a neighbor, a police patrol turned up a few minutes later, and an ambulance arrived to carry away the worst injured. The police took Marcel back to the precinct to get his witness statement. Victor had to go and rescue him at three in the morning, because he was so upset he didn't want to cycle home.

An extremist left-wing movement sprang up calling for armed struggle, tired of waiting for the revolution to triumph by peaceful means. At the same time, so too did a Fascist one that didn't believe in civilized compromises either. "If we have to fight, let's get on with it," both sides said. In order to escape Jordi's clinging affection for a few hours, Carme took part in the huge demonstrations that crowded the streets in support of the government, but also the equally big opposition ones. She would leave in her sneakers with a lemon and a handkerchief soaked in vinegar to counteract the tear gas, and return soaked to the skin from the water cannon the police used to try to impose order. "Everything is a mess," she would say. "It will only take a spark for the whole thing to explode."

Isidro del Solar's estate wasn't expropriated, but was taken over by the peasant farmers. He regarded it as having been lost temporarily, because, as he told everyone, decency and morality would be restored sooner or later, and concentrated on saving his wool export business before the rabble ate his animals. He hired *huasos* from the south who knew the paths and shortcuts through the Andes, and sent his sheep to Argentine Patagonia, as other ranchers did with their cattle. Also, he transferred his family to Buenos Aires. They left en masse, including the married daughters, their husbands, and the grandchildren with their nannies. Juana Nancucheo stayed behind to look after the Calle Mar del Plata house. Laura had to be dragged along, stupefied with tranquilizers and sweets, after she was promised that in her absence Felipe would make sure there were always fresh flowers on Leonardo's grave. Felipe was the only one of the family who stayed; he carried on working at his legal practice, although the other two lawyers left to open a branch in Montevideo.

In those days he would often pay a visit to the Dalmaus in their house in the traditional Nuñoa district, where nobody from his own class lived. He dropped in with a couple of bottles of wine and a desire to talk. He no longer felt at ease with his lifelong friends, but couldn't fit in with his few acquaintances on the Left either. They reproached him about his affected manners copied from the English, as well as the vagueness of his political position. The Club of the Enraged had long ago dissolved. He dedicated himself to acquiring, at knockdown prices, antiquities and works of art from families who were leaving the country in a hurry, until before long he had no room to move about in his house. He began looking for a larger one, taking advantage of the fact that property was well-nigh being given away. He laughed at himself, recalling how in his youth he had criticized the extravagance of his parents' home. When Roser asked him what he would do with all his trinkets if, as he often said, he decided to leave the country, he replied that he would store them in a warehouse until his return, because Chile wasn't Russia or Cuba, and the famous Chilean-style revolution wasn't going to last very long. He seemed so certain of this that Victor suspected his friend was in the know about some fundamental intrigue. Just in case, he never mentioned his games of chess with the president.

Whenever Felipe drank whisky to follow the wine over dinner, his tongue was loosened, and he started railing against life and the world in general. He had become cynical, with little left of his youthful idealism and generosity. He admitted that socialism was the most just system, but in practice it led to a police state or a dictatorship as in Cuba, where anybody who didn't agree with the regime either escaped to Miami or ended up in prison. His aristocratic nature abhorred the disorder of equality, revolutionary clichés, dogmatic slogans, vulgar manners, bushy beards, and the ugly handicrafts: cane furniture and jute carpets, rope sandals, seed necklaces, crocheted skirts. It was all a huge disaster. "I don't see why we should dress like beggars," he maintained. Not to mention what was called popular culture, which had nothing cultural about it. It was a Chilean version of the Soviets' horrible socialist realism, with their murals of miners raising their fists and Che Guevara portraits, singer-songwriters preaching sermons with their tedious little tunes. "Even instruments like the Mapuche *trutruca* and the *quena* of the Quechuas have become fashionable!"

However, when Felipe was with his usual right-wing friends, he would subject them to an equally devastating critique of the recalcitrant, conspiratorial upper classes who were stuck in the past and remained blind and deaf to the people's demands, only too ready to defend their privileges at the cost of democracy and of their country. They were traitors. In short, nobody could stomach him, and he became increasingly isolated. His bachelor's solitude weighed heavily on him, and he was full of aches and pains.

Victor, who had been so pleased with the improvements in public health, from the daily glass of milk for every child as a palliative against malnutrition to the building of new hospitals, found he had no antibiotics, anesthetics, needles, syringes, or basic medicines. There was also a shortage of people to care for the sick, because many doctors had left Chile to ride out the feared Soviet tyranny that the opposition propaganda was predicting, and because the School of Medicine had declared a strike, which most of his colleagues joined. He continued working double shifts, falling asleep on his feet, weary to the core, and feeling as though he had lived through the same thing during the Spanish Civil War. Other professional associations, factory owners, and business organizations also imposed a shutdown. When truck drivers refused to work, the long, thin country was left without transport. Fish rotted in the north, vegetables and fruit in the south, while in Santiago there were shortages of essentials. Allende roundly denounced North American intervention in their financing of the truck drivers and right-wing conspiracies. Students added to the chaos, barricading themselves in university lecture halls. When they blockaded the faculty entrance with sandbags, Roser arranged to see her students in the park and gave her theory classes in the open air, under umbrellas if necessary. She took attendance and gave grades as usual, only sad that she couldn't drag a grand piano out there. People grew accustomed to the sight of the police in riot gear, protest placards and banners, inflammatory posters, the threats and catastrophic warnings in the press, the shouts from one side and the other, everyone against everyone. And yet there was unanimous consensus over the complete nationalization of mining.

"It was about time," Marcel Dalmau told his grandmother. "Copper is Chile's paycheck, it's what sustains the economy."

"If copper is Chilean, I don't see why it has to be nationalized."

"It's always been in the hands of North American companies, *Àvia*. The government took it back and refused to indemnify the Americans, because they owe the country billions of dollars in excessive profits and tax evasion."

"The Americans aren't going to like that. Take heed of what I'm saying, Marcel, there's going to be trouble," Carme told him.

"When the Americans leave the mining industry, we're going to need more Chilean engineers and geologists. I'm going to be in demand, *Àvia*."

"I'm glad. Will they pay you more?"

"I don't know. Why?"

"So that you can get married, Marcel. If you don't hurry up, I'm not going to get to know my great-grandchildren. You're thirty-one, it's time for you to settle down."

"I am settled."

"I can't see any women in your life. That's not normal. Have you never been in love? Or are you one of those who . . . ? Well, you know what I mean."

"How nosy you are, *Àvia!*"

"This comes from the vice of riding a bicycle. It crushes the testicles and causes impotence and sterility."

"Aha."

"I read it in a magazine at the hairdresser's. And it's not that you're bad-looking, Marcel. If you got rid of that beard and cut that mop of hair of yours, you'd look just like Dominguin."

"Who?"

"The bullfighter, of course. And you're not stupid either. Wake up a bit. You're like a Trappist monk."

Carme hadn't anticipated that one consequence of the nationalization would be that the copper corporation gave her grandson a grant to go to the United States. She got it into her head she would never see him again. Marcel left for Colorado, to a city at the foot of the Rocky Mountains founded during the gold rush, to study geology. He took his dismantled bike with him because it was specially made for him, together with his Victor Jara records. "I'll write to you," was the last thing Àvia told him in the airport.

Marcel had studied English with the same quiet obstinacy that made him refuse to speak Catalan, and was able to adapt after only a few weeks in Colorado. He arrived at the start of a golden fall, and a couple of months later was shoveling snow. He joined bike enthusiasts training to cross the United States from the Pacific to the Atlantic, and another group that climbed mountains. Victor was never able to go and see him; with all the disturbances, demonstrations, shutdowns, strikes, and overwork, he couldn't find time to travel. But Roser visited him a couple of times and was able to inform the rest of the family that her son had possibly said more in English in Colorado than he had in Spanish in all his previous life. He had shaved off his beard and wore a short ponytail. Àvia was right, he did look like Dominguin.

Far from his family's scrutiny, free from the conflicts and injustices taking place in Chile, and in the intellectual oasis of the university, where he spent his time deciphering the secret nature of rocks, for the first time he felt comfortable in his own skin. In Colorado he wasn't the son of refugees, nobody had heard of the Spanish Civil War, and only a few people could place Chile on a map, much less Catalonia. In this foreign reality and in a different language he made friends, and within a few months was living in a tiny apartment with his first love, a young Jamaican woman who studied literature and wrote for newspapers. On Roser's second visit, she met the girlfriend and returned to Chile commenting that as well as being beautiful, she was as bubbly and talkative as Marcel was introverted. "Don't worry, Doña Carme, your grandson is finally wising up. The Jamaican girl is teaching him to dance to her country's rhythms. If you saw him writhing around to the sound of drums and maracas, you wouldn't believe it."

AS SHE FEARED, *Àvia* never embraced her grandson again, nor did she meet the Jamaican girl or any of his other girlfriends, or the great-grandchildren who would have prolonged the Dalmau lineage. She died in her bed on the morning of her eighty-seventh birthday, when the tent and tables for the party had already been set up behind the house. She had gone to bed with her smoker's cough as always, but in good health and looking forward to the celebration. Jordi Moline woke to the daylight filtering in through the slats in the shutters. He lay around in bed, waiting for the smell of toast to tell him it was time to get up, put his slippers on, and have breakfast. It took him several minutes to realize that Carme was still alongside him, motionless and cold as marble. Taking her by the hand, he lay there quietly, sobbing gently as he took in the terrible betrayal of her going first and leaving him all alone.

Roser discovered Carme around one o'clock that afternoon, when she appeared at the house with the birthday cake and a car full of balloons to set the tables before the caterer and his assistants arrived. She was surprised by the silence and darkness in the house, the closed shutters and stale air. She called out to her mother-in-law and Jordi from the living room before going to look for them in the kitchen and then venturing into the bedroom. Afterward, as soon as she could react, she picked up the telephone and first dialed Victor's number at the hospital and then Marcel's at his hotel in Buenos Aires, where by chance he had been visiting with a group of students. She told them *Àvia* had died, and Jordi had disappeared.

Carme had said on more than one occasion that if she died in Chile she wished to be buried in Spain, where her husband and son Guillem were laid to rest, but if she died in Spain she wanted to be buried in Chile, to be near the rest of her family. Why? Well just to cause trouble, she would say with a laugh. And yet it wasn't simply a joke, it was the anguish of divided love, separation, of living and dying far from one's loved ones.

Marcel was able to fly to Santiago the next day. They kept vigil over the grandmother in the house where she had lived with Jordi Moline for nineteen years. There was no religious ceremony, because the last time Carme had set foot in church was as a little girl, before she fell in love with Marcel Lluis Dalmau. However, without being asked, two Maryknoll priests who lived nearby turned up. In the past, Carme had traded serrano ham and manchego cheese Jordi obtained illegally for cigarettes the priests had been sent from New York. The two improvised a funeral service with a guitar and singing that would have pleased Carme.

The only inconsolable member of the family was her grandson, Marcel, who had enjoyed the closest relationship with *Àvia*. He drank two glasses of *pisco* and sat and wept for all he hadn't managed to say to her, for the lost tenderness he had been ashamed of showing her, for having refused to talk to her in Catalan, for having made fun of her disastrous cooking, for not having answered every single one of her letters. He was the one closest to the heart of that rebellious, bossy grandmother who had written him a daily letter after he left for Colorado until the day before she died. From then on, the only thing that went with Marcel wherever he happened to live was the shoe box tied up with string that contained the three hundred and fifty-nine letters from his *Àvia*. Quiet and sad, Victor sat down next to Marcel, reflecting that his small family had lost the cornerstone that held it up. Much later that night, he said as much to Roser when they were alone in their bedroom. "You're the cornerstone that's always held us up," Roser told him.

Among the mourners at the wake were neighbors, former colleagues, and students from the school where Carme had taught for years, friends from the days when she accompanied Jordi to the Winnipeg tavern, and friends of Victor and Roser. At eight o'clock that night the police arrived on motorcycles and blocked off the whole street to allow three blue Fiats to enter. One of them contained the president, who had come to offer his condolences to his chess-playing friend.

Victor bought a plot in the cemetery big enough to accommodate not only his mother, but Jordi and possibly his father's remains, if in the future they succeeded in bringing them from Spain. He realized that from this moment on he belonged definitively to Chile. "Our homeland is where our dead are buried," Carme always used to insist.

The police meanwhile were searching for Jordi Moline. The old man had no family, and his friends were the same as Carme's. None of them had seen him. Thinking that due to his slight dementia he might have gotten lost, the Dalmaus put up his photograph on posters in local shops, and left the door to his house unlocked in case he returned. Roser thought he must have left in pajamas and slippers, because it seemed to her all his clothes were still in his wardrobe, but she couldn't be sure. This was confirmed the following summer, when the level of the Mapocho River dropped and they finally found what was left of the old man caught in some reeds. The only items of clothing recovered were shreds of his pajamas. A whole month went by before he was definitely identified and handed over to the Dalmau family for burial beside Carme.

———

DESPITE PROBLEMS OF EVERY KIND, galloping inflation, and the catastrophic news spread by the press, the Allende government still had popular support. This was demonstrated in the parliamentary elections, when its share of the vote grew unexpectedly, making it plain that the economic crisis and the hate campaign would not be enough to get rid of Allende.

"The right wing is arming itself, Doctor," Victor was warned by the patient who brought him toilet paper. "I know, because in my factory there are rooms locked with metal bars and padlocks. Nobody can enter."

"That doesn't prove anything."

"Some comrades take turns to be on guard day and night because of possible sabotage. They've seen crates being unloaded from trucks. Since they looked different from the usual loads, they decided to investigate. They're certain they were full of weapons. There's going to be a bloodbath here, Doctor, because the youth in the revolutionary movement are armed as well."

That night Victor commented on this to Allende. They were finishing a game they had postponed for several days. The house, purchased by the government as a presidential residence, was Spanish-style, with arched windows, red tiles, a mosaic with the national coat of arms over the entrance, and two tall palm trees visible from the street. The guards knew Victor, and no one was surprised he should turn up late at night. He and Allende played chess in the living room, where there was always a board set up, surrounded by books and works of art.

Allende was not surprised by what Victor had to say. He was already aware of the situation, but legally it was impossible to raid either that factory or any others where doubtless the same thing was occurring. "Don't worry, Victor. As long as the armed forces remain loyal to the government, there's nothing to fear. I trust the commander in chief, he's an honorable man." He added that the vociferous left-wing extremists who were demanding a Cuban-style revolution were just as dangerous; those hotheads did as much harm to the government as the right wing.

At the end of that year a mass homage to Pablo Neruda was held in the National Stadium. This would be the poet's last public appearance. The previous year, he had received the Nobel Prize from the hands of the elderly Swedish monarch. Neruda quit his position as ambassador to France and withdrew to the anarchic house at Isla Negra that he loved so much. He was ill, but continued writing in his small study with the angry sea pounding the rocks outside his window. Over the next few months Victor visited him several times as a friend, and on two occasions as a doctor. Neruda would greet him in his indigenous poncho and beret, affable and as much a gourmand as ever, more than ready to share a sea bass baked in the oven and a bottle of Chilean wine and to talk about life. No longer was he the playful joker who dressed up to entertain his friends and wrote odes to a happy day. Although he was flooded with invitations, prizes, and admiring messages from all over the world, his heart was heavy. He was afraid for Chile.

He was writing his memoirs, in which the Spanish Civil War and the *Winnipeg* filled several pages. He grew emotional when he recalled all the many Spanish friends who had been murdered or were missing. "I don't want to die before Franco," he would say. Victor assured him he would live for many years: his illness was slow-moving and under control, but he too suspected the Caudillo was immortal: he had clung to power with an iron fist for thirty-three years already. Victor's memory of Spain was increasingly vague. At midnight every year he proposed a toast to the New Year and for a swift return to his home country, but he did so only out of tradition, without any real hope or desire. He suspected that the Spain where he was born, the Spain he knew and had fought for, no longer existed. In all the years dominated by uniforms and cassocks, it must have become a place to which he no longer belonged.

Like Neruda, he too was afraid for Chile. Rumors of a possible military coup that had been heard for two years now suddenly grew louder. The president still trusted the armed forces, even though he knew they were split. By the start of spring 1973, violence from the opposition had reached unprecedented levels, while discontent among the military had become a threat. Undermined by his officers' insubordination, the commander in chief resigned in late August. He explained to the president that his duty as a soldier was to step down to avoid the breakdown of military discipline. His gesture proved useless. At five in the morning on September 11, the feared military coup took place. Within a few hours Chilean reality was turned upside down, and nothing was ever the same again.

Victor left early for the hospital. He found streets blocked by tanks, lines of green trucks transporting troops, and helicopters buzzing low in the sky like birds of ill omen. Soldiers in combat gear and faces painted like Comanches rifle-butted the few civilians out at that time of the morning. Victor understood immediately what was going on and returned home, calling Roser in Caracas and Marcel in Colorado. They both announced they would catch the next available plane back to Chile, but he convinced them they ought to wait for the worst of the storm to blow over. He tried in vain to get in touch with the president and political leaders he knew. There was no news. The television channels were in the hands of the rebels, and so were all the radio stations apart from one, which confirmed what he suspected. The operation to silence the country, directed from the U.S. embassy, was precise and efficient. Censorship began at once.

Victor decided his place was at the hospital, and so threw a change of clothes and his toothbrush into a bag and drove there along backstreets in his old Citroën. He had with him a transistor radio that was transmitting, amid harsh screeches, the voice of the president denouncing the betrayal of the armed forces and the Fascist coup. He urged the people to stay calm in their workplaces and not permit themselves to be provoked or massacred, repeating that he would remain at his post defending the legitimate government. "Placed in a historic transition, I will pay for loyalty to the people with my life." Victor's tears prevented him from driving on, and he came to a halt just as the fighter planes roared overhead. Almost immediately he heard the first bombs being dropped. He saw thick clouds of smoke in the distance and calculated, to his astonishment, that they were bombing the presidential palace.

THE FOUR GENERALS OF the military junta controlling the country's destiny appeared several times a day on television with their edicts and proclamations. They were in uniform, framed by the national flag and coat of arms, with military marches playing in the background. All information was tightly censored. They said Salvador Allende had committed suicide in the palace, although Victor suspected they had killed him as they had so many others. It was only then that he understood how grave the situation was. There would be no going back.

Government ministers were arrested, Congress was declared in permanent recess, political parties were banned, press freedom and citizens' rights were suspended until further notice. Anyone in military barracks who hesitated to join the coup was arrested, and many of them shot, although this didn't become known until much later, because the armed forces had to give the impression they were monolithic and indestructible. To avoid being murdered by his own comrades in arms, the former commander in chief fled to Argentina, but a year later a bomb was put in his car and he died, blown to pieces together with his wife.

General Augusto Pinochet led the military junta, and soon came to personify the dictatorship. Repression was instantaneous, brutal, and thorough. It was announced that no stone would remain un-turned, that the Marxists would be dragged out of their hiding places wherever they were, and the fatherland would be cleansed of the communist cancer at any cost. While in the bourgeois neighborhoods they finally celebrated with the champagne put aside for almost three years, in the working-class barrios and in the shantytowns there was a reign of terror.

Victor didn't return home for nine days, at first because there was a seventy-two-hour curfew and nobody could go out into the street, and afterward because the hospital was full to overflowing. There was a stream of patients with bullet wounds, and the morgue filled with unidentified corpses. Victor ate what he could find in the cafeteria, slept fitfully in a chair, washed his body with a sponge, and was able to change clothes only once. It took him several hours to place an international call. He phoned Roser from the hospital, ordering her not to return for any reason until he said she could, and telling her to pass the message on to Marcel. The university had been shut down, and any attempt at resistance was stifled by gunfire. He was told that the walls of the School of Journalism and other faculties were smeared with blood. He couldn't tell Roser anything about the situation in the Conservatory of Music or her students. The doctors' strike came to an end at once, and his colleagues returned to work in a cheerful mood. The purge had begun of hospital staff and even of patients, who were pulled from their beds by the security forces. A colonel was put in charge of the hospital, and machine gun–toting soldiers guarded the entrances and exits, corridors, wards, and even operating rooms. Many left-wing doctors were arrested, and others fled or sought asylum, and yet Victor went on working with an irrational sense of impunity.

When he finally went home to bathe and change clothes, Victor was confronted by an unrecognizable city, clean and painted white. In those few days the revolutionary murals and banners inciting hatred had disappeared, as had the garbage, the bearded men and women in trousers. He noticed in shop windows products that previously had been available only on the black market, but there were few customers because prices had soared. Soldiers and armed police were keeping watch; there were tanks on street corners and closed vans hurtled by, howling like jackals. The spotless order of barracks and the artificial peace of fear reigned everywhere.

As he was entering his home, Victor greeted his neighbor of many years, who poked her head out at that moment. She didn't return his greeting, slamming shut her window. That should have served as a warning, but he simply shrugged, thinking the poor woman was as bewildered as he was by the latest events. His house was exactly as he had left it in his hurry to get to the hospital on the day of the coup: the unmade bed, clothes strewn about, food with green mold in the kitchen. He didn't have the heart to tidy up. He fell flat on his back in bed and slept for fourteen hours.

IT WAS AROUND THIS TIME that Pablo Neruda died. The military coup had been the culmination of his worst fears. He couldn't withstand it, and his health suddenly declined. While he was being taken by ambulance to a Santiago clinic, troops raided his home at Isla Negra, trashed his papers, and trampled on his collections of bottles and all kinds of shells, searching for weapons and guerrilla fighters. Victor went to visit him at the clinic, where the guards frisked him, took his fingerprints, photographed him, and in the end the soldier guarding the door to the poet's room blocked the entrance.

From what he knew of Neruda's illness, and because he had seen him looking well only a month earlier, Victor was surprised at the suddenness of his death. He wasn't the only one who was suspicious: a rumor soon went around that Neruda had been poisoned. Three days before he was interned in the clinic, the poet wrote the final pages of his memoir filled with the bitter disappointment of seeing his country divided and subjugated, and his friend Salvador Allende buried in an inconspicuous spot with his widow the only mourner . . . *that glorious dead figure was riddled and ripped to pieces by the machine guns of Chile's soldiers, who had betrayed Chile once more,* he wrote. He was right to say the Chilean military had rebelled before against a legitimate government, but the weak collective memory had erased those earlier betrayals from history. The poet's funeral was the first protest against the coup-mongers, and it wasn't prohibited because the eyes of the world were watching. Victor was operating on a gravely ill patient and couldn't leave the hospital. He learned the details several days later from one of his patients.

"There weren't many people, Doctor. Do you remember the huge crowd in the National Stadium when there was that homage to the poet? Well, I think there must have been about two hundred of us at most in the cemetery."

"The news of his death has just come out in the newspapers, so it was too late. Not many people knew either of his death or his burial."

"People are scared."

"Many of Neruda's friends and admirers must be in hiding or in prison. Tell me what it was like."

"I was up at the front. I was a bit frightened, because there were soldiers with submachine guns lining the route in the cemetery. The coffin was covered with flowers. We were walking along in silence until somebody shouted: 'Comrade Pablo Neruda!' and we all shouted back 'Here, now and forever!'"

"What did the soldiers do?"

"Nothing. Then one brave guy shouted 'Comrade President!' and we all shouted 'Here, now and forever!' It was so moving, Doctor. We also shouted that the people united would never be defeated. The soldiers did nothing, but there were some guys taking photos of those of us in the cortege. Who knows what they want them for."

Victor was suspicious of everything. Reality had become hard to grasp, people lived in the midst of lies, omissions, and euphemisms, in grotesque exaltation of the blessed fatherland, brave soldiers, and traditional morality. The word "comrade" was erased: nobody dared pronounce it. There were whispered rumors about concentration camps, summary executions, thousands and thousands of people, fugitives and exiles, arrested or disappeared, stories of torture centers where dogs were used to rape women. Victor wondered where the torturers and informers had been before, as he had never seen them. They seemed to have emerged in the space of a few hours, ready and organized as if they'd been in training for years. The deep Chile of the Fascists had always been there, beneath the surface, just waiting to emerge. It was the triumph of the arrogant Right, the defeat of the people who believed in that utopian revolution.

He learned that, like so many others, Isidro del Solar had returned to Chile a few days after the coup, ready to reclaim their privileges and the reins of the economy, although not political power. For the time being, that lay with the generals while they restored order to the chaos into which Marxism had plunged the country. No one apart from the generals imagined how long the dictatorship would last.

IT WAS HIS NEIGHBOR who denounced Victor Dalmau. The same woman who two years earlier had asked him to use his friendship with the president to secure a place for her son in the police force, the same one on whom he had operated to insert a couple of heart valves, the same one who swapped sugar and rice with Roser, the same one who attended Carme's funeral in tears.

Victor was arrested at the hospital. Three men in civilian clothes who didn't identify themselves came to look for him while he was in the operating room. At least they had the decency to wait until he finished operating.

"Come with us, Doctor, it's just routine," they ordered him brusquely. Out in the street they pushed him into a black automobile, handcuffed and blindfolded him. The first punch was to his stomach.

Victor Dalmau had no idea where he was until two days later, when they had finally had enough of their interrogations and dragged him out of the bowels of the building, took off the blindfold and handcuffs, and he was able to breathe fresh air. It took him several minutes to adjust his eyes to the blinding midday light and recover his balance so that he could stand up. He was in the National Stadium. A very young conscript gave him a blanket, took him by the arm without violence, and led him slowly over to the stand he had been assigned to. Victor found it hard to walk: his whole body was aching from the beatings and electric shocks, he was as thirsty as a shipwrecked sailor and couldn't figure out what day it was, or remember exactly what had happened. He could have been in the hands of his torturers for a week or only a few hours. What had they asked him? Allende, chess, Plan Z. What on earth was Plan Z? He had no idea. There were others in similar cells, noise from giant ventilators, hair-raising screams, bullets. "They shot them, they shot them," murmured Victor.

He saw thousands of prisoners in the stands, guarded by soldiers. He had been there before for soccer matches and cultural events, like the homage to Pablo Neruda. When the conscript who had brought him there moved away, another prisoner came up to Victor. He took him to a seat and offered him water from a thermos. "Don't worry, comrade, I'm sure the worst has passed." The prisoner let him empty the thermos, then helped him lie down and put a rolled-up blanket under his head. "Get some rest. We're going to be here a long while." He was a metalworker who was arrested two days after the coup and had been in the stadium for weeks. At dusk, when the heat lessened and Victor could sit up, he explained the routine.

"Don't attract attention. Stay still and silent—they can use any excuse to beat you to death with their rifles. They're wild animals."

"So much hatred, so much cruelty . . . I don't understand," Victor mumbled. His mouth was dry, and the words stuck in his throat.

"We can all turn into savages if we're given a rifle and an order," said another prisoner who had come over to them.

"Not me, comrade," the metalworker responded. "I saw how these thugs destroyed Victor Jara's hands. 'Sing now, you jerk,' they shouted at him. They beat him and then riddled him with bullets."

"The most important thing is for someone outside here to know where you are," the other man said. "That way they can follow your trail, if you disappear. A lot of people disappear and are never heard of again. Are you married?"

"Yes," replied Victor.

"Give me your wife's address or telephone number. My daughter can get word to her. She spends all day outside the stadium with members of other prisoners' families waiting for news."

Victor, though, didn't give him either, fearing he might be an informer planted to get information.

One of the nurses from the San Juan de Dios hospital who had seen Victor being arrested finally managed to reach Roser by telephone in Venezuela and tell her what had happened. As soon as she heard this, Roser called Marcel to give him the bad news and order him to stay where he was, because he could be more useful outside the country than in Chile. She, however, was going to return immediately. She bought a plane ticket, and before boarding went to see Valentin Sanchez. "Once we know what they've done with your husband, we'll rescue him," her friend promised her. He gave her a letter for the current Venezuelan ambassador in Chile, a colleague from his days as a diplomat. There were already hundreds of people seeking asylum in his Santiago residence, waiting for safe-conducts to go into exile. His was one of the few embassies willing to offer refuge to fugitives. Hundreds of Chileans began to arrive in Caracas; soon there would be thousands.

Roser landed in Chile at the end of October, but it wasn't until November that she learned her husband had been taken to the National Stadium. When the Venezuelan ambassador went there to ask after him, he was assured Dalmau had never been there. By this time they were evacuating the prisoners and distributing them in concentration camps throughout Chile. Roser spent months searching for him, using her friends and international contacts, knocking on the doors of different organizations, consulting lists of the disappeared put up in churches. His name was nowhere to be found. He had vanished into thin air.

Together with other political prisoners, Victor Dalmau had been taken in a caravan of trucks that traveled a whole day and night. They ended up at a camp for saltpeter miners in the north that had been abandoned for decades and was now converted into a prison. These were the first two hundred men to occupy the makeshift installations in huts that had once accommodated the saltpeter workers. The camp was surrounded by electrified barbed-wire fences and tall watchtowers, with soldiers carrying submachine guns, a tank patrolling the perimeter, and every so often air force planes. The commander was a police officer who barked orders and sweated in a uniform that was too tight for him. He was a stone-hearted bully who announced over the loudspeaker that he intended to keep the prisoners in a fist for the crimes they had committed and those they were thinking of committing. As soon as the prisoners climbed down from the trucks they were forced to strip and left in the hot desert sun for hours without food or water, while he walked along insulting and kicking them one by one. From the outset he doled out arbitrary punishments to break his victims' morale, and his men imitated him.

Because of the months spent in Argeles-sur-Mer, Victor thought he was better prepared than the other prisoners to resist, but that had been years ago, when he was young. Now he was about to turn sixty, but until the moment of his arrest he had never had time to think about his age. There in the north, with burning hot days and icy nights on the saltpeter flats, he longed to die of weariness. It was impossible to escape: the camp was surrounded by the immense desert, hundreds of kilometers of dry earth, sand, rocks, and wind. He felt like an old man.

CHAPTER 11

1974–1983

Now I'll tell you:
my land will be yours,
I'm going to conquer it,
not just to give it to you,
but to everyone,
to all my people.

— PABLO NERUDA
"Letter on the Way"
THE CAPTAIN'S VERSES

DURING THE ELEVEN MONTHS VICTOR DALMAU spent in the concentration camp, he didn't die of weariness as he had expected. Instead, his body and mind were strengthened. He had always been thin, but there he was reduced to nothing but skin and bones. His skin was burned by the unrelenting sun, salt, and sand, his features sharpened: he was a Giacometti sculpture in cast iron. He wasn't defeated by the absurd military exercises, pushups, races in the scorching heat, the hours lying still in the freezing night, the blows and beatings, being forced to work at pointless tasks, humiliated, ravenous. He yielded to his condition as a prisoner, abandoning all pretense that he could control anything in his existence. He was in his captors' hands: they had absolute power and impunity, he was master only of his emotions. He repeated to himself the metaphor of the birch tree, which bends in a storm but doesn't break. He had already endured this in other circumstances. He protected himself from the sadism and stupidity of his jailers by withdrawing into silent memories, certain only that Roser was searching for him and would one day find him. He spoke so little that the other prisoners nicknamed him "the mute." He thought of Marcel, who had spent the first thirty years of his life saying next to nothing because he didn't want to talk. Victor didn't want to either, because there was nothing to say. His companions in misfortune kept their spirits up whispering out of earshot of the guards, while he thought of Roser with great nostalgia, of all they had lived through together, how much he loved her.

To keep his mind sharp he obsessively went over the most famous games in the history of chess, as well as some of those he had played with the president. He once dreamed of carving chess pieces from the camp's porous stones so that he could play with some of the others, but that was impossible due to the guards' despotic surveillance. These soldiers came from the working class. Their families were poor, and perhaps most of them had been sympathetic to the socialist revolution, but they obeyed orders with great cruelty, as though the prisoners' past actions were personal insults.

Each week, inmates were taken to other concentration camps or were shot, their bodies blown up with dynamite in the desert, and yet many more arrived than left. Victor calculated there were more than fifteen hundred altogether. They came from across the country, were of different ages and occupations; the only thing they had in common was the fact that they were being persecuted. They were enemies of the fatherland. Like Victor, some of them had not belonged to a party or held any political position; they were there due to a vengeful denunciation or a bureaucratic mistake.

———

IT WAS THE START of spring, and the prisoners were already fearing the arrival of summer, which turned the camp into a hell during the daylight hours, when an abrupt change came in Victor Dalmau's fortunes. The camp commander suffered a heart attack just as he was giving his morning harangue to the prisoners, who were lined up in the yard barefoot and in their underwear. The commandant fell to his knees, managed to gasp for breath, then slumped to the ground before the nearest soldiers could catch him. Not a single prisoner moved; no one made a sound. To Victor it was as if everything was happening in slow motion, in silence and in another dimension, as if it were part of a nightmare. He saw two soldiers trying to lift the commandant, while others ran to call the nurse.

With no thought for the consequences, he stepped forward through the lines of prisoners as though sleepwalking. Everybody was staring at the fallen man, and by the time they noticed Victor and ordered him to stop and throw himself facedown on the ground, he had already reached the front of the ranks. "He's a doctor!" shouted one of the prisoners. Victor continued to trot forward, and in a few seconds reached the unconscious commandant. He kneeled down beside the commandant without anyone stopping him: the soldiers stepped back to give him room. He checked that the commandant wasn't breathing. He signaled to one of the closest guards to loosen his clothing, while he gave him artificial respiration and pressed down hard on his chest with both hands. He knew there was a manual defibrillator in the sick bay because it was occasionally used to resuscitate torture victims.

A few minutes later the nurse came running up, followed by an assistant with oxygen and the defibrillator. He helped Victor restart the commandant's heart.

"A helicopter! We have to get him to a hospital at once!" Victor insisted as soon as he realized the heart was beating once more. They carried the commandant to the sick bay, where Victor kept him alive until the helicopter on standby at the edge of the camp was ready to take off. They were thirty-five minutes from the nearest hospital. Victor was ordered to accompany the patient and was handed an army shirt, trousers, and boots.

It was a small but well-equipped provincial hospital. In normal times it would have had sufficient resources for an emergency of this kind, but now there were only two doctors. They both knew Victor Dalmau by reputation and greeted him respectfully. Thanks to an irony typical of those days, Victor was told the chief surgeon and the cardiologist had both been arrested. Victor had no time to wonder where they could have been taken, as neither of them was among the prisoners in his camp. An operating room had been his workplace for decades, and as he always told his students, the heart is a muscular organ that contains no mysteries; those attributed to it are entirely subjective. In no time at all he gave the necessary instructions, scrubbed his hands, prepared the commandant, and then, assisted by one of the hospital doctors, proceeded to carry out the operation he had performed hundreds of times. He discovered that his hands' memory was intact: they moved by themselves.

Victor spent the night awake with his patient, more euphoric than exhausted. In the hospital nobody stood guard over him with a submachine gun; he was treated with deference and admiration, and given steak with mashed potatoes, a glass of red wine, and ice cream for dessert. For a few hours he became Doctor Dalmau again rather than a number. He had forgotten what life was like before his arrest. In midmorning, when his patient was still critical but stable, an army cardiologist arrived by plane from Santiago. Victor was ordered to return to the concentration camp, but he managed to ask the doctor who had assisted him in the operation to contact Roser. This was a risk, because the man was undoubtedly right-wing, but over the hours they worked together their mutual respect was plain. Victor was certain Roser had returned to Chile to look for him, because that is what he would have done for her.

The new concentration camp commandant turned out to be as brutal as his predecessor, but Victor only had to put up with him for five days. That morning, when they had finished the roll call and separated out the prisoners to be taken away, his name was called. For the prisoners, this was the worst moment of the day, as they could be transferred to a torture center, a camp still more terrible than this one, or taken out and shot. After waiting three hours standing up, the group was led to a truck. The guard checking the names on his list stopped Victor from climbing on board with the others. "You stay here, asshole." He had to wait another hour before he was led to the camp office, where the commandant himself told him he was in luck and handed him a sheet of paper. He had been granted parole. "If it was up to me, I'd open the gate and make you walk, you communist son of a bitch. But it turns out you're to be taken back to the hospital," the man told him.

Roser and a Venezuelan embassy official were waiting for him there. Victor hugged his wife with the despair of those long months of uncertainty when he had thought of her with a love he had never clearly expressed. "Oh, Roser, how much I love you, how much I've missed you," he whispered, burying his nose in her hair. Both of them were weeping.

BEING ON PAROLE MEANT going every day to a police station to sign a register. Depending on the mood of the duty officer, this could take a long while. Victor signed in twice before deciding to seek asylum in the Venezuelan embassy. It had taken him those two days to realize that having been a prisoner condemned him to being ostracized. He couldn't go back to work at the hospital; his friends avoided him, and he ran the risk of being rearrested at any moment. The caution and fear all around him were in sharp contrast to the defiant, vengeful optimism shown by the dictatorship's supporters. What was really going on in the shadows was never mentioned. Nobody protested; the crushed workers had lost their rights: they could be fired at any moment and were grateful for whatever wages they received, because there was a line of unemployed waiting at the door to be given an opportunity. It was the employers' paradise. The official version was of an orderly, clean, and pacified country heading for prosperity. Victor couldn't help thinking of those tortured or killed, the faces of the men he had met in prison and those who had disappeared. People had changed; he found it hard to recognize the country that had received him with such a fervent embrace thirty-five years earlier, and which he loved as if it were his own.

By the second day he confessed to Roser he couldn't bear the dictatorship. "I couldn't do so in Spain, and I can't here. I'm too old to live in fear, Roser; but a second exile is as unbearable as staying in Chile and facing the consequences." She argued it would only be temporary: the military regime would soon end because, as everyone said, Chile had a solid democratic tradition, and so they could return. Her argument crumbled in the face of the fact that Franco had been in power for more than thirty years, and Pinochet could imitate him. Victor spent a sleepless night contemplating whether to leave or not, lying in the darkness with Roser curled up beside him, listening to the noises from the street.

At three in the morning he heard a car pull up outside the house. That could only mean they were coming for him again; during curfew only military and security service vehicles were allowed on the streets. There was no way he could run or hide. He lay there in a cold sweat, his heart beating like a drum. Roser peeped out through the curtains and saw a second black automobile pull up behind the first one. "Get dressed quickly," she ordered Victor.

But then she saw several men get out of the cars in a leisurely way: no rushing, shouting, or pulling out weapons. They stood there for a while smoking and chatting, and eventually drove off again. Trembling, arms around each other, Victor and Roser waited at the window until it began to grow light, then five o'clock struck and the curfew ended.

Roser arranged for the Venezuelan ambassador to collect Victor in a car with diplomatic license plates. By this time, most of the asylum-seekers in embassies had left for the countries that accepted them, and surveillance was less strict. Victor entered the embassy curled up in the trunk. A month later he was given a safe-conduct. Two Venezuelan officials accompanied him to the door of the plane, where Roser was waiting for him. He was clean, freshly shaven, and calm. On the same plane was another exile, who had his handcuffs removed once he was in his seat. He was filthy, disheveled, and shaking. Victor couldn't help noticing him, and when they were in the air, approached him. He had difficulty striking up a conversation and convincing the man he wasn't a secret policeman. He saw the man had no front teeth, and several of his fingers were crushed.

"How can I be of help, comrade?" he said.

"They're going to make the plane turn around . . . They're going to take me back to . . ." the man said, bursting into tears.

"Stay calm, we've been in the air for almost an hour, I'm sure we're not going back to Santiago. This is a direct flight to Caracas; you'll be safe there, you'll have help. I'll get you a drink, you need it."

"Make it something to eat," the other man begged him.

ROSER HAD SPENT LONG PERIODS in Venezuela with the Ancient Music Orchestra. She gave concerts, had made friends, and moved easily in a society whose rules of behavior were different from those of Chile. Valentin Sanchez had introduced her to everyone worth knowing, and opened the doors to the world of culture. Her love affair with Aitor Ibarra had ended years before, but they were still friends, and she visited him from time to time. His stroke had left him a semi-invalid, and he had some difficulty getting his words out, but it hadn't affected his mind or diminished his instinct for dreaming up new businesses, which his eldest son supervised. His house was high up in Cumbres de Curumo, with a panoramic view over Caracas. He grew orchids, collected exotic birds and custom-made cars. It was a gated community with a leafy park containing several houses, protected by a barrier wall and an armed guard. Two of his married children also lived there, and several grandchildren.

According to Aitor, his wife never suspected the lengthy relationship he had had with Roser. Roser doubted this was true, as they must have left many clues over the years. She concluded that the beauty queen had tacitly accepted that her husband was a womanizer, like many men for whom that was a proof of virility, but chose to ignore it. She was the legitimate wife, the mother of his children, the only one who counted. After Aitor was left paralyzed, she had him all to herself, and she came to love him more than before, because she discovered his great virtues, ones she hadn't been able to appreciate in the hustle and bustle of their previous existence. They were growing old together in perfect harmony, surrounded by their children.

"As you can see, Roser, every cloud has a silver lining, as the saying goes. In this wheelchair I'm a better husband, father, and grandfather than I would be if I were able to walk. And even though you might not believe me, I'm happy," Aitor told Roser on one of her visits. In order not to disturb her friend's peace of mind, she chose not to tell him how important the memory of those afternoons of kisses and white wine was to her.

They had both promised they would never reveal this past love to their partners—why hurt them?—but Roser didn't keep her side of the bargain. In the two days between Victor's liberation from the camp and his asylum in the embassy, they fell in love as if they had just met. It was a luminous discovery. They had missed each other so much that when they reunited they didn't see each other as they really were, but as they had been when they were sad youngsters pretending to make love with whispers and chaste caresses in the *Winnipeg* life-boat. She fell in love with a tall, tough stranger, his features sculpted like dark wood, his eyes gentle and his clothes freshly ironed, some-one who was capable of surprising her and making her laugh with silly remarks, who gave her pleasure as if he had memorized the map of her body, who cradled her all night long so that she fell asleep and woke nestled against his shoulder, who told her what she had never expected to hear, as if suffering had demolished his defenses and made him sentimental.

Victor fell in love with the woman he had previously loved with a brother's incestuous love. She had been his wife for thirty-five years, but it was only during those days of their re-encounter that he saw her stripped of the burdens of the past: her role as Guillem's widow and Marcel's mother. She was a youthful, fresh apparition. In her fifties, Roser was revealed to him as sensual, filled with enthusiasm, with an endless reserve of fearless energy. She detested the dictatorship as much as he did, but she didn't fear it. Victor realized that, in fact, she had never shown any sign of fearing anything, apart from traveling by plane, not even in the last days of the Spanish Civil War. She was facing exile now with the same courage as she had done then, without complaining, without looking back, her eyes fixed on the future.

What kind of indestructible material was Roser made of? How was it that he had been so lucky to have her for so many years? And how could he have been so stupid not to love her from the start the way he loved her now? He never imagined that at his age he could fall in love like an adolescent or feel desire like wildfire. He looked at her enraptured, because still intact beneath her appearance as a mature woman was the innocent, formidable little girl Roser must have been when she looked after goats on a hillside in Catalonia. He wanted to protect and care for her, even though he knew she was stronger than he was whenever they suffered misfortune. He told her all this and much more in the days after their reunion, and he was to go on repeating them all the days that followed.

It was during those evenings of confessions and memories—when they shared glories, wretchedness, and secrets—that she first told him about Aitor Ibarra. Listening to her, Victor felt a bullet in his chest that knocked the wind out of him. The fact that, as Roser assured him, their adventure had ended long ago only partly consoled him. He had always suspected that on her travels she had taken a lover, or perhaps even several, but the confirmation of this longstanding, serious love awoke in him retrospective jealousy that would have destroyed the happiness of the moment had Roser allowed it. With her implacable common sense, she showed him she had not robbed him of anything to give to Aitor. She had not loved him any the less, because that love was always hidden in another chamber of her heart and didn't interfere with the rest of her life. "Back then you and I were great friends, confidants, accomplices, and spouses, but not lovers the way we are now. If I'd told you about him at the time it would have upset you a lot less, because you wouldn't have seen it as betrayal. And anyway, you've been unfaithful to me as well." This comment startled Victor, as his own infidelities had been so insignificant he could scarcely recall them, and he never imagined she knew about them. He grudgingly accepted her argument, but continued sulking for a while, until he eventually realized it was useless to stay bogged down in the past. As his mother used to say, "What's done is done."

Venezuela received Victor with the same easygoing generosity with which it took in thousands of immigrants from many parts of the world, the most recent of whom were refugees from the dictatorship in Chile and the dirty wars in Argentina and Uruguay, as well as Colombians who crossed the frontier illegally, fleeing poverty. Venezuela was one of the few democracies left in a continent dominated by heartless regimes and thuggish military juntas. Thanks to the endless flow of oil from the ground, it was one of the wealthiest countries in the world, and was also blessed with other minerals, an exuberant nature, and a privileged position on the map. There were so many natural resources that nobody killed themselves working; there was plenty of space and opportunity for whoever wanted to come and set themselves up. Life was one long party, with a great sense of freedom and a profound sense of equality. Any excuse was good enough to celebrate with music, dancing, and alcohol. Money seemed to pour out endlessly; everyone benefited from corruption.

"Don't be deceived, there's a great deal of poverty, especially in the provinces," Valentin Sanchez warned Roser. "Every government has forgotten the poor. That creates violence, and sooner or later the country will pay for that oversight." To Victor, who came from a sober, cautious, prissy Chile now repressed by the dictatorship, such exuberant joy seemed shocking. He thought people were superficial, that nothing was taken seriously; there was too much wastefulness and ostentation, everything was for the moment and fleeting. He complained that at his age it was impossible for him to adapt, that he wouldn't live long enough, but Roser argued that if at sixty he could make love like a youngster, to adapt to this wonderful country would be easy. "Relax, Victor. Going around in a sulk will get you nowhere. Pain is unavoidable, but suffering is optional."

His fame as a doctor had reached Venezuela, because several surgeons who studied in Chile had been students of his. He didn't have to earn a living driving taxis or waiting tables like so many other exiled professionals whose past was erased with a stroke. He was able to validate his qualifications, and very soon was operating in Caracas's oldest hospital. He lacked for nothing, but felt himself irredeemably foreign and followed the news to see when he could return to Chile. Roser was having great success with her orchestra and concerts, and

Marcel, who had completed his doctorate in Colorado, was working in the Venezuelan state oil company. Although they were content, they continued to think of Chile in hopes of going back there again one day.

VICTOR WAS STILL AWAITING their return to Chile when Franco died on November 20, 1975, after a long final illness. For the first time in many years, Victor was tempted to go back to Spain. "So the Caudillo was mortal after all" was the only comment made by Marcel, who had not the slightest curiosity about the land of his ancestors; he was a Chilean, heart and soul. Roser, though, decided to accompany Victor. Any separation, however brief, made them anxious. It was to tempt fate; they might never get together again. Entropy is the natural law of the universe, everything tends toward disorder, to break down, to disperse. People get lost: look how many vanished during the Retreat; feelings fade, and forgetfulness slips into lives like mist. It takes heroic willpower just to keep everything in place. Those are a refugee's forebodings, said Roser. No, they're the forebodings of someone in love, Victor corrected her.

They saw Franco's funeral on television, his coffin escorted by a squadron of lancers from Madrid to the Valley of the Fallen. Crowds of people paid homage to the Caudillo: weeping women on their knees, the Catholic Church with its pomp and ceremony of bishops in their elaborate vestments for High Mass, politicians and dignitaries in strict mourning, with the exception of the Chilean dictator in his imperial cloak. An endless parade of the Spanish armed forces, with the question hanging in the air: what was going to happen to Spain after Franco?

Roser convinced Victor to wait a year before attempting a return to his native country. During the months that followed, they watched from afar the transition to freedom headed by a king who turned out not to be the Francoist puppet everyone had expected, but someone determined to lead the country peacefully toward democracy. To do that he had to avoid all the obstacles put in his path by an intransigent right wing that refused any change and was afraid of losing all their privileges once Franco was gone. The rest of the country was clamoring for the unavoidable reforms to be brought in as quickly as possible, so that Spain could take up its place in twentieth-century Europe.

In November of the following year, Victor and Roser Dalmau landed in their homeland for the first time since those desperate days of the Retreat. They spent little time in Madrid, which was still the beautiful imperial capital it had always been. Victor showed Roser the neighborhoods and buildings that had been destroyed by bombs but were now restored. He took her to the university city to see the bullet holes that were still visible in some walls. They went to the area near the River Ebro where they thought Guillem had fallen, but found no reminders of the bloodiest battle of the war. In Barcelona they looked for the house in the Raval district that had once belonged to the Dalmaus. The names of the streets had been changed, and they had some trouble finding their way. The house was still there, though by now it was a ruin, so dilapidated it barely stood upright. From outside it appeared uninhabited, but they knocked on the door and after a long while it was opened by a young woman with eyes edged with kohl and a filthy Indian skirt. She smelled of marijuana and patchouli, and had some difficulty understanding what this couple of strangers wanted because she was so high she was in some other dimension. Eventually, however, she asked them in. The house had recently been taken over by a commune of young squatters who had rather belatedly adopted hippie culture, which would not have been tolerated in the days of Franco. Victor and Roser looked around the rooms with an empty feeling in their stomachs. The walls were crumbling and daubed with graffiti. There were people smoking or dozing on the floors, garbage was everywhere, the toilet and bathroom were disgusting. Doors and shutters dangled precariously from their hinges, and everywhere there was the smell of dirt, stale air, and marijuana. "You see, Victor, you can't bring back the past," Roser commented as they left.

Just as they didn't recognize the Dalmau family house, so they couldn't recognize Spain. Forty years of Francoism had left a deep imprint noticeable in the way people related to one another, and in every aspect of culture. Catalonia, the last bastion of Republican Spain, had suffered the victors' most savage revenge, the cruelest repression. They were surprised that Franco still cast such a long shadow. People complained about unemployment and inflation; the reforms being implemented and those that weren't; the power the conservatives had, or the chaos of the socialists. Some advocated for Catalonia to separate from Spain; others that it should be more closely integrated. Many of those the war had forced into exile began to come back. Most of them were elderly and disillusioned, and there was no longer any place for them. Nobody remembered them.

Victor went to the Rocinante bar. It still existed on the same corner with the same name. He drank a beer in honor of his father and his domino pals, the old men who sang at his funeral. Over the years, the Rocinante had been modernized; instead of hams hanging from the ceiling and the smell of sour wine, it boasted acrylic tables and air-conditioning. The manager said Spain had gone to hell after Franco. It was nothing but chaos and rudeness, strikes, protests, demonstrations, whores and queers and communists. Nobody respected the values of family or fatherland, nobody remembered God; the king was a nincompoop, what a mistake the Caudillo had made appointing him as his successor.

They rented a small apartment in the Gracia district, where they lived for six seemingly endless months. This "dis-exile," as they called the return to the land they had quit so many years earlier, was almost as hard as going into exile itself in 1939 when they crossed the border into France. It took them those six months to admit how alienated they were: him out of pride, and her out of stoicism. Neither of them found work, partly because there was none for people their age, and partly due to a lack of contacts. They didn't know anyone. Love saved them from depression, because they were like a newly married couple on their honeymoon rather than two mature, idle, and solitary people who spent the morning wandering round the city, and the evenings at the movies watching the same old films. They prolonged the illusion as long as possible until one boring Sunday that was no different from any other boring day, they had had enough. They were warming themselves up with thick hot chocolate and sugar cakes in a shop on Petritxol Street when Roser suddenly came out with a phrase that was to define their plans for years to come: "I'm fed up with being outsiders. Let's go back to Chile. That's where we're from." Victor exhaled as loudly as a dragon and bent forward to kiss her on the mouth. "We'll do that as soon as we can, Roser, I promise. But for now we're returning to Venezuela."

Several years were to go by before he could keep his promise to return to Chile. They spent them in Venezuela, where Marcel was living and where they had work and friends. The Chilean colony grew daily because, in addition to political exiles, others arrived in search of economic opportunities. In their Palos Grandes neighborhood a Chilean accent was more common than a Venezuelan one. Most of those who came remained isolated within their own community, licking their wounds and concerned above all about the situation in Chile, which showed no signs of changing despite the promising snippets of news that passed from mouth to mouth but were never confirmed. The fact was that the dictatorship was still solid. Roser suggested to Victor that the only healthy way to grow old was to integrate into Venezuelan society. They had to live in the present, making the most of everything that agreeable country had to offer, grateful they were well received and had work, without wallowing in the past. The return to Chile was left pending for some future date. They didn't allow it to spoil their present, as that future could be a long way off. Roser prevented him from living in nostalgia and hope, introducing him to the art of having a good time without feeling guilty. This, together with generosity, was the best lesson Venezuela had to give. In his sixties, Victor changed more than he had done in all his previous life. He attributed this to his continuing infatuation, Roser's constant efforts to smooth the rough edges of his nature, as well as the positive influence of the Caribbean chaos. This was how he described the institutionalized indolence that undermined his serious attitude, at least for a few years. He learned to dance salsa and play the four-stringed guitar.

IT WAS THEN THAT Victor Dalmau met Ofelia del Solar again. Over the years, he had sporadically had news of her, but had never seen her because they moved in very different circles and she had spent most of her life in other countries due to her husband's profession. He had also done his best to avoid her, concerned that the ashes of that frustrated youthful love might still contain burning embers that could disrupt his orderly existence or his relationship with Roser. He had never understood why Ofelia had cut him out of her life so completely, with no explanation apart from a short letter written in the tone of a capricious young girl that he could not match with the woman who escaped from her art classes to make love with him in a seedy hotel. At first, when he had finished feeling sorry for himself and cursing her in secret, he came to detest her. He attributed to her all the worst defects of her class: lack of awareness, egotism, arrogance, pretentiousness. His loathing slowly subsided, leaving him with the fond memory of the most beautiful woman he had ever known, her infectious laughter and her seductiveness. As time went by, he seldom thought of Ofelia, and never felt the impulse to find out about her. Prior to the dictatorship in Chile, he had heard random scraps about her life, usually from some comment by Felipe del Solar, whom he saw a couple of times a year in order to artificially preserve a friendship based entirely on Victor's sense of gratitude. He had seen some not-exactly-flattering images of her in newspaper social pages, but nothing in the Arts sections; her work was unknown in Chile. "Well, the same happens with other talented national artists, and more so if they're women," Roser remarked, when she once brought back a magazine from Miami that had four full-color pages showing Ofelia's work. Victor studied the two photos of the artist that accompanied the article. The eyes were those of the Ofelia he knew, but the rest had changed a lot—although that could have been the camera's fault.

Roser arrived with the news that there was an exhibit of the latest works by Ofelia del Solar in the Caracas Athenaeum. "Did you see she uses her maiden name?" she said. Victor pointed out this had always been the case, especially among Chilean women, and that Matias Eyzaguirre had died years earlier. If she hadn't taken her husband's name during his lifetime, why would she do so as a widow? "Well, whatever. Let's go to the opening," said Roser.

His automatic reaction was to say no, but curiosity got the better of him. There weren't many works in the exhibit, but each was the size of a door, so they filled three rooms. Ofelia had not escaped the influence of Guayasamin, the great Ecuadorean painter under whom she had studied. Her canvases were of a similar style, with strong brushstrokes, dark lines, and abstract figures. They didn't, though, have any of his humanitarian message; there was no denunciation of cruelty or exploitation, nothing of the historical or political conflicts of the time. Instead they were sensual images, some of them very explicit, couples entwined in twisted or violent embraces, women yielding to pleasure or suffering. They confused Victor, as they didn't correspond to the idea he had of the artist. He remembered Ofelia in the first flush of womanhood, the pampered, naïve, and impulsive girl he had fallen in love with, who painted watercolor landscapes and bouquets of flowers. All he knew of her was that since those far-off days she had been the wife and then the widow of a diplomat; she was a traditional woman, accepting her role. But these paintings showed an ardent temperament and a surprisingly erotic imagination. It was as if the passion he had caught a glimpse of in the dingy hotel where they made love had remained suppressed inside her and its only means of escape was through brushes and paint. Her last canvas, displayed on its own on one wall of the gallery, made a strong impression on him. It was a naked man holding a rifle, painted in white, black, and gray. Victor studied it for several minutes, stirred without knowing why. He went closer to read the title: *Militiaman, 1973.* "It's not for sale," a voice next to him said. It was Ofelia. She looked different from how he remembered her, and from the few photographs he had seen: older, more faded.

"It's the first of this series, and it marks the end of a stage for me. That's why I'm not selling it."

"That's the year of the military coup in Chile," Victor said.

"It has nothing to do with Chile. That was the year I liberated myself as an artist."

Until that moment she hadn't looked at Victor, but had been talking while staring at the canvas. When she turned to continue the conversation, she didn't recognize him. More than forty years had passed since they had been together, and she was at a disadvantage, because in all that time she had never seen a photograph of him. Stretching out his hand, Victor introduced himself. It took Ofelia several seconds to remember the name, and when she did, she gave such a spontaneous little cry that Victor was convinced she had no idea who he was. What for him had been a stab to the heart had left no trace in her.

He invited her for a drink in the café and went in search of Roser. When he saw the two women together, he was struck by how time had treated them so differently. He would have thought that the beautiful, frivolous, rich, and refined Ofelia would have withstood the passage of the years more easily, and yet she appeared older than Roser. Her gray hair looked singed, her hands were gnarled, and the demands of her profession had left her stooped. She was wearing a brick-colored linen tunic that hung loosely to disguise the extra pounds, carried a huge multicolored woven Guatemalan bag, and wore Franciscan sandals.

She was still beautiful. Her blue eyes shone as they had done when she was twenty, but in a face tanned by too much sun and crisscrossed by wrinkles. Roser, who was not vain and had never appeared particularly attractive, dyed her gray hairs and wore lipstick. She took care of her pianist's hands, her posture, and her weight, and that night was wearing a pair of black pants and a white blouse with the discreet elegance that was her trademark. She greeted Ofelia warmly, but made excuses for not accompanying them: she had to rush off for an orchestra rehearsal. Victor looked at her quizzically, guessing she wanted to leave him alone with Ofelia. He felt a moment's panic.

AT A TABLE ON the Athenaeum patio, surrounded by modern sculptures and tropical plants, Ofelia and Victor caught up on all the most significant events of those forty years. They made no mention of the passion that had once engulfed them. Victor didn't dare refer to it, much less ask why she had vanished, as this seemed to him humiliating. Nor did she bring it up, because the only man who had counted in her life was Matias Eyzaguirre. Compared to the immense love she had with him, the brief adventure with Victor was a childish folly that would have been forgotten were it not for that tiny grave in a rural cemetery in Chile. She didn't mention that to Victor either, because she had shared the secret only with her husband. She bore the responsibility for her mistake without broadcasting it, as Father Vicente Urbina had instructed her.

They were able to talk a long while as if they were good friends. Ofelia told him she had two children and had lived happily for thirty-five years alongside Matias Eyzaguirre, who loved her in the same steadfast way as he had pursued her hand in marriage. He loved her so much and so exclusively that their children felt excluded.

"He changed very little. He was always a tranquil, generous man who was unconditionally loyal to me. Over the years, his virtues only became more pronounced. I assisted him as best I could in his profession. Diplomacy is difficult. We changed countries every two or three years—we had to uproot ourselves, leave friends, and start again somewhere else. It wasn't easy for the children either. What was worse was the social life: I'm no good at cocktail parties or lengthy meals."

"Were you able to paint?"

"I tried, but it was only part-time: there was always something more important or urgent to do. When my children went to university I told Matias I was retiring from my job as mother and spouse, and was going to devote myself to serious painting. That seemed fair to him. He gave me a free hand and no longer asked me to accompany him on the social engagements that were what I found most irksome."

"Goodness, one man in a million."

"A shame you never knew him."

"I saw him only once. He stamped my entry visa for Chile on board the *Winnipeg* in 1939. I've never forgotten it. Your Matias was an honorable man, Ofelia."

"He rejoiced in everything I did. For example, he took classes in order to appreciate my paintings because he said he didn't understand art, and then he financed my first exhibit. He was taken by a sudden heart attack six years ago. I still cry when I go to sleep every night because he isn't with me," Ofelia confessed in an outpouring of emotion that left Victor flushing.

She added that ever since then she had freed herself of the chores that had kept her from her vocation. She lived a rural life on a piece of land two hundred kilometers from Santiago, where she grew fruit trees and reared dwarf long-eared goats to sell as pets. Above all, she painted and painted. Apart from traveling to visit her son and daughter, one in Brazil and the other in Argentina, or for an exhibit, or to visit her mother once a month, she didn't move from her studio.

"You knew my father died, didn't you?"

"Yes, it was in the press. Chilean newspapers take some time to get here, but they do arrive. He was prominent in the Pinochet government, wasn't he?"

"That was at the beginning. He died in 1975. After his death, my mother flourished. My father was a despot."

She told him that Doña Laura became less devoted to compulsive praying and good works, and more interested in games of canasta and spiritualism with a group of esoteric old ladies who communicated with the souls of people in the Great Beyond. This was how she kept in touch with Leonardo, her adored Baby. Father Vicente Urbina was unaware of this fresh sin staining the del Solar family, because Doña Laura was careful not to tell him. She knew summoning the dead was a demonic practice roundly condemned by the Church. Ofelia spoke of the priest with sarcasm. She said that at eighty-something years old, Urbina was a bishop and an eloquent defender of the dictatorship's methods, which he saw as fully justified in their protection of Western Christian civilization against the perversity of Marxism. The Chilean cardinal, who had set up an organization to protect the persecuted and keep a record of the disappeared, had to call him to order when in his enthusiasm he defended torture and summary executions. The bishop was tireless in his mission to save souls, especially those of the well-to-do faithful. He continued as the spiritual adviser to the del Solar family, in a much more powerful position since the death of the patriarch. Doña Laura, her daughters, sons-in-law, grandchildren, and great-grandchildren all depended on his wisdom for both big and small decisions.

"I escaped his influence because I loathe him. He's a sinister man. Fortunately, I've nearly always lived far from Chile. Felipe also escaped, because he's the most intelligent one in the family, and because he lives half his life in England."

"What's become of him?"

"He endured the three years of Allende's government, certain it wasn't going to last. But he couldn't stand the junta's barracks mentality, because he foresaw they could remain in power forever. You know how he admires everything English. He detests Chilean hypocrisy and sanctimony. He goes back on regular visits to see my mother and look after the family finances."

"Didn't you have another brother? One who measured typhoons and hurricanes?"

"He settled in Hawaii. He came back to Chile only once to claim his share of the inheritance after my father's death. Do you remember Juana, our housekeeper, who adored your son, Marcel? She's exactly the same. No one, not even she herself, knows how old she is, but she still looks after the house and cares for my mother, who's over ninety and quite mad. There are a lot of lunatics in my family. Well, I've brought you up to date about us. Now tell me about you."

Victor summed up his life in five minutes. He mentioned only briefly the year he had been a prisoner, and skipped over the worst moments, partly because it seemed to him in bad taste to mention them, and also because he thought Ofelia would prefer not to know. If she guessed at any of it she refrained from asking him, merely commenting that Matias had been conservative in his political ideas, but had served Chile as a diplomat throughout the three years of socialism without questioning his duty. On the other hand, he had felt ashamed to be representing the military regime because of the bad reputation it had throughout the world. She added that she had never been interested in politics, that art was her thing, and that she lived in peace in Chile, with her trees and animals, never reading the press. Her life was the same, with or without the dictatorship.

They said goodbye, promising they would stay in touch, although they knew this was a mere formality. Victor felt relieved: if one lives long enough, circles close. The Ofelia del Solar circle closed neatly for him in that Athenaeum café, without leaving any ashes. The embers had died long ago. He decided he didn't like her character or her painting. The only thing memorable about her was her sky-blue eyes.

Roser was waiting at home for him rather anxiously, but she only had to glance at him to burst out laughing. Her husband looked several years younger. Victor gave her the news of the del Solar family, and in conclusion commented that Ofelia smelled of withered gardenias. He was convinced Roser had foreseen his disappointment: that was why she took him to the exhibit and left him alone with his former love. His wife had taken too big a risk: it could have happened that rather than being disenchanted with Ofelia, he would fall in love with her again. Evidently that possibility didn't worry Roser at all. *The problem with us,* he reflected, *is that she takes me for granted, whereas I keep thinking she might run off with somebody else.*

CHAPTER 12

1983–1991

I live now in a country as soft
As the autumn skin of grapes.

—PABLO NERUDA
"Country"
BARREN TERRAIN

THE NEWS THAT IN CHILE THERE WAS A NEW LIST
of eighteen hundred exiles authorized to return was
published in the Sunday edition of *El Universal,* the
only day that the Dalmaus read the newspaper from
start to finish. Roser went to the Chilean consulate to
see the list posted in the window. Victor Dalmau's
name was on it. The earth opened beneath her feet.
They had been waiting for this moment for nine years,
but when it finally happened she couldn't rejoice, because it meant leaving everything they had, including
Marcel, to return to the country they had left because
they couldn't bear the repression. She wondered what
sense there was in going back if nothing had changed,
but talking it over that night with Victor, he argued
that if they didn't do it soon, they never would.

"We've started from nothing several times, Roser.

We can do it one more time. I'm sixty-nine, and I want to die in Chile." A line from Neruda came into his mind: *How can I live so far from what I loved, from what I love?*

Marcel not only agreed, he offered to go and scout out the terrain, and within a week was in Santiago. He called to tell them that on the surface the country was modern and prosperous, but that one only had to dig down a little to see the damage underneath. The degree of inequality was staggering: three-quarters of the wealth was in the hands of twenty families. The middle class survived on credit; there was poverty for the many and opulence for the few: shantytowns contrasting with glass skyscrapers and mansions behind walls. Well-being and security for some, unemployment and repression for others. The economic miracle of recent years, based on absolute freedom for capital and a lack of basic rights for workers, had burst like a bubble. Marcel told them there was a feeling in the air that things were going to change. People were less afraid, and there were massive protests against the government. He thought the dictatorship would collapse; it was the right moment to return.

He added that soon after he arrived, he was offered a job at the same copper corporation where he had first worked after graduating. Nobody asked him about his political ideas; the only things that counted were his U.S. doctorate and his professional experience. "I'm going to stay here. I'm Chilean." This was the clincher, because despite everything they had been through, they too were Chilean. Besides, there was no way they were going to be apart from their son.

In less than three months, the Dalmaus sold their possessions and said goodbye to their Venezuelan friends and colleagues. Valentin Sanchez suggested that Roser go back in triumph, head held high, as she had never been on a blacklist or in the sights of the security forces as her husband had. She was to return with the entire Ancient Music Orchestra and give a series of free concerts in parks, churches, and high schools. When she wanted to know how all this would be financed, he told her it was a gift from the people of Venezuela to the people of Chile. The Venezuelan budget for culture was generous, and in Chile they wouldn't dare refuse—that would cause an international scandal.

The return was harder for Victor than for Roser. He left his post at the Caracas hospital with its economic security for the uncertainty of a place where exiles were regarded with suspicion. Many on the Left blamed them for leaving rather than staying to fight the regime from inside, while the right wing labeled them Marxists and terrorists, claiming there must have been some reason for them to be expelled.

When he turned up at the San Juan de Dios hospital where he had worked for almost thirty years, he was received with hugs and even tears by nurses and some doctors from before, who remembered him and had escaped the purges of the first years when hundreds of medical personnel with progressive ideas were dismissed, arrested, or killed. The hospital director, a military man, greeted him in person and invited him into his office.

"I know you saved the life of Commandant Osorio. That was a praiseworthy act for someone in your situation," he said.

"You mean as a prisoner in a concentration camp? I'm a doctor, I attend whoever needs me, whatever the circumstances. How is the commandant?"

"Long since retired, but well."

"I worked many years in this hospital and I'd like to return," said Victor.

"I understand, but you have to consider your age . . ."

"I'm not seventy yet. Until two weeks ago, I was in charge of the cardiology department at the Vargas hospital in Caracas."

"Unfortunately, with your record as a political prisoner and an exile, it's impossible to employ you in any public hospital. Officially, you're suspended until further notice."

"Does that mean I won't be able to work in Chile?"

"Believe me, I'm truly sorry. It's not my decision. I suggest you apply at a private clinic," the director said by way of farewell, giving him a firm handshake.

The military government had decided public services should be in private hands. Health was not a right, but a consumer good to be bought and sold. In those years when everything that could be privatized had been, from electricity to airlines, a plethora of private clinics had sprung up, with state-of-the-art buildings and facilities for those who could afford them. After years of absence, Victor's professional prestige was still high, and he immediately secured a position in Santiago's most exclusive clinic, at a salary far higher than the one he would have accepted in a public hospital.

On one of his frequent visits to Chile, Felipe del Solar went to visit Victor. It had been a long time since they had last seen each other, and though they had never been close friends or had a great deal in common, they hugged each other with real affection.

"I heard you had returned, Victor. I'm really pleased. This country needs good people like you to come back and work."

"Are you back in Chile as well?" asked Victor.

"Nobody needs me here. I live in London: can't you tell?"

"Yes, I can. You look like an English lord."

"I have to come quite often for family reasons, even though I can't stand any of them except for Juana Nancucheo, who brought me up. But you can't choose your family."

They sat on a bench in the garden opposite a modern fountain that spouted jets of water like a whale, and caught up with the news from their respective families. Felipe spoke of Ofelia, shut away in the countryside, working on paintings nobody bought. Laura del Solar had senile dementia and was in a wheelchair, while Felipe's sisters had turned into unbearable snobs.

"My brothers-in-law have made fortunes in recent years, Victor. My father looked down on them: he said my sisters had married well-dressed idiots. If he could see his sons-in-law now, he'd have to eat his words," Felipe added.

"This is a paradise for business and businessmen," said Victor.

"There's nothing wrong with making money if the system and laws permit it. But you, Victor, how are you?"

"Trying to adapt and understand what's happened here. Chile is unrecognizable."

"You have to admit it's much better. The military putsch saved the country from Allende's chaos and a Marxist dictatorship."

"And to prevent that imagined left-wing dictatorship, an implacable right-wing one has been imposed, Felipe."

"Listen, Victor, keep those views to yourself. They don't go down well here. You can't deny we're much better off, we have a prosperous country."

"But at a very high social cost. You live abroad, you know about the atrocities that are never mentioned here."

"Don't start with that refrain about human rights. That's such a bore, Victor," Felipe interrupted him. "They are excesses committed by a few stupid military men. Nobody can condemn the governing junta, much less President Pinochet, for those exceptions to the rule. The important thing is that the country is calm and we have an impeccable economy. We were always a country of layabouts, but now people have to work and make an effort. The free market system favors competition and promotes wealth."

"This isn't a free market, because the labor force is repressed, with their most basic human rights suspended. Do you think this system could be implanted in a democracy?"

"This is an authoritarian, protected democracy."

"You've changed a lot, Felipe."

"What makes you say that?"

"I remembered you as more open, iconoclastic, quite cynical and critical. Against everything and everyone, sarcastic and brilliant."

"I still am in some respects, Victor. But as you grow older you have to take up a position. I've always been a monarchist," Felipe said with a smile. "At any rate, my friend, be careful with your opinions."

"I am careful, Felipe, but not with my friends."

TO ALLEVIATE THE EMBARRASSMENT he felt at treating medicine as a commodity, Victor worked as a volunteer in a makeshift consulting room in one of the Santiago shantytowns. They had sprung up with the migration of workers from the countryside and the saltpeter industry half a century earlier, and had since multiplied. About six thousand people lived crammed into the one where Victor worked. There he could assess the repression, the discontent, and the courage of the poorest people. His patients lived in shacks made of cardboard and wooden planks with beaten earth floors, and had no running water, electricity, or latrines. They had to endure summer dust and winter mud surrounded by garbage, packs of stray dogs, rats, and flies. Most of them had no proper work, earning a minimum for survival in desperate jobs such as scavenging in the garbage heaps for plastic, glass, and paper to sell, or doing heavy manual work for the day in anything that came along, trafficking or stealing. The government had plans to eradicate the problem of the shanties, but the solutions kept being delayed, and in the meantime they raised walls to hide this wretched spectacle that made the city look ugly.

"What's most impressive are the women," Victor told Roser. "They're steadfast, long-suffering, more combative than the men, mothers of their own children as well as the relatives they take in. They put up with the alcoholism, violence, and abandonment of their transient partners. But they don't give in."

"Do they at least get some help?"

"Yes, from churches, especially the evangelical ones, from charities, and volunteers. But it's the children I'm worried about, Roser.

They grow up out of control, often go to bed hungry, attend school when they can, not always, and reach adolescence with no more prospects than gangs, drugs, or the street."

"I know you, Victor. I know you're happier there than anywhere else," was Roser's reply.

It was true. By the third day of serving in this community together with a couple of nurses and other idealistic doctors who worked shifts, Victor rediscovered his youthful enthusiastic flame. He would return home weary as a dog, heavyhearted and with many tragic stories, yet impatient to return to the consulting room the next day. His life had a meaning as clear as during the Civil War, when his role in this world had been beyond question.

"If you could only see how they organize themselves, Roser. Those who are able contribute something to the common pot cooked in giant cauldrons on braziers in the open air. The idea is to give everyone a hot meal, although sometimes there's not enough to go around."

"Now I know where your salary goes."

"It's not just food that's needed, Roser. We also need everything in the consulting room."

He explained that the shantytown dwellers kept order themselves to avoid raids by the police, who usually came in heavily armed. Their impossible dream was to have their own houses and plots of land to live on. In the past they had simply taken over land and stubbornly resisted being thrown off. These "takeovers" began with a few people arriving surreptitiously. Then more and more would appear, in a stealthy, uncontainable procession that advanced with their few possessions on carts and wheelbarrows, in sacks slung over their shoulders, and what little material they had for a roof, pieces of cardboard, blankets, carrying their children and followed by their dogs. By the time the authorities came to see what was going on, there were thousands of people installed, ready to defend themselves. But in the current climate, that sort of thing would have been rash to the point of suicide: the forces of law and order could come in with tanks and open fire without a second thought.

"Just suggesting a protest is all it takes for someone to disappear. If they're seen again, it's as a dead body that appears in the entrance to the shanty as a warning to the others. That was where they dumped the maimed body of the singer Victor Jara, with more than forty bullet wounds. Or so I've been told."

In the consulting room they dealt with emergencies, cases of burns, broken bones, wounds from knife or bottle fights, domestic violence. None of this was any great challenge to Victor, but simply by being there he gave the shanty dwellers a sense of security. He dispatched the most serious cases to the nearest hospital and since there was no ambulance, often took them there himself in his car. He had been warned about robberies, and was told it was unwise to arrive there in a vehicle, because it could be dismantled and the parts sold at the Persian Market, but one of the female leaders, a still-young grandmother with the character of an amazon, warned the inhabitants, especially the wayward youngsters, that the first one who touched the doctor's car would be in deep trouble. That was enough: Victor never had any problems.

The Dalmaus ended up living off their savings and what Roser earned, because Victor's salary from the clinic was devoted entirely to buying essential items for the consulting room. Roser saw he was so happy she decided to accompany him. She bought instruments with money from Valentin Sanchez, who sent a substantial check and a shipment from Venezuela, and went to the shantytown on the same days as her husband, to teach music. She discovered this brought them closer together than making love, but didn't tell him so. She gave reports and photographs to Valentin Sanchez. "In a year we'll have a children's choir and a youth orchestra, you'll have to come and see it with your own eyes. But for now we need good recording equipment and loudspeakers for our open-air concerts," she explained, knowing her friend would find a way to come up with more funds.

SOMEWHAT ENVIOUS OF OFELIA del Solar's bucolic description of life in the countryside, Victor convinced Roser they should find somewhere to live on the outskirts of Santiago. The city was a nightmare of traffic and scurrying, bad-tempered pedestrians, and in the early morning was often covered by a cloud of toxic fog. They found what they were looking for: a stone and wood rustic dwelling that the architect had capriciously adorned with a thatched roof that was intended to camouflage it in the rural landscape. Three decades earlier, when it was built, access was along a snaking track that zigzagged between steep precipices, but the capital gradually had spread up the mountainsides, and by the time they bought the property, this area of small plots of lands and vegetable gardens was part of the city. There was no public transport or mail, but they could sleep in the deep silence of nature, and wake to a bird chorus. On weekdays they got up at five in the morning to go to work, and didn't return until after dark, but the time they spent in their new house gave them the strength to take on any challenge.

The property was empty during the day, and in the first two years burglars broke in eleven times. These were such unimportant thefts there was no point getting angry or calling the police: the garden hose and hens, kitchen utensils, a transistor radio, and other insignificant items. Their first television set was also taken, as were another two replacements, so they decided to do without—there was hardly anything worth watching anyway. They were considering the possibility of always leaving the door open to avoid having their windows smashed by the thieves, when Marcel brought two big dogs rescued from the municipal dog pound that barked loudly but were gentle, and a small one that did bite. That solved the problem.

Marcel lived and worked among people Victor loosely called "privileged" for want of a more precise definition, because compared to his patients in the shantytown, that's what they were. Marcel resented this description, which couldn't be applied generally to all his friends, but didn't want to get into any tangled argument with his parents. "You two are relics from the past. You're stuck in the seventies and need to get up to date." He called them daily and visited them every Sunday to share the obligatory barbecue Victor insisted on. He came accompanied by different women of a similar style— tall and slender, with long straight hair, laid-back and almost always vegetarian—completely different from the passionate Jamaican girl who had first taught him to love. His father could never manage to distinguish the latest of them from the previous ones, or learn their names before Marcel changed to another, almost exactly similar one. When he arrived, Marcel would whisper in Victor's ear for him not to mention exile or his consulting room in the shantytown, because he had only just met the girl and wasn't certain about her political tendencies, if she had any. "You only need to look at her, Marcel. She lives in a bubble, with no idea of the past, or of what's going on now. Your generation has no ideals," Victor would retort. They would end up arguing in the pantry while Roser tried to entertain the visitor. Later, their differences forgotten, Marcel would barbecue bloody steaks while Victor boiled spinach for the long-haired girlfriend.

They were often joined by their neighbors, Meche and Ramiro, who brought a basket of fresh vegetables from their kitchen garden and a couple of jars of homemade jam. Even though Ramiro was in good health, Roser insisted to Victor he was going to die at any moment, and in fact this is what happened. He was knocked down and killed by a drunken driver. When Victor asked his wife how on earth she had known, she told him she could see it in Ramiro's eyes: he was marked by death. "When you become a widower, marry Meche, understand?" Roser whispered to him during the poor man's funeral. Victor nodded, sure as he was that Roser would long outlive him.

Victor and Roser worked as volunteers for three years in the shantytown, winning the trust of the inhabitants, but then the government ordered the evacuation of the families to other locations on the edge of the capital, farther away from middle-class neighborhoods. Santiago was one of the most segregated cities in the world: none of the poor lived within sight of the rich on the hillsides. The police arrived, followed by soldiers, separated people at gunpoint, and took them away in army trucks escorted by motorcycles. They were distributed among identical new settlements, with unmade roads and lines of dwellings like boxes dumped on the dusty ground. Fifteen thousand people were transferred in record time without the rest of the city being aware of it. The poor became invisible. Each family was allotted a basic wooden dwelling made up of one multipurpose room, a bathroom, and kitchen. This was better than the huts they came from, but it meant that at a stroke their community was destroyed. The shantytown inhabitants were left divided, uprooted, isolated, and vulnerable: everyone had to look out for themselves. The operation was carried out so efficiently that Victor and Roser only found out the next day when they arrived to work as usual, only to find bulldozers clearing the ground where the shanties had been, in order to build apartment blocks.

It took them a week to track down some of the displaced groups, but that same evening they were warned by police agents that they were under surveillance, and any contact with the shanty dwellers would be seen as a threat to law and order. This hit Victor hard. He had no intention of retiring: he was still in charge of the most complicated cases at the clinic, but neither practicing the surgery he loved nor the money he earned could compensate for losing his shantytown patients.

Under pressure from popular protests at home, and internationally from the poor reputation it had, in 1987 the dictatorship ended the curfew and relaxed the press censorship that had been in place for fourteen years. They also authorized political parties and the return of all remaining exiles. When the opposition demanded free elections, the government responded by imposing a referendum in October 1988 to decide whether Pinochet was to remain in power for eight more years. Victor, who had never gotten involved in politics but had suffered the consequences anyway, thought the time had come to commit himself openly. He joined the opposition, which was faced with the herculean task of mobilizing the country to defeat the military government in the plebiscite. When police agents just like those who had threatened him before turned up on his doorstep, he threw them out. Instead of leading him away in handcuffs with a hood over his head, they responded with feeble threats and went their way. "They'll be back," said a furious Roser, but days and weeks went by without her forecast being fulfilled. This showed the couple that at last things were changing in Chile, as Marcel had suggested four years earlier. The dictatorship's impunity was slipping away.

The referendum took place in a calm atmosphere that surprised everyone. International observers and journalists from all over the world kept a close eye on the proceedings. Nobody failed to vote: not even old people in wheelchairs, women in labor, the sick on stretchers. And at the end of the day, making a mockery of the junta's cleverest maneuvers, the dictatorship was beaten at its own game, by its own laws. That night, faced with the incontrovertible results, Pinochet, hardened by the arrogance of absolute power and cut off from reality by many years of complete impunity, proposed another coup to keep himself on the presidential throne indefinitely. This time, however, the U.S. intelligence officials who had supported him before, and the generals he himself had handpicked, refused to back him. Unable to concede defeat until the very last moment, he finally gave in. Months later, he handed his post to a civilian to begin the transition to a restricted, cautious democracy, but he maintained tight control over the armed forces and kept the country in fear. By the time he left office in March 1990, seventeen years had gone by since the military coup.

WITH THE RETURN TO DEMOCRACY, Victor Dalmau left the private clinic to devote himself exclusively to the San Juan de Dios hospital, which he rejoined in the same position he had held before his arrest. The new director, who had been a student of Victor's at the university, refrained from pointing out that his former professor was more than old enough to retire and enjoy his old age. When Victor arrived one Monday in his white coat and carrying a briefcase battered by forty years' use, he was greeted in the lobby by a crowd of some fifty people—doctors, nurses, and administrative staff—with balloons and an enormous cake smothered in meringue. They had gathered to offer him the welcome they couldn't give before.

Goodness, I'm growing old, thought Victor when he felt tears welling in his eyes. It had been many years since he had cried. The few exiles who returned to the hospital were received with much less fanfare, because it was unwise to attract attention. This was the tacit slogan throughout the country: don't provoke the military, so as to pretend the recent past was buried and in the process of being forgotten. Doctor Dalmau, however, had left a long-lasting impression of decency and competence among his colleagues, as well as of kindness among his juniors, who could turn to him at any moment and know they would be well received. Even his ideological opponents respected him, which meant none of them had denounced him: Victor's years in jail and exile were simply the result of a resentful neighbor who knew of his friendship with Salvador Allende. Victor was soon invited to give classes at the School of Medicine and to occupy the post of undersecretary at the Health Ministry. He accepted the first offer, but rejected the second, because the condition was that he join one of the governing parties. He knew he wasn't a political animal, and never would be.

He felt twenty years younger and was euphoric. After suffering punishment and ostracism in Chile and having been a foreigner for many years, overnight his luck had changed: now he was Professor Dalmau, head of cardiology, the most admired specialist in the country, capable of carrying out feats with his scalpel that others wouldn't dare attempt, and a noted public speaker. Even his enemies turned to him, as he discovered on more than one occasion when he found himself operating on two high-ranking members of the still-powerful armed forces, and one of the most passionate strategists of repression during the dictatorship. When it was a question of saving their own lives, these men came to consult him with their tails between their legs: fear has no shame, as Roser liked to say.

This was Victor's moment: he was at the pinnacle of his career. He felt that in some mysterious way he embodied Chile's transformation; the shadows had been dispelled, freedom was dawning, and so he too was living a glorious dawn. He devoted himself to his work, and for the first time in his introverted life sought attention and enjoyed whatever opportunities he had to shine in public.

"Be careful, Victor, success is intoxicating you. Remember life has many peaks and troughs," Roser warned him. She had been observing him with some concern, thinking he was growing conceited, noticing his pedantic tone, his superior air, his tendency to talk about himself—something he had never done in the past—his categorical assertions, his hasty, impatient manner, even with her. When she pointed all this out, he replied he had many responsibilities and couldn't be treading on eggshells at home.

Roser saw him having lunch in the faculty cafeteria surrounded by young students listening to him with the veneration of disciples. She could see how Victor enjoyed this reverence, especially from the female students, who applauded his banal observations with unjustified admiration. Roser knew him inside out, every nook and cranny, and this belated vanity surprised her for being so unexpected. It made her feel sorry for her husband: she was discovering how vulnerable to flattery a conceited old man could be. It never crossed her mind that she would be the one to cause the reversal of fortune that punctured Victor's vanity.

THIRTEEN MONTHS LATER, Roser began to suspect a stealthy disease was slowly eating away at her, but since her husband hadn't noticed anything, she convinced herself these must be symptoms of age or her imagination. Victor was so caught up in his success he had neglected his relationship with her, although when they were together he was still her best friend and the lover who made her feel beautiful and desired at the age of seventy-three. He also knew her inside out. If her weight loss, the yellowish tinge to her skin, and her nausea didn't worry Victor, it must be something unimportant. It was another month before she decided to consult someone, because in addition to her previous symptoms, she was waking up shivering with fever. Out of a vague feeling of embarrassment, and to avoid giving Victor the impression she was complaining, she went to see one of his colleagues. When she was handed the results a few days later, she came home with the desperate news that she had terminal cancer. She had to say it twice for Victor to snap out of his stupor and react.

From then on, both their lives suffered a dramatic transformation. The only thing they really wanted was to prolong and enjoy the time they had left together. Victor's vanity was well and truly pricked. He descended from Olympus to the hell of illness. He asked for indefinite leave from the hospital and gave up his classes to be with Roser. "We're going to spend our time well for as long as we can, Victor. Maybe the war against this cancer is lost, but meanwhile we can win a few battles." Victor took her on a honeymoon to a southern lake, an emerald-colored mirror that reflected forests, waterfalls, hills, and the snowcapped peaks of three volcanoes. They stayed in a rustic cabin in the midst of this serene landscape, far from everything and everyone. There they went back over every stage of their lives, from the days when she was a skinny young girl in love with Guillem, to the present, when for Victor she had become the most beautiful woman in the world. She insisted on swimming in the lake, as though that icy, pristine water could wash her inside and out, purify her, and restore her health. She also wanted to take walks, but wasn't strong enough to go as far as she wished, and so they ended up strolling gently, her clinging to her husband's arm and with a stick in her other hand. She was visibly losing weight.

Victor had spent his life fighting suffering and death. He was familiar with the volcanic emotions a patient facing the end goes through, because he had taught them at the university: denial of one's fate, immense anger at becoming ill, bargaining with destiny and the divinity to prolong one's existence, succumbing to despair, and finally, at best, resigning oneself to the inevitable. Roser skipped all the earlier stages and from the outset accepted her passing with astonishing calm and good humor. She refused to follow the alternative treatments that Meche and other well-intentioned female friends suggested: she didn't want to know about homeopathy, herbs from Amazonia, healers, or exorcisms. "I'm going to die: so what? Everybody has to die." She took advantage of the hours when she felt well to listen to music, play the piano, and read poetry with the cat Meche had given them on her lap. It looked like an Egyptian goddess but had always been half-feral, distant, and solitary. Sometimes it disappeared for days on end, and would often come back bearing the bloody remains of a rodent, which it deposited on their marital bed as an offering. Now it seemed to understand that something had changed, and overnight became gentle and affectionate, refusing to leave Roser.

At first, Victor was obsessed with existing treatments and experimental ones. He read reports, studied every drug, and memorized statistics selectively, rejecting the most pessimistic and clinging to any shred of hope. He remembered Lazaro, the boy soldier from Estacion del Norte, who came back from death because he had such a strong desire to live. He thought that if he could inject Roser's spirit and immune system with a similar passion for life, she could defeat cancer. There were such cases. Miracles did exist. "You're strong, Roser, you always have been. You've never been ill, you're made of iron and will get over it, this illness isn't always fatal," he repeated like a mantra, without managing to instill in her any of this baseless optimism that as a professional he would have discouraged in his patients. Roser went along with him as long as she was able to. Just to please him, she underwent chemotherapy and radiation, although she was convinced this only meant prolonging a process that was becoming more painful by the day. With the stoicism that was her birthright, she put up with the horror of the drugs without ever complaining. All her hair fell out, even her eyelashes, and she was so weak and thin that Victor could pick her up without effort. He carried her in his arms from bed to armchair, to the bathroom, out into the garden to see the hummingbirds in the fuchsia bush and the hares bounding past, mocking the dogs already too old to bother to chase them. She lost her appetite but made an effort to swallow at least a couple of mouthfuls of the dishes he prepared by following recipe books. Toward the end she could only keep down the Catalan custard dessert that Carme used to make for Marcel on Sundays. "When I'm gone, I want you to cry for a day or two to show respect, comfort poor Marcel, and then go back to the hospital and your teaching. But with a bit more humility, Victor, because you've been unbearable lately," Roser told him on one occasion.

Right to the end, the thatched stone house was their sanctuary. They had spent six happy years there, but it was only now, when every minute of the day and night was precious, that they fully appreciated it. When they bought it, the house was already in poor condition, but they had postponed the necessary repairs indefinitely. They should have replaced the shutters hanging off their hinges, redecorated the bathrooms with their pink tiles and rusty pipes, rehung doors that wouldn't shut and others they couldn't open, gotten rid of the rotting thatch on the roof where mice nested, swept away the cobwebs, moss, and moths, and beat the dusty carpets. But they saw none of this. The house wrapped itself around them like an embrace, protecting them from pointless distractions, the curiosity and pity of others.

Marcel was their only regular visitor. He arrived every so often laden with bags of groceries from the market, food for the dogs, the cat, and the parrot, who always greeted him with an enthusiastic "Hello, handsome!" He also brought CDs of classical music for his mother, videos to entertain them, and newspapers and magazines that neither Victor nor Roser read, because they found the outside world exhausting. Marcel tried to be discreet, taking his shoes off in the doorway so as not to make noise, but he was a big man, and his looming presence and feigned cheerfulness made the house seem small. His parents missed him if he didn't come to see them for a day, and when he was with them, he left them with their heads in a whirl. Their neighbor Meche also came to quietly leave food on the porch and ask if they needed anything. She stayed only a few moments, understanding that the most precious thing the Dalmaus had was the time they spent together, the time to say goodbye.

The day came when, sitting side by side on the wicker chair on the porch, with the cat on her lap, dogs at their feet, and a view of the golden hills and blue sky of evening, Roser asked her husband to please let her go, because she was very weary. "Don't take me to the hospital for any reason. I want to die in our bed, holding your hand." Defeated at last, Victor had to accept his own powerlessness. He couldn't save her, and he couldn't imagine life without her. He realized in horror that the half century they had spent together had galloped by. Where had the days and years gone? The future without her was the huge empty room without doors and windows that appeared in his nightmares. He dreamed he was escaping from war, blood, and shattered bodies. He ran and ran through the night until suddenly he found himself in that sealed room where he was safe from everything but himself. The energy and enthusiasm of the previous months when he thought age could not touch him drained from his bones. The woman beside him also grew old in a few minutes. Moments earlier she was still as he had always seen her and as he remembered her in her absence: the twenty-two-year-old with a newborn babe in her arms, the woman who married him without love but loved him more than anyone else in the world, his lifelong companion. With her he had lived everything that was worth living. The proximity of death made the intensity of his love as unbearable as an acid burn. He wanted to shake her, shout at her not to go, they still had years ahead of them to love each other more than ever, to be together and not be apart a single day: *Please, please, Roser, don't leave me.* And yet he said none of this to her, because he would have had to be blind not to see Death in the garden, waiting for his wife with the patience of a specter.

There was a chill breeze, and Victor had wrapped Roser in two blankets that came up to her nostrils. Only a skeletal hand poked out of the bundle, gripping him with more strength than she seemed capable of. "I'm not afraid of dying, Victor. I'm happy: I want to know what comes next. You shouldn't be afraid either, because I'll always be with you in this life and in others. It's our karma." Victor began to weep like a baby, in despairing sobs. Roser let him cry until he ran out of tears and resigned himself to what she had accepted months earlier. "I'm not going to let you suffer anymore," was all Victor could offer her. As she did every night, she nestled in the crook of his arm and let herself be rocked and lulled to sleep. It was dark already. Victor lifted off the cat, picked up Roser carefully so as not to wake her, and carried her to bed. She weighed almost nothing. The dogs followed him.

CHAPTER 13

1994

And yet.
Here are the roots of my dream,
This is the harsh light we love.

— PABLO NERUDA
"Return"
SAILINGS AND RETURNS

THREE YEARS AFTER ROSER'S DEATH, VICTOR Dalmau was about to turn eighty in the home in the hills where they had lived ever since their return to Chile in 1983. The house was an aging, trembling, and disheveled monarch, but still noble. Solitary from childhood, Victor found being a widower more of a burden than he had anticipated. Theirs had been the happiest of marriages, as anyone meeting them would have said who didn't know the details of their remote past.

After Roser died he found himself unable to get used to her absence as rapidly as she herself would have wished. "When I die, remarry quickly. You're going to need someone to look after you when you're decrepit and demented. Meche wouldn't be a bad choice . . ." she ordered him toward the end, between inhaling through her oxygen mask. Despite his loneliness, Victor liked his empty house, which seemed to have grown larger somehow. He enjoyed its silence, disorder, the smell of the closed rooms, the cold and the drafts his wife had battled against much more fiercely than the rodents in the roof.

The wind had been howling all day, the windows were covered with hoar frost, and the fire in the hearth was a ridiculous attempt to combat the winter rain and hail. After more than half a century of matrimonial sharing, it was strange being a widower: he missed Roser so much that sometimes he felt her absence as a physical pain. He didn't want to accept being old. Advanced age is a distortion of a familiar reality, it changes the body as well as circumstances. You gradually lose control and have to depend on the kindness of others—but Victor had thought he would die before this happened. The problem was how hard it sometimes can be to die swiftly and with dignity. It seemed unlikely he would suffer a heart attack, because his heart was fine. His doctor assured him of this during his annual checkup, and this comment invariably reminded Victor forcefully of the boy soldier whose heart he had held in his hands.

Victor didn't share his fears for the immediate future with his son. He decided to postpone worrying about more distant days until some other time.

"Anything could happen to you, Papa. If you have a fall or some kind of attack while I'm away, you could be lying there without help for days. What would you do?"

"I'd simply die, Marcel, and pray that nobody came to spoil my final moments. And don't worry about the animals. They always have food and water for several days."

"What if you get ill? Who'll look after you then?"

"That used to worry your mother. We'll see. I'm old, but not ancient. You've got more wrong with you than I have."

This was true. At the age of fifty-five, Marcel had already had a knee replaced; he had broken several ribs and the same collarbone twice. In Victor's view, this came from overdoing exercise: it's fine to stay fit, but who on earth wants to run if no one's chasing you, or to cross continents on a bike? Marcel ought to get married, then he would have less time to pedal about, and fewer ailments. Marriage suits men, although not women. When it came to marriage, though, Victor wasn't keen on following his own advice. He wasn't worried about his health. He had adopted the theory that to stay healthy, the best thing was to ignore any bodily or mental alarm signals and always keep busy. You have to have a purpose in life, he told himself. It was inevitable that over the years he was growing weaker: his bones must be as yellow as his teeth by now, his inner organs had to be wearing out, and his brain cells were gradually dying, and yet this drama was taking place invisibly. From the outside his appearance was still passable: who cares what the liver looks like if you have all your teeth? He tried to ignore the dark blotches that appeared spontaneously on his skin; the unavoidable fact that he found it increasingly hard to walk the dogs uphill or button his shirt; his tired eyes, deafness, and the trembling hands that had forced him to retire from practicing surgery.

Yet he wasn't idle. He continued seeing patients at San Juan de Dios hospital and giving classes at the university. He no longer had to prepare any of these: sixty years' experience, including the harshest ones during the Spanish Civil War, were preparation enough. He was square-shouldered, with a firm body. He still had hair on his head, and stood ramrod straight to compensate for the limp and the fact that it was becoming gradually more difficult for him to bend his knees and waist.

He was careful never to voice how hard he found it being a widower, so as not to upset Marcel, who worried about him like a mother hen. Victor did not see death as an irremediable separation. He imagined his wife traveling ahead through sidereal space, where perhaps the souls of the dead ended up, while he was waiting his turn to join her, more curious than concerned. He would be there with his brother, his parents, Jordi Moline, and all those friends who had died in battle. For a rationalist agnostic with scientific training like he was, this theory had fundamental weaknesses, but it comforted him. More than once Roser had warned him, only half joking, that he would never be free of her because they were destined to be together in this life and others. In the past they had not always been man and wife, she would say: most likely in other lives they were mother and son or brother and sister, which would explain the unconditional love that bound them together. Victor felt nervous at the idea of an infinite repetition with the same person, although if repetition were inevitable, better it was with Roser than anybody else. At any rate, this possibility was no more than poetic speculation, because he didn't believe in either destiny or reincarnation. He thought the first of these was a TV soap opera gimmick, and the second scientifically impossible. According to his wife, who tended to be seduced by spiritual practices from remote regions like Tibet, science could not explain reality's multiple dimensions, but Victor thought this was a specious argument.

The possibility of getting married again sent a shiver down his spine; he was happy with the company of his animals. It wasn't true that he talked to himself; he was talking to the dogs, the parrot, and the cat. The hens didn't count, because they didn't have their own names; they came and went as they liked, and they hid their eggs. He would arrive home at night to tell his pets all that had happened during the day. They were his audience on those rare occasions he became sentimental, and listened to him when he closed his eyes and named objects in the house or the flora and fauna in the garden. That was his way of focusing his memory and his attention, the way other old people did crossword puzzles.

When he had time during the long evenings to reflect on his life, he would go over the short list of his loves. The first had been Elisabeth Eidenbenz, whom he had known long ago, in 1936. Whenever he thought of her, he imagined her white and sweet, like an almond cake. Back then he had promised himself that after all the battles, when the rubble and dust had settled on the earth, he would look for her; but that was not how things had turned out. When the wars were over, he was far away, married, and with a child. Much later on, he did try to find her, out of simple curiosity. He discovered Elisabeth was living in an Austrian village, watering her plants and oblivious to tales of her heroism. When he had found her address, Victor sent her a letter she never answered. Perhaps now that he was on his own it was time to write her another one. There would be no risk in it, because there was no way they would see each other again: Austria and Chile were a thousand light-years away. He preferred not to dwell on Ofelia del Solar, his second brief but passionate love. There had been few others. More than loves, they had been flashes of emotion. Yet he liked to think of them, and magnify their importance, if only to ward off unbearable memories. The only woman who counted was Roser.

He would celebrate his eightieth birthday with his animals, sharing the meal he always made on that date in homage to the happiest moments of his childhood and youth. His mother, Carme, had always been less of a cook and more of a teacher, which kept her busy during the week. On Sundays and holidays she didn't go into the kitchen either, because she would go to dance *sardanas* outside the cathedral in Barcelona's Gothic quarter, and from there to a bar to enjoy a glass of red wine with her women friends. Victor, his brother, and his father dined each day on bread smeared with tomato, sardines, and milky coffee, but every so often his mother woke up inspired and surprised her family with the only traditional Catalan dish she knew how to prepare: *arròs negre*. In Victor's mind, the memory of its fragrance was forever associated with a celebration. In honor of this sentimental legacy, the day before his birthday he would go down to the Mercado Central in search of the ingredients for the *fumet*, and fresh squid for the rice. Catalan through and through, Roser used to say. She herself never collaborated in the homespun creation of this festive dinner, instead contributing a piano recital from the living room or sitting on a kitchen stool to read Victor verses from Neruda, often an ode with a marine flavor, such as *in Chile's tempestuous sea lives the pink conger, that giant eel with snow-white flesh.* It was pointless for Victor to inform her time and again that the dish in question didn't contain conger, the king of aristocratic dinner tables, but the humble fish heads and tails of a proletarian soup. Or while Victor fried the onion and pepper in olive oil, then added the peeled and sliced squid, cloves of garlic, a few chopped tomatoes, and the rice, ending with hot stock that was black with squid ink and the obligatory fresh bay leaf, she would share gossip with him in Catalan in order to refresh their mother tongue, grown rusty from all their wanderings.

THE RICE COOKED SLOWLY in a big pan. He prepared three times the stated amount, even if he had to eat the same meal for the rest of the week. The legendary aroma invaded the house and his soul, while Victor waited with a small plate of Spanish anchovies and olives, available everywhere in Chile. As Marcel said to provoke him, that was one of the advantages of capitalism. Victor preferred to buy Chilean products, because it was patriotic to support national industry, but his idealism wavered when it came to such sacred items as olives and anchovies. A bottle of rosé wine was chilling in the fridge for a toast with Roser once dinner was ready. He had laid the linen tablecloth and bought half a dozen greenhouse roses and two candles to decorate the table. Ever impatient, Roser would have opened the bottle a long while earlier, but in her present state she would have to wait. There was also a Catalan custard dessert in the fridge. He wasn't fond of sweet things, and that would end up in the dogs' mouths. The telephone startled him.

"Happy birthday, Papa. What are you doing?"

"Remembering and repenting."

"For what?"

"For the sins I didn't commit."

"And apart from that?"

"I'm cooking, son. Where are you?"

"In Peru. At a conference."

"Another one? That's all you ever do."

"Are you cooking the usual?"

"Yes, the house smells of Barcelona."

"I suppose you've invited Meche."

"Mmm."

Meche . . . Meche, the enchanting neighbor his son was forcing on him, determined to resolve the problem of his widowhood with drastic measures. Victor admitted that her liveliness and happy disposition were attractive: alongside her, he felt like a pachyderm. Meche, with her open and positive mind, her exuberant sculptures of women with impressive buttocks, and her vegetable patch, would be forever young. With the tendency he had to cut himself off, he, on the other hand, was aging rapidly. Marcel had adored his mother, and Victor suspected he still shed tears for her in secret, but he was convinced that without a wife his father would turn into a tramp. To distract him, Victor had spoken of his intention to get in touch with a nurse he had known in his youth, but once he got an idea in his mind, Marcel would never let go. Meche lived three hundred meters away. Between them were two plots of land separated by rows of poplars, but Victor thought of her as his only neighbor, because he hardly said a word to the others, who accused him of being a communist for having been exiled and working in a hospital catering to the poor. As a rule, he avoided the company of others because he had sufficient contact with colleagues and patients, but he had not managed to keep Meche away. Marcel saw her as an ideal partner: she was no longer young, she was widowed, had children and grandchildren, and no obvious vices. She was eight years his junior, cheerful and creative. Last but not least, she loved animals.

"You promised me, Papa. You owe her lots of favors."

"She gave me the cat because she was tired of having to come here to fetch it back. And I don't know why you imagine any normal woman would be interested in a lame, unsociable, and badly dressed old man like me. Unless she was desperate, and in that case why would I want her?"

"Don't be silly."

This perfect woman also baked biscuits and grew tomatoes. She brought them over discreetly and left them in a basket she hung from a hook in the doorway. She wasn't offended when he forgot to thank her. To him, her boundless enthusiasm seemed suspect. Quite often, she would turn up with strange dishes like cold zucchini soup or chicken with cinnamon and peaches. Victor saw these offerings as bribes. To him it seemed only wise to keep her at bay: he was planning to spend his old age in peace and quiet.

"I'm sorry you're on your own for your birthday, Papa."

"I have company. Your mother."

A lengthy silence on the line forced Victor to insist he was still in his right mind. The idea of having dinner with his dead wife was similar to going to Midnight Mass at Christmas, an annual metaphorical ritual. It had nothing to do with ghosts, it was simply a few hours enjoying her memory, and a toast to a good wife who, with a few ups and downs, had put up with him for many decades.

"Good night, then. Make sure you go to bed early, it must be very cold down there."

"And you spend the night partying and go to bed with the dawn. You could do with it."

It was just past seven in the evening. The sky was dark, it was pouring outside, and the winter temperature had dropped several degrees. In Barcelona nobody would eat black rice before nine, and in Chile the custom was more or less the same. Having dinner at seven was for old people. Victor sat down to wait in his favorite armchair, whose battered frame was molded to the shape of his body. He breathed in the aroma of the hawthorn logs burning on the fire, anticipating the pleasure the meal would give him. He had the book he was currently reading, and a small glass of *pisco* just as he liked it, with no ice or any other addition. This was the only strong drink he allowed himself at the end of the day, convinced that loneliness could lead to alcoholism. The contents of the pan were tempting, but he was determined to resist them until the proper time.

All of a sudden the dogs, who had gone out to do their business before settling down for the night, interrupted his thoughts with a chorus of fierce barking. It must be a skunk, thought Victor, but then he heard a vehicle in the garden and a shudder ran through him: damn it, it must be Meche. He didn't have time to switch off the lights and pretend he was asleep. Usually the dogs ran to greet her in a state of ridiculous excitement, but this time they continued barking. He was surprised to hear the sound of a car horn. His neighbor never normally used hers, unless she needed help to unload some dreadful present, like a roast suckling pig or another of her works of art. Meche had won a reputation for her sculptures of fat naked women, some of them so big and heavy they in fact resembled pigs. Victor had several hidden in corners of his house, as well as one in his consulting room, which proved useful as a surprise for his patients and helped relax the tension of their first visit.

He struggled to his feet, grumbling, and went over to the window with his hands on his kidneys, one of the most vulnerable parts of his body. His back was weakened by his limp, and this obliged him to put more weight on his right leg. The pin with four screws inserted in the base of his spine, and his unshakable decision always to maintain good posture, had alleviated the problem somewhat, but hadn't resolved it. That was yet another reason to defend his position as a widower: the freedom to talk to himself, to curse and complain without witnesses about the private discomforts he would never admit to in public. Pride. That was what his wife and son had often accused him of, but his determination to appear hale and healthy to everyone else was not pride but vanity, a trick to defend himself against decrepitude. As well as walking erect and disguising his tiredness, he also tried to avoid other symptoms of old age: meanness, mistrust, ill temper, resentment, and bad habits such as no longer shaving every day, repeating the same stories over and over, talking about himself, his ailments, or money.

By the yellow light of the two porch lamps he saw a van outside his front door. When the horn sounded a second time, he guessed the driver must be afraid of the dogs, so whistled for them to come to him. They obeyed reluctantly, still growling softly.

"Who's there?" he called out.

"Your daughter. Please, Doctor Dalmau, control your dogs."

She didn't wait for him to invite her in but hurried past him, afraid of the dogs. The two large ones sniffed at her from too close, and the small one that always seemed angry continued growling at her, fangs bared. Taken aback, Victor followed her, and unthinkingly helped her out of her coat, laying it on the bench in the hallway. Shaking herself like a wet animal, she commented on the downpour outside, and timidly extended her hand.

"Good evening, Doctor. I'm Ingrid Schnake. May I come in?"

"I think you already have."

By the dim lamps and firelight in the living room, Victor examined the intruder. She was wearing faded jeans, men's boots, and a white woolen turtleneck sweater. No sign of jewelry or makeup. She wasn't as young as he had thought at first: she was an adult woman with wrinkles around her eyes, and yet gave a different impression because she was slender, long-haired, and swift in her movements. She reminded him of someone.

"Excuse me for coming here like this all of a sudden, without any warning. I live a long way off, in the south of the country, and I don't know my way around Santiago. I didn't think I'd arrive here so late."

"That's all right. How can I help you?"

"Mmm. What's that delicious smell?"

Victor Dalmau was about to forcibly eject this stranger who had the nerve to turn up at night and invade his house uninvited, but curiosity overcame his irritation.

"Rice with squid."

"I see you've already set the table. I'm interrupting, I can come back tomorrow at a more suitable time. You're expecting guests, aren't you?"

"You, apparently. What did you say your name was?"

"Ingrid Schnake. You don't know me, but I know a lot about you. I've been trying to track you down for a long while."

"Do you like rosé wine?"

"I like it any color. I'm afraid you're also going to have to offer me some of your rice, I haven't eaten a thing since breakfast. Do you have enough?"

"There's more than enough for us as well as the neighbors. It's ready. Let's sit down and you can tell me why a pretty young girl like you is trying to find me."

"I already told you, I'm your daughter. And I'm no young girl, I'm fifty-two well-lived years old, and—"

"My only child is called Marcel," Victor cut in.

"Believe me, Doctor, I haven't come to upset you. I just wanted to meet you."

"Let's get comfortable, Ingrid. I can see we have a lot to talk about."

"Yes, I've got a lot of questions. Do you mind if we start with your life? Afterward I'll tell you about mine, if you wish . . ."

THE NEXT DAY, VICTOR'S phone call roused Marcel shortly after dawn. "Our family's just become bigger, son," he began. "You have a sister, a brother-in-law, a nephew, and two nieces. Your sister's called Ingrid, and she's going to stay with me for a couple of days. We have a lot to tell each other."

While he was talking with Marcel, the woman who had burst into his house the previous evening was fast asleep in her clothes on the battered living room sofa, wrapped in blankets. Victor had always suffered from insomnia, and so a night without sleep didn't have much effect on him. In the morning he felt more wide awake than he had since Roser's death. His visitor, however, was exhausted after spending ten hours listening to Victor's story and telling him hers. She had revealed that her mother was Ofelia del Solar, and from what she understood, he was her father. It had taken her months to discover this, and had it not been for an old woman's uneasy conscience, she might never have done so.

So that was how, more than fifty years later, Victor learned that Ofelia had become pregnant during the time they had their affair. That was why she disappeared from his life, why her passion had turned to resentment, and led her to break with him without any proper explanation. "I think she felt trapped, robbed of her future through making one mistake. At least, that's the explanation she gave me," said Ingrid, who went on to tell him the details surrounding her birth.

When Ofelia wouldn't cooperate, Father Vicente Urbina took the matter of adoption into his own hands. Once she had promised never to reveal it, the only other person to participate in the plan was Laura del Solar. It was a necessary white lie, forgiven in the confessional and sanctioned by heaven. The midwife, someone by the name of Orinda Naranjo, took it upon herself to follow the priest's instructions, and kept Ofelia in a semiconscious state before the birth, and sedated during and after it. Then, with the grandmother's help, she whisked the baby away before anyone in the convent could ask questions. When Ofelia emerged from her stupor a few days later, they explained she had given birth to a baby boy, who died a few minutes after being born. "But it was a girl. And it was me," Ingrid told Victor. Her mother was told it had been a boy as a precaution, to confuse her and prevent her finding her daughter if at some hypothetical future moment she came to suspect what had happened. Doña Laura, who had agreed to deceive her daughter in this way, meekly accepted the rest of the plan, including the farce of the cemetery, where they erected a cross over a tiny empty coffin. None of this was her responsibility; it was dreamed up by someone far more devious than her, a wise man of God, Father Urbina.

Over the following years, seeing Ofelia in a good marriage, with two healthy, well-behaved children and leading a successful life, Doña Laura buried her doubts in the deepest recesses of her memory. From the outset, Father Urbina told her the baby girl had been adopted by a Catholic couple in the south of Chile. That was all he could tell her. Later on, when she plucked up courage to ask for more details, he reminded her curtly she should consider the grandchild as dead: she had never belonged to the del Solar family, even if she had their blood in her veins. God had given her to other parents. The couple who adopted the girl were descendants of Germans on both sides—big, tall, blond, and blue-eyed. They lived more than eight hundred kilometers south of Santiago in a lovely town by a river with trees and lots of rain (although the grandmother never knew this). It was when this couple had lost hope of having their own children that they took in the newborn baby offered them by the priest. A year later, the wife became pregnant. In the years that followed, they had two children as Teutonic in appearance as themselves. Compared to them, Ingrid, who was small and had dark hair and eyes, stood out like a genetic mistake. "From childhood I felt different, but my parents spoiled me terribly, and never told me I was adopted. Even now, when the whole family knows, if I mention adoption my mother starts to cry," Ingrid explained to Victor.

Seeing her sleeping on the sofa, Victor could study her closely. She wasn't the same woman he had been talking to hours earlier; asleep she looked like the young Ofelia, with the same delicate features, childish dimples in her cheeks, arched eyebrows, widow's peak, light golden skin that must become tanned in summer. The only thing missing were the blue eyes; otherwise she would have been almost identical to her mother. When she first arrived, Victor had thought he knew her from somewhere, but didn't connect her to Ofelia. Now that she was lying there relaxed, he could see not only how similar they looked, but how different their characters were. Ingrid had none of the superficial coquettishness of the young Ofelia he had loved. She was intense, serious, and formal, a woman from the provinces, with a conservative, religious background. Her life must have been placid until she learned of her origins and set out to find her father. Victor also reflected that she didn't seem to have inherited much from him: neither his lanky, tough body, his aquiline nose, spiky hair, stern expression, nor his introverted character. She was gentle, and he guessed she must be very maternal and loving.

He tried to imagine what a daughter with Roser would have been like, and regretted never having had one. At first they hadn't felt they were properly married: they were together only temporarily as the result of a convenient agreement between the two of them; and by the time they realized they were more married than anyone, twenty years had gone by and it was too late to think of children. It would take Victor an effort to get used to Ingrid, because until the previous night Marcel had been all the family he had. He thought Ofelia del Solar must be as surprised as he was; after all, she too was discovering late in life that she had an unexpected daughter. Not only that, but Ingrid had given them three grandchildren.

Ingrid's husband was also of German extraction, like her adoptive parents and many others in some southern provinces colonized by Germans from the nineteenth century on, thanks to a selective immigration policy. The idea had been to populate the land with true-blooded white immigrants to bring discipline and a work ethic to Chileans, who had the reputation of being lazy. In the photos Ingrid had shown him of her children, Victor saw a young man and two girls who looked like Valkyries and seemed to have inherited none of his traits. He found it hard to recognize them as his descendants.

"Ingrid's son is married, and his wife is pregnant. I'll soon be a great-grandfather," Victor told Marcel toward the end of their phone conversation.

"And I'm an uncle to Ingrid's children. What will I be to the one about to be born?"

"I think you'd be something like a great-uncle."

"Wow! I feel really old. I can't help thinking of *Àvia*. Do you remember how she wanted me to give her great-grandchildren? Poor thing, she died without knowing she already had them. A granddaughter and three great-grandchildren!"

"We'll have to go and visit these people from a different race, Marcel. They're all Germans. Besides, they're right-wing and were supporters of Pinochet, so we're going to have to bite our tongues in front of them."

"What's important is that we're family, Papa. We're not going to fight over politics."

"I'll also have to establish some regular communication with Ingrid and the grandchildren. They've fallen on my head like apples from a tree. All these complications: maybe I was better off before, alone and peaceful."

"Don't talk nonsense, Papa. I'm dying to meet my new sibling. Well, cousin, all the same."

Victor calculated that if the family got together he would inevitably meet Ofelia del Solar once more. That didn't seem such a bad thing: he had long since recovered from any nostalgia he felt for her, and yet he was curious to see her again and correct the bad impression he had of her from the Caracas Athenaeum eleven years earlier. Hopefully he would have the chance to tell her that, thanks to her, he had deep roots in Chile, deeper than any he had in Spain. It was ironic he was linked in this way to the del Solar family, who had been so against the immigration of the Spanish refugees on the *Winnipeg*. Ofelia had offered him an amazing gift: she had opened up the future for him. He was no longer an old man with only his animals for company. Now he had several Chilean descendants as well as Marcel, who never considered himself as anything else.

Ofelia had been far more important in his life than he had ever thought. He had never really understood her: she was more complex, more tormented than he believed. He thought about those strange canvases of hers, and reasoned that by marrying and choosing a conventional life, the security of a marriage and her place in society, Ofelia had exiled herself from herself, renouncing an essential part of her soul, although possibly she had partly regained it in later life and in solitude. But then he recalled what she had said about her husband, Matias Eyzaguirre, and guessed that she had not renounced that part of her out of laziness or frivolity, but from a very special love.

A YEAR EARLIER, INGRID SCHNAKE had received a letter from a stranger claiming to be her mother. It didn't come as a complete surprise, as she had always felt different from the rest of her family. First she confronted her adoptive parents, who eventually admitted the truth. Then she prepared to receive the visit of Ofelia and Felipe del Solar, who arrived accompanied by a little old woman wearing deep mourning: Juana Nancucheo. None of them had the slightest doubt Ingrid was Ofelia's long-lost daughter: the resemblance was only too obvious. Since then, Ofelia had seen her daughter on three occasions. Ingrid treated her with the stilted courtesy of a distant relation, because her real mother was Helga Schnake. This visitor with paint-stained hands and the bad habit of constantly complaining was a stranger to her. Aware of the similarity in their appearance, Ingrid was worried she might also have inherited her mother's defects, and that as she grew older she would become as narcissistic as Ofelia was. She learned the story of her birth little by little, and it was only at their third meeting that she discovered her father's name.

Ofelia considered her past dead and buried, and avoided talking about it. She had obeyed Father Urbina's instruction to stay silent, and she so resolutely refused to mention the dead boy buried in the rural cemetery that this youthful episode became lost in the fog of reiterated omission. She recalled it briefly when she had to bury her husband and wanted to keep the promise they made when they married that one day the baby boy would be laid to rest with them in Santiago's Catholic cemetery. This would have been the moment to transfer the baby's remains, but her brother Felipe persuaded her not to do so, as she would have had to explain it to her children and the rest of the family.

By the time Laura del Solar's health began to decline, Ofelia had been living alone for years, painting in her studio in the Chilean countryside. Her elder son was building a dam in Brazil, while her daughter was working in a museum in Buenos Aires. Doña Laura, who was about to turn a hundred, had for a long time been suffering from dementia. Two selfless caretakers looked after her day and night, under the strict supervision of Juana Nancucheo, almost as old as Laura but looking fifteen years younger. She had served the family forever and intended to continue to do so for as long as Doña Laura needed her. It was her duty to look after her until her dying breath. Her mistress was confined to bed, lying there on feather pillows and embroidered linen sheets in her silk nightdresses imported from France, surrounded by the precious objects her husband had bought her with no regard for cost. After his death, Doña Laura freed herself from the iron straitjacket of her marriage to such an overbearing man. She was able to do exactly as she pleased for a while, until old age crippled her and senility prevented her from communicating with the ghost of Leonardo, her Baby, in spiritualist séances. She gradually lost her mind, couldn't figure out where she was in the house, and when she saw herself in the mirror asked with alarm who the ugly old woman in her bathroom was, and why she came every day to pester her. Soon, the arthritis in her legs and feet meant they couldn't support her, and she was unable to stand up. Enclosed in her bedroom, she alternated between weeping and prolonged drowsy spells, calling out to Baby with an inexplicable anxiety and terror that her doctor tried in vain to lessen with antidepressants. During those final days of her illness, her whole family thought she was suffering from the loss of Leonardo as if it had only just happened.

Felipe del Solar, the head of the clan since his father's death, had flown in from London to take charge of things, settle debts, and distribute the family's possessions. People said he must have made a pact with the devil, because, contrary to his own hypochondriac predictions, he seemed never to age. He had a thousand things wrong with him, and every week discovered a new one. Everything hurt, even his hair, but thanks to one of life's injustices, none of this was visible. He was a distinguished gentleman straight out of an English comedy, wearing a vest, a bow tie, and a supercilious expression. He put his healthy appearance down to London fog, Scotch whisky, and his Dutch pipe tobacco. He brought with him the documents for the sale of the Calle Mar del Plata house; the land it was built on in the heart of the capital was worth a fortune. He only had to wait for his mother to die to finalize the deal.

Reduced to little more than skin and bone, Doña Laura went on calling out to her Baby until her dying breath, unable to find peace either in her medicines or her prayers. Juana Nancucheo closed Laura's mouth and eyes, said a Hail Mary, and dragged herself wearily away. At nine the next morning, while the funeral directors were preparing the house for the wake, the coffin in the living room festooned with floral wreaths, candles, black cloths and ribbons, Felipe gathered his sisters and brothers-in-law in the library to inform them of the forthcoming sale of the house. Afterward he called in Juana to tell her the same.

"They're going to knock down the house to build an apartment block, Juana. But you won't go short of anything. Tell me how and where you'd like to live."

"What can I say, *niño* Felipe? I don't have any family, friends, or acquaintances. I can see I get in the way. You're going to put me into a home, aren't you?"

"Some old people's homes are very good, Juana, but I won't do anything you don't want. Would you like to live with Ofelia or any of my other sisters?"

"I'm going to die in a year, and I don't care where. Dying is dying, that's all there is to it. You finally get some rest."

"My poor mother didn't think that . . ."

"Doña Laura felt very guilty, that's why she was afraid to die."

"For goodness' sake, what did my mother have to feel guilty about, Juana?"

"That's why she cried so much."

"She had dementia and was obsessed with Leonardo," Felipe said.

"With Leonardo?"

"Yes, Baby."

"No, *niño* Felipe, she didn't even remember him. She was crying over little Ofelia's baby."

"I don't understand, Juana."

"Do you remember she became pregnant before she was married? The thing is, that baby didn't die, as everyone said."

"But I've seen his grave!"

"It's empty. And it was a girl. She was taken away by that woman—I can't recall her name—the midwife. Doña Laura told me all this, and that's why she was weeping, because she listened to Father Urbina and stole little Ofelia's daughter from her. She spent her whole life with that lie gnawing away inside her."

Felipe was tempted to put this macabre story down to his mother's dementia, or even Juana's senile ideas, and dismiss it as absurd. He also thought that even if the tale were true it would be best to ignore it, because it would be unnecessarily cruel to tell Ofelia. However, Juana insisted she had promised Doña Laura she would find the child so that Laura could go to heaven rather than be trapped in purgatory, and promises to the dying were sacred. At this, Felipe realized there was no way to keep Juana quiet. He would have to deal with the matter before Ofelia and the rest of the family came to hear of it. So he promised Juana he would look into it and keep her informed.

"Let's start with the priest, *niño* Felipe. I'll go with you." He couldn't shake her off. The complicity built up between them over eighty years and his certainty that she could read his intentions forced him to take action.

By now, Father Urbina had retired. He was living in a residence for old priests, looked after by nuns. It was a simple matter to find him and arrange an interview: he was lucid and remembered his former flock very well, especially the del Solar family. He greeted Felipe and Juana with an apology for not having been able to give Doña Laura extreme unction himself. He had undergone an intestinal operation, and the recovery was taking far too long. Getting straight to the point, Felipe repeated what Juana had told him. As an experienced lawyer, he had been prepared for a difficult cross-examination to corner the bishop and force him to confess, but this proved completely unnecessary.

"I did what was best for the family. I was always very careful in my choice of adoptive parents. They were all practicing Catholics," said Urbina.

"You mean Ofelia wasn't the only one?"

"There were many girls like Ofelia, but none of them as stubborn. Generally, they agreed to let the baby go. What else could they do?"

"In other words, you didn't have to lie to them to steal the baby."

"I won't permit you to insult me, Felipe! They were girls from good families. My duty was to protect them and avoid any scandal."

"The scandal is that you, shielded by the Church, committed a crime—or rather, many crimes. By law, that should be paid for by a prison sentence. You're too old now to face the consequences, but I demand you tell me who you gave Ofelia's daughter to. I'm going to get to the bottom of this."

Vicente Urbina hadn't kept a register of the couples who received the babies, or of the children themselves. He took care of the transaction personally: the midwife, Orinda Naranjo, only helped with the delivery, and besides, she had died long ago. At that point Juana Nancucheo butted in to say that according to Doña Laura the baby had been given to a German couple in the south of Chile. Father Urbina had let that slip on one occasion, and Doña Laura had never forgotten it.

"German, you say? They must be from Valdivia," muttered the bishop.

Their name escaped him, but he was sure the girl had a decent home and didn't lack for anything; the family was well-off. This comment led Felipe to deduce that in these dealings money changed hands: in other words, the bishop was selling babies. At this, Felipe gave up trying to pry anything more out of him, and decided to concentrate on following the trail of donations the Catholic Church had received through Vicente Urbina around that date. It would be difficult, but not impossible, to gain access to those records; he would have to find the right person to investigate. He guessed that money always left some trace of its passage through the world, and he wasn't mistaken.

He had to wait eight months until he finally obtained the information. He spent those months in London, pursued from afar by postcards with two-line missives from Juana Nancucheo, littered with grammatical and spelling mistakes, reminding him of his duty. The aged servant struggled to write them without help from anyone, because she had promised to keep the secret until Felipe resolved the mystery. He kept telling her she must be patient, but she couldn't offer herself that luxury, because she was counting the days that remained to her in this world. Before she left it, she had to find the child and save Doña Laura from purgatory. When Felipe asked her how she could be so sure of the date of her impending death, she simply said she had put a red circle around it on the kitchen calendar. She was installed in Ofelia's house, with nothing to do for the first time in her life, apart from preparing her own funeral.

One winter day, a letter brought Felipe the details of the donations received by Father Vicente Urbina in 1942. The only one that caught his attention was from Walter and Helga Schnake, the owners of a furniture factory. According to his investigator, they had done very well, and had branches in several southern cities run by their sons and son-in-law. As Urbina had said, theirs was a wealthy family. The time had come to return to Chile and confront Ofelia.

Felipe found his sister mixing paints in her studio, a freezing shed reeking of turpentine and embroidered with cobwebs. She had grown fatter and more ragged, her hair was a dirty white mop, and she was wearing an orthopedic corset for her backache. Ensconced in a corner and wearing an overcoat, gloves, and woolen hat, Juana was the same as ever. "You don't look as if you're about to die," said Felipe by way of greeting, and kissed her on the forehead. He had carefully constructed the most compassionate phrases he could use to tell his sister she had a daughter, but there was no need for any such precautions. She reacted with only vague curiosity, as if it was gossip about someone else. "I assume you want to meet her," her brother said. She explained he would have to wait awhile, because she was busy painting a mural. Juana said in that case she would go, because she had to see the girl with her own eyes so that she could die in peace. In the end, all three of them went.

Juana Nancucheo saw Ingrid only once. Reassured by that visit, she communicated with Doña Laura as she did every night between two prayers, and explained that her granddaughter had been found, her guilt had been atoned for, and she could arrange her transfer to heaven. Juana herself had twenty-four days left on the calendar. She lay down on her bed surrounded by her bedside saints and photographs of her loved ones—all from the del Solar family—and prepared to die of hunger. From that moment on, she neither ate nor drank, accepting only some ice to moisten her parched mouth. She left this world without fuss or pain a few days before the scheduled day. "She was in a hurry," said a desolate, orphaned Felipe. He rejected the simple pine coffin Juana had bought and had placed standing in a corner of her bedroom. Instead, he made sure she had a High Mass and was buried in a walnut casket with bronze fittings in the del Solar mausoleum, alongside his parents.

ON THE THIRD DAY the storm finally abated. The sun came out, defying the winter, and that morning the poplars guarding Victor Dalmau's property like sentinels were freshly washed. Snow covered the mountains and reflected the violet color of the clear sky. The two big dogs were able to shake off the lethargy of being in for so long, although the small one, who in dog years was as old as his master, stayed by the fireside.

Ingrid Schnake had spent those days with Victor. She was accustomed to the rain of her southern province, and stayed not so much to ride out the bad weather as to give time to this first encounter, to allow them to get to know each other. She had carefully planned this meeting for months, and had been firm with her husband and children that they were not to accompany her. "You understand I had to do this on my own, don't you? I found it hard, because it's the first time I've traveled alone, and I didn't know how you would receive me," she told Victor. Unlike her experience with her mother, with whom she found it impossible to bridge the gap of more than fifty years' absence, she and Victor became friends easily. Both of them understood he could never compete with her love for Walter Schnake, her beloved adoptive father, the only one she recognized. "He's very old, Victor, he's going to die on me at any moment," she told him.

They discovered they both played the guitar for consolation, were fans of the same soccer team, read spy novels, and could recite from memory many of Neruda's verses. She knew the love poems; he the militant ones. That wasn't all they had in common: they both had a tendency toward melancholy, which he kept at bay by plunging into work, and she with antidepressants and by sheltering in the unshakable haven of her family. Victor lamented the fact that his daughter had been bequeathed this trait, whereas she had inherited neither Ofelia's artistic temperament nor her cerulean blue eyes.

"When I'm depressed, it's affection that helps me most," Ingrid told him. She added that this had never been lacking: she was her parents' favorite, was spoiled by her younger siblings, and was married to a honey-colored bear of a man who could lift her up with one arm and who gave her the quiet love of a big dog. In his turn, Victor told her that Roser's love had always helped him keep at bay that sly melancholy that pursued him like an enemy and sometimes threatened to crush him with its weight of bad memories. With Roser gone, he was lost. His inner fire had gone out; all that was left were the ashes of a grief he had been dragging round with him for three years now. He surprised himself with his hoarse confession: he had never before spoken of that cold hollow in his chest, not even to Marcel.

He felt as if even his soul was shriveling. He was retreating into an old man's manias, a mineral silence, into his widower's solitude. He had gradually given up the few friends he had from before; he no longer sought buddies to play chess or the guitar with; the Sunday barbecues were a thing of the past. He carried on working, because this obliged him to connect to his patients and students, but kept an insuperable distance, as if looking at them on a screen. During the years he spent in Venezuela he thought he had once and for all overcome the solemnity that had been an essential part of his nature from childhood, as though he was in mourning for all the world's suffering, violence, and evil. Faced with so many disasters, happiness seemed to him obscene. In love with Roser in the green, warm country of Venezuela, he had vanquished the temptation to cloak himself in sadness. As she would often tell him, this was less a mantle of dignity, more a contempt for life. But his serious nature had returned agonizingly: without Roser he was withering away. He was touched only by Marcel and his animals.

"Sadness, my enemy, is gaining ground, Ingrid. At this rate in the years I have left I'm going to turn into a hermit."

"That would be death in life, Victor. Do as I do. Don't wait to defend yourself against that enemy, go out and confront it. It took me years in therapy to learn that."

"What reasons do you have to be sad, child?"

"That's what my husband asks me. I don't know, Victor, I suppose you don't need reasons; it's part of your nature."

"It's very difficult to change your nature. For me it's too late, there's nothing for it but to accept myself the way I am. I'm eighty years old: it was my birthday the day you arrived. That's the age of memory, Ingrid. The age of making an inventory of life," he said.

"Forgive me if I'm intruding, but can you tell me what's in your inventory?"

"My life has been a series of journeys. I've traveled from one side of the world to the other. I've been a foreigner without realizing I had deep roots . . . My spirit has sailed as well. But I don't see the point in making these observations now; I should have done so a long time ago."

"I don't think anybody reflects on their life when they're young, Victor, and most people never do. It would never occur to my parents, for example, and they're almost ninety. They simply live for the day and are happy."

"It's a shame we only make this kind of inventory when we're old, Ingrid, when there's no time left to make amends."

"You can't change the past, but perhaps you can banish the worst memories . . ."

"Listen, Ingrid, the most important events, the ones that determine our fate, are almost always completely beyond our control. In my case, when I take stock, I see my life was marked by the Spanish Civil War in my youth, and later on by the military coup, by the concentration camps and my exiles. I didn't choose any of that: it simply happened to me."

"But there must be things you did choose . . . like medicine, for example."

"That's true, and it's given me a great deal of satisfaction. But do you know what I'm most grateful for? Love. That has marked me more than anything else. I was incredibly lucky to have Roser. She'll always be the love of my life. Thanks to her I have Marcel. Being a father has also been essential for me; it's allowed me to keep faith in what's best in the human condition. Without Marcel that would have been crushed. I've seen too much cruelty, Ingrid. I know what mankind is capable of. I also loved your mother a great deal, although that didn't last long."

"Why? What happened exactly?"

"Those were different times. Chile and the world have changed a lot in the past half century. Ofelia and I were separated by a social and economic gulf."

"If you loved each other so much, you would have run the risk . . ."

"She once suggested we escape to some tropical country to live our love beneath the palm trees. Just imagine! In those days Ofelia was passionate and had an adventurous spirit. But I was married to Roser, I had nothing to offer her, and knew that if she left with me she'd regret it within a week. Was that cowardice on my part? I've often wondered. I think it was a lack of empathy. I didn't measure the consequences of my relationship with Ofelia. I did her a lot of unintentional damage. I never knew she was pregnant. She never knew she'd given birth to a little girl, who lived. If we had known, it would have been a different story. There's no point digging up the past, Ingrid. But anyway, you're a child of love. You should never doubt that."

"Eighty is a perfect age, Victor. You've already more than fulfilled your obligations, you can do whatever you like."

"Such as what, daughter?" Victor said with a smile.

"Go off on another adventure, for example. I'd love to go on safari in Africa. I've been dreaming of it for years, and one day, when I manage to convince my husband, we'll go. And you could fall in love again. You've nothing to lose, and it could be fun, couldn't it?"

It seemed to Victor he was listening to Roser in her final moments, reminding him that we human beings are gregarious, we're not programmed for solitude, but to give and receive. That was why she insisted he mustn't withdraw into old age, and even chose him a new partner. He suddenly thought tenderly of Meche, the kindhearted neighbor who gave him the cat, brought him tomatoes and herbs from her garden, the tiny woman who sculpted fat nymphs. He decided that as soon as his daughter had left, he would take Meche what was left of his *arròs negre* with squid, and the Catalan dessert. Sailing on, he thought, on until the end.

ACKNOWLEDGMENTS

I FIRST HEARD ABOUT THE *WINNIPEG*, THE SHIP OF HOPE, IN my childhood, at my grandfather's. Many years later I heard that evocative name once more in conversation with Victor Pey in Venezuela, where we were both exiles. In those days I wasn't a writer and didn't imagine I would become one, but the story of that boat stayed in my memory. It's only now, forty years later, that I can tell it. This is a novel, but the events and historical individuals are real. The characters are fictional, inspired by people I've known. I have had to imagine very little, because as I was doing the exhaustive research I carry out for each novel, I found I had more than enough material. This book wrote itself, as if it had been dictated to me.

Heartfelt thanks to:

Victor Pey, who died at 103, with whom I had a copious correspondence to get the details right.

Dr. Arturo Jirón, my friend in exile.

Pablo Neruda for taking the Spanish refugees to Chile, and for his poetry, which has always accompanied me.

My son Nicolás Frías, who carried out the first meticulous reading, and my brother Juan Allende, who corrected the manuscript page by page several times, and helped me with research into the period covered by this story, from 1936 to 1994.

My Spanish editors, Nuria Tey and Johanna Castillo.

My English editor, Jennifer Hershey.

My loyal researcher, Sarah Hillesheim.

My agents, Lluis Miquel Palomares, Gloria Gutierrez, Maribel Luque, and Johanna Castillo.

Alfonso Bolado, who carefully checks my manuscripts out of pure affection, because he's already retired. He forces me to do my best.

Jorge Manzanilla, the ruthless (and according to him, good-looking) reader who corrects my slips, because after forty years of living in English, I commit dreadful grammatical and other mistakes.

Adam Hochschild, for his extraordinary book *Spain in Our Hearts,* and fifty or more other authors whose books were invaluable for my historical research.

Born in Peru and raised in Chile, ISABEL ALLENDE is the author of a number of bestselling and critically acclaimed books, including *The House of the Spirits, Of Love and Shadows, Eva Luna, The Stories of Eva Luna,* and *Paula.* Her books have been translated into more than forty-two languages and have sold more than seventy-four million copies worldwide. She lives in California.

IsabelAllende.com

Facebook.com/IsabelAllende

Twitter: @isabelallende

Instagram: @allendeisabel

ABOUT THE TYPE

This book was set in Fournier, a typeface named for Pierre-Simon Fournier (1712–68), the youngest son of a French printing family. He started out engraving woodblocks and large capitals, then moved on to fonts of type. In 1736 he began his own foundry and made several important contributions in the field of type design; he is said to have cut 147 alphabets of his own creation. Fournier is probably best remembered as the designer of St. Augustine Ordinaire, a face that served as the model for the Monotype Corporation's Fournier, which was released in 1925.